8 - 27　　　SALG

FATAL MISTAKE

Center Point
Large Print

Books are produced in the United States using U.S.-based materials

Books are printed using a revolutionary new process called THINKtech™ that lowers energy usage by 70% and increases overall quality

Books are durable and flexible because of smythe-sewing

Paper is sourced using environmentally responsible foresting methods and the paper is acid-free

This Large Print Book carries the Seal of Approval of N.A.V.H.

FATAL MISTAKE

SUSAN SLEEMAN

CENTER POINT LARGE PRINT
THORNDIKE, MAINE

This Center Point Large Print edition is published in the year 2017 by arrangement with FaithWords, a division of Hachette Book Group, Inc.

The text of this Large Print edition is unabridged. In other aspects, this book may vary from the original edition. Printed in the United States of America on permanent paper. Set in 16-point Times New Roman type.

ISBN: 978-1-68324-442-4

Library of Congress Cataloging-in-Publication Data

Names: Sleeman, Susan, author.
Title: Fatal mistake / Susan Sleeman.
Description: Center Point Large Print edition. | Thorndike, Maine : Center Point Large Print, 2017. | Series: White knights ; 1
Identifiers: LCCN 2017013447 | ISBN 9781683244424 (hardcover : alk. paper)
Subjects: LCSH: Witnesses—Protection—Fiction. | Terrorism—Prevention—Fiction. | Man-woman relationships—Fiction. | Large type books. | BISAC: FICTION / Christian / Suspense. | FICTION / Christian / Romance. | FICTION / Romance / Suspense. | GSAFD: Romantic suspense fiction. | Suspense fiction. | Christian fiction. | Love stories.
Classification: LCC PS3619.L44 F38 2017b | DDC 813/.6—dc23
LC record available at https://lccn.loc.gov/2017013447

For my family.
Your support and love has allowed
my writing dreams to come true.

CHAPTER 1

Spotsylvania County, Virginia
Thursday, April 28
7:50 p.m.

He was coming for her, and he was close.

He'd parked on the driveway and would soon head for the pump house, taking long strides. Spaced evenly, methodical, as she knew Mr. Perfectionist would take, his footsteps rustling over dead grass, bringing him closer.

At the door, he would twist the rusty knob. Step inside. Spot her. She could almost hear his thoughts when he did.

I was sloppy. Now she knows. Do I let her live? Kill her? How can I dispose of the body?

The body. Ha! *Her.* He was going to kill *her.* She'd grown up with him. Lived next door for years, but he had no choice now. He had to know she wouldn't keep quiet about this . . . this what? She didn't even know what to call it.

She swept her gaze over the rough-hewn table, pausing at neat piles of white blocks covered in green cellophane. Explosives—military grade, like she'd seen in briefings in her job as a government translator. The blocks sat solidly among triggers, wires, pipes, and items she couldn't identify. Items for a bomb. Maybe several bombs. Pages and pages of diagrams, maps, and other papers were scattered beside the equipment.

Recent television news stories raced through her brain. Explosions on the first of every month. The destruction. Chaos and confusion. Nothing more than burned-out shells left behind. Death. Muslim women. Always women.

Oh my gosh! Oren. Her childhood best friend was a killer. A terrorist. The Lone Wolf Bomber. No . . . no. Couldn't be, right? But the evidence . . .

His car door slammed in the distance, the echo reverberating through the quiet.

He's coming.

She had to escape, but how? The only door and window in the tiny building led to the path he'd take.

Think, Tara, think. Hurry! Hurry!

She reached for her phone. The smooth case slipped through her fingers and tumbled to the floor.

Father, please. Help me!

She dropped to her knees, her fingers crawling over the dirt floor until they curled around the cool metal. She woke it up and lifted a finger to tap in 911.

No. She should call the FBI's hotline. The bright red letters, 1-800-THE-BOMB, had scrolled across the television screen nearly every newscast for the last few months. They were better prepared than local police to deal with a lunatic bomber. She punched in the number and the phone rang.

"Hotline, this is Special Agent Cal Riggins," the deep male voice said.

Good. She'd gotten an actual agent.

"My aunt's tenant, Oren Keeler." Her words tumbled out, rushing over each other. "He has . . . oh my gosh . . . this can't be happening. I'm . . . I'm in the pump house. Behind my aunt's home. There are bomb-making materials here."

"Calm down," Agent Riggins said. "What's your name?"

Calm down? Is he nuts? "I can't calm down. Oren just drove up. Once he finds me here, he'll kill me."

"It would help if I had your name," Agent Riggins said evenly when her body revved on high octane.

He was so infuriatingly composed, Tara wanted to shout at him to take her seriously, but Oren would hear her. "My name's Tara. Tara Parrish."

"Hello, Tara."

She didn't have time for pleasantries. "I need you to get someone over here now. Before he comes inside and discovers me."

"What's your address?"

She rattled off the farm address in rural Virginia about an hour and a half from her home in Washington, D.C. "I'm down the drive. In the pump house. It's not more than a shed behind the hired hand's house Oren rents. He grew up next door, but his mother died last year and he recently lost the farm. My aunt invited him to live here."

"Why are you in the pump house?"

"My aunt . . . She wasn't getting any water at the main house, so she asked me to check the pump. The door was locked, but I broke in and found . . . oh, no . . . no. I can't believe this is happening."

Her heart rate skyrocketed, and she shot across the room, putting as much distance as possible between her and the door.

"Where is Keeler now?"

"He just got out of his car and will be here soon. He wasn't supposed to be home, but he came back early. He's gonna . . . oh my gosh . . . he'll . . ." She couldn't say the words aloud, as everything suddenly seemed terrifyingly real.

"Is there another way out of the shed?" Agent Riggins asked, that infuriating calm remaining in place.

"Nothing he can't see. I can't . . ." A sob stole her words, and tears pricked at her eyes, itching, burning for release. She swallowed hard to fight them off.

"Hey, hey, now, Tara," he soothed.

She heard clicking on the line, then silence. Terrifying, horrible silence.

"Are you still there?" she cried out.

"Don't worry, I'm here. I'll get you through this. My team is already dispatching a sheriff's deputy."

What? He was passing her off. Unbelievable.

Tears gave way to anger. "But what about you? You're the FBI. You should be here, too. To arrest Oren. He could be the Lone Wolf. The bomber you're looking for. I thought you'd make this a priority."

"It *is* a priority, and I'm on my way. But even with a chopper on standby, it'll take twenty minutes or so for me to arrive." She heard activity in the background of the call, and his breathing picked up as if he was on the move. "The deputy can arrive sooner. Until then, I need you to take proactive measures."

"What can I do other than blow up one of his bombs?" Hysterical laughter bubbled up, and she swallowed it down.

"Does the door open in?" he asked, ignoring her panic.

"Yes."

"If you're not by the door, go over there."

"But that's where *he'll* be."

"Just trust me, Tara. Go to the door. Stand behind it so when he pushes it open he doesn't see you."

He sounded so certain, so sure, that she did as he asked and crossed the room.

"Okay, I'm there," she whispered, but didn't have peace about moving closer to Oren.

Agent Riggins might be able to give directions that he thought would help, but he didn't know Oren. Didn't know his tenacity. She did. Had experienced it when he declared his love three months ago, and she'd let him down not too gently, but he still needed a giant stick upside the head to get a clue.

"Now find something big and hard that you can strike him with," Agent Riggins continued. "If the deputy doesn't arrive before Keeler enters the building, you'll have to disable him."

She looked around the room and found a thick, jagged piece of wood. She almost laughed, as it was looking like Oren would get that whack upside the head he sorely needed, but there was nothing funny about her situation.

She lowered her voice to keep Oren from hearing her. "Okay. I found a board. It should work."

"Good. Now you're ready to take action if needed," Agent Riggins said over the sound of his footsteps pounding in the background of the call.

"I . . . he . . ." She lost her voice. Lost her breath. Concentrated but couldn't seem to draw in enough air. She was suffocating.

"Let's not focus on Keeler," he said. "Why don't you describe the items on the table?"

Right. Forget the man who walked up the path ready to kill her.

"Come on, Tara," Agent Riggins commanded. "Breathe deep and look at the table. Tell me what you see."

She could at least give it a try. She glanced at her aunt's old potting bench with chipped and peeling green paint. "There's a cardboard box. It's labeled 'Explosives Dangerous Handle Carefully.' Next to it are white blocks. They're wrapped in green shrink-wrap."

"How many packs?"

"I don't know. Fifteen. Maybe more."

A low whistle came over the phone.

"That's bad, right? I knew it. Really bad." She moved her focus farther down the table. "There's also a bunch of PVC pipe connected with elbows to look like a C."

"C," he mumbled.

"Yeah. Is that bad?"

"Can be."

"Does the Lone Wolf use pipes like these?" she asked, knowing reporters had never revealed specifics of his bombs.

"Sorry. I can't discuss that with you."

Translated, yeah, the Lone Wolf used PVC pipe and odds of Oren being the bomber were growing by the minute.

Panic finally won out, and she clutched a corroded pipe to stay upright. "With the way Oren changed, I should have known something like this could happen. We were friends growing up, but he got weird in high school. Always spouting off about causes that no one cared about. Then he changed religions and tried to get us to convert to the Islamic faith. So I guess this isn't unbelievable. Or maybe it is. I mean bombs. Who does that? Not someone in my life."

Her thoughts traveled to her aunt waiting for her at the main house. "Oh my gosh, my aunt June. She's going to freak when she hears the Lone Wolf is living on her property."

"You could be wrong about this. Maybe Keeler's letting a friend use the space."

"Oren? Friends? No . . . no, he doesn't have any friends. He's a loner."

A car trunk slammed, and then footsteps crunched over gravel.

Her heart skipped a beat. "How long will it take for the deputy to get here?"

"He's five minutes out."

"That's too long." She whispered to keep from being heard. "Oren's coming to the door. What do I do?"

"First, take a deep breath, Tara." Agent Riggins's soothing voice returned, serene, almost melodic, yet deep and strong.

She thought she'd like him if she lived to meet him.

"C'mon," he continued. "Breathe. In through your nose. Out through your mouth."

She tried it. Managed two cycles before she

heard Oren's footsteps stop. Her throat closed.

"He's right outside. I can hear him." The words came out on an exhale.

Her hand shook so badly she almost dropped the phone.

"Calm down, Tara. Put the phone in your pocket so Keeler doesn't know you've called to report him. It'll also free your hands to take a better hold on the wood you found."

"Hang up? What? No. No. I don't want to hang up. Don't leave me alone."

"I won't. Just put the phone in your pocket, and I can continue to listen in. We'll stay connected. Okay?"

The doorknob turned, a click of the metal sounding like an explosion in her head. "Please stay with me, Agent Riggins. Please."

"Don't worry, Tara. I'm not going anywhere. I'm here for you."

Right, he'd said that, but he wasn't here, now, was he? Her life was in her own hands. Hers alone.

CHAPTER 2

Spotsylvania County, Virginia
8:10 p.m.

The Black Hawk's rotors thundered over Cal's head as he pressed his phone against his ear and listened hard for any word from Tara. He'd transferred her call to his cell and despite her phone remaining in her pocket, he'd picked up enough of her movements to stay current on her situation.

He'd heard the board crack against Keeler's body and Tara's footsteps as they'd pounded away from the pump house. And then . . . then . . . man, it had been gut-wrenching when a gunshot rang through her phone, and she'd issued a desperate plea for help. Every protective instinct in Cal's body sat up and took notice. But even worse, the sound was followed by silence.

Deadly silence.

"ETA, four minutes." Chopper pilot Zach Lawson's voice came over Cal's earbud.

"Copy that," Cal said, trying not to snap at Zach.

Cal was worried about Tara—that was a given —but he also didn't like this op. Didn't like it one bit. His six-person team should be suited up and onboard with him. An FBI Critical Incident

16

Response team, they always had aircraft and pilots on standby and could have wheels up in, say, an hour or so, but Tara couldn't wait for an hour. He'd had to move on the fly.

So no backup. No team. No trained operators carrying out their assignment alongside him. Tonight he had only the phone connection to Tara, the red blip of her cell on his GPS, and an aerial map of the farm for intel.

Could be worse, he supposed. At least she'd thought to call the hotline manned by agents 24/7 so they could instantly respond to credible threats. If she'd called 911, the deputy who Cal instructed to stand down at the pump house| could be racing after Tara and Keeler, getting both of them killed or even causing a SWAT situation that the deputy wasn't prepared to handle.

"Three minutes," Zach announced.

Cal couldn't sit any longer. He needed to pace but with the small space he settled for standing, his shoulders and head bent to keep from hitting the overhead. He stared down at the boots he'd worn as a SEAL on too many hostage rescue missions to count. Missions that ended in more failures than Cal could accept. He slammed a fist into the chopper's metal hull, the pain stinging up his arm and taking away some of the anger.

Some.

The rage had been simmering in his gut since a rescue gone bad where a seven-year-old boy died in his arms. Cal carried a boatload of regret from that op, and now, women dying at the Lone Wolf's hands? That had added even more guilt to the equation. Too many lives lost on his watch. He wouldn't let the same thing happen to Tara.

He jerked out his phone and checked her GPS dot. She continued to move deeper into the woods, and it would take him longer to get to her.

"Two minutes," Zach said.

Cal shrugged into his pack and double-checked his assault rifle and ammo before stepping to the door. Outside the city, black clouds obscured the moon and stars. Obscured his landing.

Once they were on target, he'd fast-rope down to the road and be on Keeler's tail without the guy even sensing his arrival. Perhaps Keeler would hear a chopper whirling overhead, hovering for a moment, then moving on, but nothing to put the guy on alert. Give it another hour or so and the full squad of operators would arrive.

Now *that* thought was smile worthy.

"One minute," Zach said.

Cal lowered his night-vision goggles. He waited for his eyes to adjust to the greenish color tinting his vision and pulled on his assault gloves. Made with a Nomex and Kevlar blend for protection, they had a gun-cut finger for increased dexterity.

The helo went into a hover, and Cal glanced at Zach, who gave a thumbs-up.

Go time.

A burst of adrenaline raced through Cal's blood, but he regulated his breathing. He nodded at Zach and jerked open the door. Air roared past, sucking and swirling. He kicked out the rope and grabbed it. Sliding down, the friction burned into his gloves. Thankfully, the Nomex shielded his hand. He hit the road hard, jarring his whole body. He wasted no time but signaled a successful landing, and the helo departed like a hummingbird whirling into the black of night.

He took a moment to get his bearings. To his right sat an open grain field. On his left, a thick grove of trees mixed with the darkness. He pulled out the GPS device and followed the red dot about five hundred yards ahead in the stand of trees. Still moving, Tara had slowed her pace. Probably tiring. Made her more vulnerable.

He had to move. Now!

He crept through the woods. Silently. Carefully.

Step. Step. Step. Break. A quick check of his surroundings.

Rinse and repeat. Over and over.

A tedious way to advance, but standard operating procedure for a hostage rescue professional dictated a cautious approach to arrive undetected and alive. After all, he had to protect himself first if he hoped to save another person.

In the thick of the trees now, Cal heard an owl hoot above, but otherwise deafening silence greeted him as he crept forward. Muggy spring

19

air closed in, the forest feeling like a sauna, and sweat dripped from his body.

Fifty yards away from Tara's location, he lifted his goggles and raised his rifle. He sighted in the area ahead and looked through the red crosshairs, but found no one.

He crept closer and swung the rifle to his right. Held his breath. Searched. Twenty feet ahead, Tara stood with her back to a tree, her chest rapidly rising and falling. No sign of Keeler.

Cal backed up and skirted behind trees to edge closer for a better look. He wanted to call out to her, but his sixth sense told him something was hinky. He took a stand behind a tree and scanned the area.

A branch snapped to his right, echoing through the still of the night.

He swung the scope, saw nothing, but dropped his finger to the trigger anyway. If Keeler and the Lone Wolf were one and the same, Cal wanted to take him alive to gain much-needed ISIS intel. But the most important thing right now—the most important thing at all times to a law enforcement officer—was to protect innocent life. Sure, if he brought the bomber in, or even put two in his chest, Cal might be stopping a future attack, but that attack wasn't certain.

Tara's life was on the line right now.

He ran his scope over the area, seeing nothing, but his frog sense kept screaming he was missing something. He continued to scan.

C'mon, c'mon, c'mon. Show yourself.

A sudden explosion in the distance thundered through the air. The ground rumbled beneath his feet in rolling waves, and the sky flashed with brilliant reds and oranges. He estimated the blast came from the pump house, and now any evidence they might have recovered to locate Keeler should he get away burned in a red-hot inferno.

A gunshot split the night. A cry of distress followed. Cal swung his scope back to Tara in time to catch sight of her collapsing to the ground. He stifled a shout of rage and scanned the area. Saw no one.

"FBI. Don't move," Cal called out, though he didn't have eyes on Keeler.

Cal remained in position, his finger itching to jerk the trigger, but he couldn't very well go firing at random into the forest, hoping to hit a person who may or may not be the Lone Wolf. Who may or may not have just shot Tara. Cal needed more information to discharge his weapon.

Deep laughter rumbled through the trees behind Tara. "Nice try, Secret Agent Man, but I think you'll want to check on Tara instead of chasing after me. Adios."

The guy charged through the trees, the sound of snapping branches and crunching leaves soon trailing off. A sense of urgency to bolt toward Tara ate at Cal's stomach, but he eased his way up to her, scanning the area with each step, looking for a trap. She lay on her back, and even in the thick of the night, he clearly saw through his NVGs the dark spot pooling on her abdomen.

A gut shot, one of the worst places to take a hit. She wouldn't survive if he didn't stop the bleeding and get her to the hospital.

Memories of the day the young boy lost his life on the raid came rushing back, filling Cal's chest with apprehension, but he kept moving and grabbed his radio to connect with Zach.

"Alpha One, this is Alpha Two requesting exfil at secondary location." A cold feeling of dread twisted through his body. "Hostage has taken a bullet. Radio the ER and let them know we're bringing her in with a gunshot wound to the left abdomen. And get word to standby deputies that Keeler's on the move. He's armed and dangerous and heading due west of my coordinates."

"Roger that," Zach said calmly, the way all operators on the team would respond.

Cal stowed his radio, grabbed his flashlight, and ran the beam over Tara's face. Her eyes were closed and her mouth pinched. He swung the light over her body, stopping at the wound. He positioned himself above her yet kept an eye on the location where Keeler had fled.

"Tara." Cal put cheer he didn't feel into his voice. "It's me, Cal. I told you I'd get here."

Her eyes fluttered open.

"I . . . he . . ." Her voice, a mere whisper, evaporated into the inky black sky.

"Don't talk." Cal tore off his gloves and ripped his medical kit from his pack. He flipped on his headlamp and pressed gauze pads on the wound.

She moaned, and the phone she clutched in her hand fell to the ground.

"It's okay, Tara. I'm going to get you through this," he soothed as her blood easily saturated the gauze, increasing his concern.

He grabbed a couple rolls of Kerlix and pressed hard. She groaned, a drawn-out, tortured expression of pain, but it was weaker this time. He rested his fingers on her wrist to find a fast and thready pulse.

Not a good sign. Not a good sign at all.

He turned his attention back to her face and cringed at the tightness he found there. He gently swept a strand of hair from her eyes and bent low. Her agony sent a visceral pain piercing his body, hitting him in a place in his heart he thought long dead.

"We're going to take a little trip, sweetheart." He did his best to keep his concern from his voice. "But don't worry. I'm going with you, and I'll get you to the ER in plenty of time."

He picked up her phone, then lifted her into his arms, his promise hanging in the air. Why had he made another promise? Like the one he'd made to the boy on his failed rescue. Just a kid who didn't make it.

What good was a promise when he had no control over the endgame and it was up to God to save her life?

12:20 a.m.

Pain kept Tara's eyes clamped down tight, but she was vaguely aware of bright lights overhead, and the medical staff's frenzied tones as they hurried her toward the ER and shouted words like *peritoneal cavity, hematocrits,* and *pancreas.* She remembered having a CT scan, but then her hematocrit had fallen, whatever that meant, and they now rushed her toward a surgical suite.

The gurney bumped through swinging doors and came to a rest, but she couldn't summon the energy to open her eyes. The nurse cooed something in her direction. Wooziness along with peace floated around her, and she drifted toward sleep.

Memories of a man's face lit by a beam of light from his helmet settled in her brain. He had a wide jaw and nose, high cheekbones, eyes that were dark and narrowed holding strength and conviction, but that wasn't all. As he'd gazed down on her, they'd softened and filled with concern and compassion that she'd never witnessed in a man's eyes.

Agent Cal Riggins, he'd said his name was. The

FBI agent she'd called. He'd told her on the phone that he was there for her, and he had been. Just like he promised. Well, almost anyway. Maybe a few minutes too late. But he had come, and as she'd gone in and out of consciousness on the helicopter, she found him holding her hand every time she woke up, warming her heart. Chasing out her fears as she tried to recall everything she'd seen.

She remembered running in fear from Oren. He'd pursued her and shot at her, bullets racing past her head. Her arms. Shoulders. Then a fiery explosion shook the earth, and he'd fired his handgun again. She could feel the pain slicing through her stomach. Feel the cold ground rise up to meet her. Agent Riggins tending to her, his hands urgent and inflicting even more pain, yet his comforting gaze and tone holding regret over having to do so.

She'd wanted to tell him something as he'd cared for her, but what? Could it be something she'd seen on the way out of the pump house? At the pump house?

She tried to remember, honestly she did, but the images danced out of her reach and sleep pulled harder. She gave in, letting her body sink into the black void and drag her under.

The next thing she knew was light and an insistent male voice.

"Wake up, Tara," he commanded.

Hoping Agent Riggins stood beside her bed, she fought through the haze, struggling to climb free and lift her eyelids. She spotted a man, tall and string-bean thin. She worked hard to focus in on his face, but she needn't have. With his slight frame, he couldn't have carried her through the woods and held her close on the chopper. He was *so* not Agent Riggins.

But Aunt June was there, her warm hand wrapped around Tara's fingers, a smile washing over the anxiety in her face. Tara squeezed her hand.

"You came through surgery fine," the man said. "The bullet bruised a few internal organs, but barring any post-op infection, you should be back to normal soon."

He ran a hand over a shiny scalp with little tufts of hair sticking out the sides. He reminded her of an asparagus stalk wearing a doctor's white coat. Laughter bubbled up inside, but his frown stifled it.

"Any questions for me?" Impatience narrowed his gaze.

Questions? She could barely keep her eyes open much less summon up any questions. She shook her head but managed to move it only a fraction of an inch.

"Don't worry, Tara. You'll be just fine. You just rest for now," Aunt June said. She glanced at the doctor. "We may have questions tomorrow."

He gave a clipped nod of his pointy head. "I'll stop by in the morning to assess your progress, and we'll take things from there." He headed for the door, this tall stalk of asparagus, moving fluidly and quickly away.

She closed her eyes, sleep waiting again with the promise of peace. Though comforted by Aunt June, Tara hoped when she next woke that Agent Riggins would be waiting at the door. His strong presence would be a comfort in itself, until . . . until he filled in the voids in her memory, and her worst nightmare once again became a reality.

CHAPTER 3

3:10 a.m.

Cal leaned against the wall in Tara's hospital room. Her aunt had gone home reluctantly after Cal's solemn assurance that they'd call if Tara's condition changed. She lay asleep in the bed, her face as pale as the bleached pillowcase. Layers of auburn hair poked out at odd angles, likely from the cap she'd worn in surgery. And yet, even in such disarray, men would find her very attractive. After all, he did, but he didn't have the time or energy to think of her as a woman right now, only as a person who witnessed important information that could help him catch the Lone Wolf.

Oren Keeler. They now knew his name. A disappointingly plain name for a notorious bomber. Cal had spent hours during Tara's surgery researching the man. His appearance was the only thing extraordinary about him. He had a long face, crooked nose, and buckteeth. Cal suspected women found him homely, far from the confident sort of man you'd expect to be brave enough to withstand the threat of an accidental detonation as he built his devices.

Tara stirred and moaned.

"No!" She shot upright, her eyes wild and searching. She locked gazes with him, then collapsed back.

He approached her bed.

"Do you need me to get the nurse, Tara . . . Ms. Parrish?" From her call and rescue, he'd come to think of her as Tara, but as a law enforcement officer, he needed to keep things professional and wait for her to suggest he call her Tara. Even then, he shouldn't do so, as he couldn't let her suffering distract him from his purpose.

"No, I . . ." She bit her lip, then took in several deep breaths and firmed her shoulders with a resolve he didn't expect. "Unless my memories are wrong, you're the agent I spoke to on the phone."

"Agent Cal Riggins." He flashed his credentials, then held out his hand.

She slipped her slender fingers into his, and he was surprised to find them warm. "I'm Tara Parrish, but then you already know that. Thank you for saving my life. If you hadn't come when you did—"

"Let's not go there, okay?" He smiled as much for himself as her. Three women had already lost their lives from Keeler's bombs and Cal didn't want to think about how close another woman had come to dying on his watch. "Are you up for answering a few questions, Ms. Parrish?"

"Tara, it's Tara."

"And you can call me Cal." Now where had that come from when only a moment ago he'd vowed to keep things professional?

Her brows knitted in worry. "Do you really think Oren is the Lone Wolf? That he's actually killing for ISIS?"

"My team and I have spent the last few hours researching him, and we're certain he's the Lone Wolf. Whether he's motivated by his misguided beliefs or not has yet to be determined."

"But all the news reports about him mention ISIS."

"News reports can be inaccurate, but I can't go into details." He wished he could share more with her so she better understood the sense of urgency he had in finding Keeler, but Cal's team had just begun a comprehensive background investigation on her and would hardly share sensitive informa-tion until she was fully vetted. Maybe not even then.

They kept many investigative details private. Details like the fact that Keeler used necklace bombs and drew a skull and crossbones on the front of his devices. At first they'd thought the common symbol of death was meaningless, but the literal translation of the symbol told another story. The X shape of the skull and crossbones was often interpreted as man being wrong about the truth and therefore he died. ISIS believed that anyone who didn't hold their beliefs should die. A perfect symbol for Keeler's cleansing.

Tara closed her eyes and sighed. "Oren and I were once such good friends. I didn't think any-thing could ever come between us."

Had she sighed because she'd learned a friend was a bomber, or because she was still involved with Keeler and was lamenting the guy choosing to turn on her and shoot her?

It sent Cal's gut churning to think this woman lying in front of him could be helping Keeler, but until their background check on her was complete, he had to at least consider the possibility. "Tell me more about your friendship with Keeler."

She pressed the remote to raise her bed, her face contorting in pain as the frame groaned upward. "There's not much to tell. I think I mentioned on the phone that we grew up next door to each other. My parents owned a farm until they died in a car crash. I was only thirteen, so I went to live with my aunt June. Oren's family farm was located between June's and my parents' place."

Cal grabbed a chair and slid it over to the bed. "But the Keelers lost that property to foreclosure about seven months ago."

Her eyebrow lifted. "Your research, right? Did you learn anything else that I should know?"

"I'm afraid I can't share details of my investigation."

"I understand." She ran a hand over her face, and he doubted that she could begin to understand the complexity of this investigation. "This is all so surreal. My friendship with Oren might have ended in junior high, but still, how could . . . I mean . . . he . . . I can't believe he shot me. I just can't."

"When's the last time you saw him?"

"Last time?" She peered up at the ceiling. "In January, I guess. At June's place. Before that, I hadn't seen him since his mother's funeral. We both lost our mothers in a car crash, so I reached out to him. But he didn't want to talk."

"You also mentioned on the phone about his conversion to the Islamic faith. Did his family convert, too?"

"No. No." She shook her head hard, the wayward strands of hair settling in place on her shoulders. "He did that all on his own, and his parents didn't support the change."

"Do you have any idea why he converted?"

"I'm not sure, but I think it was timing more than anything. Our freshman year, kids were starting to date, and I think he felt left out." Her eyes narrowed. "I imagine by now you've seen a picture of him."

Cal nodded.

"There's not a nice way of saying it, but he's not a good-looking man, and he wasn't a good-looking teenager. All gangly and disproportioned. He was teased a lot, and girls didn't find him attractive. So I think he chose a Goth lifestyle because it made him seem odd on purpose. And he changed faiths for added shock value."

Interesting. "Did he tell you that?"

"No. Just a guess. I tried to get him to talk to me about it in high school, but he refused and became withdrawn. That's when our friendship totally fell apart, and we barely talked to each other."

Cal nodded and wanted to dig deeper, but he'd hold additional questions until the team had completed their preliminary research on Keeler. Then, when Cal knew the right questions to ask, he'd come back to her relationship with Keeler.

"You're a government translator and work out of D.C.," he stated, as their research had proved that, and he wanted to get her take on it.

She nodded. "I work for the State Department translating documents, conversations, videos. You know, that kind of stuff."

"What language?" He hoped she didn't claim a Middle Eastern language, potentially tying her to a terrorist cell.

"Depends on the day."

"So you speak more than one foreign language?"

"I'm fluent in Spanish, French, and Russian."

He almost sighed out his relief, and he hated that he didn't want her to be involved when he was desperate for a lead on Keeler. Any lead. "How did you decide to major in languages?"

"I've always been good at math, so my teachers wanted me to go into a math career or IT and languages. I have no interest in IT. Math would have been okay, but as a child, I spent a lot of nights staring at the stars and dreamed of discovering what was outside my little town." A wistful smile found her lips.

"So you want to travel. Maybe visit the countries where they speak your languages?"

"Yes, absolutely. In fact my friend Penny and I have been planning a trip to Russia now that I'm free."

"Free?" he asked, and her open expression closed down.

"And after Oren is caught, of course," she quickly added, her avoidance of his question raising a red flag. "So what happens next in finding him?"

"Are you up to telling me about the pump house?"

"Sure, but I can't. I mean, for some reason,

running from Oren keeps coming back. But no matter how hard I try, my time at the pump house is fuzzy." She sighed. "Truth be told, I don't actually want to remember the details of getting shot."

Maybe a red flag, maybe not. "Memory loss happens in traumatic situations. Things are likely to come back in bits and pieces."

"I'll be sure to let you know if it does."

"About that," he said, and leaned forward. "I'll stop in to see you each day to try to jog your memory. If possible, I'd also like to get your assistance in finding Keeler."

She eyed him cautiously. "How?"

"For starters, you can share every detail you know about Keeler with my team. And we can also put you in situations that could help bring back your memories."

"I suppose I could." She wrapped her arms around her waist. "Maybe . . . I guess, anyway. This is all new to me. I've never been involved in anything like this, and . . ." She shook her head. "How long will it take to come to grips with Oren being a bomber? A killer . . . women . . . he kills women, and he shot me. Tried to kill me, too. I mean . . ." Tears flooded her eyes, and she covered her mouth with her hand.

He reached out to take her hand, then snapped his back before he made this personal. "It's hard to comprehend something like this."

"Maybe Oren didn't mean it."

"Oh, he meant it, all right. He didn't accidentally chase you through the woods and fire a gun at you."

"You're right, I suppose." She nipped at her lower lip.

"Look, Tara," he said, putting force into his tone to get her full attention. "I get that this is hard to handle, but you can't doubt Keeler's intentions. He wanted you to die, and the worst thing you can do for your safety right now is underestimate him. You need to remember that he's a dangerous man. So dangerous that while you're in the hospital, I'll have an agent outside your door at all times. In fact, Agent Fields is already standing duty in the hallway."

"He's out there now?" She shot a look at the window. "Because you think Oren will try to kill me again?"

Cal nodded, but at her anguished expression he wished he hadn't had to admit his concerns.

"But how can he . . . he was . . . we were friends. Good friends once. This's crazy. My life. It was good. Now this. How will I ever get back to normal? *Will* I get back to normal?"

"Not until Keeler is caught."

"But, he . . ." She shrugged and started crying softly.

She still didn't believe Keeler was a serial killer, and Cal couldn't risk her underestimating

Keeler or she could wind up dead, too. Cal wouldn't lose another woman on his watch. He firmed his resolve to keep this woman's pain from distracting him.

"I'll be here for you, Tara," he said, meaning watching over her, not helping her deal with her emotional trauma. "Like I was with the helicopter. We'll all keep you safe. Are you willing to help me?"

"Yes."

"Good," he replied. "Because we only have a few days until the first of the month, when Keeler is sure to detonate another bomb."

4:30 a.m.

Darkness cloaked Tara's room when she drifted out of sleep. The nurse had come in as Cal was leaving and given her something through her IV. She didn't remember anything since. How long had she slept?

She rubbed her eyes and raised the bed. Movement in the window overlooking the hallway grabbed her attention. Groggy from the pain meds, she concentrated until a man standing on the far side of the hall became clear. He stepped closer.

Had Agent Riggins come back, or was it Agent Fields?

She blinked hard and squinted until the guy came into focus.

No. Oh, no.

Oren. It was Oren. There in the hallway, standing less than twenty feet away. A sneer on his face. A challenge in his eyes.

"You're dead," he mouthed, and slashed a hand across his throat before disappearing down the hall.

Panic curled through her body. Help. She needed help. She tried to get up. To call out, but the tiniest of movements sent the room spinning. Nausea followed, curling into her stomach and leaving it roiling. She closed her eyes and tried hard to move past the undulating waves of dizziness to think.

Oh, God, please. What should I do?

Agent Riggins. She needed him here by her side, but where had he gone?

He'd promised to be there for her, but he'd disappeared. Left her alone to fend for herself. Let Oren get to her. He'd probably gone back to his job, his office, having forgotten all about her.

"Help," she finally got out.

She waited for a response from anyone.

She cried out again.

Nothing. No one.

Where was this Agent Fields? Why wasn't he coming to her aid, or even challenging Oren?

She peered at the window. Reality hit, settling in and stealing her breath.

She was alone. All alone and vulnerable.

If Oren could step into the hospital and come this close to her, he could certainly locate her D.C. row house and pounce.

She'd be a sitting duck. Exposed.

Her brain cleared for a moment and it hit her then. Hard.

She wasn't safe. Not here. Not anywhere. Not as long as Oren ran free.

CHAPTER 4

Dallas, Texas
Monday, August 1
12:25 p.m.

Cal curled his fingers and slammed his fist into the Honda Accord's charred body. The metal sizzled from water blasted through firefighters' hoses and heat from the explosion scorched his knuckles, sending pain radiating up his fingers.

Too bad. He deserved to suffer. He should have prevented Keeler from setting off his latest bomb. Could have prevented it if he'd only worked harder, smarter, longer. Anything but this destruction. With it being the first of August, Cal had known Keeler would detonate a bomb. Yet Cal had failed, adding an additional ulcer in his gut. Worse yet, Keeler had now departed from his pattern of targeting Muslim women to killing women Tara Parrish had recently befriended.

Choosing women outside the D.C. area made Keeler unpredictable. A loose cannon and even harder to find.

Cal hit the frame another time. Then again and again. Once for each of Keeler's victims. Heat blistered his knuckles, the pain intensifying, but he didn't care. He'd arrived too late today, much like the day Keeler had nearly killed Tara.

Even three months later, Cal's failure to capture the Lone Wolf haunted his dreams. He'd had a split-second decision to make in the woods that fateful night, and he'd chosen not to go after Keeler to save Tara's life. Now Keeler had strapped a necklace bomb around this woman's throat and claimed his seventh victim.

Cal stared at the car's burned-out shell. The horror this woman must have experienced lingered in the air and ate at Cal's insides. Four more women had died since he'd last laid eyes on Tara in the hospital. Innocents. All of them. They didn't deserve death or this horrific treatment. They deserved better from Cal. So did the others. The ones he continued to seek justice for.

Cal thrust another fist at the car. Something he'd taken to doing all the time. A wall. A door. Any solid object that could take his pummeling. He had to get out his anger at Keeler, at himself for failing, or he'd explode.

He tightened his fist and lifted his hand.

"Stand down, Riggins." Max White's voice came from behind.

The leader of their team, he was the reason for their team nickname. Reporters had combined his last name with the team's many heroic rescues and conflict resolutions and dubbed them the White Knights.

Max curled his fingers around Cal's wrist and dragged him off to the side where shadows from tall trees hid them from voracious reporters circling like buzzards ready to pick apart the carnage for a story.

Cal's breath came fast and deep, and he stood under Max's stare without looking at his boss. Max gave his team the freedom to take any steps necessary to get the job done and didn't often interfere, but when one of their team needed restraining, he stepped in.

Max plunged his hand into his hair, leaving it even more rumpled than usual as he scowled at Cal. "The last thing we need right now is for you to give the press something to fuel their special reports. So get a grip. Now."

"I don't care," Cal said, and truth be told, he didn't. He'd seen some horrendous things as a SEAL, and during his year as the explosives expert on the Knights, he could honestly say he'd never wanted to lay down his credentials and walk away until today. "This woman should be alive. If I had—"

"Had what?" Max interrupted. "Become Superman and located Keeler on your own when the whole team hasn't been able to do it? Our team's the best, and we *will* get him. Why take it all on yourself?"

"Why? Because it's personal," Cal said. "I had him, Max. Could've brought him in and I let him go. I—"

"Stop right there. Tara Parrish was bleeding out. You chose to save her life and hoped she'd help us hunt him down later. All of us would have done the same thing, and if you were faced with a similar choice today, you'd do it again."

"You're right. I would, but letting Keeler go? That . . ." Rage wormed its way through his body, and he shook his head in disgust. "That makes this personal, as is every stinking bomb the psychopath has detonated since then."

"If you hold on to the fact that you saved Tara's life instead of feeling guilty for the others, you'll be far better off."

He shoved his hands into his pockets, the blistered skin on his knuckles ripping open, the pain a welcome distraction. "I would have put her life first no matter what, but her leaving us in a lurch? *That* I didn't see coming."

"You couldn't." Max frowned. "Shoot, we still don't know why she bolted from the hospital. Especially not after we'd cleared her of any involvement with Keeler. Doesn't make sense for a civilian like her to think she can do a better job of staying alive on her own rather than having our team watch over her."

Tara had been lucky. Her wound had looked bad, but she'd only sustained bruised internal organs. Three days after checking into the hospital, she'd taken off and disappeared. At first Cal thought Keeler had gotten to her, but there'd been no sign of foul play, just a bamboozled FBI agent unable to explain how she'd disappeared on his watch.

A month later, Cal had discovered her working as a waitress in Atlanta, but by the time he got to Atlanta, she'd run again, leaving fellow coworkers to confirm she'd once lived there. Then Keeler killed one of these coworkers, and yesterday, an anonymous VoIP call came into the hotline telling them Keeler was likely targeting employees of Pecos Palace in Dallas. The team hopped a plane while trying to track the call through Internet servers, but they hadn't yet come up with the origin of the call.

They *had* learned that Tara worked at the Pecos Palace for three weeks before disappearing again. Now Cal had no idea where she'd gone, just that she continued to run, and Keeler killed another woman she'd worked with.

"She obviously hasn't figured out that the explosions in cities where she's recently lived means Keeler's tracking her," Max said. "I'd like to think if she knew Keeler was targeting her, she'd be smart enough come in."

"I don't know, man. She clearly doesn't trust us." *Trust me.* Cal tightened his fingers. "We have to find her before he does, though. Besides, I'm still convinced she's the only one who can help us track him down."

"We *are* going to get him, you know. With Tara or without her." Max made strong eye contact. "If you don't tuck tail and run away like the big baby you were acting like a minute ago. Throwing a tantrum."

"I'm not running," Cal said, ignoring the tantrum comment.

"Tell you what," Max said. "Let's get out of here and let Brynn do her thing with the forensics. We'll gather the rest of the team and go back to the hotel. Then we'll run the investigation one more time with fresh eyes."

Cal turned to look at forensic expert Brynn Young squatting near the burned-out car. Cal had been a part of a team since he joined the navy at eighteen, and he liked working in that capacity even now. Each of them came together to intervene in a critical situation, to use their strengths to bring order to chaos, and to apply their unique skills in an investigative capacity. His teammates were more than capable, and he could leave any one of them to handle this scene today, but as lead case agent, he wasn't going anywhere.

He faced Max. "We'll see how things go. I have witness statements to take—"

"No," Max snapped. "This is a direct order."

Max set his mouth in a hard line and pulled back wide shoulders built from hours in a gym. His military-perfect posture was born from ten years as an Army Ranger. Still, bleeding military or not, he never ordered them to do anything—never—proving his stress level now, too. The powers that be, all the way up to the president, were pressuring him to bring in the Lone Wolf.

Or maybe since Max handled pressure better than most, he was using reverse psychology that often worked on the team. They weren't three-year-olds, but tell them something couldn't be done, and with most of them former military spec ops personnel, they'd prove him wrong. No matter what it took, even if it meant bending the rules to get the job done.

"A direct order, huh?" Cal cracked a smile, likely Max's goal. "In other words, you don't want me to do it."

"Nah." Max scowled. "I want you to take a break, but I needed to shake you up to get you to comply."

Cal stared at Max. "I need a few more minutes here first."

Max arched a brow.

"If you want me to step away for a while, give me a few minutes with Brynn to get up to speed on forensics and to talk with the eyewitnesses. It'll help with our briefing, too."

"Fine. Take thirty, but then we're out of here." Max eyed him. "Keep that temper in check."

Max marched across the road to the mobile command truck rolled in by County five minutes before the Knights had arrived. Cal and the team had gotten the bombing call at 1200 hours. The Knights were already in Dallas tracking Tara, so they'd arrived on scene quickly and had taken charge. County transported the body, took preliminary statements from eyewitnesses, and set up the church down the street for the grieving family.

Cal hadn't been over there yet, but after the briefing he'd give his condolences to each and every person. He'd have to question them, too, a particularly nasty thing to do in their grief, but a career in law enforcement often meant having the emotional courage to do the right thing. He'd do his job no matter how much it hurt. Max could count on that.

Cal picked his way through the debris to Brynn. She wore a white Tyvek suit over her team uniform as she sifted through the wreckage, pausing every so often to place a numbered marker next to crucial evidence.

She looked up, every strand of chin-length blond hair in place as usual. "Looks like a necklace bomb. His signature device."

Cal nodded and ran his gaze over the debris

field. "With the air pushed outward in a blast and sucking everything back into the vacuum it creates, the components for this device are nearby. I want you to find every piece down to the tiniest of fragments."

Brynn frowned. "He's packing a ton of C-4 into these devices, and there won't be many intact pieces for your study."

"True, but each blast gives me more. Assuming, of course, Keeler doesn't change the device's blueprint." Cal thought of the fragments from the last bomb in D.C. He may have reconstructed it, but Keeler's near degree in electrical engineering had given him the knowledge to build compli-cated bombs, and Cal couldn't be certain they hadn't missed vital switches, leaving him unable to render safe one of Keeler's bombs.

"So what's your take on the C-4?" Brynn asked. "Outside of military operations it's so hard to come by that you'd think we'd have figured out where he's getting it by now."

"Most every Tom, Dick, and Harry who've worked military demo has unopened packs from training in a small stockpile in their garage. With Keeler's army days, he's bound to know a few guys."

"A few guys?" Brynn planted gloved hands on her hips. "With the quantity he's coming up with, he has to know Tom, Dick, *and* Harry." She shook her head in disgust and gestured at the FBI's local three-person Evidence Response Team. "I should get back to it. These guys will likely screw things up if I don't watch their every move."

She stepped off, making a beeline for the group of techs who lingered outside a small rental truck serving as a temporary evidence locker. Brynn would supervise the work and make sure they marked each piece of evidence with a number, recorded the details in the official logbook, and took copious photographs before properly packaging and shipping the evidence back to the FBI's only lab in Quantico, Virginia. Cal wished they weren't breaking for Max's meeting, as they already had a long night ahead of them in reviewing the evidence to determine the most probative leads, but it couldn't be helped.

On his way to the detective who'd taken witness names, Cal spotted the Knights' cyber expert, Kaci North, frantically waving at him from behind fluttering yellow tape cordoning off the scene. Her whole body vibrated with anticipation like she wanted to hurdle the barriers to get to him. She wouldn't, though. She might be their computer expert, but she knew better than to unnecessarily enter a scene and potentially contaminate the area.

Cal made his way over to her, ignoring the callouts from reporters pleading for details. When he reached her, a self-satisfied smile settled on her lips.

"I found her." She pushed large black glasses up the bridge of her nose to stare at him.

Cal lowered his voice. "Her as in Tara?"

"Yes," Kaci said, that smile widening. "I have finally found your missing Tara Parrish."

CHAPTER 5

An adrenaline rush urged Cal to take action, but he forced himself to calm down before he said something the people surrounding them had no business hearing. He looked around the area, searching for much-needed privacy for this conversation with Kaci. His gaze landed on County's command truck.

"Follow me," he said, and marched to the vehicle. He took both stairs in one leap and heard Kaci follow.

A uniformed deputy sat behind a console running the length of the vehicle about the size of a package delivery truck. He looked up, a question in his gaze.

Cal eyed him and held out his credentials. "Leave us."

The deputy with a gleaming bald head and stern expression watched him for a moment, but then stood and brushed past them before stomping down the stairs. Cal tried to be nicer to local officers, as the country's well-being depended on local law enforcement, but right now Cal didn't have the time or patience for anything but obtaining details on Tara Parrish's location. And he didn't even have patience to wait for that. He spun on Kaci.

"Tell me where she is," he demanded without apology for his pushy behavior.

"Her PO Box is in Dufur, Oregon," Kaci replied. "It's a small town outside the Mount Hood National Forest. She's working at the Fivemile Butte Lookout Tower as a fire lookout."

Cal blinked a few times, processing the news. "Oregon isn't on her list of places she's vacationed and doesn't fit her pattern."

"No, but you have to admit a fire tower is a perfect place to go to ground." Kaci took off her glasses and settled them on top of her head, pushing back gleaming dark hair. "She lives in the tower full-time, not meeting face-to-face with people, and she only comes to town to get supplies and use the post office."

"You're sure it's Tara?"

Kaci bobbed her head. "The postal worker in Dufur ID'd a picture of her."

"Wait a minute. Back up." Cal took a step closer. "You have the worker identifying Tara, but how did you find her in the first place?"

A cocky grin slid across Kaci's lips. An expert in cyber investigations, she knew her skills were second to none. "Remember I told you about Etsy."

Cal nodded. "The online site where Tara once sold her animal photos. You said her account was inactive."

"*That* account is, but she's selling landscape pictures under a new account. Not in her name, of course."

"So how'd you track her?" Cal flashed up his hand. "And if this is one of those geek kind of things, dumb it down for me, okay?"

"It isn't complicated at all, and even *you* can understand it." She chuckled and didn't seem the least bit put-upon to explain yet one more bit of technology. "With the waitress jobs Tara's been taking, we all figured she'd need extra money to live on, right? So I took that a step further. As an amateur photographer, she successfully sold photos before. What better way to make money anonymously than selling pictures again? I figured she'd have an online storage account for her pictures so she could access and sell from anywhere."

"And did she?"

Kaci nodded. "I found a link on the desktop computer in her row house. So I cracked her password and found a whole slew of marketable landscape pictures. I had my team regularly upload these pictures into Google's reverse image search. Finally the search engine hit on one, which led me to her new Etsy account."

"Explain the Google thing."

"On Google's image page, you can click on the camera icon in the search box. It then gives you the option to upload a picture. After you do, Google runs a search and returns links for any web address where the image has been posted online."

"Really?" he asked, trying to make sense of her statement. "So I could upload a picture of myself and Google would find it if someone's posted it online?"

"Yes, but one caveat. Google's Internet bots would have to crawl the Net and index the files from the picture sites. The bots don't crawl every website, and the ones they do crawl aren't necessarily done in the same time span. And webmasters can use their robots.txt file to block Google bots, too."

"Okay, now you're getting into terms I'm not familiar with. I get the gist of what you're saying, so please stop before you make my head spin."

"Aw." She laughed. "What fun is there in that?"

He grinned and had to admit smiling felt good, until the thought of going to Oregon and surprising Tara—seeing her again—took it away. It would be no hardship to lay eyes on this woman who was so vital to his case, but she was also the woman who hadn't left his thoughts for three months and not only for professional reasons. Still, that wouldn't stop him from traveling to Oregon to get the information he needed from her. Not for one second.

"Why didn't you tell me you were working on this?" he asked.

"Honestly?"

He nodded.

"You've been so frustrated with all the dead ends that I didn't want to get your hopes up if this didn't pan out."

"Well, it did, and I owe you big-time," he said sincerely.

"And you know I'll collect, right?"

He nodded, but his mind had already transitioned to his next move. Since he had no way of knowing if Tara still resided in Oregon, he'd go alone and leave the team in Dallas to work the scene. If he did locate her, he'd call in the Knights to assist in her transport back to D.C.

He checked his watch. Nearly two o'clock. It would take an hour or so for their pilot to be ready for takeoff, and then a four-hour flight to Portland, giving him plenty of time to get his emotions in check so when he came face-to-face with Tara again, he didn't let the frustrations over her taking off on him interfere in his hunt for Keeler.

"Okay." He clapped his hands. "Since Max is in town, he can take charge here, and I'll leave for Portland right away."

"One thing, though," Kaci added, this time frowning. "We both know from tracking Keeler that he has strong tech skills. So you also have to know if I located Tara, Keeler can find her, too."

Mount Hood National Forest, Oregon
8:05 p.m.

The oppressive, sultry night settled over the Mount Hood National Forest. Tara raised her binoculars and ran them over the trees. She was on alert 24/7. She had to be. Not only as her new job as a forest fire lookout, but also in search for Oren before he made good on his warning to kill her.

She rested her elbows on the rough deck railing surrounding her thirty-foot-tall tower and scanned the horizon still warm with the sun's sinking rays. Finding the area free from smoke, she dropped her focus to the ground and ran the binoculars along the edge of the clearing below.

Sudden movement in the brush sent a jolt of fear racing through her body. She zoomed in and found a deer, a smaller five-point buck edging through the trees. Fitting for the Fivemile Butte Lookout Tower, she supposed.

She blew out a breath and leaned over the railing to complete her search on the south side of the platform. The long scar on her stomach pulled tight, drawing her thoughts to Agent Cal Riggins's rescue as happened every time the now-familiar ache ran through her abdomen. If he hadn't shown up moments after Oren had shot her, she would've bled out.

As a former SEAL, Agent Riggins possessed

extensive first aid skills. At least he'd told her he'd been a SEAL. He certainly had the body and intensity that she associated with a SEAL, \and with the exceptional team he belonged to, she supposed.

She owed her life to him gallantly sweeping in on a chopper. He'd only wanted her help in return. Easy, right? Wrong. She'd planned to help him, but then Oren had shown up at the hospital, and she couldn't stay even if she hadn't sufficiently recovered and getting around was painful.

She still wanted to help, though. She would do anything to assist in finding Oren, but no matter how hard she tried, the night at the pump house remained fuzzy. Who knew, maybe the terror from Oren's threat kept her mind locked down. She couldn't come up with details needed to help find him, but his visit? That she remembered. Clearly. His eyes, the hatred, the vengeance, all sent a shudder raking over her body.

She slipped her finger under a thick red rubber band circling her wrist, snapped it, and let the resounding sting take her attention and stave off her fear. She'd discovered this pattern breaker on the Internet and used it to help let go of her anxiety and choose a new behavior. She pulled again.

Snap. The pain sizzled up her arm, but the anxiety sat on her shoulders like the weight of Mount Hood in the distance.

She should have known one snap wouldn't

work today—the first of the month, Oren's scheduled day to detonate a bomb. After moving to Dallas to make it harder for Oren to find her, she'd discovered he'd killed a coworker in Atlanta, likely because he couldn't get to her, and she didn't want the same thing to happen in Dallas. So she'd warned her coworkers at Pecos Palace and moved to Oregon. But she kept fearing for their lives, so yesterday she'd risked the FBI finding her and made a computer call to their hotline, begging them to protect her friends in Dallas.

If only she'd caught on to Oren's plan sooner.

Snap.

He would likely detonate a bomb today. Who would he kill?

Snap. Snap.

Hopefully Agent Riggins and his team were in Dallas with her friends.

Snap. Snap. Snap.

The rubber band failed to calm her for the first time ever. Maybe finishing her search would help. She moved to the other side of the tower. Perched on a hill that fell off into a rocky cliff, the tower couldn't be approached from the west side. Still, she lifted the binoculars to sweep the area, looking for any hint of smoke. Black meant structures or vehicles were burning. Sometimes pines thick with resin would first burn dark. White smoke signaled lighter fuels like grass, twigs, and pine needles.

No fires in sight, but she wouldn't end her sweep until she made certain Oren wasn't lurking nearby. She left nothing to chance anymore. She trusted no one and questioned everything. Even FBI agents. They disappeared when needed. She now planned each move. Calculated each step. No more mistakes. Finding the bombs and running had almost been fatal. Another mistake could cost her life.

She shifted and her view landed on Mount Hood, the top barely peppered with snow due to a dry spring and warmer-than-normal summer temperatures. Heavy clouds clung to the peak, but the forecast didn't hold rain. A cool breeze drifted across the deck as her binoculars traveled farther west, landing on headlights slinking into the driveway, the vehicle coming to a stop at the gate about a quarter mile out.

She zoomed the lens closer, but in the fading light she couldn't make out the driver sitting behind the wheel.

Oren?

Was it really him?

Only authorized forestry personnel could open the gate, but a simple lock wouldn't stop Oren. Nothing would.

She had no time to waste. She had to move. Now!

She raced inside the cabin and grabbed the bag she'd prepared for a day such as this. She'd run the escape drill several times, and she went on autopilot. At twenty miles per hour, the top speed at which any vehicle could take the pitted drive, it took a minute to reach the tower. Add unlocking the gate, getting out, punching in the code, lifting the lock, getting back into the car, then making the drive, and that equaled four minutes at a minimum. She could collect her bag and rifle and get down three flights of stairs to take cover in her blind in the woods in two minutes flat, well before anyone spotted her.

She snatched the rifle hanging by the door before hitting the circuit breaker for the outside light, dousing the area in a dusky haze. She bolted for the stairs. Her pulse raced as she descended, one foot after the other landing on the metal treads by rote memory, sure and swift like she'd practiced. She counted them down, fifteen to each landing, times three.

She hit the ground hard, and a puff of gritty dust filtered into the air. Her breathing accelerated, and she silently crept across the flat land. Over dormant grass dotted with weeds. Past the picnic table and fire pit. The outhouse.

She slipped into the camouflaged hunting blind she'd staked at the edge of the woods and secured the fabric door before rolling up the opening meant for targeting and firing a weapon at an animal. She lifted her binoculars into the opening.

The light waned, the sky now purple and

ominous. She'd scanned down the drive toward the car. A dark fog colored her vision, but she saw no one behind the wheel.

He's on his way.

Adrenaline spiking, her hands trembling, she jostled the binoculars as she scanned up the drive. Slowly. Inch by inch.

No one.

At least she didn't think anyone was sneaking down the driveway, but the sun had made its final plunge below the horizon, and cloaking shadows now obscured the drive. He would have to show up at dusk. Of course he would. Easier to sneak up on her. But she'd planned for this—for every situation she could imagine, and her imagination had been vivid all these days since she'd run from him.

A shiver ran over her, and her whole body shook.

"Get a grip," she whispered. "You're prepared. Just follow your plan."

She dug into her bag. Pulled out night-vision binoculars she'd purchased should an occasion like this arise. She lifted them into the opening and scanned, her breath catching in her throat. Still nothing. No one. She blinked hard, clearing her eyes, and looked again. Whoever had come calling had to have taken to the woods.

Fine. The scrub was thick and tangled. No way he could get through that brush without her hearing his movements, but not from inside the blind.

She sat back to think. She was safer in the blind. Especially with nightfall. She'd blend in with the trees.

Time ticked by. Minute after minute. Waiting.

"Enough," she whispered.

She wouldn't keep sitting there, waiting for him to come kill her. She'd never be a victim again like she was at the pump house. She lived through that nightmare and was stronger now. Prepared and experienced. She would take action, leave the protection of the blind, stay a few steps ahead of Oren to get to the truck she'd hidden down the road, and flee from Oregon.

She flipped open the door, the soft sound of the polyester fabric whispering into the quiet.

She got to her knees and shouldered her bag. After a deep breath of resolve, she made ready to leave while staying low to the ground to minimize the target she presented.

"Hello, Tara." A male voice came from just outside her blind, in the black of night, paralyzing her and leaving no time to grab her rifle for protection.

CHAPTER 6

Cal flipped on his Maglite and aimed it above Tara's head. Her face bone-white, she didn't respond to his greeting, but seemed frozen in place, drawing in air and blowing it out.

He holstered his gun and gave her a moment to compose herself while he ran his gaze over her to be sure her race from the tower hadn't resulted in an injury.

Her cutoff jeans and tank top gave him a good look at her body that had turned to hard muscle the last three months. She'd been working out, likely to ensure she had the physical stamina to evade Keeler. And the bright yellow socks embroidered with black cats sticking out of her hiking boots? They weren't at all helpful in evading a bomber, but maybe they made her smile.

She crossed her arms and stared at him. He felt bad for sneaking up on her, but he wouldn't apologize. She'd given him no choice. She'd bailed on him once, so when he'd arrived and she'd taken off from the tower, the element of surprise had been his only option.

Besides, she might be frightened now, but he'd found her before Keeler caught up to her, and she would get over her fear. Death at Keeler's hands . . . not so much. She was alive, and he could keep her that way. *If* she listened to him, which he had no confidence that she could do, considering she'd gone into hiding for months.

It made his head hurt just to think of the challenge facing him.

She sat up straighter. "What are you doing here, Agent Riggins?"

And let the sparring begin. "I still need your help to bring in Keeler and want you to come back to D.C. with me."

She tightened her arms. "I'm sure you have other ways of finding him."

Interesting response. "Is that why you ran from the hospital? Because you thought we could find him without you?"

She watched him with wary eyes, but he chose to wait for her answer. He certainly wouldn't say something foolish and spook her into running again when he needed her help.

She sighed out a long breath and dropped her arms to her side, looking defeated. Surprisingly, he preferred the lifted chin and challenging look, but the crushed expression was more likely to get him what he needed.

"I left because I'd told you everything I knew about Oren, and I couldn't give you any other help," she said. "But mostly, I ran because your agent failed."

"What agent? When?" he asked, honestly confused.

"The man you put in charge of protecting me at the hospital."

"Agent Fields? How?"

"He left his station outside my door, and Oren came to the window. He glared at me and mouthed, 'You're dead.' It wasn't hard to figure out if he could get to me with an agent in charge, he could get to me anywhere."

"Impossible." Cal clenched his hands. "Maybe you dreamt seeing Keeler."

She shook her head hard, sending her hair swinging over bare shoulders, and she planted her hands on curvy hips. "This is why I didn't tell you about it at the hospital. I knew you'd stick up for your agent, and you wouldn't believe me. But trust me, the incident is real. I can recount it for you in vivid detail if you'd like, but all you need to know is that it *did* happen. Ask your agent. If he's truthful, he'll tell you he left me alone."

He trusted Agent Fields, who hadn't reported stepping away from Tara's door, but her story was convincing. "Even if it did happen that's no reason to run."

"Isn't it?" She arched an eyebrow, and her gaze lingered on him for a moment. "Oren proved he could get to me. I couldn't rely on any of you and had to disappear."

"And how's that working out for you?" he snapped, but instantly regretted it when her shoulders drooped a fraction before rising again into a hard line. He should have kept his anger in check, but he hated that she couldn't rely on him. Hated that it was another in a long list of failures of late. But that wasn't her fault, and he shouldn't take it out on her.

"I'm sorry," he said sincerely. "That was uncalled for. If Agent Fields was negligent, I'll make sure he's taken to task. And going forward, I won't trust your care to anyone else. I'll personally see to your safety."

She didn't move, didn't change expressions, but shifted to stare over his shoulder. He could almost hear the thoughts racing through her head. Could she trust him? Was it better to be with an agent than on her own? Should she even listen to him?

"Look," he said before she voiced additional opposition. "Why don't we go up to the tower to talk about this?"

Her gaze returned to him and locked on like a heat-seeking missile. "There's nothing to talk about."

He counteracted her intensity with a smile. "Humor me, okay? Give me five more minutes of your time."

"Fine. Five minutes, and then you hit the road." She grabbed her rifle and brushed past him to march across the clearing to the stairs.

Her pack on one shoulder, the rifle strap over the other, she stormed up the metal treads. He followed, his eyes locked on her toned legs, and his thoughts took a very unprofessional path.

He dragged his gaze away and ran it over the area. For some reason, his frog sense that warned him on SEAL missions to take extra care crawled up his back and left him uneasy. Why, he didn't know, but he'd keep his eyes open.

At the top landing, she stepped through the open door and flipped on a light switch.

He gestured at her rifle. "Do you know how to use that, or do I have to worry about stray bullets?"

"I learned to hunt as a kid, and I'll bet I've spent more hours at a firing range in the last few months than you have." Her chin shot up again.

She was trying to look tough, but he saw her as a cute, irresistible woman who was willing to take on her own personal Goliath to survive, and dang if the uneasiness that had been plaguing him for months didn't nearly melt on the spot to be replaced with his interest for her as a woman.

She caught his gaze—his intent—and frowned as she spun away.

Good. She didn't want to have anything to do with him. Her attitude stung, but it would help keep him on track when he had no business thinking about her as a woman. She was a witness and a vital part of this investigation, for goodness' sake, and he needed to keep things professional so he didn't get distracted and miss an important lead or put her in danger.

He took a quick look at the single room measuring a couple hundred square feet. White cabinets with aged Formica tops ringed the lower portion of the walls. The upper walls were made of solid glass. Not a good place to defend against an attack.

She went straight to the corner, stowed her bag in a cabinet, then hopped up on top. Leaning back, she rested her feet on the rung of a wooden folding chair with a canvas sling that he suspected had occupied the tower since the fifties. She rested the rifle on her knees as if she thought she needed protection against him.

"There's no point in pleading your case," she said. "Since I don't know anything that can help you, I won't put myself in a position to allow Oren to get to me. That means I won't be going back to D.C. with you. I'm good on my own."

Cal crossed the space and leaned against the ledge of a wide viewing window, trying to act causal and ignore his mounting frustration. "Okay, let's say for a minute that's true—and I'm not in any way saying it is—can you honestly turn your back on women whose lives could depend on your help in stopping Keeler?"

Her gaze wavered, and she nibbled on her full lower lip, telling him more about her character than anything had so far. She wanted to help, but fear had gotten the best of her, overpowering her desire to do the right thing.

Once upon a time, he might have promised more than seeing to her safety and gone on to assure her that he could keep her alive. All in the name of gaining her assistance, but now he was wiser. Far wiser, and he recognized that no one could make such a promise, especially not him. He had no control over life-or-death matters. Only God had the power to save lives. When it came to Cal, the big guy had been silent far too long, and Cal had no faith that God would break His silence now.

Still, Cal's job required him to persuade Tara to accompany him to Washington. He'd do that job to give her the best chance at surviving and to put another bad guy behind bars. "I remain convinced that you saw something that can lead us to Keeler."

She held up her hand. "I wasn't lying at the hospital when I told you the details of my time in the pump house are fuzzy. And nothing has changed."

He peered into eyes clear from guile and deceit. "It's not that I don't believe you, but if you'll come back to D.C., our team will help draw out those memories. We can play the audio of your call from the pump house, and even though the building was destroyed, a visit to the ruins could help stir your memories."

He pushed off the ledge and stepped closer.

She shot a panicked look around the space as if she wanted to flee.

He came to a stop to keep from threatening her more. "You're reluctant to do this. I get it, and I wouldn't put you through it if there was any other way to stop Keeler."

"Do you get it?" She jumped to her feet and crossed her arms over the rifle. "Oren killed a woman I cared about in Atlanta. I have to stay away from people—all people—if I don't want him to kill more of my friends. I couldn't live with myself if another person died because of me."

Surprised by her response, Cal was at a loss for words. He was wrong. Fear for her own safety wasn't holding her back; it was fear for others and guilt. Emotions he was on a first-name basis with. He deserved his guilt. She didn't.

He gentled his voice. "You didn't set those bombs, Tara. Keeler did. This is all on him, not you. You can't live your life thinking your actions cause him to kill. I won't have you feeling guilty."

Her chin lifted higher. "I'm not sure you can stop it."

"Guilt will cloud many things in your life if you let it," he said, knowing full well the repercussions in his own life. "Your judgment will be compromised. That could interfere in finding Keeler."

She recoiled but quickly hid her response, and he had no idea what had caused such a visceral reaction from her.

"What is it?" he asked.

She took a breath and blew it out, as if clearing the discussion from her brain. Or maybe clearing him from her brain. "How did you find me?"

She'd changed the subject. Avoidance, pure and simple. If she was to be effective in helping them, he would need to keep an eye out for any impact her guilt had on their hunt for Keeler. For now, he'd let it go and answer her question. "Your aunt."

"Not possible. I purposely didn't contact June so she couldn't be put on the spot by you or Oren. I love her far too much to put her in harm's way."

"She didn't give us your location," he said. "But she did give us access to your things and shared your vacation pictures. I work with an extraordinary team, and it only takes a scrap of information for us to succeed."

"Okay, so you got my pictures and figured out that I was moving to cities where I'd vacationed. Doesn't explain how you came to Oregon. I've never been here before."

"True, but our computer expert discovered you'd previously sold photos on Etsy." He explained the search process as Kaci had explained it to him and hoped he'd gotten it right.

Tara's eyes widened. "You can do that?"

He nodded. "Once she found your online storefront at Etsy, it was easy to locate the rest of your information." He met her gaze head-on and dreaded telling her the next bit, but if it got her to come back to D.C. and remain under his watchful protection, it was worth scaring her. "You know Keeler has strong tech skills. He can find you, too."

She grabbed a rubber band at her wrist and snapped it. One. Two. Three times. Her gaze shot around the space and panic lodged in her eyes as it had that horrible night three months ago.

Memories often faded over time, but that one hadn't left Cal's mind. He could see her stomach ripped open, a silent plea for help as she bled out. He remembered pressing the gauze. The blood seeping through his fingers. Her tortured groans as he hoofed it through the woods, her body cradled in his arms. The pain on her face as she gazed up at him, then looking like an injured puppy in the hospital, and he'd wanted to take her home. Care for her. Vanquish this man who had shot her and left her for dead. To bring back her old life, follow this unwelcome interest in her and maybe be a part of that life.

And that's where this crazy thinking had to end.

He shouldn't have let even a hint of his attraction gain a foothold in his mind, let alone allow the thoughts to take as much space as they already did.

She was an integral part of his investigation. The key to locating Keeler. The man who'd killed seven women so far. Seven! And Cal had been powerless to stop him like the day he'd been powerless to save the young boy cradled in his arms.

Cal had failed them all.

Guilt pressed in from all sides, and he shook his head to clear his mind. He couldn't be thinking about the past. About Tara like this. He had to focus.

He couldn't—no, wouldn't—do anything to jeopardize his hunt for the Lone Wolf.

CHAPTER 7

Tara tuned out Agent Riggins's continued attempts to convince her to accompany him back to D.C. She avoided looking at his ruggedly handsome face and peered at his suit that fit the wide planes of his chest and shoulders like a glove. Pricey, she thought, as were the loafers polished to military precision.

Odd that he'd chosen to wear a suit in the woods, but maybe he thought it would make him seem more intimidating. Or not, as he'd once asked her to call him Cal and that wasn't intimidating. More likely his way of manipulating her into thinking he was a friend. Well, he wasn't a friend. They had a professional relationship, nothing more, and she'd stick with the formality of calling him Agent Riggins like she'd decided to do at the hospital.

Keeping things strictly business was even more necessary now that he'd proved his agenda was in direct opposition to hers. She wanted to stay alive. He wanted to find Oren, no matter what, even if she got hurt in the process.

Oh, for a moment she'd thought he'd been trying to help her come to grips with her guilt—a brief little inkling in time filled with hope—but then, when he'd brought it all back to finding Oren, poof, her good feelings evaporated.

"You're not listening," he said.

His accusatory tone set her teeth on edge. "The five minutes you requested was up long ago."

He arched an eyebrow. "Then I need your answer."

She didn't have one, and until she did, she'd use the opportunity to gain information that she'd craved for the last few months. "Suppose you answer a question for me first."

He continued to watch her, his eyes guarded. "Go ahead."

"I'm worried about my aunt June. Oren cares about her, so I don't think he'll hurt her, but I need to know if she's in danger, too."

"She's fine. I've had a team with her round the clock since you took off."

Surprise. "I didn't think the FBI had money for full-time protection like that."

He averted his gaze and became unnaturally still. A behavior she recognized courtesy of her former fiancé, Nolan, who'd acted the same way when he'd tried to hide things from her.

Exactly what was Agent Riggins hiding? Did it have to do with June?

"Wait," she said as thoughts popped into her head. "You didn't put the agents there to watch over June. You did it because you hoped Oren would show up and you could capture him."

Agent Riggins didn't answer, and time ticked by, but she held her tongue and waited him out.

"My motives were mixed," he finally said, but didn't elaborate. "As they are with you. I need your help, but I don't want to inflict additional pain on you. I hope you'll voluntarily accompany me back to Washington."

After his high-handed behavior, she hadn't expected his kindness, and it brought to mind his care and compassion as he'd rescued her and held her hand on the chopper ride to the hospital. Since he'd arrived tonight, she'd focused on his negatives. No one was one-sided—well, maybe Nolan had been after his true colors had come out—but she doubted the compassionate agent she'd seen at her rescue was the monster she was making him out to be.

That didn't mean she was eager to go back to D.C. "What happens if I choose not to go with you?"

He remained motionless for a long moment, then pulled a piece of paper from his interior jacket pocket and handed it to her. She felt his eyes on her as she unfolded the page, but he didn't have to watch for long. The title of the document showed his intent. She slowly refolded the paper and looked up to find hesitation in his gaze, but she didn't care what he was thinking. She cared only about the message he'd just sent.

"You have a warrant for my arrest?"

"You gave me no choice."

She wanted to give him the benefit of the doubt, but he'd gone too far. Pushing, prodding, now threatening her. After she'd broken off her engagement to Nolan, a real control freak, she swore she'd never let anyone push her around like Agent Riggins was trying to do, but this was a legal document, and short of becoming a fugitive, she could do nothing about it.

That didn't mean she'd roll over and let him get away with this strong-arm tactic. "I didn't do anything wrong, and you can't prove I did."

"By taking off as you did, you gave us probable cause to name you as a suspect and allowed us to obtain a warrant to question you."

"That's ridiculous." She stood and shoved the paper back into his hands. "You talked to me that night. You heard my voice and how terrified I was. Then you grilled me at the hospital and must have seen the same thing."

"Okay, fine. We know you're not working with Keeler, but I *do* know that you can help us. And you should know . . ." His gaze darkened with an intensity that reminded her of her last conversation with Nolan when she'd handed back his ring and walked out the door. "I'll do anything it takes to bring in the Lone Wolf. If that means I have to arrest you to get you back to D.C., I will."

At the thought of returning to the bombed-out shell of the pump house, anxiety rose up and tried to smother her. She snapped the bands as a palpable pull seemed to draw her toward the door, but she couldn't go running off into the night. Oren might be right behind Agent Riggins.

"So will you come with me?" he asked.

"I need more time to think about it," she replied, in hopes of coming up with an effective argument to his warrant.

"Sorry, no can do. Keeler could be closing in on us, and we should get going now."

She widened her stance and drew her shoulders back, though at her height of five seven to his over six feet, she knew he didn't see her as a serious physical threat. At least such a stance hadn't affected Nolan in any way.

Nevertheless, she remained locked in position. "I'm not leaving here until a replacement lookout is in place."

"That could take time."

"Then it'll take time. I ran when Oren got close before, and he killed a friend because of me. I won't run now and risk a forest fire killing more people."

"Fine." The agent who had so quickly become a pain in her side worked the muscles in his jaw. "We'll spend the night here. You think about whether you'll come willingly or not, and I'll pull some strings to get another lookout here ASAP. Does that work with you?"

"I'd rather have the time alone to think."

"Not an option. Not with the chance that Keeler knows about this location." He took his own wide stance, and the powerful planting of his feet was far more effective than hers had been. "You go ahead and get some rest. I'll take watch while I make a few calls."

"Are you kidding me?" Her voice shot up before she controlled it to keep from showing him how much he riled her. "First, I haven't agreed to you calling in a replacement. Second, I didn't say you could stay here. And third, if I do agree, there's no way I'm going to sleep and leave you in charge."

"Oh, I'm staying, all right. With or without your permission." His tone put up a solid brick wall that would be tough to break through. "I'm trained to spot threats—you're not—making me the best one to take watch."

"I may not have your fancy FBI training, but

I've lived the school of hard knocks the last few months, and I've done fine on my own."

He arched a brow. "Have you?"

"I'm alive, and Oren hasn't found me."

"Yet." One word, but the deadly implication lingered in the air.

"All the more reason for me to stay awake and remain vigilant."

"We'll compromise and take turns standing watch." He paused and locked eyes with her. "Because when people get tired, they make mistakes. And in your case, Tara, any mistake you make could be fatal."

10:05 p.m.

Cal disconnected his call with Sheriff Gorton to reaffirm his deputies continued to stand watch. After Cal had confirmed Tara's identity, he'd arranged with the sheriff to set up a perimeter in the area until the Knights could arrive and assist Cal in escorting her back to Washington. Unfortunately, that only prevented Keeler from driving up to the property. It wouldn't stop him from hiking through acres of surrounding forest. Cal needed to remain alert, and despite saying he planned to take turns standing watch, he'd be on guard every minute of the night.

He stepped onto the balcony. A soft breeze whispered through the trees and carried cooler air, relieving the heat from inside. Tara had dragged out the sling-back chair and announced she would sit in it for the rest of the night.

He didn't like her being outside and exposed, but he'd pushed her far enough for one night, and if he ordered her to come inside, she'd probably try to fling him off the edge.

Despite the potential danger surrounding them, thoughts of her trying to pick him up and heave him over the rail made him smile. She'd become one tough little cookie. Not that even with her new strength she could accomplish such a feat, but he could see her trying.

He let his gaze settle on her face bathed in the moon's golden glow. He studied her big, bright eyes ringed with long lashes, her high cheekbones, and her makeup-free, flawless complexion, and his heart took a tumble.

She was beautiful, no doubt, but it was more than that. As she'd asked about his reasons for putting a detail on her aunt, he couldn't answer right away because he actually cared about what she thought about him. That was a new one for him. He hadn't cared about other people's opinions for eons, and the thought had kept his mouth closed.

She caught him staring at her and frowned. "I've got the first watch if you want to take a beauty nap."

"I'm pretty enough, thank you very much," he joked, hoping to lighten the mood. It only gained him a roll of her eyes. "Since we're both awake, what say I run a few things past you for your opinion?"

"What kind of things?" Suspicion lingered in her eyes.

He liked the strength she'd acquired, but not this guarded attitude that said she'd lost her innocence. He couldn't even remember a time when he thought people were basically good. Certainly not since he landed on foreign soil and took part in Operation Iraqi Freedom followed by years of deployment in Afghanistan. He'd experienced terrorism firsthand, learning lessons that she was coming to understand in a very graphic way. He'd been a big part of painting that picture for her. Now, he would play an even bigger role, and he didn't like being the one to chase out her faith in her fellow man. But his opinion didn't matter. Not with a killer to apprehend.

He firmed his resolve to do his job. "I've lived in Keeler's head for the last six months. I've walked in his shoes and talked to everyone who's had anything to do with him since he was born." He crossed over to her and rested against the railing. "We're hunting him based on my conclusions, and it would help if you shot holes in it if I'm incorrect."

"Go on," she said, not really admitting she'd help him.

"First, you should know, with the number of lives Keeler has taken, he fits the definition of a serial killer." He glanced at Tara to see her reaction, but her expression remained blank.

"These killers," Cal continued, "are driven by motives and reasons that are uniquely theirs. But there are certain interpersonal traits common to serial murderers. They include superficial charm, a grandiose sense of self-worth, pathological lying, and the manipulation of others. Does any of this sound like Keeler?"

"Maybe," she said, sounding unaffected by his question, but the snap of a rubber band on her wrist told him otherwise.

He didn't know what was up with the bands, but logic said she used them as a coping mechanism. He chose not to make her uncomfortable by questioning her about them and waited for her to continue.

"Oren was far from charming in high school. He embraced the Goth look and gave everyone an attitude, including me. Oddly enough, even when he showed such a hard exterior, I always thought he had a naïve outlook. I know it's been months, but I can still hardly believe he's the bomber."

Cal knew Keeler was as far from naïve as they come. "What I don't understand is why someone so into Goth would enlist in the army."

"I never got that either. I know his dad forced that issue. His mom didn't want to talk about it.

Our friendship had ended, so I don't know the details except that he stayed in for four years and then went to college on Uncle Sam's money to get a degree in electrical engineering."

"But his father's death ended that, right?"

She nodded. "His dad had a heart attack in Oren's third year. He had to go home to run the farm. As it turns out, he ran it into the ground. Maybe if he'd finished college he'd have gotten a good job instead of assembling security systems and things would be different."

"Degree or not, those three years in college gave him the skills to create very complicated bombs."

She frowned but didn't comment.

"Tell me about after high school," Cal said. "How often did you see him then?"

"I was in college when his dad died, but when I came home to see June, I'd occasionally run into him. By then, he'd let go of the clean-cut military look and was back to the Goth style. And as I told you before, the last time I saw him was at June's house in January. He'd cleaned up his act and was quite charming."

"Charm and manipulation," Cal muttered. "True hallmarks of a serial killer."

She met his gaze. "That charm and manipulation is true of you, too, but you're not a serial killer."

He deserved her comment but that didn't stop him from cringing and looking back at the night scenery. "Serial killers fail to accept responsibility for their actions. They're irresponsible and impulsive and lack empathy, guilt, or remorse. They also don't have realistic life goals and exhibit poor behavioral controls." He met her gaze again and made sure to keep his tone light. "None of this can be said for me."

"Touché. Your need to find Oren at any cost is very clear, telling me how goal oriented you are."

Cal still needed her to answer his questions, so he let her comment slide, which in itself confirmed her claim. "Keeler has the added distinction of having been radicalized."

"Which means what exactly?"

"Our research says he turned his back on his country, accepted ISIS's views, and aligned himself with them. We don't believe he's acting as an official part of the group. More like a loner with loose ties to the organization, hence the Lone Wolf name assigned to him."

She shifted to face him, and he could tell he'd gained her interest. "Isn't that odd? Going off on his own like that?"

"In today's world, no. He's one of thousands across the country committed to Islamic groups but only possessing a shallow understanding of Islam."

"Then why join them?"

"People like Keeler are restless and feel trapped in an uneventful life. They're disenfranchised or alienated. They long to belong to something where they're welcomed and their grievances are validated. At the same time, they become obsessed with deadly terrorist acts carried out in the name of faith. They think committing these acts will relieve their emotional distress. No cause. Just self-serving violence."

She sighed and twisted her hands together. At least she wasn't snapping the rubber bands and making her wrist even redder.

"I don't know about the acts in the name of faith," she finally said. "But the rest of what you described sounds very much like the Oren I knew in high school."

"So my thoughts are on target?"

She nodded and got up to stare over the balcony. "You've never told me how Oren killed them. I mean, I know he used bombs, but you didn't share any details. Or did you on the phone that night? I can't remember."

"No," he replied, and wished she hadn't chosen this topic for tonight.

She'd said she'd only heard about one woman killed by Keeler since she'd left D.C., meaning she didn't know about today's bombing. He would have to tell her about that and share the details of other bombs at some point, but he didn't want to mention it tonight and spook her into taking off again.

"Maybe that should wait," he suggested. "Until later."

She spun so quickly, if she'd been an attacker, he couldn't have reacted fast enough, and as a former SEAL, he moved lightning fast.

"Please stop trying to control every little thing. My ex was a master at pushing me around, and I won't stand for it." Barely contained anger vibrated in her voice.

Cal was hot and tired, and if she continued to argue with him he might snap, but June had told him about the jerk Tara had split with, and Cal didn't want to add to her distress, so he held his frustration in check for now.

"We'll talk about it another day." He forced out a smile to make peace with her. "I promise."

"I need the information tonight to make my decision," she insisted, sending him over the edge.

"Okay, fine. You know best. You want to know about the bombs? You got it." He snapped his phone from his belt clip with more force than necessary and navigated to his photos.

Despite his irritation, he kept the device at an angle to prevent her from seeing horrific pictures from bomb scenes and photos of the actual device Keeler had reconstructed.

He paused at a sketch he'd drawn of the bomb minus Keeler's skull and crossbones and held out his phone. "His devices are made of white PVC. Do you remember seeing something like this at the pump house?"

She shook her head. "I wish I could remember, but nothing comes to mind. What is it?"

"It's called a necklace bomb because it's placed around the victim's neck."

Her eyes flashed wide exactly like he expected would happen when she learned of the horror behind Keeler's bomb choice.

"The explosives are in the pipe?"

He nodded. "He fastens it around their neck and the device has a motion switch inside so the woman can't move without setting off the bomb. He then leaves and detonates it from a remote location so he doesn't get hurt."

"It . . . oh my . . . oh . . . the bomb must blow—"

"It does," he interrupted before she spoke aloud words that would make the situation even more unpalatable for her.

She blinked hard. "And that's what Oren is doing?"

Cal nodded and waited for her reaction. She didn't lash out, cry, or make any noise, for that matter. She nodded and went pale.

"It's worse than I thought," she whispered, her fingers going for a rubber band and pulling hard. "I can't believe someone I know is capable of doing something so terrible."

She closed her eyes and leaned her head back, her finger snapping the band over and over. He reached out and held her hand so she couldn't release the rubber band.

Her eyes flashed open, and she jerked her hand free. "Don't. Don't do that. I need something to help me handle my stress. But then you probably think I'm foolish and the rubber bands are a big waste of time."

"Hardly," he replied, and tucked his hand back into his pocket. "I know what you're feeling, Tara. Believe me, I know. If there was any way I could take the pain and distress from you, I would."

CHAPTER 8

Surprised to see the sun, Tara blinked a few times and stared up at treetops dusted with the golden glow of morning sunlight. She'd slept deeply and had a nightmare-free night for the first time since she'd discovered Oren's bomb-making supplies.

She closed her eyes again and savored the sun's warmth, the soft breeze drifting through the window, and the melodic birds singing from surrounding pines. Peace. Heaven-sent peace.

Movement sounded from the far end of the room, and her eyes flew open, her heart racing like a Thoroughbred. Agent Riggins stood looking out the far window, his back to her.

Right. It's him. He's still here. Waiting for an answer.

She stifled a sigh to keep from drawing his

attention. She'd forgotten that this superagent, this man who infuriated her one minute and sent her pulse tripping faster the next, was in her little home away from the world.

She hadn't meant to fall asleep, but around two a.m., when the air turned too cool to stay outside, she'd dragged her chair inside, dropped into it to rest her eyes for a moment, and apparently nodded off. At some time, he'd covered her with a blanket. She couldn't believe she hadn't felt it.

If it had been Oren . . .

A shiver raked down her spine, and she forced her attention back to the man who seemed to take up all the space in the room. He'd shed his jacket, revealing a custom-tailored white shirt, wide at the shoulders and narrowing to a trim waist, and he'd rolled up the sleeves. His body looked like it was sculpted from marble, and his heart likely was, too, though he'd shown enough emotions last night to prove that he had a physical attraction to her, one he didn't want to have.

And here she was letting him get to her, too, even when his actions resembled Nolan's. If that wasn't enough reason to guard her heart, Agent Riggins had a singular purpose. Find Oren, and if he had to use people like her or her aunt along the way, then it seemed as if he had no qualms in doing so.

Putting up a solid wall on her emotions, she removed the blanket and folded it. He glanced at her. She waited for his first question of the day—for him to ask if she would voluntarily go back with him or if he'd need to take her into custody as he'd threatened.

He held up a steaming mug. "Hope you don't mind, but I made coffee."

She gaped at him. How had she missed the coffeemaker's ready beep? She really had zonked out if she hadn't heard the shrill alarm, not to mention feeling the blanket settling over her.

"You needed the rest," he said, as if reading her mind, before he resumed looking out the window. "Oh, and you should know. I've arranged for someone to take your place in the tower. She'll be here in a few hours."

Tara eyed him. "You had no right to call anyone, let alone put the wheels in motion without my input."

"Something you need to know about me." He turned and faced her full-on, the look of a hunter in his eyes. "I'm relentless in my pursuit of Keeler. I might step on your toes along the way, but I mean no harm in my actions."

She crossed her arms. "You think a blanket apology in advance will excuse all of your future actions?"

He shrugged.

"Do most people let you get away with taking over like this, Agent Riggins?"

He narrowed his eyes. "I'm not sure what you

mean by 'most people,' but if you're asking if I behave like this in my personal life, I don't have a life outside of work, so there's no one to offend."

"But would you?" she asked, though she had no business going down this path.

He shook his head. "Relationships require mutual respect. Nothing respectful about not including you in plans that impact your life."

"And yet you know it bothers me, and you'd do it again?"

"If it moved us closer to Keeler at a faster pace and helped us stop another woman from losing her life?" His breath came in hard fast bursts, his emotions churning in a melee on his face. "You better believe I'd do it again. In a heartbeat."

She stood watching his chest rise and fall with the passion he exuded for his work. His continued overbearing and controlling attitude should be putting her off. Instead, all she could think was that if he really meant what he'd said about mutual respect between a man and woman, he wasn't as superficial as she'd first thought, and he would be worth getting to know as a man and not this relentless agent.

Their gazes met and held for a moment, the air seeming to heat up in the space, but she ignored it, he ignored it, and a silent message of understanding passed between them. Though they were attracted to each other, neither would act upon it.

Never had she communicated so much in a single look.

He lazily drew his focus away to glance at his watch. "Now that the sun is up, if Keeler has tracked you, we can't risk him seeing my car at the gate. I'll stash it in the woods and grab a change of clothes while I'm out there."

"Or you could get in the car and drive back to the airport." *Or I could take off while you're gone.*

"I'm not leaving town without you. You can be certain of that." He grabbed his jacket from the chair and crossed over to her, each step reminding her of a panther stalking his prey. His piercing gaze pinned her in place.

"Don't even think about leaving," he said.

"You're a mind reader now?" she asked, hating that he was right.

He didn't speak but held her gaze for a moment before heading for the door. "I should be back in ten minutes or less."

He stepped onto the landing, and she let out a pent-up breath of frustration. She heard the outside padlock snick into place.

"Really," she called out. "You're locking me in?"

"You give me no choice."

Just like him to assume she'd take off. She supposed since she'd been thinking that very thing he was justified in his interpretation, but still. "Maybe you should have thought about it first. I have the key, and you won't be getting back inside until my replacement shows up."

"Are you sure?"

Keys jingled on the other side of the door, and she ran to her hiding place to jerk open the drawer. She found it empty. *Great.* He'd taken her keys while she'd slept, too. She wanted to stomp her foot in frustration, but she resisted displaying her anger for him to gloat over.

Not anger. Not really. She had no real intention of leaving before her replacement arrived. Still, she wouldn't let anyone bark orders at her.

She glanced out the window and caught sight of him as he skirted the edge of the clearing. A big, powerful guy, a real man's man, he also possessed the grace of a dancer and the tenacity of a bull.

He disappeared into the woods near her hunting blind. He was doing everything in his power to catch Oren, and for that she should be thankful and help him track Oren down.

So what if Agent Riggins was bossy and controlling? She knew how to handle that behavior. She'd learned the hard way when Nolan did an about-face after he'd put the engagement ring on her finger. He'd gone from a kind man to a guy who thought of her as his property and demanded she comply with his wishes. She didn't put up with his need to control her every step for long, but broke off their engagement and had only recently gotten her life back on track.

There was no way she would ever enter into a relationship with a man like that again.

But what about staying alive and getting her old life back? How did that work with going to D.C. and putting herself in Oren's path?

It didn't, but could she live with herself if Oren killed another person when she could have helped Agent Riggins stop him?

The answer was simple. No. She'd go to D.C. to help locate Oren, but she wouldn't let anything personal develop with Agent Riggins. And she wouldn't let down her guard and count on him for her protection. She might accompany him, but she would live as she had for the last three months, relying on herself alone to stay safe, as she still couldn't trust him to be there for her while he was so focused on capturing Oren.

"So you're going to D.C.," she whispered to the empty room, as if it could talk back and reinforce her decision, and she hoped—no, she prayed—she wasn't making the biggest mistake of her life.

Cal stepped through knee-high grass, seeds clinging to his dress slacks. He should have worn tactical clothes instead of the suit, but he thought Tara would respond better to the professional agent look he reluctantly took on when his job required it. He'd planned to march up to her tower last night, make a proper entrance, and offer a professional plea for her help.

"That went according to plan," he muttered as he slipped under the limb of a tall maple.

When she'd run again, he'd had no choice but to come after her. Then emotions had flown high between them in this ridiculous undercurrent that seemed to swirl round them. He made sure his presence kept people from crossing him or arguing, but Tara? She didn't care. She stood up to him. Impressed the heck out of him as much as it frustrated him.

He'd always been able to control his emotions, but, man. With her it was like she had antiaircraft ready to shoot down his defenses. That made him mad at himself. He got grumpy and fired back.

And if his behavior wasn't enough to make her run screaming, he'd come here to ask for her help, and what had he done in return? Nothing. Well, he'd locked her in the tower. That was less than nothing. He would never have done so if she didn't have a rifle and could handle it if needed.

His behavior was going to change starting the moment he returned to the tower. He'd control the way he responded to her and point out that she couldn't run on her own forever. That despite Agent Fields's failure to keep Keeler away from her at the hospital, the Knights would protect her—*he* would protect her. He'd remind her that she was needed to help catch Oren, and once he was caught, she'd be safe and could go back to a normal life. Then maybe she'd agree to accompany him back to D.C., and he could do right by her.

A twig snapped ahead, and he swung around to see a rabbit hop into the undergrowth. It could have been Keeler, and Cal's head was all wrapped up in Tara.

"Not good, man," he whispered to himself. "Focus."

One second of underestimating the enemy and people died.

God had given Cal the ability to save people, but He allowed them to die anyway. What point was there in women losing their lives in these bombs? In allowing a stray bullet to take Willy's life?

What a disaster that had been. Cal carried the boy as they fled from the drug cartel who had taken Willy and his missionary family hostage. Shocked, Cal had stood frozen in place, the boy cradled close, his heart no longer beating. Cal's second in command basically dragged him out of the compound so they could get to their exfil location in time. They boarded the aircraft, and for the whole flight to Dallas, he listened to the mother's keening wails and the father's mumbled prayers. It was the longest flight of Cal's life, and his palms sweat just thinking about it.

Where were you, God? Didn't these parents deserve their precious son?

He waited for an answer, but why? He'd been asking the same question for too long. Never finding answers. Never finding peace, and nothing he'd done or could do would erase the pain of losing a child. Sure, everyone's life was precious —these women Keeler had taken and others Cal had lost during his SEAL career—but the death of an innocent child was far harder to bear, and as a result Cal had left the SEALs behind and had tried to make sense of the loss.

Anger rose up and tried to suffocate him, but he swallowed it down and refocused before another tragedy occurred. He moved from tree to tree, scanning the area until he came upon his car. He took a few minutes to look deeper into the woods, and after he was convinced that no one lurked nearby, he slipped into his car and drove down the road, moving slowly and keeping his head on a swivel.

On his initial scouting of the area last night, he'd spotted a rusty old pickup in the brush up ahead. He'd jimmied the lock and found a tote bag filled with items Tara would use for a quick getaway, which was why he'd had to lock her inside the tower. He'd also pulled the distributor cap on the truck just in case. Even if she decided to run again, he could find her at the truck, so he bumped his vehicle off the road next to it. Once parked, he slipped out of his suit and into tactical pants and a team logo shirt. He resettled his holster and Glock before grabbing his comms unit. He clipped the radio on his belt and wove under his shirt the cord with a mic that sat at chest level and terminated in earbuds.

He inserted the buds in his ears, then pressed the talk switch. "Alpha Two. You in range?"

"Roger that." Brynn's voice came through his earbud. "We're ten minutes out."

"Report," he demanded without any pleasantries.

"We've reviewed satellite images and the op is set. County deputies are still in formation in a wide perimeter, and they'll remain in place until we move our package. I'll set up our command post at their rear and the rest of the team will set an interior line of defense. I'll also intercept the fire lookout when she arrives and deliver her safely to the tower. Then you and I will move the package to the command station. If things go according to plan, we'll have a county escort to the airport and have the package onboard our Cessna winging her way to D.C. by noon."

"According to plan," he muttered. "Let's make sure that happens, and we keep the package safe."

Calling Tara a package felt odd, but on the off chance that someone intercepted their communication, they couldn't risk mentioning her name. He signed off with the team and shrugged his go pack over his shoulders before heading toward the tower to share the plan with Tara.

He didn't have to give her reaction to the team's assistance much thought. She was already mad about him obtaining a warrant for her arrest, calling in a replacement, and then locking her in the tower. When she learned that he'd enlisted the team and the sheriff to ensure that she got on that plane whether she wanted to or not, she'd fire that heated gaze his way. He'd take any guff she threw at him and continue with his plan.

With a longer hike now, he picked up his speed, glad to be wearing tactical boots and less restrictive clothes that allowed him to move with ease. He jogged over rough terrain, pausing to listen at intervals.

A rifle boomed in the distance, the sound coming through the external hear-thru microphones on his earbuds. The report reverberated through the air and sent birds squawking into the sky.

A hunter? Not likely with deer season occurring in the fall.

The tower? Had Keeler arrived after Cal had departed and fired on Tara in the tower?

Another shot ripped through the air, sounding from the gate.

He jerked out his gun and froze to evaluate. The driveway was about six hundred yards long and a basic hunting rifle could easily fire that distance.

Tara!

"Shooter at the gate," he said into his comms unit, though the team wouldn't be able to help for another few minutes. "I'm going for the package. You take the gate when you arrive."

"Roger that," Brynn replied.

Cal took off running, his heart thumping hard against his chest. He hadn't prepared for sniper fire, as Keeler was a bomber not a shooter. Without a rifle, Cal was defenseless against a long gun in the hands of a skilled shooter.

What had he been thinking leaving Tara in the tower like a sitting duck?

It didn't matter. It was too late to rethink his decision. He had to hope she hadn't exaggerated her ability to use a rifle, or this could end as disastrously as the horrific vision racing through his mind.

CHAPTER 9

"Oren!" Tara hit the floor. "Don't let him be here. Please. Not him."

Another bullet zipped through the wall above her head, and she rolled to the side. She had to get out of there, but she couldn't exit by the door Agent Riggins locked. Not that she'd take that exit anyway. Oren would expect that.

She scooted to the far corner, pulled open the bottom drawer of built-in shelving, and tugged out the same backpack from last night.

Crack. A bullet whizzed through the wall, then another, sending splinters of wood pelting her body. She rolled to her side and used her feet to push a cabinet off a hidden trapdoor before prying the heavy wood open.

Fresh air rushed through the hatch, and hope for escape blew in with it, allowing her to breathe again. She opened a container holding the emergency stairs that resembled a fire escape ladder made for two-story homes. She dropped the ladder down.

Yes! Perfect, just as she planned. As was the thick cardboard she'd attached to an outside post to hide her escape ladder in the event of an attack. Oren couldn't possibly see her movements until she ran for brush surrounding the clearing. Even then, depending on his location, he wouldn't catch sight of her.

She scrambled down the ladder and hit the ground hard, creating a mini dust storm. She paused for a moment to get her bearings. She counted to five and ran. Straight ahead. Hard. Fast. Over the packed dirt. Across clumps of crabgrass and past a thicket of wild raspberry bushes.

Her bare arm caught on a bramble, ripping her skin, but she didn't stop. Getting to her truck was the only thing on her mind. She'd run this route every day to keep the crabgrass flattened down and the path free, so she made good time. She plunged down the final incline to her truck and spotted an SUV parked next to it.

She came up short and stood panting, evaluating.

Agent Riggins's or Oren's car? It could belong to either one.

She dropped into a squat behind high grasses and slithered to the side of the SUV. She popped up, took a quick look. Agent Riggins's pricey suit hung in the back. Sighing, she dropped down to catch her breath and listen.

Birds had resumed their chatter, and a soft breeze stirred the grasses, swaying them in a gentle rhythm. No footsteps pounding her way or twigs snapping or leaves crunching—no sounds that Oren would make if he was coming after her. Cal was another story. He'd be silent and quick. Something she wouldn't mind right now.

Digging her keys from her pocket, she bolted for her truck. Trembling hands fumbled to fit the key in the lock, but she soon jerked open the rusty hinged door and slid onto cracked vinyl seats. She inserted the key and cranked.

No response. Nothing. Zilch.

She tried again. Just a click.

Agent Riggins. He must have disabled it. She pounded her hand on the wheel. She knew nothing about engines and couldn't possibly fix it, but owning an ancient truck, she'd prepared for this possibility. Only one thing to do.

"Hoof it." She reached for her secondary escape bag but came up empty-handed. Agent Riggins again, she supposed. Too bad for him. He didn't realize the lengths she'd go to. She had another identity in her backpack. She'd felt dirty when she'd met with the forger in Atlanta, but she'd obtained several IDs and now she'd used them all.

She slipped out of the truck, squatted behind the door for safety, and peeked around the edge. Leaves swished in the breeze, the sun shone warm on her face, but somewhere in the idyllic setting a killer waited with a bullet for her. Still, there had been no additional gunfire, and she'd moved well out of rifle range from where the shots had originated at the gate.

She couldn't underestimate Oren, though. They'd learned to hunt together. She was a better shot, but he was more willing to kill anything in sight, so he wouldn't easily give up. Perhaps he crept through the scrub, heading her way, or maybe Agent Riggins had stopped him.

She couldn't hang around to find out. She searched the area one more time, focusing in on the surrounding forest, but saw no suspicious activity.

In one sure move, she got up and bolted for the other side of the road, where she dove into the ditch. She landed with an *oomph*. Her knees and hands razored across rocks and gravel. She gasped for air, filling her lungs with dust and grit. She lay still, waiting for gunfire, for a bullet in the back.

Nothing happened. She counted to thirty. Poked her head up to look around.

A gunshot cracked through the air, the sound

coming from across the road. She ducked her head, but the bullet didn't land anywhere near her.

Odd.

Her truck suddenly erupted in a deafening explosion.

She clamped her hands over her ears and curled up as a ball of orange-and-yellow fire whooshed across the road and debris pummeled her body.

Cal spun, the ground reverberating under his location just shy of the tower. A fireball rose into the sky. It had to be Tara's truck. Had she somehow gotten out of the tower? Was she sitting inside, cranking the engine he'd sabotaged, and the twist of the ignition had set off a bomb? Or worse, had Keeler climbed the tower and dragged her to the truck where he'd put a necklace bomb around her neck?

God, no, please, Cal pled silently, though his experience said God wasn't listening.

His heart constricting, he spun, and not caring for his own life, he plunged into the bushes. He found a well-worn path that Tara must have groomed for an escape that he'd foiled any chance of happening.

He ran hard, his gut cramping for the danger he'd put her in. Knowing she'd parked the truck just over the rise, he kicked harder and barreled down the incline. The heat hit his face before he caught sight of the fire.

Red-hot flames engulfed Tara's truck and his SUV. He tried to ease closer. Held his hands up against the heat, but the searing temperature forced him to back away.

"Tara." The anguished cry escaped his lips.

Was she in that fiery inferno? Had another person died on his watch? How could he have let that happen—how could God have allowed it to happen?

He shifted to his right, skirted the blaze, and searched for a better angle to attempt a rescue.

Movement in the ditch across the road caught his eye, and he came to a skidding stop to take cover behind a tree. An arm, a hand, small and graceful, reached up to the shoulder of the road.

Tara? Could she be alive?

Cal found a path to the road, scanned the area, and bolted toward her.

A gunshot rang out.

He dove for the ditch, the bullet whizzing overhead. He rolled to his side, lifted his handgun, and aimed at the tree where the shot had originated. He fired off a few rounds to lay down cover, allowing him to move forward. He crawled ahead—frantic, quick movements. He saw hiking boots, and Tara's yellow cat socks, but she lay motionless as in death.

He scrambled forward. "Tara?"

No answer.

He continued clawing at the ground and moving

on his elbows. All of the drills he'd learned as a SEAL became more important than he'd ever known. He reached ahead and shook her foot.

No response.

Please, God. Let her be alive.

He shimmied up next to her and took her wrist to check her pulse.

She stirred. Turned to look at him. "Agent Riggins, thank goodness! I think there was a bomb. In the truck."

A rifle shot split the air, the bullet piercing the ground inches from her head. She recoiled. He pushed to his arms and covered her body, shifting to access his microphone.

Tara struggled to get out from under him.

Right. She didn't trust him. Even here. She considered him the enemy when he only wanted to keep her safe. His anger boiled up.

"Don't move, for Pete's sake," he snapped. "My team is nearly in place, and we need to wait for them before we can get out of here. And for the last time, call me Cal."

She didn't respond. It could be because her ears were ringing from the explosion or she didn't want to speak. Right now it didn't matter.

Static played over his earbud, and he pressed his finger over it until it quieted. He activated his mic. "Alpha Two, report."

"We have you on GPS." Brynn's voice came in loud and clear, and Cal detected a note of relief in her voice. "We're a mile due south and exiting the vehicles now. I've got County holding the perimeter."

Perfect. The last thing he needed was an inexperienced deputy racing in and trying to be a hero. "Bring my vest and long gun, and you better make this the fastest mile you've ever covered in full gear."

"I thought you were wearing a vest," Tara cried out. "You need to move to safety. Without a vest he could kill you."

He ignored her panic and settled in to wait for his team. "If it keeps you safe, that's a risk I'm willing to take."

A high, tinny wail sounded through Tara's head, and she couldn't breathe. Terror raced along her nerves, and she didn't feel safe. Not even with the heavy weight of Agent Riggins's body protecting her from gunfire. No, not Agent Riggins any longer. She'd call him Cal from now on as he'd asked. If a man would take a bullet for her, they should certainly be on a first-name basis.

The shooting stopped, and she became more aware of him. He felt like a big old security blanket gently cradling her body, his back exposed to a bullet if the shooter started firing again. His life was on the line. A man who sacrificed himself for her, no matter her arguments, which had been many. He'd even brought in his team to help. Or did he have other motives?

A bad feeling settled in her stomach. She wiggled around and craned her neck to look up at him. To read his eyes. "Did you plan this? Set me up as bait to bring Oren out here so your team could arrest him?"

"No, of course, not," he said, and she struggled to hear him through the ringing. "The team is here because I wanted to be prepared in case Keeler followed you again. As it stands, I'm glad I did."

Eyes the color of dark coffee riveted to her with an intensity that gave her a glimpse into his world. A world where he'd been a Navy SEAL. The focus and strength he had, the change of his suit to tactical gear, and the corded muscles of his forearm as he clutched his gun all said he was fierce and dangerous. A guy with combat skills she couldn't even begin to imagine.

He pressed his finger against his chest.

"Roger that." He gave her a terse smile. "We're cleared for exfil."

His military lingo only added to her impression of his incredible skills, leaving her uneasy and in awe at the same time as she waited for direction.

"Be ready," he said. "Once the team lays down cover from secure locations we'll move behind their line. When you hear me say go, I'll roll off, and you come to your feet. Ignore the gunfire, grab on to my side, and cling to me. Got that?"

"Yes," she replied, but she didn't know if her shaky legs would allow her to move.

"You can do it, Tara," he said, as if reading her mind. "I've seen how strong you are."

She replied with a nod and stared up at his transformation into war hero. He'd sustained a large cut to his forehead with blood running down to his eyebrow.

"You're bleeding."

"No biggie. Let's just focus on what we have to do."

"Right, run through gunfire."

"Don't worry so much." He gently rested his fingers on her cheek. "This jerk's no match for our team. Most of us are old spec ops guys. Keeler may have done a stint in the army, but his skills at stalking in the bush don't come anywhere close to ours."

She didn't mention that, so far, Oren had bested them.

Suddenly, a barrage of bullets started flying.

"Okay, we're a go." Cal rolled off.

She jumped up, and he clamped her tight to his side. Then suddenly they were running while bullets flew in all directions. Hitting the ground. Sending up puffs of dirt. His team firing way more bullets in the shooter's direction.

He'd told her to ignore the gunfire, but she couldn't think about anything else.

The sounds echoed through the trees, and she

flinched at each one. She soon tired and lagged behind. Cal wrapped a strong arm around her waist and carried her the final distance to a secured area. He immediately released her, grabbed a vest from the back of an SUV, and strapped her into it before donning one for himself. He adjusted his radio before he inserted earbuds back into his ears and added a helmet.

"How can you hear me with earbuds?" she asked, suddenly wondering if he'd even been listening to her.

"The earbuds have microphones that pick up external sounds so we can hear the team and what's going on in our surroundings at the same time." He shifted the vest that fit him like a custom piece of clothing while hers hung like sagging laundry on the clothesline.

She was shaking and wished they were far away from this horrible scene or that he'd take a moment to reassure her. Maybe with another touch of his hand.

Instead, he picked up a submachine gun and pressed a hand to his chest. "Stand down. Package secure. Brynn, I need you here."

Tara had no idea what *package secure* meant, but the shooting stopped, and a woman soon came out of the brush. Dressed like Cal, she held a matching gun in one hand. In the other, she clasped a large black shield with a clear window in the top. Audio cords dangled from her ears and disappeared into her vest matching Cal's.

"This is Brynn," he said.

Standing two inches taller than Tara, Brynn had grayish-blue eyes that were direct and held a guarded expression. She'd set her mouth in a grim line. Tara figured the woman possessed skills very similar to Cal's, but Tara had no idea the role she played on the team.

Tara looked back at Cal.

"Stay with Brynn," he said. "She'll move you to the command post until I'm free."

"Wait, what?" Tara cried out. "You're leaving?"

"Keeler." He gestured over his shoulder.

Brynn handed her shield to Cal, and the muscles in his arm bulged from exertion. Tara had no idea how Brynn could even hold something that strained his muscles.

"I have to go." Cal met Tara's gaze over the shield. He offered her an apologetic look, and after the beat of a few seconds, he bolted.

Really? Just like that, he'd gone. He'd promised to provide security for her and not leave her in anyone else's hands, but they hadn't even left town, and he'd walked away. Maybe worse, he could be walking into a hail of bullets.

"Don't look at him like that." Brynn gestured for Tara to join her in the SUV. When they were settled, Brynn peered at Tara. "Cal knows you're safe with me, and after a grueling hunt for Keeler, there's no way Cal's not going to be in the fight to bring the creep in."

"Trust me, I get it." Tara swatted the big vest out of the way and buckled her seat belt. "He's obsessed with catching him."

"Obsessed? Maybe . . . but not in the sense that you know *obsessed*."

"There's a difference?"

"To me there is. Obsession for me denotes personal gain or satisfaction. Cal isn't doing this for himself. He's doing it to keep people alive."

"Is he?" Tara asked. "I don't know him at all, but it seems to me he's got something to prove and something's driving him beyond apprehending a killer."

Brynn's eyebrow lifted, but she didn't respond as she wedged her gun between her knees and turned the key.

Right. Close down like Cal.

Try to get personal with either of them and they shut down. The whole team could be like that for all Tara knew.

Brynn shifted into drive and drew her handgun. She rested it on her lap before looking at Tara again. "Our drive is short, but you may find your adrenaline subsiding and fatigue settling in. I need you to stay alert and keep your focus. Eyes open and directed out the window as we roll. If you see anything out of the ordinary, tell me. If I tell you to hit the floorboards, you do so. Got it?"

"Yes," Tara answered.

Brynn gave a firm nod and set the vehicle rolling down the road. Tara kept her focus out the window as instructed and watched the wooded property pass by. A property that for nearly a month had been the closest place to a refuge that she'd found since taking off from the hospital. Now, Oren sat in some tree, firing at this team—at the guy who'd offered his life for hers—and she didn't know very much about any of them.

She glanced at Brynn. "I wondered if—"

"No talking until we get to the command post."

Tara wished Brynn had asked nicely, but there wasn't anything nice about this situation. It was big and nasty and ugly, like a two-headed gargoyle, and Tara wanted it to be over.

She leaned forward and resumed her watch out the window. Before long they approached a large truck like the ones that delivered packages to her doorstep, but this one held the local sheriff's office information and emblem on the side.

Brynn bumped the SUV onto the gravel shoulder and shifted into park. "Wait here."

Her handgun outstretched and the submachine gun slung over her shoulder, she came around to open Tara's door. "Stay by my side and climb into the back of the truck in front of me."

Tara followed directions, and Brynn escorted her across the road, standing guard while Tara took the three stairs to the truck. She quickly looked over the space where cabinets lined both walls and cutout sections housed small desks. A deputy with wild red hair sat behind the wheel.

Brynn brushed past Tara and dropped into a seat behind a laptop. "I'll have the team's feed up in a few seconds."

Brynn tapped a few keys on the computer and a barrage of gunshots sounded from the speakers. Tara turned her focus to the screen where she saw large maple trees and Douglas firs mixed with quaking aspens, their white trunks vivid in the shadowed forest.

"Take cover," Cal called out as the video panned through the trees.

"Cal's wearing the camera?" Tara asked Brynn, who nodded. "Is he the leader?"

Brynn shook her head. "He's lead on this investigation, but Max White is our leader. He's back in D.C. watching the same feed."

Tara didn't bother explaining that she'd read about Agent White on the Internet and only wondered about the group coming under fire. "Can they hear us?"

"I've muted our mic to prevent any distractions. I'll let you know if that changes."

Tara listened to the exchange of bullets, heard Cal's deep breathing and the deafening report of his gun. Oren could kill Cal. Just like that, with one well-placed shot, which Oren had the skills to land.

Her mouth went dry as she kept her gaze glued to the action.

The camera panned to the other team members as if Cal had turned. "We've got him pinned down. Now it's just a matter of bringing him in."

"Just," the man sitting next to Cal said, "all depends on his stockpile of ammo."

"And on us keeping our heads down until it's depleted," a woman's voice joined in.

"Don't even think about going after him, Riggins." A deeper authoritative voice came over the speaker. "I don't need a dead hero. I need a living operator."

"Max?" Tara asked Brynn.

She gave a clipped nod.

Tara stepped back until she could no longer see the screen. If the team leader didn't want Cal to go after Oren, she didn't want to see if Cal disobeyed and tried to apprehend Oren like she thought he would do. Gunfire sounded from the speakers again.

"Riggins!" Max yelled.

Even across the space she heard Cal's heavy breathing and the continued gunshots. So he'd gone after Oren. A crazy thing to do, but not surprising in the least.

The monitor beckoned Tara, and yet she couldn't make her feet move. She wanted to see the action but couldn't bear to witness Cal being gunned down.

The gunfire escalated in quick bursts like a packet of firecrackers ignited at the same time. It could be the team laying down cover as Cal had described them doing earlier, or Oren firing at Cal. Above it all, she heard a rustle sounding like static.

"Stand down," Cal called out, and the gunfire stopped.

The scratching sound grew louder, but she had no idea the origin of the noise. She couldn't stand back any longer. She approached the monitor where a tree trunk, branches, and leaves holding the distinct shape of a maple leaf slipped past. Cal was climbing a tree. Likely headed for the shooter. For Oren.

Could the standoff be over? Yes! Her heart soared.

His movement stopped, and Tara's breath caught. A gun that looked like the one Cal carried flashed past the camera and the focus of the lens moved up to a man's feet in scraggly once-white sneakers perched on a branch.

"Freeze, Keeler," Cal shouted.

"What the . . ." a male responded, the words muffled and barely recognizable.

"Hand down your rifle, butt first," Cal commanded. "Nice and easy."

A rifle stock slowly lowered in front of the camera.

"We're secure," Cal announced. "Keeler's ours."

A loud cheer went up.

Tara exhaled loudly, and she noted Brynn did the same thing.

"So," Cal said. "You're going to back yourself down the tree. You can manage that, right?"

"Yeah, I got myself up here." The other man's voice came through loud and clear now. "I can get down."

"No, oh, no." Tara took a step back, her gaze going to Brynn. "The voice. It's wrong. You've got the wrong guy. Tell Cal. This man. The one he captured. It's not Oren. So totally not Oren."

CHAPTER 10

Cal punched his fist into the side of County's command truck that they'd moved to the crime scene. He'd probably startled Brynn and Tara inside, but he didn't care. He'd failed to arrest Keeler again, and Tara had gotten banged up.

Double fail. Triple fail if you counted his plan to have Tara safely in D.C. by now, not sitting in this truck in the Oregon boonies while he worked another bomb scene.

He looked at Tara's pickup, now a mangled twist of metal with debris littering the road. Tara had almost lost her life, and it was all his fault.

How had he agreed to let her spend the night in the tower? Hadn't he learned anything from losing countless women to Keeler's bombs?

He should have forced Tara to leave the tower last night, even if he had to carry her out. But he'd let her get to him, and he'd acquiesced to her desire to make her own decision. That wouldn't happen again. Not even if she thought him controlling and demanding.

He raised his fist again, but a redheaded deputy stepped from the command truck and fixed his focus on Cal.

Great, just what Cal needed. A pimple-faced, wet-behind-the-ears deputy giving him the stink eye. At least Max wasn't here with a ready lecture about Cal climbing the tree.

Cal swallowed hard and turned to the suspect sitting near the truck's front bumper. Team ballistics and hostage rescue expert Rick Cannon held his rifle on the cuffed man, his glare even more intense than Cal's. Team negotiator Shane Erwin stood at attention at the front of the truck scanning the area for any additional threat.

Kaci had confirmed the shooter was sixty-two-year-old Lonnie Hickson. His address listed him in northeast Portland, but Kaci learned he'd been evicted. He had ground-in dirt on his hands and under his nails, and he wore a pair of jeans that were so dirty they could stand on their own. Cal believed the guy was homeless. He sure wasn't the kind of person who would own the thousand-dollar Browning hunter rifle he'd been using.

Stepping to the man, Cal held out his phone

displaying a picture of Keeler. "Is this the guy you're working for?"

"It's not a guy," Hickson said, as if he didn't have a care in the world.

"Then who sent you?"

"A pretty little lady."

"Explain."

Hickson peered into the distance, his gaze losing focus. "I was minding my own business outside the Rescue Mission yesterday when a lady paid me a thousand bucks to take a ride with her and fire a few potshots at the girl."

"Potshots as in you weren't supposed to hit her?"

"Right. Just scare her." He narrowed his eyes. "I'm not a killer, man, and wouldn't have taken her out for a thousand bucks. Or even more money."

Cal rarely trusted suspects because most of them lied, but something in Hickson's tone rang true. Plus, they'd found the cash in his back pocket. Cal doubted he'd legitimately come upon that much money.

"You got a cigarette?" Lonnie ran his hands over his salt-and-pepper beard that made him look more like Santa Claus than a killer.

Cal ignored the request. "So you started firing from the gate, then moved to this tree?"

"Gate? Nah, man. I've been here the whole time."

Right. Maybe Cal's belief in Hickson was misplaced. "Then who was firing at the gate?"

Hickson shrugged.

"What about the truck?" Cal asked, as Tara had said that a gunshot had hit the truck before the explosion. "You fire that shot, too?"

Hickson's head swung side to side, his beard floating in the wind. "Surprised the heck out of me when another shooter got into the game and the truck blew." He chuckled as if this was a game to him. "Had to hang on to a branch. Thought I was a goner for sure."

Had there been another shooter in addition to Hickson? Maybe Keeler or this mystery woman who appeared to be working for him?

Cal took a step closer to Hickson. "Why would someone walk up to you on the street and hire you for something like this?"

"Guess she thought I was down on my luck and needed the money." He held out an arm with a wildly colored tattoo sleeve poking out of a stained T-shirt featuring the Grateful Dead. "Maybe she saw the tat of our flag on my wrist and thought I was a vet who knew his way around a gun." His puffy lips split in a grin, wrinkling weatherworn cheeks. "Which I am and I do."

Hickson's smile vanished. "I suppose you're gonna keep the money. I coulda used it, man." Even if this guy needed cash, he'd go away for a long time after this stunt and wouldn't need much money.

"Describe the woman who gave you the cash," Cal said.

"She was from one of those Middle Eastern countries but she spoke good English. Just a hint of an accent. Not that she said much. She was also wearing one of those black thingies that covered everything but her eyes, so there's not much else I can tell you."

"A headscarf," Cal said, his mind already racing over the implication of this news. Either this woman was tied to Keeler and ISIS or someone wanted them to think there was a connection.

"Yeah, sure, whatever you call it, it was black, and she had on black gloves, too. Kind of freaked me out at first, but then the cash came out and . . ." He shrugged.

"What about other physical characteristics?"

"She was small . . . maybe five six. Had big brown eyes. Made me want to see what she was hiding under all that fabric if you know what I mean." He grinned, obviously not having a clue as to the trouble he was in.

"Any idea of her age?" Cal asked, though it was unlikely that he could make an accurate assessment with her body almost fully covered.

"Like I said, she was all covered up, but she didn't have any wrinkles by her eyes, and she moved like a younger woman."

"What happened after she paid you?"

"She drove me out here and left. Said to find my own way back to town." He shook his head.

"Would've been a long hike out. 'Course maybe she didn't think I'd be hiking out of here after a battle with guys like you."

Cal had thought the same thing, but he didn't acknowledge it. "What kind of car did she drive?"

"Toyota Corolla."

One of the most popular cars in America. She likely knew that and hoped it would make her harder to track down. "Did you catch the license plates?"

"Nah, didn't have a reason to. I did notice they were from Oregon, though." He frowned. "Oh, and I saw a rental contract on the console."

"Which agency?"

"I dunno, man. She got me a fifth of gin before we took off and my memory's not so clear."

"And the Browning? Did she give you that, too?"

"Yeah, man. Sweet gun. She said I could keep it."

A vehicle rolled down the road, grabbing Cal's focus. He clapped a hand on his holster. Rick came to attention, and Shane lifted his rifle.

"It's Kaci with equipment," Shane called out.

The rental SUV came up just short of the command truck, and Kaci hopped down.

She'd shed her tactical gear and marched across the road, her SLR already hanging around her neck on a Star Wars Chewbacca camera strap. "What'd I miss?"

Cal brought her up to speed on Hickson's

119

confession. "Once you're done with the scene photos, I need you to look for this woman who supposedly paid him and drove him here."

Kaci stared at Hickson. "Odd, isn't it—to learn a Muslim woman is working with Keeler when he targets Muslim women for his bombs?"

Their profiler believed the necklace bombs were Keeler's way of beheading an infidel, meaning these women must have violated the Muslim faith in some way. Unfortunately, the team had found no proof of that. All they'd discovered thus far was that the women all assimilated into the Western world, and until Tara left town, they all lived in the D.C. metro area.

"It might make more sense if we were sure why he's targeting them in the first place," Cal said.

Kaci frowned. "We've got to be missing something."

Cal nodded. "Once we get this scene processed, we need to discuss that. But for now, start with the Rescue Mission where he claims the woman picked him up. Maybe they have outside cameras. And follow up with the rental car agencies in the area."

"You got it." She took the lens cap off her camera. "How soon before you'll have the scene cordoned off, and I can get my long shots?"

"I'm done with Hickson, so Rick and I can secure things now."

She nodded, but her attention had already gone

to her camera, and she didn't look up. Kaci was a single-folder kind of person who didn't multitask well, so they often had to pull her focus from her electronics.

Cal stepped over to Shane. "Cuff Hickson to the truck's push bars so you can keep an eye on him and the road at the same time."

"Gladly." Shane stepped over to Hickson and jerked him to his feet while Rick held his gun at the ready in case Hickson tried to bolt.

Cal went to the SUV to grab a roll of crime scene tape. He joined Rick and didn't need to offer direction. After seven fatal explosions courtesy of Keeler, Rick knew the drill, and there was no guy better than Rick to share the job. They'd walk the area around the scene to establish a perimeter that included an entry and exit to keep contamination to a minimum from personnel arriving on scene. Along the way, they'd also look for secondary devices, unconsumed explosives, or other hazardous materials in the rubble. Cal was glad to have Rick's help. Perfection was expected from Marine Scout Snipers, and as a former sniper, Rick had come to expect that perfection in every area of his life. He wouldn't miss a thing.

Cal tied the end of the bright yellow tape around a tree trunk.

"You think Tara's recollection of the truck blowing after a gunshot is accurate?" Rick asked, his smooth southern drawl controlled and clipped.

"Meaning what?" Cal asked.

"Meaning do you think the shot set off the explosion?" Rick looked up at the tree where they'd apprehended Hickson.

Cal was well versed in weaponry, but Rick served as their ballistics expert, and Cal respected his teammate's opinion. "You look like you have a theory."

"Just speculation, but Keeler could have used Tannerite for this bomb."

Cal glanced at the twisted hull of Tara's pickup. "There's no question the truck was the seat of the explosion, but Tannerite? I don't know. He's never used it before."

"He could change his MO. And with Tannerite so cheap and readily available, he wouldn't have to hunt for a source of C-4 after arriving in Oregon."

A binary substance made of ammonium nitrate and aluminum powder used in exploding rifle targets, Tannerite was readily available both in retail stores and on the Internet, so Keeler could quite easily get his hands on an unlimited supply without raising any questions.

"Plus it only takes a high-powered bullet to ignite the bomb instead of relying on a cell or other wireless signal that could be iffy out here," Rick continued. "And since a hypersonic shock is the only thing that sets off Tannerite, a large-caliber bullet is the fastest and easiest way to provide that shock. After a quick mix of the stuff in a storage container, he could have set it in the cab or even the truck bed."

Cal thought about his visit to the truck. "I looked at the vehicle right before it went up. There was nothing in the cab, but Tara had a storage box in the bed. Keeler could have put it in there, I suppose."

"Or, with all the dense vegetation in the area, he watched you until you took off and added the Tannerite after you left."

Cal didn't want to think Keeler could have been hunkering down in the woods today, rubbing his grubby hands together and smiling in glee while Cal had been totally unaware of him and missed the opportunity to apprehend him.

But Cal couldn't rule out the possibility. "Hickson claims he didn't fire at the truck, but he could be lying."

"If Keeler placed the bomb, he could have been the shooter, too."

"Which corroborates Hickson's account of a second shooter. I'll have Brynn test for Tannerite and look for the slug," Cal said. "Even odder to me, though, is that Keeler didn't shoot Tara when he had a chance, or detonate the bomb when she was in the truck. Why give her the chance to escape?"

"Seems like he was sending a message. Telling

her that no matter who's protecting her, he can get to her. Either to mess with her, or maybe it was a warning, telling her not to help us."

"Then Keeler must think she knows something that will lead us to him, and we're right on track in obtaining her help."

"Or . . ." Rick paused and met Cal's gaze. "He's waiting until she's alone so he can use one of his necklace bombs on her and revel in her terror."

"Something a psychopath like Keeler would do for sure." Cal hissed out a breath. "Not that everyone isn't doing their best as it is, but we need to up our game on protecting Tara."

"Agreed," Rick said, and started forward again.

Cal continued walking next to Rick until they'd checked every inch of the area for explosives and strung the tape in a large square, leaving an opening by County's command truck.

Back at the SUV, Cal stowed the roll of tape, and Rick grabbed equipment to draw the scene to scale. With his constant attention to the smallest of details, he was charged with measuring and sketching their crime scenes for the case files.

The deputy who'd given Cal the stink eye paced around the area. Cal didn't like idle hands at a scene. It often led to interference and screwups.

He grabbed a worn clipboard holding the access control log and shoved it at the guy whose name tag read JON ANDREWS. "You're in charge of access to the scene. Stand here and do not leave without my permission. The team can come and go as needed, but no one else is allowed in without my say-so. Not even your supervisor or any other County brass who might show up. Are we clear?"

"As a bell." Instead of looking frustrated over having to perform such a mundane job, the deputy's eyes gleamed with excitement. Cal pegged him as a rookie, and the guy would have huge bragging rights as the only deputy allowed to work the investigation today.

"Out of my way, people," Kaci called as she peered out from behind a tripod with a boxy camera mounted on top.

"What's that thing?" Andrews asked.

"A 3-D scanner," Brynn said from the doorway of the truck. "It uses eye-safe laser light to scan the crime scene and create a 3-D rendering that's uploaded to a computer. In addition to the pictures, it captures measurements so the model is scaled."

"Cool."

"More than cool," Brynn added as she jumped down and lingered by the door. "It's a great way for a DA to show the crime scene to a jury or for investigators to refresh their memory as time passes."

"If you don't mind," Kaci yelled from a distance, her tone filled with sarcasm, "can you all carry on your conversation in the truck or behind it so when I turn the camera on it doesn't catch you in the frames?"

The deputy looked up at Cal for direction, but Cal had more interest in the transport vehicle arriving to haul Hickson to Northern Oregon Regional Corrections Facility, a joint jail used by many of Oregon's rural counties.

Cal turned to Andrews. "You can step away this time to get Hickson ready for transport, but I want you right back here when Kaci's done filming."

"Yes, sir." He stepped off.

Cal turned to Brynn. "FYI, we might be looking at Tannerite instead of Keeler's usual C-4."

"Interesting," she said. "You think the shooter ignited it?"

"It's seeming like a good possibility, so once Kaci is done, I want you to focus on locating a slug in the truck debris. And, of course, I'll need you to test for Tannerite."

Tara came to the door of the truck. She'd sustained scrapes and bruises, and her clothes were dirty and torn. Cal wasn't worried so much about her physical injuries, as they were minor, but her defeated look had his concerns rising. Not concerns related to the investigation, but personal ones, and he should turn and walk away, far away, but he couldn't leave her looking so broken without trying to help.

CHAPTER 11

Tara saw Cal looking her way, and she backed up to avoid his questioning gaze. She didn't need him coming to check on her and adding the stress of fighting her attraction for him while still in a vulnerable state. She resumed pacing down the narrow aisle she'd prowled for an hour now. Back and forth, she walked, thankful Brynn had stepped out, leaving her alone. The air was steamy and thick and the walls closed in on her. She wanted to head outside for fresh air, but Cal had commanded her to remain in the truck for her own safety.

Her safety. Ha! What safety? She'd almost been shot, blown to bits in a bomb, and her heart couldn't seem to gain a normal rhythm again. And even if she could get it under control, Cal storming into the truck earlier to bark orders at her added to her unease.

She paused near the driver's seat, grabbed the rubber band on her wrist, and snapped. Once. Twice. Three, four times. The sting radiated up her arm. It didn't help. She tried it again and again. Nothing. Maybe she'd moved beyond using the bands to contain her stress. Maybe she needed something different. Like more pacing.

She spun to resume her steps only to find Cal

standing in the rear of the truck, his shoulder resting on a cabinet, his body cutting off the hint of sunlight that had been filtering through the opening.

His warm gaze settled on her face. "How are you holding up?"

"I'm doing okay." She looked away before she let his concern warm her heart but not fast enough to miss seeing that the large gash on his forehead remained untreated. She was trained in first aid and could do something about his injury instead of standing idly by and giving her time to wonder about how he could affect her so much with one little look. To wonder anything about him.

"Your forehead." She pushed past him. "I'll grab the first aid kit and clean it up."

"It's nothing."

She ignored him and reached for the kit she'd spotted by the back door.

"Sit, Cal." She gestured at a bench and eyed him until he complied.

"You decided to call me Cal." His expression remained neutral, his voice flat as he moved to the bench seat.

Of course, he didn't give her even a hint of what he thought about it, so she didn't bother to explain her reasoning.

He stretched out his long legs that didn't fit under the tabletop. His thigh muscles strained the fabric of his khakis, and he'd opened a few shirt buttons, revealing a thickly muscled neck. Not that she was noticing. Okay, fine, she was, and her response to him unsettled her more.

He peered up at her, a glint of humor in his eyes. "Are you always this bossy?"

Thankfully, he hadn't noticed her study. "Talk about taking one to know one."

"So you think I'm bossy."

She snorted, earning a chuckle from him, proving he had a sense of humor when she'd thought he was all business.

A flutter of nerves sent her senses reeling, so she ignored the resulting grin and turned her attention to the first aid kit. She dug out an antiseptic wipe and leaned over him. "This will probably sting."

His response was more of a grunt than anything.

She carefully dabbed at the gaping wound, expecting him to flinch, but he didn't move or even change his breathing. With an even in and out, his powerful chest rose and fell beneath her.

"I'm not a doctor," she said, ignoring the fact that she'd underestimated his effect on her or she wouldn't have chosen to get this close to him. "But this looks like it could use some stitches."

He grabbed a butterfly bandage from the kit. "Put one of these on, and I'll take care of stitching it up later."

Shocked at his response, she met his gaze.

"You're telling me you plan to sew this up yourself?"

"Sure. Wouldn't be the first time."

She stood back and stared down at him. "Who are you anyway?"

He chuckled again, and his eyes lit with humor.

"What's so funny?"

"That look of horror on your face. I'm just a regular guy who learned how to close wounds downrange."

"Right, regular guy." She shook her head. "Like regular guys use the word 'downrange.' What does that even mean?"

"In the military it often refers to an overseas deployment in a war zone."

She could see him in a war, taking care of himself and others around him as he snapped out directions. She dabbed the wound a few more times to clean up the last of the blood, then blew on it to dry the skin so the bandage would stick.

He suddenly jolted back and pushed her away with firm hands planted on her shoulders. "Let's get this done so we can move on."

Surprised at his terse tone, she stared at him for a moment before she took the bandage from his hand.

He let out a long breath. "Sorry. I'm kind of jumpy. Adrenaline, you know? I'm sure you're still feeling the residual effects. Which, by the way, will soon make you feel very tired if it hasn't already."

She pressed the first bandage at the top of his cut. "I can take a nap on the plane."

He looked into her eyes. "Does this mean you've decided to come back with me?"

"I saw you guys handcuff Hickson and thought it'd be a good idea to avoid my own cuffs," she joked to play down her decision, maybe lighten up her mood. "So yeah, I'm all yours."

She expected a nod of acknowledgment if not an outright smile, and she received a frown instead. "About our trip. Our departure is delayed indefinitely. The team needs to remain on site to work the scene."

Processing the news, she ripped open a second bandage. Not more than a few hours ago, she hadn't wanted to go to D.C. Now, with Oren or people working with him nearby, she wished she could leave the area as soon as possible. "Delayed how long?"

"Hard to tell. We think there were at least two shooters. Hickson, of course, and if what he said is true, another shooter to detonate the bomb. There could also be a third shooter at the gate or the guy who detonated the bomb had moved over here. Either way, we'll search for another weapon."

"Then you think the shooter ditched the rifle."

"If Keeler was the second shooter, it's very possible. He didn't fly cross-country with a rifle, so I'm guessing he stole the weapon he used or it was provided by his ISIS contacts. In either case, if he was in a hurry to escape unseen, he could ditch it to move more freely through the scrub. And if that's not reason enough, if he was driving home and was stopped by a law enforcement officer for any number of reasons—speeding, taillight out, et cetera—Keeler wouldn't want the gun in his car."

"Makes sense, I guess."

"We'll get a search started, but we have a large, heavily wooded area to cover. Depending on the resources available to us, that could take days, and we won't get home for some time."

"Home? So you're based in D.C., then?" she asked, despite knowing that posing a question about his private life wasn't a good idea.

He nodded. "Our team is part of the FBI's Critical Incident Response Group out of FBI national headquarters."

She applied the second butterfly strip at the bottom of the gash. "I didn't realize I was considered a critical incident."

He scowled but said nothing for a moment, and the air between them sizzled with tension.

"Someone will go for food at some point," he said, ignoring her comment. "And I'll arrange a safe house for tonight." He met her gaze for a long stressful moment, then escaped from his seat and eased past her without touching her.

"I hate that you have to sit in here all day, and I'll do my best to get you out of here as soon as possible."

"It's okay," she replied, though she couldn't imagine what she might do for the rest of the day in this tin can of a vehicle, but maybe she could concentrate on the pump house and try to remember additional details. "When we do get back to D.C., will it be possible for me to call June and my friend Penny? I'm sure they're both worried about me."

"I can arrange for you to see June when we take you to the pump house, but I'm afraid contacting Penny is too dangerous right now for you *and* her."

Tara wouldn't put anyone else in danger, so she nodded her understanding and settled for the fact that she would soon see June.

Instead of leaving as she'd expected him to do, he leaned against the wall and crossed his ankles. "Tell me more about Keeler before your friendship ended."

"You've asked me about him so many times, I'm sure I shared everything that's pertinent."

"The tiniest detail that you left out could have meaning to the investigation."

"What do you want to know?"

"When you hung out, were you involved with video games, computers, music, that sort of thing?"

She closed the first aid kit and thought back to her childhood with Oren. "Computers weren't big in those days. Neither of our families had one. Oren did get a PlayStation in junior high, and we played that together. We both listened to music, but we didn't share it."

"Why not?"

"Oren was into heavy metal bands like Fear Factory and Marilyn Manson. I liked alternative rock. We didn't agree on tastes, so we both listened to our own stuff. But I don't see how any of that could be important."

"Love of heavy metal music is a way to express dissatisfaction in life and can be one of many predictors for radicalization." He held up a hand. "Now before you think everyone who listens to heavy metal is a bomber, that's not true and the music doesn't turn them into terrorists. It's only one predictive trait in a slew of marks that helps behavioral analysts create a profile."

"But it sounds like you think Oren's love of this music might have been a sign."

"Perhaps. More important is finding out what happened in his life to kick off his bombing spree."

"I don't follow."

"Our research shows that he's been involved with ISIS for quite a few years without taking any action. He didn't just wake up one morning and decide to begin targeting and killing women.

We've tried to find a connection between them to make sense of his bombs. But despite running down thousands of leads in the past six months, the only thing the women in the first bombings have in common is their Muslim faith. So we continue to look for a catalyst of some sort that set off his spree."

She thought back to everything she'd learned about the current-day Oren and came up empty. "I don't know what it could be. Like I said, I haven't really known much about how he thinks or feels since he started acting really weird in high school."

"You've mentioned weird before." Cal arched a brow. "What exactly do you mean by 'weird'?"

"We went to the same church growing up and were active in our youth group in junior high. When we started high school, he suddenly stopped attending. He kept passing it off like he was too cool for church, but one day I heard June and his mom talking. She said he'd converted to the Islamic faith. At first, I didn't believe her, so I asked him about it. He confirmed it and even tried to get me to convert."

"Did you ever consider it?"

She fixed her gaze on his. "Do you think I'd do that?"

"No, not after everything I've learned about you in my research, but I have to ask to cover all bases."

"I was raised in a traditional home with Christian values, and I'd never turn my back on my faith. It's too important to me," she said, but the moment the words came out she knew she'd overstated her current trust in God to protect her from Oren.

Cal frowned. "You might think that now. I once did, anyway. But trust me when I say I've been in situations where it doesn't seem so far-fetched to turn your back on your faith. I'm not saying converting to another religion, just letting go of innocent childhood beliefs."

So he was a man of faith. Or maybe not anymore. His comments were too cryptic to tell, but she hoped he had faith to sustain him during all of the difficult trials he must face on the job.

Of course, she'd experienced horrific events lately, too, and what had she done? Trusted in God? No, when He let Oren get to her at the hospital, she'd taken things into her own hands and fled from D.C., and as Cal had suggested, that wasn't working out so well for her.

Maybe Cal would explain turning his back on his faith, and that could help her, too. She opened her mouth to ask for an explanation, but as usual when they got sidetracked in an area where he might need to share something of himself, he rushed on. "So after this conversion, what happened to your friendship?"

"By the end of that year, he'd gotten into the

whole underground Goth thing, and we had nothing in common. He became a real loner. Sure, we said hi when we passed in the halls at school, but that was it." She shook her head. "Maybe I had a part in his weird changes when I turned him down."

"Turned him down as in dating? You didn't mention that before."

"It was no biggie. He asked me on one date. I said no. Turns out he had a thing for me for years, but I didn't know it until after we both left for college."

Cal pushed off the wall, his attention rapt and unyielding. "Did he ever ask you out again or make his feelings for you known?"

Uncomfortable rehashing such private information, she didn't want to answer. She looked down at her wrist and twisted the band around her finger until it cut off the blood flow, and then she released it in a big snap.

"Tara?" he prodded.

"Like I told you at the hospital, I ran into him at my aunt's place in January. He wasn't as harsh and withdrawn, and I was more comfortable around him. We started talking . . . catching up, you know? And when my aunt left the room, he asked me out again."

"He asked you out, as on a date?"

She sighed at the memory. "He wouldn't take no for an answer, pushing and pushing, relentless like Nolan."

"Your former fiancé, right?' "

She nodded, hating that Cal had dug into her life and knew all about her when she hadn't a clue about his life beyond his job.

"So what happened with Keeler?" he asked.

"I'd just managed to get my life back from my disastrous engagement to Nolan, and Oren's attitude rubbed me wrong. So I snapped, and I didn't let him down very gently."

Cal stepped closer, intensity burning bright in his eyes. "He was upset? Maybe mad?"

At Cal's over-the-top reaction, alarms began going off in her head. "Both, actually. He stormed out and slammed the door. I watched him march down the driveway to the hired hand's house. He kicked stones on the way. Got in his car and raced off, sending gravel flying."

"Why didn't you mention this before?"

"I didn't think it was relevant, but clearly you do."

"Maybe," he replied.

His vague answers whenever she asked him a question grated on her last nerve. She pushed to her feet and looked him in the eye. "You've been grilling me like a well-done steak since you found me, and it would be nice if you answered at least one of my questions."

She crossed her arms and waited for him to argue, but he gave a quick nod. "Our profiler believes with Keeler targeting women, a woman hurt him in the past, and he's using the bombs as a means to vent his frustration." Cal met her gaze and held it. "We thought the loss of his mother was the catalyst for the bombings, but he started killing women on the first of February, mere days after what you're describing, so . . ."

"You're not saying that . . ." A fist squeezed her heart, and she couldn't drag in any air. "It's me, right? You think I'm the reason Oren's killing women. But I have no connection to the Muslim community."

"True, but you rejected him, and for some reason he's taking out that rejection on these women. We may not figure out why he chose Muslim women until we catch him. And even then, he may not tell us. And, of course, this is a working theory, so we could be wrong about the catalyst, or there's an added component in his desire to target Muslim women, but—"

"But you think he started killing because I turned him down." She clamped a hand over her mouth, then as the shock settled in, let it fall to her lap. "If it wasn't for me, these women would be alive."

Five hours later, Cal wrapped up his reports and headed toward the command truck to escort Tara to the SUV for their trip to the safe house. Temperatures had mounted, hitting the mid-nineties, and he couldn't wait to get out of the heat and humidity that had the entire team wilting. And he couldn't wait to move Tara into a more secure location. He wasn't about to let Keeler get to her again.

Brynn waylaid him and held out a clear plastic evidence bag with a severely deformed slug. "Found this near the truck bed. It's looking like Rick is right about the Tannerite."

Cal took the bag and didn't have to look too closely to identify the bullet. "A .30-06. Hickson's Browning uses that caliber. Maybe he lied to me."

"Wouldn't be surprising," she said.

Cal studied the slug. He found very few land and groove impressions from the rifle barrel, but only firearms specialists with proper equipment could determine if a sound comparison could be made under a microscope. He'd get the slug to the Firearms and Toolmarks Unit at the FBI lab.

Cal looked at Brynn. "If Hickson's telling the truth, and there is a second shooter, we can compare the slugs from the tower with this one and hopefully prove the same weapon was used for both."

"I'll get a tech over to the tower right away to process the area," Brynn said.

"And how about Tannerite? Any idea on when we'll know about that?"

"I'll run the tests the minute I get back to the lab. With the way things are going, that won't be until tomorrow night at the soonest."

"We can't land at our airstrip in D.C. or Tara will learn the location," Cal said. "Might as well put down at Turner Field, where we can pop over to the lab and drop off the slug, rifle, and sample to check for Tannerite at the same time."

"Perfect. I'll make sure everything's packaged for transport."

"Let's go ahead and assume you're going to find Tannerite. I'll get analysts on the task force to start tracking down large purchases in the area." The potential lead should have cheered Cal up, but even that hadn't helped alleviate the tightness in his chest. "Is there anything you need from me before I take off?"

"No." She sounded offended. "I come prepared."

"I didn't mean that, I . . ." He shoved a hand into his hair to stem off his ongoing frustration. "With this change in Keeler's methods, he's become unpredictable, and it's throwing me off my game."

"It definitely provides more of a challenge in finding him."

"Exactly. And it could mean he's escalating in his need to inflict harm. We could be dealing with another necklace bomb sooner than the first of next month. Means this scene is more important than ever, and we have to find something here to stop him."

"I hate to interrupt, Agent Riggins," Deputy Andrews called out from the truck as he jumped down and hurried over to them. "My sergeant just contacted me. Keeler's been spotted, and we have a lead on his current whereabouts."

"Credible lead?" Cal asked, adrenaline already racing through his body.

Andrews bobbed his head. "We have an eye-witness who can take us right to the cabin where the jerk's been hiding out."

CHAPTER 12

Dufur, Oregon
3:05 p.m.

On a hill above Keeler's rental cabin, Cal walked the length of the lot, making a final assessment before he and Rick breached the door. The one-room log cabin with a red metal roof and stone chimney sat at the base of a hill, cowering in a thick stand of tall pines much the way Cal thought Keeler would cower when they barged through the door.

The FBI SWAT team had arrived from Portland, and they, along with Cal and Rick, were on hold while their sniper crept into position. Then it would take the rest of their team a few minutes to set their outer perimeter and take a secondary stance at the back door.

Cal stopped next to Rick, who lay behind a log, his binoculars trained on the house. "Any movement?"

"None." Rick swatted at a mosquito buzzing around his head, but he didn't take his eyes from the cabin.

"Then either Keeler's not home or he's hunkered down. We'll follow standard protocol in case he's there. You sure you don't want to take the long shot?"

"Where's the challenge? The range is so short any trained sniper can make that shot." Rick offered a rare grin and came to his feet. "I'd rather bust down the door with you."

"Nothing like the rush of not knowing what's waiting on the other side." Cal strode to their SUV, Rick following.

Before picking up his weapon, Cal dialed Shane. "Everything good back there?"

"Quiet as can be. That is if you don't count Kaci's bad jokes." Shane laughed. His easygoing attitude was legendary for a man in such a high-pressure job.

"We're about to breach the door, and I'm going silent," Cal said. "Text me with any issues, and I'll look at them on the other side."

"Roger that," Shane replied. "And, hey man, relax. We've got this."

"See that you do." Cal clicked off, and after silencing and stowing his phone, he glanced at Rick. "Ready to do this?"

Rick stood silently appraising Cal with a focus so pointed that it cut to Cal's soul. "You know

I was born ready. It's you I'm worried about."

"Me? I'm good."

"You sure about that?" Rick strapped on his helmet. "You seem distracted."

Cal couldn't lie and say the disappointment on Tara's face before he left for this raid didn't keep playing in his mind. He'd promised to put her safety first, but then something came up requiring his attention, and he reneged.

Right. Required.

The well-trained SWAT team could handle this raid without his or Rick's help, but Cal wanted to be there to see the look on Keeler's face when they slapped handcuffs on his wrists. To be there to put away another bad guy so he could chip away at his guilt.

You've put away a lot of bad guys this past year. The thought popped into his mind. *And has that honestly made your life better?*

"I'm talking about looks like that one." Rick picked up a Heckler and Koch MP5, the standard-issue submachine gun for their team. "You're a million miles away."

As a former sniper, Rick had to understand and deal with guilt that the loss of life caused.

"You ever lose someone on a mission or on the job, and you can't let it go?" Cal asked.

Rick nodded. "We've all got our incidents that we can't shake. Most everyone in the military and law enforcement does."

"And does it ever get in your way?"

"In the way like here on a mission?" He tapped his rifle. "Nah, I'm good to go on the job."

"But it might affect your personal life?"

Rick went motionless, his fierce sniper gaze homing in on Cal. "Sounds like that's what's going on with you, but maybe it's spilling over into the job, too."

"It's Tara," Cal said before thinking it over. "Keeler's killed women right under our noses and man, that's hitting me hard, you know? But him going after Tara? That's different. We didn't know the other women, but we know Tara, and we're getting to know her better every day. If Keeler gets past us . . . gets to her . . . I . . ." He shook his head.

Rick arched a brow but said nothing. Cal had never seen Rick open up, and Cal should have thought of that before beginning the conversation. It was patently clear now that he'd chosen the wrong guy to talk to. He should have spoken to Shane instead. Better yet, he should keep his big mouth shut and his thoughts on the job.

"Never mind, man." Cal picked up his gun. "I've got my head in the game, and you don't need to worry about your back."

"Team in position." The SWAT commander's voice came over Cal's earbud.

"Roger that, we're a go in five," Cal replied, and looked at Rick, who gave his nod of readiness.

Cal shouldered a backpack of entry tools and lifted his weapon. They crept forward and reached the clearing where they bolted across the grass and flattened their backs against the wall on the porch. Cal dropped to his knees and slid a snake camera under the door to check for explosive devices or triggers Keeler might have rigged on the door.

"We're clear," Cal whispered, and tucked the camera into his vest. He fractured the door with a battering ram, sending the door swinging inward.

"FBI," Rick called out as he entered.

Cal followed and surveyed the small room, noting a door to the bathroom. A small kitchen was located on one end of the room, an unmade bed on the other. A plump sofa and chair in the middle. No one in sight.

Rick signaled his plan to search the bathroom, and Cal covered him by standing at attention for an attack from any direction. Rick disappeared into the room, and soon the rings of a shower curtain grated along a rod.

"Clear," Rick called out.

Cal approached the edge of the bed. Hoping to find Keeler hiding underneath, he dropped to the floor and lifted the dust ruffle. Empty, but on the far side between the bed and the wall, a bright ray of sun filtered through the white fabric ruffle, and his gut said someone was lying on the floor.

He came to his feet and signaled to Rick to cover him. Silently, Cal inched toward the foot of the bed. His heart racing with the thrill of the chase, he swung around the end and trained his weapon on the floor.

He exhaled, coming up short.

"What is it?" Rick asked.

Shaking his head, Cal eased closer and dropped to the ground next to a Caucasian woman who looked like she was in her early fifties.

Rick joined him. "Oh, man."

"Man is right." Cal laid his fingers aside her neck to check for a pulse, then sat back on his heels and looked up at Rick. "I was hoping to find someone here, but not a woman, and definitely not one who isn't alive."

"You think we were meant to find her?" Rick asked.

"Maybe." Cal stood. "Or this place could be set to blow, maybe set to take us out, and we got here before the device detonated."

"Your thoughts seem more on target."

"Then let's sweep this place and clear the exterior," Cal replied.

They moved forward in silence and searched the small cabin, quickly determining that no threat existed inside.

"As much as I want to check for ID on the woman," Cal said. "The exterior could be hot."

Rick nodded and backed to the door.

Cal informed the SWAT commander of their movements, and they backtracked outside. A narrow crawl space ran under the cabin, protected from animals by wooden lattice, a perfect place to hide an explosive device.

Cal circled the building, checking drain spouts and looking for sections where the lattice had been disturbed or the vegetation mashed down. Rick stepped along with Cal, his gun at the ready.

"No obvious disturbance," Cal said. "I'll check underneath to be sure."

He ripped off the front lattice. With a flashlight in hand, he shimmied into the dank space. Spiderwebs caught at his helmet, sending creepy crawlies running, but he tuned them out and shone his flashlight at the underside of the house and the supports. At the far side, he noticed something affixed to a support beam beneath the area where the woman lay.

Cal pressed his mic. "Possible device spotted on northeast corner of cabin. Everyone evacuate to a safe distance."

Rick peered into the space. "What can I do?"

Already crawling ahead on his elbows, Cal called over his shoulder, "Let me get a good look at the device, and I'll let you know."

At the corner, he flipped onto his back and shined his flashlight up at a simple bomb made with a rudimentary timer strapped to four sticks of dynamite. The timer counted down, hitting five minutes as he watched.

"Basic device," Cal shouted, but didn't take his eyes from the bomb.

Simple or not, devices malfunctioned all the time. The men could make it out of range before the timer hit zero and no one would be hurt, but Cal wouldn't let the device destroy forensic evidence in the cabin. Not to mention tearing apart the woman above.

Cal dug his tool kit from his pack as he saw Rick scooting toward him.

"You should take off," Cal said.

Rick came to a stop by Cal and stared up at the device. "You can see the entire bomb and there's no anti-removal device. If you can't render that one safe without taking us both out, you shouldn't be on our team."

Rick's teasing gave Cal a chuckle and helped diffuse the tension.

Cal tuned Rick out and set to work, removing the power source from the device and halting the timer at two minutes forty-nine seconds.

Cal sighed out a breath and dropped his arms to the ground. "Max is going to let us have it for not properly suiting up before tackling this bomb."

"We'll need to redirect him to the fact that we preserved evidence that could bring in Keeler."

"Good luck with that." Cal huffed a laugh. "Do

you think this bomb was meant for us or to cover up the woman's murder?"

"Hard to tell without tracking back the person who reported this place."

"Are you up for running it down?" Cal asked.

"I'm up for anything that gets me out of this sweaty Kevlar." Rick grimaced. "And I have to admit, I'd like to figure out the woman's ID and how she's connected to Keeler."

"I didn't notice a purse or luggage inside that could provide an ID, did you?"

"No. Nothing."

"Then we need to get the medical examiner out here ASAP to search and fingerprint her." Cal dug out his phone. "I'll take a few pictures of the device and call Sheriff Gorton to rush the ME."

"I'll be at the truck." Rick scrambled out from under the house while Cal shot photos with his phone and then scooted out, too. He ripped of his helmet before getting to his feet and joining Rick at the SUV. The breeze, though hot and sticky, cooled his perspiration-soaked head.

Cal removed his Kevlar vest and set it next to Rick's in the cargo area, where they would let them dry out before placing them back in their bags. He dug out his phone and sat on the tailgate to dial Sheriff Gorton.

"Man, oh, man," Gorton said after Cal explained the situation. "This hasn't been my day."

"I hate this as much as you do," Cal replied.

"But if you get the ME out here we'll be able to move forward."

Gorton sighed. "I don't know, man. I mean, we're a small office. I haven't had a single murder in my ten years in this job. I honestly don't know if our examiner is up to handling this situation to your satisfaction. Maybe we should take our time here. You know, get someone in from the state medical examiner's office instead."

"Time is not a luxury I have," Cal said forcefully. "Get your examiner out here ASAP, and if they're not up to speed on proper forensic protocol, I'll walk them through procedures."

"But I—"

"Now, Sheriff! Get them out here now." Frustrated, Cal hung up before the guy voiced additional objections.

"Not cooperating?" Rick asked.

"No, he's cooperating, but he's freaked out by the whole thing." Cal shook his head. "Remind me never to work a crime in a rural county."

"I'm guessing you won't want such a reminder if Keeler strikes in the boonies again."

"You're right. I won't." Cal shoved his phone into his pocket. "Go ahead and take the SUV back to the team and send Brynn over here with her equipment."

"You sure you got this?" Rick appraised him.

Cal was getting perturbed at everyone questioning his emotional stability. He gave a sour laugh. "Nothing to do here except wait for the ME to show up and for SWAT to finish their search. Which is unlikely to produce Keeler as he runs from his bombs. So yeah, I think I can handle things on my own."

CHAPTER 13

Mount Hood National Forest, Oregon
4:50 p.m.

Cal had given Tara an impossible choice. Stay in the command truck where they'd turned off the air-conditioning to save fuel and it was inferno hot, or go with him to the cabin he'd arranged for their overnight stay. On the surface, the cabin seemed the best choice, but the rest of the team would stay at the crime scene until later in the day, and she'd be alone with Cal. Not a good thing with the way they'd been alternating between butting heads and fighting an obvious attraction. But maybe she didn't need to worry. Not with the way he'd arrived back on site, his lips in a flat line that discouraged discussion and his shoulders rigid as he marched to the rental SUV.

She followed at a slower pace and took a few moments to pull her damp shirt away from her body and flap the fabric in the breeze.

Cal jerked open her car door and huffed out

an impatient sigh. "This is no place to dawdle."

She peered at him. "Do you actually think Oren is still hanging out somewhere near here?"

"You're here, aren't you?" he said matter-of-factly.

He didn't have to say anything else. He was right. If Oren wanted her dead, he'd have to be within shooting or bombing range. Not a comforting thought.

She climbed into the SUV, but Cal shielded his eyes from the sun and surveyed the area before he took the driver's seat. She wanted to think his cautionary approach was overkill, but he'd just convinced her that danger followed her everywhere, and she needed to heed the warning. With that being true, she wouldn't roll over and count on him to protect her. She'd continue to stay alert and use the self-protection skills she'd learned over the past few months.

Protect yourself. Of course. But what about God? Shouldn't she ask for His protection, too, or had she turned her back like Cal suggested? If not, where did God fit in all of this?

He didn't. Or at least He hadn't. If He wanted her to be safe, would He have let Oren shoot her and get away with it? He could have arranged for Cal to arrest Oren at the pump house and many times since then, ending her terror and the loss of additional life, but He hadn't done so.

No, she believed in Him, in His mighty power,

but she wasn't sure about Him knowing what was best for her right now, and she needed to focus on what *she* could do to remain safe.

She kept her gaze moving over the roads and through the dark forested area until they reached a gated driveway. Cal punched a code into the lockbox and moved the car onto the drive before the gate swung closed with a solid clang behind them. They wound up the drive until it opened to a wide clearing holding a two-story house with five different rooflines, a two-car garage, and three decks visible from the front. Rough cedar covered the exterior and brick wrapped the corners.

"This place is huge." She glanced at Cal. "I thought you said it was a cabin."

Cal used a remote to open the garage door. "That's what Sheriff Gorton told me, but we obviously have differing definitions of 'cabin.' "

"I was picturing small and quaint, and that the team would be cramped into a little space. Now we won't be crowding each other."

Cal shifted into park. "I'll take your bag in and come back for the groceries."

They got out and she met him at the tailgate, where he lifted her tote from the back.

"I can carry it." She took the bag from him in an effort to prove her independence, but more likely, she needed to believe she retained some control of her life.

He didn't seem to give her actions much

thought, but he crossed over to the steel entry door leading into the house. He unlocked it and punched in the security code for the alarm. Tara watched and memorized the code in case she had to take off without alerting him.

She left him to fetch the groceries that were delivered to the crime scene by a deputy and stepped into the wonderfully cool air-conditioned home where vaulted ceilings covered in rustic pine and rough-hewn log beams soared high. Perfect. She could actually breathe in the wide-open space. She stepped into the family room that included floor-to-ceiling windows overlooking another large deck with steps leading down to a small creek and lush woods.

"Wow." Cal entered and paused to look around before carrying the groceries to the adjoining kitchen.

The scenic calm of the outdoors called to Tara. She stepped to the windows to gaze over the yard. Peace and tranquility sat on the other side of the glass. She rested a hand on the pane, feeling like a prisoner. How she wanted to go outside, sit in the cool of the shade, and draw in fresh air and clear out her fear and frustration. Maybe look for God in the beauty surrounding them and believe He really was watching over her.

Cal joined her, standing so close he took over her thoughts and reminded her to keep a solid wall between them.

She moved a few steps away. "Amazing view, right?"

"Not defensible, though," he mumbled. "I'll need you to stay away from these windows."

She spun to look at him. "Oren can't possibly know where I am right now, can he?"

"I can assure you we weren't followed, but locals arranged this place, so anything is possible." He offered her a flicker of a smile, but she'd gotten to know him well enough to tell it was forced. "For now, join me in the kitchen, and we can put away the groceries."

He led the way, and she followed, glancing back at the window and now seeing what Cal had seen, walls of glass that Oren could shatter and step through to kill her.

"Omelets okay for dinner?" Cal asked as he unloaded contents from a paper bag onto the white quartz countertop.

She pulled another bag closer and dug inside. "I'm not very hungry."

"But you will eat." He eyed her. "You need to keep up your strength, and you didn't eat lunch."

She shot him a look over the bag. "You noticed?"

"I notice everything about you, Tara."

She should have expected he wouldn't miss anything, but the tone of his response had nothing to do with his role as an investigator. He'd moved into the personal realm, and she wouldn't go there with him.

She turned back to the bag and lifted out a loaf of hearty wheat bread. "Looks like we have a good selection of food."

Cal held up a bottle of orange juice. "Would you like some?"

She nodded, and while he grabbed glasses, she searched for a safe topic that didn't involve Oren. But what did they have to talk about other than Oren or their personal lives?

Cal set a tall glass in front of her, poured thick, pulpy juice, then made eye contact.

"Do you like your job?" she said quickly before she fell prey to his bottomless brown eyes.

He set down the container, never taking his gaze from hers. "Do I make it seem like I don't?"

Perfect. Irritate her by avoiding an answer again, and there was no danger that she'd fall prey to her developing feelings for him. "Do you ever answer a question instead of offering another question?"

"Sorry. I guess it's a habit from my SEAL days, and to a great extent, something I need to practice as an FBI agent."

"So do you like it?" she asked again. This time she was honestly interested and wasn't making small talk.

"Most days." He put the juice in the refrigerator.

"And on those other days?"

He shrugged and folded the paper bag. Was he

as cool and in control as he always seemed, or was he a master at hiding his stress?

She suddenly wanted to know. "How do you deal with all the bad things you see on the job?"

He looked like he wanted to fire off an easy answer, but he planted his hands on the counter and met her gaze in earnest. "SEALs have a motto that explains it, I guess. The only easy day was yesterday."

"Which means what when it comes to coping?"

"I prepare for the worst at the start of each day." Staring down at the counter, he didn't move. "Sometimes the day turns out to be the worst— like the first of the month when Keeler strikes." He shook his head, then looked up and plastered one of his fake smiles on his face. "But terrible events like that don't happen every day."

"You mentioned earlier about situations where turning your back on faith doesn't seem so far-fetched. Days like those must be the ones that challenge your beliefs."

He remained silent for a long time, his lips pressed together. "My faith has pretty much been on the rocks for a while now."

"And that's why you don't ever let down your guard," she said, and ignored the fact that her lack of trust in God resembled Cal's struggle.

He shrugged and looked away.

Right. He didn't plan to talk about it, and she wouldn't keep heading that direction either.

He took over emptying her grocery bag and gestured at a stool. "What about you? Tell me more about your job."

"Way to change the subject."

"Hey." A tight smile spread across his mouth. "You asked about me, so it's only fair that I ask about your job."

"I suppose you mean the government translator job that I had before Oren tried to kill me."

"Right. They probably didn't hold it for you, did they?" He set apples next to the bananas. "I'd be glad to talk to your boss and let him know you had no control over this situation. Maybe they'll give you back your job."

She settled on the stool and considered how to respond to him. One minute he acted hard as nails, not open to talking, demanding, pushing her around, and the next, he appeared genuinely considerate, doing things like offering to help her get her job back. Or even more importantly, he was willing to sacrifice his life for hers. She was smart enough to know he could be both controlling and kind. The big question for her was how he lived out those characteristics off the job, but to find out, she'd have to breach a wall to his personal life that was best left in place.

His phone rang, and he looked at the screen. "I need to take this call."

"Brynn," he said into the phone as he left the room.

Tara understood that he had to be careful about discussing the investigation in front of her, but she didn't like being left in the dark when her life was on the line. She finished unpacking the groceries, and he returned in short order.

His tortured gaze landed on her, and she didn't have to wonder if Brynn gave him bad news, just the specifics of the news.

"What is it?" she asked.

He came back to the island and took the stool next to her. "I have something difficult to share."

"Is it Aunt June?"

"June is fine." He set his phone on the sleek countertop.

Tara exhaled. "Then what?"

"You know that we didn't find Keeler at the cabin, but I didn't tell you that we found a body. A woman."

She opened her mouth to ask for details, but his phone dinged, stealing his attention.

He picked it up and tapped the screen. "We haven't been able to identify her through any of our methods, and we need you to look at the woman's picture to see if you know her."

"But I don't know anyone in Oregon. I purposefully made sure of that."

"I need you to look. Just in case." He pressed the button to unlock his phone. "She's been dead for some time, so you should prepare yourself for what you're about to see. It's nothing gory, but still . . ."

Tara took a deep breath and turned his hand to look at the picture.

"Oh, no." Her stomach sent the orange juice roiling, and she clapped a hand over her mouth.

"You know her," Cal said in his usual straightforward tone.

Tara nodded and fought for enough composure to speak. "I don't actually *know* her or even know her name. She worked in the post office in Dufur. I talked to her when I picked up my mail."

Tara wrapped her arms around her waist. "She was such a sweet person. She always went the extra mile for me, and now . . ." Tara's sorrow begging for release, she shook her head. " . . . now because I talked to her, she's dead."

Wondering how to help Tara, Cal watched her. Swirls of dirt covered her clothes and a few blades of grass clung to her hair. She'd pulled it into a ponytail that morning, but the force of the truck blast had freed sections, leaving them sticking out like porcupine quills.

All he could think to do to help her handle yet another blow was reach out to pluck the grass from her hair.

"I'm not sure that will help much, but thanks." She peered at him, tears rolling down her cheeks before she turned away and he saw her shoulders shaking.

It was about time she actually cried and not just

those few tears at the hospital. She'd continued to exhibit incredible strength, too much, if you asked him. If she kept burying her emotions, the dam would eventually burst. Maybe at the wrong time, wrong place, and she could get hurt. She needed to let go and have a good cry now.

And what about you?

Okay, fine, there was no way he was ever going to sit down and cry like a little girl, but he could take his own advice and find a way to alleviate some of his stress.

Prayer. The thought came unbidden.

It hadn't helped in the past, so he shrugged it off.

But why did you call out for God's help when you thought Tara was in danger?

Old habit. Just an old habit. He dismissed the idea to focus on Tara.

Her crying snapped his tight rein on keeping a professional distance, and he took her hand. She shot him a surprised look but didn't withdraw. Tears continued to trail down her cheeks, leaving a clean path through the dirt. He lifted his free hand to swipe them away, but touching her so intimately wasn't a good idea on so many levels that he didn't know which reason topped the list, so he held back.

"So what happens next?" She looked down at their hands as if she didn't want to hear the answer.

"The team finishes processing the scene and prepares the evidence to ship to the FBI lab in Quantico. We'll all hop a plane, and when we get back to D.C., we'll debrief and make a plan while Brynn and her team pore over the evidence."

"And then you'll take me to the pump house." She went quiet for a few moments and raised his hand to stare at it. "What happened to your knuckles?"

Two knuckles sustained second-degree burns and had blistered, but today when he'd punched the truck they'd broken open to expose raw, red skin. "An on-the-job injury."

"They were burned. A bomb?" Her head shot up. "These are fresh. Another bomb. Dallas, right? Why didn't you tell me?"

"I thought you had enough on your plate right now."

She pulled her hand back and sat up straight. "Don't do that. Don't spare me. If I'm going to help find Oren, I need details of his actions. Even if it hurts, I want you to tell me about Dallas."

"Why don't we hold off until later? You can take a shower and unwind from the day. If you still want to know more after that, I'll share every piece of information within your clearance level."

She stared at him long and hard. "You want to catch Oren, right? Desperately, I mean. I see it in your eyes. In the way you put this manhunt before everything else. You should be happy that I want to know more to help."

She was the second person to comment on his drive to find Keeler in the last few hours, and they were both right. He was pushing things, but at what cost to himself, the team, and even Tara?

"The bomb," she said. "The woman in Dallas. I know her, right?"

Cal nodded. "Allison Foster."

The blue of Tara's eyes darkened, and she panted for air as if anxiety might take her at any moment. She didn't say a word but seemed to internalize the pain.

"I'm sorry, Tara." He assumed his response came across as trite, but he honestly meant it.

"I don't need to wait until later. I want to know everything about Dallas now." Her voice wavered, but she firmed her shoulders. "Then when we get back to D.C., I'll commit myself and my time one hundred percent to helping find Oren."

Cal nodded at her sudden resolve to assist in the investigation, but unfortunately, the things she would have to do would be painful for her. Equally painful as the events she'd survived thus far, and he worried she'd fold under the stress.

CHAPTER 14

Late-night pizza never tasted so good to Cal as he shared it with the Knights in the living room at the safe house. The whole team gathering under one roof lowered the odds of Keeler harming Tara and helped Cal relax a notch. Not Tara. She'd tucked her feet under her in the corner of the sectional sofa and didn't seem relaxed or hungry. She'd pushed her fork around her plate at dinner, too, eating only a few bites of the omelet despite his encouragement.

Maybe her tension now had to do with the fact that they'd finished eating and the team planned to review notes from the day. At least the ones she could be privy to.

And Cal had to begin the discussion with a particularly hard one for her. "Before we get started, I need to bring you up to speed with something Tara shared earlier today."

Her gaze shot up to him, panic riding on the surface. "Is this about Oren asking me out?"

All heads snapped in her direction, and Cal would rather face down a marauding army than share the details, but he needed to keep the team apprised of all developments. "Do you want to tell it or should I?"

"You, please." She jumped to her feet and began pacing in the attached dining area.

Cal forced himself to ignore her frantic steps. "Back in high school, Keeler asked Tara to go out with him, and it turns out he had a thing for her for years, but she didn't return his affections."

"How's that related to the bombings?" Rick asked, his gaze fixed on her, but she seemed oblivious to him.

"When she ran into Keeler back in January," Cal said. "He asked her out again."

Tara spun, her hands clenched into tight fists. "And I not only said no, but when I did, he wouldn't let it go. I got irritated at him and snapped, making a mess of the whole thing."

"And soon after that, he set his first bomb." Shane slid forward in his chair. "Likely the catalyst we've been looking for."

"Exactly," Cal said.

Tara's shoulders curved forward as if trying to make herself disappear. "And it's all my fault."

"Please don't take responsibility for Keeler's actions," Cal said, fully aware of the fact that he'd mentioned the same thing to her earlier.

Experience told him people had to hear this advice repeatedly to internalize it. He ought to know. So many people had lost their lives because of his failures at work. Sure, other people made on-the-job mistakes, but people died when he failed, and no matter his effort, no matter using the skills God had given him to the best of his ability, women were still dying, and he was to blame.

"How can I not feel responsible?" she asked. "Wouldn't these women still be alive if I'd been gentler when I let Oren down?"

"Maybe or maybe not," Shane said. "This path has already been set in Keeler's life. Even if you hadn't rejected him, something else would have set him off and made him act. We can't control his actions. Only God can do that."

But Cal knew more than any of the team members that God seemed to be silent when it came to Keeler.

"When you've had time to process this, you'll see we're right," Shane added.

Tara looked away, smoothed her hair back, and used one of the rubber bands circling her wrist to put a ponytail in place. She remained frozen in time, gazing out the patio door while everyone sat watching.

Cal stared at the slender curve of her neck, the sight beckoning him to discover if her skin was as soft as it seemed. He sat on his hands, his knuckles stinging, the pain bringing his mind back to the task at hand. He needed to remember his commitment. Remain focused on the job. Forget all about any kind of relationship, catch more bad guys, and make them pay. And maybe, just maybe, if he put enough criminals behind bars, his work would make up for some of the recent tragedies.

"What about forensics at the cabin, Brynn?" Shane asked, employing his peacemaking and negotiation skills that he often used to move the team out of a tense situation. "Did you discover anything there?"

"Keeler's fingerprints," Brynn replied. "But that only proves that Keeler is—or was—here in Oregon."

"How can you be sure they're his prints?" Tara asked from where she stood in front of the door.

"We matched them to the ones on file from his military service."

Tara turned, her expression blank. "If his motivations are related to me, why do you think he killed this woman? I didn't really know her."

Kaci sat forward to put her plate on the table. "My guess, and it's only a guess mind you, is that he tracked you the same way I did. Then he talked to the woman and became worried that she'd ID him."

"So it was senseless." Tara shook her head. "Not that any killing makes sense, but this poor woman—all the women he's killed—did nothing wrong."

Shane looked at her with the same soothing expression he offered victims and hostages. "Remember we're dealing with a psychopath, here. The murder may not make any sense to us, but it made perfect sense to Keeler."

"A psychopath, really?" Tara shook her head. "I knew killing like this wasn't normal behavior, but 'psychopath' sounds so evil."

"He *is* evil!" The words flew out before Cal could temper them or his frustration with Keeler.

Tara stared down at her fisted hands, but Cal couldn't tell if she was pondering the woman's death or his heavy-handedness.

"I'm sorry for blowing up like that," he said. "But Keeler isn't the boy you grew up with. He's a cold-blooded killer now."

"I know." Her words whispered out, and Cal had to strain to hear her. "But that doesn't mean I can accept it."

Shane eyed Cal. "I don't agree with Cal's outburst, but he's right. Even if it hurts, you have to realize that the boy you grew up with is long gone."

She nodded and smiled at Shane, a soft smile filled with her thanks for his consideration.

Jealousy, an emotion Cal had rarely felt in his life, settled over him. He would much rather receive her sweet smile than the frustrated look she fired his way most of the time. Not that it was her fault. He was to blame. He couldn't seem to do the right thing around her and, of course, there would be no thanks for his constant overbearing tactics.

He had to keep his frustrations in check in the future and remember she prized her independence. She didn't want to be coddled. She wanted to take decisive action. To end this, find Keeler, and return to her normal life. Just as he wanted in his own life, and he respected that about her, liked it even, so why did he keep trying to go against it?

"Hey, Kaci," Rick said, interrupting Cal's thoughts. "Any proof that Keeler's tried to catch a plane out of here?"

Kaci shook her head. "I have the TSA at PDX and surrounding airports on alert. In case they miss him, I also have analysts running footage for as many airports as they can manage."

"What about rental car companies?" Brynn asked.

"Got that covered, too," Kaci replied. "Though I doubt he'll head out on a road trip back to D.C., he could drive to another Oregon airport or one in a nearby state. While my team is trying to track that down, we're asking for rental records for Toyota Corollas, too, but as you can imagine, we're getting a lot of blowback about warrants. Max is working that end of things, and hopefully we can get a judge to sign off with our limited information."

"Fortunately, I didn't get any grief from the Oregon State Police when I called on Hickson's rifle," Rick said. "In fact, we got lucky. They only maintain firearms sales records for a five-year period before destroying them, and the Browning was purchased a month short of five years ago."

Cal's hope for a solid lead perked up. "So we have the owner's name?"

Rick nodded. "I talked to him this afternoon. He didn't know the rifle was missing. He has a gun cabinet in his garage, and when I called, he discovered the lock was broken. I passed this off to local agents to make a visual confirmation and to keep digging into this guy, but I doubt we'll find a connection to Keeler."

"What about the man who reported seeing Keeler at the cabin?" Cal asked. "Anything new on that?"

Rick shook his head. "I personally interviewed him, and Kaci's team ran a background check. He has no record or affiliation with radical groups. Sheriff Gorton even vouched for the guy. Still, we'll leave it in the hands of local agents, too, in case we missed anything."

Cal looked at Shane. "You've been working on Hickson's background. Anything there?"

Shane's usual good humor vanished. "He's a Vietnam vet. He holds a number of marksman awards and was decorated for his service, but he came back with issues, as many vets do."

A murmur of understanding traveled through the team, who'd all served in the military, and Cal added his, too.

"He had a drinking problem that he managed to control until his wife died about five years ago, and he's been homeless since then. He's like the guy who reported Keeler, in that he has no affiliations with ISIS, which for a vet isn't surprising."

Another buzz of agreement ran through the group. Sure, at first Cal had been angry with Hickson. After all, he'd committed a crime and he had to pay, but if the woman hadn't enticed a hungry, down-on-his-luck guy with a wad of cash, Hickson would be sitting on the curb instead of heading to prison.

"I hate that a fellow vet will be going away because of Keeler," Shane said, echoing Cal's thoughts. "That's assuming Hickson is on the up and up."

Tara returned to the corner of the sofa. "Oren is destroying lives left and right."

"I'm leaning toward believing Hickson," Kaci said.

"Why's that?" Cal asked.

"None of his shots came close to hitting us. Or am I the only one who noticed that?" She looked around the group. "It was like he possessed strong enough skills to miss, if that makes sense."

"Perfect sense. I don't know why I didn't catch that," Rick said. "At some point, odds would say with the number of shots he'd fired off that he'd get lucky and hit one of us. It's only when you master a weapon that you can miss such a close target on every shot."

Cal believed they were right, but the only proof

was Hickson's statement, so there was very little they could do to help the guy out. "If it turns out he's telling the truth, I'll do everything I can to get his prison time reduced.".

Tara swiveled to look at him and offered a flicker of a smile. Why, he had no idea.

"Since we all think Hickson told us the truth," Shane said, "we need to talk about the implication of Keeler working with a Muslim woman while also killing women of the same faith."

"I didn't think Muslim women were allowed to participate in such things," Tara said. "Certainly not with ISIS, right?"

"That's rapidly changing with women from Western countries," Cal said. "In Europe, North America, and Australia, about ten percent of ISIS's foreign recruits are women. The majority of them are between the ages of eighteen and twenty-five."

"Jihadists actually celebrate the Muslim woman warrior," Shane said. "These are not the women you see covered in a burka trailing behind a man, but educated women who reject their Western freedoms to join in the fight. They're drawn by many of the same reasons as men."

"And they're effective for the cause," Brynn added. "Because of the stereotypes of Muslim women, they're often overlooked in investigations. Good for ISIS. Bad for us."

"But the women he killed have no ties to ISIS, right?" Tara asked.

"Right," Shane said. "And his willingness to work with Muslim women says his killing spree isn't about Muslim women in general."

"This fits your theory, Shane," Cal said. "Keeler doesn't hate women per se, and the women he'd killed must have something in common that we're missing."

"Once we get back to D.C., I'll take another look through the victims' files," Shane offered.

"What you all are saying is that you think my rejection is Oren's catalyst, but you still have no idea why he targeted the women he killed." Tara sighed.

Cal peered at her and noticed the dark circles under her eyes. She was exhausted and could do with a good night's sleep. He would suggest she go to bed, but she wouldn't leave this room and miss out on something, so he should wrap up their conversation.

"So," Cal said. "It looks like our most viable lead right now is the Tannerite, which could lead us to a local dealer who might have additional information on Keeler."

"And we could find a second rifle," Brynn added.

Cal smiled at her optimism. "The local office has freed up agents to search in the morning, and that should speed things along."

Tara sat up, suddenly looking very alert. "I could help, too."

All eyes swung to focus on her.

Cal shook his head. "That's not an option."

She lifted her chin. "You need my help."

"I'm pretty sure we can handle the search." Cal hated that he came across as patronizing, but he wasn't about to let her wander around in the general area where Keeler had been spotted.

Tara came to her feet, planted her hands on her hips, and stared at him. "I know the property better than anyone. I can show you how to move through the forest on hidden routes that Oren likely used as he approached the gate and my truck. That's where you're going to find a weapon if he ditched one."

"Still," Cal said, putting force into the word. "It's not something I'll allow."

"What about the rest of you?" She ran her gaze around the group, pausing to meet each person's eyes. "If there's a rifle out there, I'm your best hope of finding it, and I'm asking you to consider letting me help."

CHAPTER 15

Tara's statement brought awkward silence to the room, but she wouldn't back down. Oren had ruined a homeless vet's life and killed another innocent woman. Sure, he hadn't killed her with a bomb, but he'd taken a life, and Tara was now more committed to doing everything possible to help catch him, even if it meant she had to put her own life on the line.

She pulled her shoulders back and ran her gaze over the group again. "I think we should put this to a vote. Who's onboard with me helping?"

Tara heard Cal inhale and blow out a breath, but she wouldn't back down. In fact, she looked at him and held his gaze, even though his expression said he wanted to wring her neck.

"Sounds like a good idea to me." Brynn's voice was strong and unwavering. "With all the acreage we have to search, Tara could really cut down the time we—"

"No." Cal's voice held a definite edge that Tara hadn't heard before. "I won't allow her to participate in the search."

"Because she's a civilian?" Rick asked before Tara could ask the same question. "Or do you have another reason you'd like to share with us?"

Cal clenched his hands. "It's too dangerous for her to wander the woods."

"You're kidding, right?" Shane, the guy who seemed the most even-tempered of the team, asked. "We'll have groups of Portland agents involved in the weapon search tomorrow, and Keeler's not going to show up. If he planned to attack, he would have done it today when you left only three of us on her detail."

"He's right," Kaci added. "And as an extra

precaution, we can put Tara in tactical gear, and she should be good to go."

"Since everyone but Cal is in favor of this," Rick said. "Our plan is clear."

Cal came to his feet. "I'd like to talk to Tara alone."

No one moved.

Looking like he wanted to crash a hand into the wall, Cal curled his fingers into tight fists and met his teammates' gazes. "Make yourselves scarce."

"We've decided, Cal," Brynn said quietly. "Leave it at that, okay?"

His jaw tightened, and a thunderous look claimed his face. "A minute with Tara is all I ask."

Rick stood and grabbed the pizza box. "There's a media room downstairs filled with DVDs. We can unwind with a movie." He headed for the stairs.

Tara stood in place, but Cal went to the large window looking over the yard and faced outside. One by one, each teammate cast him a long look, but he remained peering out at the night, so he couldn't have seen them. However, he did have to feel their intense study as tension crackled through the room. He'd made his anger perfectly clear, but she didn't know if he was mad because she'd gone against his wishes and usurped his control, or if he felt like his team betrayed him.

Memories of Nolan going off on one of his tirades, demanding her compliance with whatever arbitrary rule he'd come up with—berating and browbeating her—left her apprehensive of the man in front of her who seemed barely in control of his emotions.

A knot formed inside her chest while she waited to be alone with him. But then she remembered that he'd offered to go to bat for Hickson simply because he felt a loyalty to a fellow vet. Nolan had no loyalties. He didn't even know the meaning of the word.

But Cal?

He'd been loyal to her, protecting her at all costs. Loyal to his quest for justice for the murdered women. To his team. He really was an incredible man if you could get over the fact that he tried to control everything. Maybe it was a good thing she couldn't get past it.

The last one to depart, Kaci started down the stairs, giving Tara a reassuring glance before disappearing from view.

She was eager to talk this out and faced Cal. "Everyone's gone."

Looking over his shoulder, he glanced around the room before stepping in her direction.

"Why don't we sit down?" he suggested, his tone not at all angry or harsh as she'd expected.

She appreciated his change in attitude, but she had to believe he would ask her to reconsider her decision, and standing made her feel more confident. "I'd like to stand."

"I don't want you to do this," he said softly, though his body language was anything but soft.

She wouldn't let that deter her. "I don't get the change in you. Last night you showed up here and begged for my help. I hate to admit it, but I put myself and my safety first when I should have been thinking of others. So now I'm thinking of them and giving you all the help I can provide, and you don't want it."

He narrowed his stance and shoved his hands into his pockets as if trying to physically withdraw from her, but as he looked away, she caught a flash of dark anguish in his eyes. She saw a tortured soul, pain, and torment that went far deeper than this disagreement with her, but his about-face said he didn't plan to share it with her.

What was he trying so hard to keep buried? Was it guilt? Sadness? Regret? The reason for turning his back on his faith? Would he ever tell her? Did she even want to know?

Enough with the questions that he'll likely never answer.

"Cal," she said to gain his attention. "I don't want to go against your wishes if helping with the search is foolish, which is why I asked your team to weigh in. If the others don't think this is a mistake, I think it's safe for me to help, don't you?"

He shook his head but didn't speak.

She stepped closer, drawing his full attention. "What's going on? You want to catch Oren more than anything, so what's changed that you don't want my help?"

He clasped a hand on the back of his neck and started massaging. "I can't explain it."

He'd never shown a loss for words before, and she wondered if he wasn't willing to talk to her. Another trait of a man needing to be in charge.

And yet . . . she couldn't let go of the fact that she'd come to see there was far more to Cal. Something that he worked very hard to keep hidden, and when she should be heeding the warning signs and running the other way, she kept wanting to find out what that something was. To get to know the real Cal Riggins. To find out if he was indeed like Nolan or if that other, deeper man that she'd seen hints of actually existed.

She groaned internally. This kind of thinking showed why she'd wound up hurt and alone in past relationships. And worse, in this case, she'd seen Cal's tendencies right up front and had no business trying to figure him out.

She had to stick with the investigation, keep up that wall between them as he was doing, and do nothing more. "Give me one good reason not to help tomorrow, and I'll back down."

He met her gaze. "I don't have a good reason, all right? I don't know why my feelings about your involvement have changed, they just have."

● ● ●

Tara's throat closed, and she clawed at her neck to dislodge the bomb. Fear, frenzied and raw, bubbled up, and she ripped the item free, then shot into an upright position and ran a frantic gaze around the space to get her bearings.

She was in her bedroom at the safe house, and the sheet had twined around her neck.

A nightmare. She'd had another one.

She pushed her sweaty hair from her forehead and kicked off the covers to rush into the attached bathroom. She ran cold water, splashed her face, and looked into the mirror. Panic lingered in her eyes and charcoal-colored slashes clung below them.

"This has got to stop," she whispered.

Last night she'd slept peacefully, and she'd honestly hoped that meant she'd feel safer with Cal around and the nightmares would stop. But tonight's nightmare had been the worst one yet, the sheets feeling like one of Oren's necklace bombs.

She now got a glimpse at his victims' terror as they waited for the bomb to detonate. They must have ached to claw at their throats but couldn't move an inch for fear of setting off the bomb. She ran her fingers over her neck above the tank top she'd slept in and tried to take a deep breath, but she couldn't manage to gain enough air.

She rushed from the room and raced for the

French doors, where she tapped in the code for the security alarm. Outside, she gulped in the coolness of the night and listened to trickling water run through the property.

Her body still overheated, she hurried down the stairs and sat at the edge of the creek to dip her feet into icy-cold water coming from the mountains. She cupped water into her hands and sloshed it down her legs, getting the hem of her shorts wet, but she didn't care. She took another handful and ran it over her face, down the back of her neck, the chilly goodness making a path between her shoulders. Feeling her breathing ease, she pulled up her knees and hugged her arms around them.

She wished Cal had never shown her the drawing of the necklace bomb. Every detail in the picture had lodged in her memory and transferred to her dreams. How ironic. She had no trouble remembering every tiny detail of Cal's drawing, but she had no recollection of the night at the pump house. Maybe the memory loss was God's way of keeping her from even worse nightmares.

Maybe . . . *if* God was listening and watching. But was He? She didn't deserve for Him to be. Not when she'd taken off without consulting Him. She'd once heard that when faced with difficulties, a person could either be fearless and courageous or be hopeless and rebellious. She'd chosen the latter and severed the cord that anchored her to trusting God. She wished she could cast out a new line, but God's plan in all of this was still hidden, and she felt helpless to act.

Heavy footsteps sounded behind her, and without looking, she knew Cal crossed the deck and came down the stairs. "You shouldn't be out here."

She glanced up at him. He'd firmed his jaw in a hard line and narrowed his eyes.

She didn't want to tell him about the nightmare. Being a guy he'd try to fix it when he could do nothing to help short of arresting Oren, and she couldn't be sure even that would work right now. Besides worrying about Oren killing her, she also feared that these nightmares would continue forever.

How could she go about life like that? She could never have a relationship that was for sure. No man would want to be saddled with such an emotionally damaged partner.

Or was Cal the kind of guy who could handle it? He obviously had his own issues, so maybe he could understand.

Enough with all of this crazy introspection. She wanted to clamp her hands over her ears and maybe her mind would quiet for once.

Without offering further chastisement, Cal dropped down next to her. Though he sat a few feet away, the heat from his body stretched between them, and she felt drawn to him.

Or maybe she imagined the warmth because she'd become so aware of him as a man. His long legs were bent, the muscles of his thighs coiled as if ready to spring into action. She had no doubt he would come to her defense and defeat any enemy that breached the security of the fence. Her own personal knight, his armor that of iron will and determination. His sword, his caring and dedication.

"You had a bad dream," he stated flatly.

How did he know? She flashed him a questioning look.

"My room is next to yours, and I heard you. Doesn't take a rocket scientist to figure out you came out here to get some air." He paused a moment, his gaze searching hers.

She didn't know how to reply, so she took hold of a rubber band and snapped it.

He pressed his hand over her wrist, the heat from his touch sending her head spinning. "I hate to see you hurt yourself like that."

She should pull her arm free, but she closed her eyes and let his touch soothe her already-heated skin. "It's the only thing that works for me."

"If I asked, would you consider taking them off?"

Would she? She didn't know, so she shrugged.

"Then will you at least consider coming inside?" His unusually gentle tone wrapped around her like a soothing heat wrap.

She wanted to comply, but she wasn't ready to be cooped up again. She also couldn't talk about the nightmare or her rubber bands.

"This guard you put up all the time," she said, turning the focus on him in hopes that he might respond to her this time. "Is it from something in your past or living the SEAL motto you told me about?"

He went quiet. Not that she expected him to respond, but at least it stopped him from asking additional questions.

"Both," he said.

Surprised that he'd answered, she swiveled to face him, her wrist pulling free, and she immediately missed his touch.

"I was a SEAL for enough years to know that if you don't keep up your defenses, people can die." He looked into her eyes. "People like you, and I wouldn't want anything bad to happen to you. I get that I'm coming on strong when it comes to protecting you, but I only want to make sure you're safe."

In the fathomless bottom of his eyes, she glimpsed a level of caring that took her breath. This hunt for Keeler was very personal for him. *She* was personal for him.

"Why?" she whispered, even though she shouldn't go down this path. "Why this deep interest in protecting me?"

"It's my job."

"And that's all it is to you?" Breath held, she waited for his answer.

Water trickled over her feet and frogs chirped in the distance, but he remained silent.

"Cal?" she asked, yet wished she'd been strong enough not to need to.

"We . . . you and me, we have something. A connection." His eyes flashed up to meet hers and held. "You can feel it, too. Right?"

Should she answer truthfully? She couldn't look him in the eye as she considered her response, so she ran her gaze over him.

He wore his tactical pants and the navy shirt that molded to his toned body. His jaw was rugged, his eyes soft and caring. He was the complete physical package, so her attraction to him made sense, but it went deeper than that and was stronger than she'd first thought. Something that hadn't happened since, well, since never.

Why now, God? Why him?

She raised her gaze to Cal's. "I don't want to be attracted to you."

"But you are?" he asked again, as if he needed to hear her admit it.

"Yes." She kept it at one word and wouldn't elaborate, as speaking it aloud would make things worse.

"Then we need to get beyond it, or at least I need to. I'm charged with finding a serial killer and making sure you don't become one of his victims." The warmth evaporated from his gaze, and his shoulders stiffened. "We need to keep things professional between us. Let's agree to avoid situations like this, especially when we're alone under the stars."

"Why, Cal Riggins, I think you're a romantic at heart," she teased, in hopes of lightening things up a bit.

"Maybe." He started to get up.

"Wait." She shot out a hand to clutch his wrist. His pulse throbbed under her fingers, making her even more aware of him as a man, but she banished thoughts of him from her mind.

"I didn't thank you for this morning, for risking your life for me," she said. "If you hadn't been there. Been willing to cover me . . ." Tears threatened, and she looked up to stem them. "So if you want me to back down on helping tomorrow, I will."

"It's your decision." His voice held no hint of his true thoughts. "I won't tell you what to do, but I hope you'll at least think about my reservations." He smiled and their gazes collided.

Emotions raced along her nerve ends so fast she couldn't even put a name to them. She opened her mouth to speak, but she didn't know what to say. How to act.

"I want to let you do this, but when you look at me like you're doing now . . ." His low, husky voice wrapped around her. "I can't think, much less entertain the thought that you would put your life on the line."

"I can't either," she whispered. "Think, that is."

His smile widened, one corner crookedly tipping higher. He gently cupped the side of her face, and then, not breaking eye contact, he got to his feet and tugged her up. She half hoped he'd stood to draw her into his arms, as she wanted nothing more than to feel the security of rock-solid arms holding her right now, but he let go of her hand and stepped back.

"We need to get inside." With gentle pressure on her back, he steered her toward the house, ending their amazing interlude. If Tara would be brutally honest with herself, she'd admit she never wanted it to end.

Chapter 16

Tara stepped into the kitchen the next morning and found Cal alone. Wearing a pressed version of yesterday's uniform, he rested against the granite countertop and cupped his hands around a mug, his focus fixed on the blue stoneware. She wondered about his pensive study, but when he looked up, his face held no sign of deep intro-spection, or he'd managed to hide it from her.

"Good morning," she said, and went straight to the refrigerator to put off telling him that she'd decided to assist in looking for the rifle today.

He mumbled a "good morning" back at her. She grabbed the orange juice and filled a large glass. She didn't have to see his eyes to know he was tracking her movements, and once she turned to face him, she'd have to share her decision.

She took a long drink of the cool juice before pivoting. Looking him square in the face, she opened her mouth, but words failed her.

He held up a hand. "You don't have to say it. You're going to lead us through the woods today."

She nodded. "You should know, though, I did take your concerns into account. But I couldn't live with myself if I didn't help and Oren hurt another person."

He set down his mug. "Trust me, I get that. Besides, I expected you'd decide in favor of helping."

"You know me that well, huh?"

He met her gaze and held it. "I'm coming to."

And she was coming to know him, too, which she doubted was a good thing.

He pushed off the counter, rising to his full height and seeming to take up all of the space in the room. "I was hoping we might reach a compromise."

Compromise from him? Mr. By-the-Book. She was all for compromise, and it thrilled her to see he knew the meaning of the word, but unfortunately, she didn't trust his motives and needed clarification before she would agree to anything.

"Compromise how?" she asked.

"We'll spend the morning searching for the rifle. If we don't find anything, we'll head to D.C."

"Interesting compromise."

"I continue to believe the pump house ruins will help you remember more about that night, and that will best serve us in the long run. But I know you want to assist in finding the rifle." He appraised her for a long moment. "Do we have a deal?"

Him considering her wishes for once? She didn't need to think twice.

"Deal." She stuck out her hand.

He engulfed her fingers in his and shook, but he quickly released her hand. "The rest of the team left for the scene hours ago. So why don't you grab something to eat, and we can get moving?"

The tension in the room seemed to ease, but she thought it better that they didn't remain in the house alone for much longer.

She picked up a banana and protein bar. "I'll eat on the way."

She expected him to argue—to insist she have a more filling meal—but he gestured at the door. In the car, her appetite returned, and she devoured her food as he launched into detailed safety procedures for their search. He gave her so many dos and don'ts that, by the time they stepped outside at the bomb site, her head spun with all the details.

Frowning, he paused by the rear of the SUV and looked up at the sky. She followed his gaze to ominous gray clouds. Humidity saturated the air, and even with the clouds obscuring the sun, the thermometer had risen above eighty degrees.

"Rain's coming," he said. "We need to get going before it does and destroys any evidence we might find."

He opened the SUV hatch and began unloading gear. Rick crossed over to the SUV. Like the other team members, he wore khaki pants and a navy shirt. The others were all neat and clean-looking, but there was an extra sharpness to Rick's attire at all times, as if he still tried to maintain military precision in his appearance. He shot a look between her and Cal, likely gauging the mood after last night's tension.

"Don't worry," Tara said. "We've reached a compromise."

Rick gave a sharp nod, then grabbed a clipboard and calculator from his bag. In order to determine the direction for their search, Cal and Rick compiled trajectory possibilities for the rifle shot that could have detonated the bomb.

She rested on the bumper and watched the pair. Their heads bent together over a clipboard with drawings filled with angles and numbers. They bandied about words like *wind speed, range,* and *bullet diameter.* It didn't take long for her to see they were both extremely knowledgeable about weapons.

Their expertise impressed Tara, but then their many skills already awed her.

Cal tapped the clipboard. "So we're agreed. We have three locations to scout."

"Affirmative." Rick stepped back. "Let's get it done."

A southern accent she'd caught the slightest hint of before today threaded through his tone, and one corner of his mouth turned up a fraction. Rick liked weapons. He made that more than clear. As he was the team's ballistics expert, it also made sense.

Cal grabbed a bag labeled with Kaci's name in black letters. "Kaci is the smallest person on the team, and she's already agreed to let you wear her gear." He pulled out an army-green vest and dropped it over Tara's shoulders.

She stood so he could help fasten the tabs, and the heavy weight threatened to buckle her knees. "Odd that this is smaller than the one I wore yesterday, but it feels heavier."

"First, you were fueled with adrenaline yesterday, making it seem lighter. And second, Kaci is a pack rat and has the vest jammed with stuff. Let me lighten the load a bit."

He removed ammunition mags from pockets, a first aid bag, and various tools clipped on the outside. "Sorry, the ceramic plates alone weigh about ten pounds, but they're needed to protect against high-caliber ammo. If you get tired, let me know, and we'll take a rest."

"Thank you," she said, wondering if Oren actually was up in a tree ready to shoot her.

She wouldn't worry. She'd remember Shane's words from last night instead and believed Oren wouldn't dare attack with the swarm of agents in the area.

Cal settled a helmet on her head. Adjusting the chin straps, he brushed his fingers against her skin, firing off her nerves. She forgot all about the weight of the vest and the heat the helmet instantly trapped next to her scalp and focused on his face.

He met her gaze and lingered, and her heart rate kicked into a higher gear.

He suddenly dropped his hands to step back. "I'm sure you can take care of the strap."

How did she allow him to do this to her? Worse, she let him see the effect his touch had on her. She needed to control her emotions. Better yet, she had to keep from letting him touch her again.

He grabbed icy-cold bottles of water and loaded the backpack. "In this heat you need to stay hydrated, so don't hesitate to ask for water breaks."

She nodded, and he handed her the GPS device where he'd entered their first coordinates and a map displayed the targeted location.

"Follow me." She set off.

"Hold up." Cal caught up to her and took her arm. "Remember we go together. Side by side or we don't go at all."

"There are some spots on this route that are too narrow for side by side."

"When that happens, we'll assess the threat and go from there. Until then, you need to pretend we're connected at the hip."

His words brought a crazy image to mind, and she laughed.

"I'm serious," he growled at her.

"Don't worry, I get it," she assured him.

With Cal at her side, Tara crossed the road, and Rick took up the rear. She stepped into knee-high grass that tangled around her feet and ankles, making the trip forward difficult.

"Clearly, this is the easy way." The sarcasm she'd come to expect from Rick wove through his voice.

"You should live by Cal's motto." She turned and smiled up at Rick. "The only easy day was yesterday."

Cal broke out in unexpected laughter, and Rick chuckled, too. She'd never heard Rick laugh, but she only cared about the cheerful sound coming from Cal. His unusual lighthearted stance gave her a glimpse at the man he did his best to hide.

She swallowed hard to ignore the way his good mood sent her pulse beating fast and gestured ahead. "It'll get easier once we reach the actual path."

Despite the moisture-wicking lining of the helmet, perspiration quickly covered her head. The skies continued to threaten rain, and if the heat wave didn't break under the rain, the highs were expected to reach one hundred degrees by afternoon. It would be a good ten degrees cooler in the shaded forest, but wearing the vest and helmet would soon sap her strength.

She slipped under low-hanging branches and moved to the right a few feet where the trees opened up to a narrow path.

"Here's the reason you brought me along." She nodded at the trail ahead.

"Sweet," Rick said, but Cal was looking up through the trees and didn't immediately respond.

"I'll lead," he finally said. "Tara next."

Tara had no reason to argue, so she nodded but added, "The path forks ahead. Veer right and your coordinates are about a hundred yards after that."

He set off. Tara followed, watching him instead of the path. How could such a large man move so fluidly and silently? She pictured him as a SEAL sneaking through a jungle, his mind set on rescuing a hostage. Focused on his mission.

If she found herself in such a situation, she wouldn't want any other man coming to her rescue. Not even Rick, who seemed more than competent, too. She felt this way about Cal for the same reason she was leery of him. He took command of a situation and approached it with everything he was made of.

Did he run his life outside the job the same way? He'd mentioned that he wouldn't be a dictator in his personal life if he even had one, but turning off this working attitude at the drop of a hat? She couldn't imagine that.

At the fork, he headed right and came to a stop.

"We'll start our search here." He caught Tara's attention. "Go ahead and take a rest at the base of the tree next to you."

She didn't want to appear to be the weak one in the group. "I'm good."

"With the possible sniper angles in this area, if you sit where I tell you, you'll be protected from rifle fire, and I can search more freely without worrying about you." He cracked a smile. "You can even take the helmet off for now." He dug out a bottle of water and handed it to her.

She lowered herself to the ground and gladly unclipped the helmet. She swiped the perspiration from her forehead and chugged the water. Sweat trickled down her neck. She must look quite a sight. Not that the guys cared about how she looked. They walked together, heads down, and stepped in an unspoken grid pattern. The heat didn't seem to bother them. She'd played softball in high school and worked the farm, but she was such a girly girl compared with the Knights. She honestly had very little in common with Cal, and yet they were attracted to each other. Clearly, there was no accounting for what the heart wanted.

"We can move on to the next location," Cal soon announced.

She clamped the helmet on her head, stowed her water bottle, and stared at Cal. "I assume you want to lead, so take the same trail back to the scrub by the road."

He nodded and they set off. Back at the knee-deep grass, she stepped ahead, and he moved to her side.

"When did you have time to find all these trails?" he asked.

"The few rainy days that we've had this summer."

"So you slogged through all of this in the rain?"

She nodded.

He shook his head. "You keep surprising me at how tough you are."

She snorted. "I was just thinking about what a wuss I am compared to you all."

"Well, that's a given." He grinned, revealing a small dimple on one side. Ah, that boyish charm she found irresistible had returned. "But still.

You're a strong person, Tara. Don't ever think otherwise."

Why had she been blessed with smiles and laughter from him today? Should she ask? No, not with Rick nearby.

She led them to the next path. It was wider, so they continued walking together until they approached their location. Cal grabbed her arm, stopping her forward progress. She tried to preempt his need to instruct her and looked for a place to sit.

"Have you been here recently?" he asked, instead of directing her to sit.

She shook her head.

He gestured ahead at the side of the path. "The trampled foliage says someone has."

Excitement and fear commingled in her stomach. "Oren, yesterday?"

"Could be."

"If I help with the search we can figure it out faster."

"Sorry," he replied. "Rules of evidence prevent me from allowing you anywhere near potential evidence before I've had a look myself."

"So you want me to sit down and wait."

He shook his head. Gone were his smiles and easygoing laughter. "I want you on alert and ready to flee if needed."

He and Rick shared a look as they raised their weapons. Cal a handgun, Rick his submachine gun. He planted the stock on his shoulder and scanned the area. Tara had no problem imagining him in his former role as a marine sniper, but his caution made her want to bolt in the other direction.

"You think Oren is here? Now?" Tara tried to keep the anxiety from her voice, but failed.

"Can't be too careful." Rick's tone mirrored Cal's.

They set off together. Rick was as light-footed as Cal, and he continued to prove his serious nature, smiling even less than Cal. Tara had seen another side to Rick, though. He was a compassionate man who wanted to help others, much like Cal. Like the whole team.

"Over here." Cal jerked his phone from his belt clip and snapped pictures of the ground.

Rick stood at attention, his gun and gaze continually sweeping over the area. She respected his discipline, which kept him from changing his focus to check out the lead Cal had located. She didn't possess the same discipline and warred with thoughts of racing over to Cal, where he now squatted in the ferns abutting the path. He dug latex gloves from his pack and snapped them on. He moved foliage aside, then jumped to his feet and shot a look at the tree line. He pointed at an area nearer to her.

"There." He strode up the path.

Rick followed right on Cal's heels, swinging his weapon in arcs, his posture and intense focus frightening Tara. Cal rushed to the tree and began shimmying up the trunk.

Amazed at the body strength that allowed him to move without much leverage, she couldn't pull her eyes away, but her thoughts went back to yesterday when the climb involved a hail of bullets.

She had to know if they were in danger. "What did you find by the path?"

"A rifle," Cal replied, but didn't stop his climb.

"Make?" Rick asked, for the first time showing interest in Cal's discovery.

"Remington 798."

"It's chambered for a .30-06, too."

They were talking about the caliber of bullets, but she didn't know the importance of this particular caliber. "Which means what exactly?"

Rick glanced at her. "The bullet we believe set off the bomb is a .30-06."

"So this could be the rifle, then." She paused to process the news and looked up at Cal. "But why climb the tree?"

"I wanted to check the firing angle to be sure." He peered down at her. "There's blood up here. Likely Keeler's."

Rick glanced around the area. "Nothing on the ground, so I doubt it's a serious wound, and he wouldn't have sought medical attention. We should still follow up with local medical facilities. Even if we strike out, at the very least, the blood could provide a physical connection to Keeler's role in detonating the bomb."

"Wouldn't there also be fingerprints on the rifle?" Tara asked.

"Could be, if he didn't wear gloves, but the blood will also place him in the right position to have fired at the truck."

Thunder rumbled from above, a rare phenomenon in this part of the country. Tara's attention went to the angry clouds rolling over each other as if trying to fight for space.

"Get back to the bomb site, Rick." A thread of urgency wove through Cal's voice. "Lead Brynn out here to preserve the evidence before it rains."

Tara opened her mouth to remind Rick of the paths they'd taken to reach this location, but then it hit her that he, like Cal, would know their exact steps and could retrace them without any help, so she turned her attention back to Cal. He'd gotten out his camera and snapped pictures of a branch.

"Tara, can you locate our exact GPS coordinates on my device and mark it?" he asked without looking at her. "Then go to the area where I found the rifle and do the same thing?"

"Sure." Not technically inclined, she hoped she could pull it off.

"Don't step off the path by the rifle or you risk contaminating the area but get as close as you can."

She punched a few buttons, located the right

settings, and marked Cal's location before doing the same with the rifle. By the time she'd finished, Cal dropped to the ground. He stepped to the rifle location, dug a tarp from his pack, and shook it out. The plastic waved in the breeze until he wrestled it under control to cover the rifle. He grabbed his phone and dialed.

"Gorton," he said, and Tara recognized the name as belonging to the local sheriff. "We have a second shooter, and I have reason to believe he's been injured. Not likely a gunshot wound, but more likely a puncture from a tree branch. I realize you have limited resources, but I need your people to check with local medical facilities for anyone recently treated for such a wound."

Cal listened for a moment. "Get back to me either way."

He stowed his phone.

Tara met his gaze. "It's great that you found the other rifle."

"We can't be sure it belongs to Keeler."

"But you can trace it and find out who it belongs to?"

"Someone filed the serial number off the rifle's receiver."

"So you can't find out who owned it, then?"

"I didn't say that." His grin and the cute dimple came back. "We have several ways to recover the number in the lab, where I plan to go the minute our plane lands on the East Coast."

CHAPTER 17

Fairfax, Virginia
Thursday, August 4
7:50 a.m.

Today was the day. The day Tara went back to the pump house. The day she dreaded, and yet she hoped the visit would help with the investigation.

She'd be lying if she said the thought of visiting the burned-out shell didn't weigh heavy on her mind. It apparently weighed on Cal, too, because breakfast at the new safe house near D.C. was a silent affair between them. She'd tried small talk for the first few minutes, but it was forced and awkward, so she turned her attention to eating her yogurt.

Cal's phone chimed, and he lifted it to read the text. His jaw tightened, and Tara took a deep breath to prepare herself for more bad news.

"The text is from Kaci." He held out his phone, showing a picture of Oren captured by a security camera.

Her stomach knotted, unsettling her breakfast. "Where was it taken?"

"Eugene airport. He chartered a jet to D.C. Kaci spoke to the pilot and confirmed Keeler took the flight and touched down in D.C. in the middle of the night. Means Keeler could be looking for you, and we need to be extra cautious."

Tara reached for her rubber bands. The first pull bit into her skin, but the ominous feeling remained. So what? She'd committed to helping catch Oren, and that meant taking risks. But she didn't have to be a fool about it.

"I'll follow your every direction today," she said to Cal, but in reality the words were meant for her.

"I hate that Keeler's back in the area, but if I'd known his arrival would make you so compliant . . ." Cal smiled.

Despite her misgivings, she couldn't resist his playful attempt to brighten her mood. She let go of the rubber band and returned his smile. The tension fled and electricity charged between them.

He freed his gaze and gestured at the door to the garage. "We should get going."

Cal said he wanted to keep his focus on the road and his mirrors, so they drove in silence. She also watched out the window, noting each and every car until they turned onto Pennsylvania Avenue and got caught up in the tourist traffic. FBI headquarters was located in the J. Edgar Hoover building, which sat between the White House and the U.S. Capitol, an area bustling with visitors on foot and in cars.

Cal fired a cautionary look in her direction. "With the congested traffic, this is the most critical zone, so stay alert. Look past the families crowding the street and search for any threat."

His focus intensified, and she tried to comply, but she couldn't see through the waves of people enjoying the sights. Tension mounting, she slid a finger under her rubber band and knotted it around her finger until Cal pulled into the secured parking area. Even then, her pulse continued to race, and settled down only after they stepped inside the FBI's fortress locked down tight with metal detectors and screeners. Oren couldn't get through the FBI's defenses, and for the first time in months, stress flooded from her body and she could finally breathe freely.

Cal stood with her while the guards cleared her, and then they rode a nearby elevator to a small foyer. Cal swiped a security card to unlock a door and headed down a pin drop–quiet hallway. Professional men and women were hurrying about their business with single focus and thankfully not paying any attention to Tara's jeans and T-shirt. She'd hoped someone on the Knights' team could have gone to her house to grab nicer clothing, but Cal said it could tip off anyone watching the place.

How she missed home, a row house on a tree-lined street with brightly painted houses as far as the eye could see. She rented the place from another translator who was temporarily assigned overseas. Since she was still paying off student loans and saving money for travel, she could never have afforded such a nice house if not for her coworker, and each day when she arrived home, she relished the place, as she'd soon have to move back into a cheaper apartment.

"Everything okay?" Cal asked as he stopped next to another door.

"Yes, just homesick."

"Understandable. You've been gone for a long time." He pressed his thumb against a digital print reader. The lock clicked, and the door popped open.

"Hold on a second," he said, and stuck his head inside. "You have a minute, Kaci?"

Cal held the door barely cracked open and tapped his foot.

Tara tried to scoot around him to see inside the room, but he blocked her view. "Seriously, what do you have in there?"

"Information," he replied cryptically. "Nothing but information."

Kaci pushed the door open and peeked out. "About time you got here. We have a—" She suddenly noticed Tara. "Oh, hi, Tara. I didn't think Cal would bring you here."

"You have a what?" Cal asked.

"A lead, but maybe that should wait until we decide if it can be shared." She tipped her head at Tara.

Cal spun to face Tara. "Would you mind waiting out here with Kaci for a moment?"

She didn't like all the cloak-and-dagger stuff,

but she'd promised to listen to Cal's directions today, so she nodded her agreement. Kaci stepped out, and Cal disappeared behind the door before pulling it closed.

"What's he up to in there?" Tara asked.

"He's most likely being read in on the latest lead and determining if we can share it with you. And since this is our strategy room, we keep a timeline of events, pictures, and other information posted on the walls. He's probably removing sensitive information that can't be shared with anyone outside the team."

"If you all want my help, why keep things from me?"

Kaci frowned. "Let me first say, we don't willingly share *any* information."

"I thought that was just Cal."

"He's a quiet one, all right." Kaci smiled and looked like a teenager instead of a woman in her thirties. "But if you really want to see someone who doesn't share much, Rick's your guy. He's so used to being held to the standard of perfection as a sniper that he weighs his words carefully before he speaks. He gives a mummy a run for his money in the silence department." Kaci laughed.

Tara laughed, too, and hoped Kaci would serve as an ally on the team. At least be someone who was more forthcoming, who Tara could go to when Cal didn't provide a straight answer.

"About the information sharing," Kaci continued.

"As a team, we decide which details, if they were leaked, could harm our investigation. We try to ensure that talk of those items never leaves the four walls of this room."

"I see." Tara's mind shifted to thinking about how many things Cal might have kept from her.

He'd shared some pretty gruesome things, but had he let her see only the tip of the iceberg when it came to Oren's depravity?

The door popped opened, and Cal stood back. They were allowing her into their inner sanctum. *Exciting.*

She stepped in and let her gaze race over the room. Her excitement plummeted. She didn't see a supersecret lair, just a plain old meeting room. She focused on a round table in the middle of the space where the team had congregated.

In keeping with her inner sanctum thoughts, she imagined King Arthur with his knights gathered around their table, and a laugh escaped before she could stop it.

Cal eyed her.

She gestured at the table. "The table. It's round."

He continued to stare at her.

"You know, like Knights of the Round Table."

Kaci chuckled behind her, and Tara didn't feel so bad about bringing it up, but the others continued to stare at her.

"C'mon, people." Kaci dropped into a chair next to Shane. "Lighten up."

"Go ahead and have a seat, Tara." Cal's serious tone was in complete opposition to Kaci's comment.

Tara didn't know how to get the happy guy from yesterday back, but she wished she could. As she crossed the windowless room, she took a closer look at the space. Bookshelves filled with dated three-ring binders going back seven months filled one wall. Another held a long workbench with a variety of tools neatly mounted above. And as Kaci had mentioned, whiteboards holding timelines for each bombing with graphic pictures and vinyl pockets containing information covered the other walls.

Tara took in the pictures of the murdered Muslim women posted on the wall next to burned-out buildings and car shells. As she read the names below, each woman became a person to her instead of a statistic, and sadness wove through her body. She spotted the names of her friends from Atlanta and Dallas, and she quickly averted her gaze before she saw any horrific pictures.

Her good mood long gone, she dropped onto the chair, wanting to be anywhere but in this room circled with death and destruction.

The door latch released and everyone looked at the door except Cal.

He kept his focus on her. "That'll be Max."

Eager to get a look at the person who commanded the very strong-willed team, Tara stared at the door.

A man about Cal's height with military-perfect posture stepped inside. He had the squarest jaw Tara had ever seen and sandy-brown hair that looked like he'd recently run his fingers through it. He wore what she now assumed was the team uniform of khaki pants and a navy shirt. With his swagger and confident look, she could easily imagine him leading the Knights.

His fierce focus traveled around the table and landed on her, where it lingered.

"Ms. Parrish." He stepped closer and offered his hand, his gaze lightening a fraction. "I'm Max White."

She accepted his hand and made sure she didn't flinch at his iron grip or close scrutiny.

"I'm sorry we have to meet under such dire circumstances."

She nodded but couldn't for the life of her come up with anything to say.

Cal clapped Max on the shoulder. "Feel free to speak your mind with Max. He can be kind of intimidating, but don't let that stop you."

"Kind of," Kaci said, and the others grunted their agreement.

"It's not intentional, I assure you," Max replied warmly, then cast a baleful look at his team. He pulled out a chair and straddled it, making Tara think he didn't plan to stay long. "So what did you need to see me about?"

Cal took a seat. "We've discovered information

on a woman who seems to be working with Keeler." He peered at Kaci. "You found the lead, so why don't you share the details with Max?"

"Happy to." She smiled and opened a laptop computer. "Hoping to collect any photos from the area before the bomb detonated, we set up LEEDIR before we left Dallas."

"LEEDIR stands for Large Emergency Event Digital Information Repository and is a database," Cal told Tara. "Basically law enforcement makes a plea to the public to upload photos they took of a specified area. It's used mostly for large events like earthquakes, the Boston bombing, that sort of thing."

Kaci nodded. "We figured it was a long shot, as there could only be so many people in the Dallas bomb vicinity. On top of that, they would need a reason to be taking pictures, but we put out a plea anyway. Last night three photos came in from a person who was visiting her sister and snapping shots of the barbeque joint next door. We cropped out the person at the barbeque place, then enhanced and enlarged the image background, revealing this woman."

Kaci clicked a button on her computer, and an image flashed onto the large television mounted on the wall. The woman had dark skin, and a strand of jet-black hair peeked out of her head covering. Kaci advanced the pictures, and the woman moved in a way that would look furtive if you were looking for something suspicious.

Rick leaned closer to the screen. "She fits the size and build of the woman Hickson described."

"I thought the same thing," Kaci said. "And she's acting odd, so we ran her through facial recognition."

"And?" Max asked.

"It returned this." She handed Max a sheet of paper.

Tara waited for Kaci to hand a page to her, but she didn't. Obviously the team had decided not to share this detail outside the group. Tara was disappointed, but she couldn't do anything about them keeping the woman's identity confidential.

Cal must have caught her questioning look as he leaned close. "She's a known ISIS associate who lives in the D.C. area."

"D.C.?" Tara muttered. "So if she was in Dallas on the day of the bombing, she could very well be connected to Oren."

"Yes, and all we need is a search warrant and we can raid her home." Rick sounded like he couldn't wait to break down the woman's door.

Max laid the paper facedown on the table and sat back. "Odds aren't good that a judge would sign off on a warrant based on such limited information and circumstantial connection. Do we have anything beyond a Middle Eastern woman looking a bit suspicious outside a restaurant near the bombing site?"

"Other than she lives here in D.C. and has an ISIS affiliation, no," Kaci said.

"You'll need to run a stakeout on her or find another connection to Keeler if you hope to get that warrant."

"We all get that, Max," Cal said. "But we were hoping due to the exigent circumstances you could work your magic with a judge."

Max pushed to his feet. "Magic is one thing, but even the great David Copperfield couldn't pull this one off." He strode to the door. "Call me when you have more."

"That went well," Kaci grumbled the moment the door closed behind Max.

"Did you expect more from the master of 'give me cold, hard facts and nothing more'?" Cal asked.

"No, but . . ."

Rick picked up the paper Max had left behind. "Let me confirm that she still lives at this address, and then I'll stake out her house."

"And I'll burn up my keyboard looking for additional information online," Kaci added.

"I'll get started on reviewing the victims' files like I promised last night," Shane said. "But is there anything else you'd like me to do first?"

"Two things," Cal replied, "but they're not related to this woman. Can you follow up with the analysts to see where they stand on Tannerite purchases in Oregon and track down any leads?"

"Got it, and what else?"

"Before you get started on the Tannerite, can you go to evidence and bring up the items recovered from Keeler's rental house so Tara can review them?"

Shane didn't respond right away, but sat in contemplative thought. "You're hoping her history with Keeler will reveal something we've missed."

Cal nodded and stood. "If any new information comes to light, you'll find me here with Tara. We'll review the evidence, and I'll be playing the audio from her call to the hotline. If that doesn't bring back any memories, we'll visit the pump house. I'll let you know if and when I need your help on that detail."

The team might as well have smacked hands together and shouted "break" like football players in a huddle, as they got up in unison, gathered their items, and moved to the exit without a word.

Cal's focus remained on the door until it closed. His gaze switched to Tara. "Would you like a cup of coffee or some water?"

"Water, please."

He crossed the room to a small refrigerator in the corner, retrieved two bottles of water, and set one in front of her.

"We spend a lot of time in this room, so we keep drinks and snacks handy. Let me know if you want anything else." He sat next to her and pulled a computer close. "Are you ready to hear your hotline call?"

She nodded, but in all honesty, she'd never be ready to hear the details of that night.

"Perhaps you'll want to close your eyes so you can focus."

She didn't know if she wanted to do that either, but it would at least keep her from looking at the horrific pictures on the wall, so she clamped her eyes closed.

"Okay, here we go."

The computer speakers crackled, and she took a deep breath.

"Hotline, this is Special Agent Cal Riggins." Cal's rumbling voice replaced the crackling.

"My aunt's tenant, Oren Keeler." Her words came pouring out, each one trying to step on the prior one. Even with vague memories of the incident, the terror in her own voice brought a wave of fear crashing over her. She focused on drawing air and blowing it out while continuing to listen carefully. Soon a hint of a memory danced on the edge of her mind, but actual visions of the night remained shrouded.

She clenched her hands in frustration and listened to the recorded conversation as Cal tried to calm her down and told her how to overpower Oren. Muffled sounds followed, making no sense to her. A gunshot cracked through the speakers.

"I remember him shooting at me. Right there by

the pump house." She opened her eyes and found Cal's focus fixed on her.

The rustling sound played once again.

"What's that noise?" she asked.

"It's the sound of your phone rubbing against your pocket as you ran from Keeler." He pressed the button on his computer and the noise stopped.

"Is that the end of the recording?"

"No."

"I want to hear it all."

Cal seemed to mull it over, but finally nodded. "I'll skip past the running noises."

He fast-forwarded the audio. She closed her eyes again, and the sound of the massive explosion tore through the speakers.

She could almost feel the ground rumbling under her chair, and she jumped. Cal took her hand, and she clasped his with an iron grip that likely had him wincing, but she didn't look to see.

All sounds ceased until the blast from a single gunshot broke the quiet. The sharp report and rumbling explosion fired off her senses, bringing back the fear as she ran from Oren, and the pain of a bullet piercing her stomach.

She gasped. Cal's other hand came over hers, giving her the strength to keep her eyes closed and continue to listen.

She remembered falling at a snail's pace, as if time had slowed. Hitting the ground and the earthy scent of the forest floor rising up to meet her. Fear raced over her that Oren would come closer and finish her off, and she'd tried to lift her phone in her hand to call for help, but couldn't raise her arm. She'd thought she would die all alone in the woods with no one to comfort her, to find her, and she wouldn't have the chance to say good-bye to June and her friends.

She'd been alone. All alone.

"No!" Her voice cried out on the recording, full of the panic now threatening to take her down.

She whipped her eyes open and jerked her hand free to wrap her arms around her stomach. Cal reached for the mute button on his computer, but the sound of footsteps pounding over the ground came through the speakers.

"Let it play," she said, and soon heard Cal radio for help. Then a much quieter sound of him telling her that he was there for her, and he would get her through this.

The anguish washed away, and her heart soared at his kindness, his help. Tears that she'd held back the last few days flowed down her cheeks, and she didn't try to stop them. "I felt so alone, but you came. Like you promised."

He scooted his chair closer and with a gentle thumb brushed away her tears. "I know this has been hard on you, but I promise to be here for you every step of the way until this is resolved."

She threw caution to the wind and stood to tug him to his feet. She wrapped her arms around the neck of this strapping man who'd flown in on a helicopter to save her life. He drew her close and held her tightly with one arm while cradling the back of her head with the other.

She rested her cheek on his broad chest and closed her eyes, reveling in the feel of his solid strength. The inky night came back again. She was lying on the ground with Cal standing above her in his tactical gear looking fierce and intimidating while at the same time anger mixed with sorrow in his gaze.

But now?

She leaned back and peered up at him. His warmth, compassion, and—dare she think— caring displayed in his expression filled her to a depth that erased all of her worries and fears of not ever getting over the shooting and being whole again. Sure, she thought the optimism was for this moment only, but she'd take the little bit that God offered right now.

Cal gently touched her cheek as if he thought she was fragile and needed to be treated with kid gloves. She smiled up at him, and he returned it with a shy, almost uneasy one of his own.

Her heart started thumping wildly. She'd really connected with him on a level far beyond anything she'd felt for a man, even Nolan, and *they'd* been engaged to marry.

The man holding her was no longer the fierce, powerful warrior who'd flown in on his chopper, who'd covered her body with his. He was the man to whom she owed her life, and the man who, despite his controlling tendencies, had wormed his way into her heart, and she knew clinging to him for the moment was the right thing to do.

Problem was, she didn't know if the stress of the situation was influencing her feelings or if she really did care about him. Sure, he was attracted to her, too. But his actions now could just be him doing his job. After all, he'd said he wasn't looking for a relationship, and she'd best remember that if she didn't want to get hurt.

CHAPTER 18

Cal stood across the table from Tara and opened the five cardboard boxes in front of him. Something had shifted between him and Tara a moment ago, and his mind had shifted along with it, moving to all the possibilities a relationship might bring. A wife, family, companionship. The easing of the ache in his gut that a simple smile from Tara brought.

If Shane hadn't delivered the evidence boxes and broken in on them, Cal didn't know what he might have done other than hold Tara tighter and kiss her until they were both breathless. He needed to figure out why she succeeded where no other woman had, unsettling him and making him forget his job, but to help keep his focus on the job, he'd asked Shane to sit in with them as she reviewed the evidence.

"That's a lot of boxes." Tara laughed nervously.

"Actually, there are more, but these boxes hold items we believe have more meaning in the investigation." Cal prepared to show them to her by sorting through each carton and choosing the evidence in the order he would display it.

"I'm glad you're looking at this stuff," Shane said from where he sat across from Tara. "I suspect Keeler's possessions will shed additional light on his personality."

Cal thought the same thing, as the evidence didn't have a forensic relationship to the bombs but was so odd it had stood out in their search of Keeler's place.

Cal sat next to Shane and looked across at Tara. "Ready?"

She nodded, but he'd have to be blind not to see her agitation. He ignored his protective urge that had him wanting to slam the lids back on the boxes and lifted out a plastic evidence bag containing a woman's scarf. He set it on the table in front of her.

She took a quick look and her head snapped up. "Oren had this?"

Cal nodded. "You obviously recognize it."

"It's mine. It went missing in eighth grade."

Cal's concern for her well-being rose, but he

forced himself to keep his tone neutral so he didn't color her thoughts. "Tell me about it."

She slid a finger under one of her rubber bands and twirled, tightening the band. "My parents went to France for their anniversary. They were killed in a car accident right after they came home." She let the band release, and when it connected, she winced but continued her story. "My mother brought this scarf home, but one day it mysteriously disappeared from my things."

"Didn't you wonder what had happened to it?" Shane asked.

"Of course. I was heartbroken when I couldn't find the small box I stored it in. I liked to take it out and dream of what it would have been like if they'd lived and they'd taken me to visit Paris, too." She worked the rubber band again.

Cal suddenly wished he could make her dreams come true and board a plane with her to Paris. Spend days, maybe weeks, exploring the city with her by his side.

"I went to live with June at that time," she continued. "And we decided that somehow the box had gotten mixed in with packing materials and tossed in the garbage. We burned all of our trash in a barrel, so there was no hope of retrieving it."

She picked up the bag, running her finger over the outside and trailing it around one of the purple paisleys. "I was so upset. Oren comforted me. Said it was meant to be. God's way and all."

Shane shook his head. "But he took it."

"Or found one like it, I suppose."

Cal wanted to fire off a scathing comment about Keeler, but that wouldn't help Tara, so he gentled his tone. "I think the odds are very much against him locating an identical scarf purchased in Paris."

"You're right, I suppose."

Her pitiful tone ripped into Cal's gut, and his anger rose at Keeler, if that was even possible. The guy was a fool. He was friends with an amazing woman like Tara, and then he threw it all away to take on a crazy mixed-up life that ended in terrorism.

Cal swallowed down his anger before continuing. "How old were you at the time?"

"Thirteen. Before my parents left for Paris, my mom and I went shopping to find the perfect dress for my eighth grade graduation." Her face lit with a bright smile, chasing away her sadness for the moment. "My mom picked out the scarf to match the dress. After she died, I wanted to wear them as a way to have her with me at the graduation."

"And Keeler ruined that," Shane stated.

"Yes, but I wore the dress, and she was still there. He didn't take that away."

"Good for you," Shane said.

She rested her hands on the table and stared at them. "Where did you find the scarf?"

"Keeler kept it in a desk drawer and wrapped it

around a number of items." Cal reached into another box and drew out a small bag. "This is one of them."

She took it from him. "My decoder ring from a box of Trix. I was like six or seven when it went missing."

"Another item that mysteriously disappeared?" Shane asked. She nodded.

Cal lifted out a pen with a fuzzy-headed troll doll on the end. "Yours too?"

She picked up the bag and shook her head in disbelief. "I was ten or so the last time I saw it."

Next, he removed a small book called *Kristy's Great Idea*.

"Oh my gosh, my first Baby-Sitters Club book." She ran her fingers over the toy block letters above the picture on the cover. "My mom was so mad at me for losing this book. We borrowed the set from a cousin who wanted it back when I was finished reading it."

Shane sat forward, steepled his hands and rested his chin on them, his gaze pensive. Cal could almost see the wheels and gears churning in his teammate's head. Before this review was over, Shane would have added to Keeler's profile.

Cal turned his thoughts back to Tara. "How old were you when he stole the book?"

"Nine or so." She came to her feet and grabbed the edge of the last box. "Is that all that you have in there?"

Before Cal could reply, she snatched up a heart necklace in another bag. "Why would he take this? He gave it to me."

Cal turned to his associate. "Want to answer that one, Shane?"

Shane nodded. "He's insecure and doesn't think he deserves your friendship, so he's proving you really do like him by looking at items that remind him of the times you shared."

"But why keep them now? I mean after our friendship ended a long time ago, why would he want them?"

"Because even if you no longer like him, after what you've told us, we can assume he's still in love with you and these things remind him of a happier time in life. A time when he thought you might become his." Shane shook his head. "Or, as it often is with a twisted mind like Keeler's, it could be the opposite. These things remind him of how you hurt him, and he used them to fuel his rage to get even with you."

She shuddered. "That's creepy."

And sick. Cal didn't bother putting voice to his thoughts, as they would only add to Tara's unease.

"These items don't help move the investigation forward, and this was a waste of time," she said.

Shane shook his head. "Anytime we gain insight into a sick mind like Keeler's, we're one step closer to understanding him and catching him."

A knock sounded on the door, startling them all. "I'll get it," Shane said.

Cal kept his focus on Tara to judge her mood. Her gaze tracked Shane to the door, and she'd twisted a rubber band around her finger so tightly her finger turned purple. As Shane talked to their visitor, Cal pointed at her finger but didn't say a word.

She looked down. "Oh . . . right . . . oh."

She released the band so by the time Shane returned carrying an overnight package, her finger had returned to a normal color.

"From the lab in Quantico." He set the box in front of Cal. "It's the fragments from the Dallas bomb."

"That was quick," Tara said.

"Brynn made sure the evidence took top priority." Cal rested a hand on the box. "I'll need to look at this before we head over to the pump house."

Tara stared at the box. "I'm confused. If the lab has already processed the fragments, why do you need to review them, too?"

"I can answer that one." Shane stepped closer. "The forensic staff at the lab is the best of the| best, but we like to think we're just a little bit better."

"Modest, too." Tara smiled, and Cal appreciated the change in her mood.

"No one would ever accuse us of that." Cal returned the smile, and she blessed him with a full-fledged grin, pushing away some of the unease in the room.

He grabbed a pair of scissors from the table to slice open the box. "This could take some time. If you want, I can have Shane find a quiet spot for you to hang out until I'm ready to go."

She shook her head hard. "I'd rather stay here with you."

Shane arched a brow, his expression filled with questions. Cal suspected his teammate's study of human behavior had him trying to figure out why she chose to remain in this room instead of finding solitude. Where some of the others on the team might have blurted out a question, Shane was the consummate professional and didn't ask.

"Call me if you change your mind." He offered a comforting smile and left the room.

"Let me know if you need anything," Cal said to Tara before taking the box to a workbench in the corner.

He turned on the lighted magnifying glass mounted on the corner of the workbench for such an occasion. He spread out fresh paper across the table and removed evidence bags to line them up in size order.

"Wow," Tara said, coming up behind him. "How many bags are there?"

Cal pulled out the inventory list. "Sixty-eight."

"And that's only pieces of the bomb, nothing more?"

He nodded.

"How do you even choose where to start?"

"I begin with the largest fragment that might yield the best evidence and work my way to the smallest."

"Makes sense, I guess."

"It's a lot like a puzzle." He selected the bag holding the largest item and held it under the magnifying glass. He turned the bag in various directions, looking at the metallic shard with fragments of wire sticking out.

Tara moved closer. "Can you even identify what you're looking at?"

"Actually, this is one of the best examples of an action circuit that we've recovered from any of Keeler's bombs." He smoothed out the bag and lifted it closer to the magnifying glass. "Odd."

"What?" she asked.

"It looks like a counterfeit switch."

"You can tell that just by looking at it?"

"I've examined countless switches over the years, and I recognize this one, but the markings are wrong."

"And that's odd why?"

He set the switch on the paper and leaned back to look at Tara. "Bombs can be unpredictable, so getting one to detonate, especially one as complicated at the ones Keeler builds, is harder than it seems. If I was building a bomb, I'd use the best-quality materials possible to be certain my device would work. So why spend so much on the other materials but buy a counterfeit switch? Just doesn't make sense."

"What if Oren didn't know it was counterfeit?"

"That's likely the best explanation," Cal said, his mind racing over what that could mean if anything. "Which is why counterfeiting is so successful."

"Where would he even buy something like this?"

Cal tapped the bag. "This switch is used for remote-controlled toys. He could have taken it from a toy he already owned, but most likely, with his plans of producing so many bombs, he purchased a number of these switches online."

Tara's forehead furrowed. "Wouldn't the package have been delivered to the house and you could have tracked it?"

"We checked all package deliveries at the rental house and his family's farm. He's smart enough to have set up an alternative mailing address such as a PO Box to keep from arousing suspicion."

"Again, couldn't you check with local post offices?"

"We did—not only near your aunt's place but near Keeler's employer. We also checked stores with rental boxes, but he didn't use his official ID to rent a box in any of these locations."

Tara frowned. "What about that woman Kaci showed the picture of? Could she be buying the supplies and giving them to him?"

He nodded. "As could other ISIS supporters."

Tara bit down on her lower lip and shook her head. "I had no idea Oren could be this devious. His thought patterns used to be so much simpler."

Cal met her gaze and held it. "The kind of terrorism he's engaging in *is* simple. Kill people. Do so publicly, with much media attention, and then don't get caught so you can do it all over again."

CHAPTER 19

Spotsylvania County, Virginia
2:00 p.m.

Despite precautions, Cal was on high alert for the drive to June's place. After he'd started analysts tracking down counterfeit RC parts, he'd sent Shane and Kaci along with four other agents to scope out the farm and to sit sentry along their travel route, but he wouldn't let down his guard until he had Tara back at the safe house.

Fortunately, she seemed more relaxed than she'd been on the drive to headquarters. She was so eager to see her aunt that her knee kept bouncing like a kid on Christmas morning. He even caught a broad smile on her face when they passed familiar countryside.

"That was my parents' farm." She pointed out the window. "I wish we could have kept it in the family, but when my uncle Earl passed away, June had her hands full and couldn't continue to run both properties." She sat back with a wistful sigh and looked at him. "You know, you've never mentioned your parents."

Not willingly. "I didn't, did I?"

"C'mon, you know all about me, and I know very little about you."

"As it should be in our business relationship."

Tara jerked back as if he'd slapped her.

Great. Now he'd hurt her feelings, and she didn't deserve it. They'd strayed from the professional long ago, and he could easily tell her about his family. He just didn't want to talk about his past where his parents bickered all the time, ignoring him in the process, and the moment he could he'd left home for the navy. Why hash over that old news or even discuss his empty personal life, which was the direction he was certain this conversation would go?

He gestured ahead on the road. "We're almost at June's place, and I need to focus on the op." The truth, but it sounded like a lie to him.

Tara clasped her hands in her lap and turned her gaze back to the side window. Cal tried to ignore the rigid set of her shoulders and watched ahead for Shane's car instead. When he spotted it parked at the end of the drive, he slowed. Shane reached out his window and waved them on, so Cal turned into the driveway. The tires crunched over gravel as the car rolled down to Kaci, where she stood guard next to the agents assigned to June's detail. Kaci gave him a nod of clearance, and he pulled up to the house.

He lifted his sunglasses to peer at Tara. "Stay close to me, okay?"

She nodded but didn't look at him. He pushed open his door and hoped his refusal to talk didn't distract her. He joined her on her side of the vehicle, where she paused to look up at the house. The white clapboard siding on the two-story home and the small front porch with worn rocking chairs seemed welcoming and a great place to grow up. So different from his family's small bungalow in a dingy suburb of Toledo.

"Looks like a place built for making good memories," he said, hoping to restore her good mood and keep her mind off the pump house for now.

"It was." He'd have to be deaf not to hear the residual disappointment in her voice and he suspected it was from his failure to share his past with her.

The screen door groaned open, and June stepped onto the porch. She wore serviceable jeans and a purple tank top. Her silvery-gray shoulder-length hair was pulled back in a ponytail, fitting her down-to-earth personality. Cal had questioned her at length, and he respected the sincerity and strength she displayed. Perhaps that's where Tara got her strong-willed attitude. June was also a woman of faith, and Cal had to admire how she remained calm and peaceful in times of adversity.

"Aunt June!" Tara ran up the steps with abandon.

Cal knew she'd forgotten all about him, but he couldn't forget about protecting her. He climbed the stairs, too.

A wide smile on her face, June opened her arms, and Tara rushed into them. A warm feeling settled into Cal's heart. They were obviously close; they had the exact thing he'd been missing all of his life. Camaraderie with his SEAL team was the closest family connection he'd ever found. He could have the same bond with the Knights, but he'd drawn a line between himself and the team so they didn't push him into opening up.

Maybe he'd been too hasty with them. His time with Tara told him he needed closer friends and letting the team in might help him cope with his stress.

And what about Tara? Should that line be erased with her as well?

"I'm so happy to see you, sweetheart." June pulled back and pushed Tara's hair from her face.

Tara flashed a dazzling smile, and pure joy washed over her face. A look of contentment—of homecoming—replaced the narrowed eyes, the clenched jaw, the uncertainly that had been present since he'd met her.

Cal's heart melted into a big old puddle of

mush. He suddenly knew as clearly as he knew he was standing in the warm sunshine that women like Tara didn't come along very often, and only a fool would write off the potential of a relationship with her.

"Car slowing by the drive." Kaci's voice came over Cal's earbud. "Will let you know if it turns in."

Relationship. Right. Not now. Not while Keeler was out to kill Tara. Maybe never.

Cal jerked his focus to the driveway meandering downhill to a bright red barn with a white silo. About halfway down the drive sat a small, single-story home that Keeler had rented. Out of sight and nearer to the barn lay the ruins from the pump house. Cal continued on and peered over miles of tall green field corn used to feed cows, not humans. His gaze landed on a metal pole barn before finishing the circle back at the women.

June stared at Tara like a person stranded in the desert might eagerly eye an oasis. "It's been so long. Let me look at you."

"You're thinner," June pronounced. "But you've been working out, and you know I believe in staying fit."

June obviously lived her belief. Cal's research put her at sixty-four, but her arms were toned and muscled. The agents on her protective detail had reported that she worked the farm with hired hands and put in a full day at their side.

"Where are my manners?" She spun to face Cal. "Agent Riggins, it's good to see you again."

Tara startled in surprise as if she didn't remember that he had a connection to her aunt or maybe even that he stood on the porch.

"We spent a lot of time talking after you took off," her aunt explained while running her gaze over him from head to toe and smiling at Tara. "He obviously believes in keeping in shape, too."

An innocent-enough comment, but Tara's face colored, and he knew where her mind had gone as he continued to admire her fresh farm-girl look, too. He liked the worn jeans, T-shirt, and boots. Her hair in a braid, her face beet red. Such simplicity he hadn't seen in years, and the corner of his mouth twitched up, but he resisted commenting.

June's casual gaze intensified. "Oh, it's that way, is it?"

Cal didn't know if he should say anything in response, so he kept his mouth closed.

Tara ignored the comment, too, and linked her arm with her aunt's. "Let's catch up before Cal grills you about Oren again, as I'm sure he plans to do so."

They stepped through the door and, after signaling to Kaci to keep her eyes open and stay alert, Cal followed the pair into the living room. A large modular sectional took up most of the room, sitting on dark hardwood floors with scrapes and scuffs from years of use. On Cal's prior visit, June mentioned that when Tara and Oren were kids, they often separated the sectional pieces, draped blankets over them, and declared them forts. June also said there were few kids in the area, so Tara and Oren mostly played alone, except when her cousins came to visit.

Cal didn't have to struggle to imagine Tara having fun like that, but Keeler? No, Cal couldn't imagine the killer anywhere near Tara, much less having fun.

She sat by her aunt on the sofa and took her hand. "So what's new in your world?"

June spent the next thirty minutes updating Tara on the neighbors and local gossip, and Cal got antsy. Peering out the window. Checking the driveway. Looking for any sign of Keeler. The longer they remained on the property, the greater chance that Keeler would make them. But Tara deserved this little chat with her aunt, so Cal tried to hide his impatience.

His mind shifted to wondering what it would be like at the end of a workday to find Tara, not in any danger, waiting for him to come home to a place much like this one.

A pipe dream. The only progress he'd made in dealing with his guilt was wishing he could get over it, and if there was one thing he knew for certain, wishing didn't make things happen.

People, determination, and grit did. And, of

course, so did God. Or at least that's how Cal remembered it. For months, Cal had tried to locate Keeler on his own and failed. Maybe it was time to give God a second chance to help not only eradicate the guilt and anger eating at Cal, but bring Keeler to justice.

Are You up there listening, watching? If so, mind giving me some sign that You're working on this and help me trust in that?

Okay, so he was rusty in the prayer department and his prayer was kind of lame, but maybe God answered lame, too. Maybe.

"Of course," June said, drawing him back. "People keep asking me about the agents sitting in the driveway."

Cal thought of the mistake Agent Fields had made at the hospital, and he pushed off the wall to step closer. "I hope they haven't been a problem for you, June."

"Quite the opposite. Agent Ingles is particularly good at hoeing the garden."

Cal gaped at her for a moment. "You got Ingles to work in your garden?"

She nodded with only a hint of an impish expression. "In all seriousness, I appreciate you providing the protection."

"You're welcome, but you must know by now that their assignment is twofold."

"Sure, they're keeping an eye out for Oren." She sighed and let go of Tara's hand. "I'm guessing since you brought Tara over to look at the pump house today that you don't have any solid leads on his whereabouts."

He couldn't acknowledge that, though they'd run down countless leads over the past six months, they'd made little progress in the investigation. "Is there anything you've remembered about Keeler since we last talked?"

"Trust me. If I thought of anything to stop Oren from killing, your agents would have been the first to know."

"Sometimes things happen that we don't realize are important. Would you mind rehashing the day of the explosion with me again?"

"I don't mind at all." A look of resolve very similar to the one Tara often wore narrowed June's eyes. "But please have a seat. You standing there all agent-like is making me nervous."

Cal would rather stand where he had a better view of the outside, but Kaci and Shane had his back, and making June uncomfortable wouldn't help her open up. He dropped onto a worn recliner across from the sofa.

She began describing the day, and Tara listened with rapt interest though June had talked about the pump house events with Tara at the hospital before she'd taken off. Cal hung on June's every word, too, but when she'd finished her story, she hadn't added anything new.

"I know Oren is still engaged in horrible

things," she continued. "But I have to say it's been weird not having him around."

"From what you told me, you spent a lot of time with him," Cal said.

"After his mother passed, I stepped in as a surrogate. We often ate dinner together, and he'd talk about his day at work." She frowned. "He hated his job and thought assembling security systems was beneath him. He said one day he would do something powerful that changed the world." She twisted her hands together in her lap. "I thought he meant finally going back to college to finish his degree."

"It was unfortunate that he had to drop out when his dad died," Tara said. "Maybe if Oren had been able to get a degree, things would be different now."

June nodded. "But even if he didn't go back, he could've used the knowledge he gained in electrical engineering to do something to make the world a better place. Not start building bombs." June shifted her focus to Cal. "Do you think this had to do with losing his parents or the farm?"

Cal shook his head but chose not to mention the connection to Tara. If she wanted June to know, she could tell her.

"Cal thinks it's about me, Aunt June, and he knows I already feel guilty, so he's being kind and not mentioning it." Tara caught his gaze and smiled a thank-you at him before explaining to her aunt about rejecting Oren.

June clutched Tara's arm. "I don't get why you and Oren didn't mention it to me."

"I didn't because, honestly, it wasn't big news for me." Tara sighed. "I guess Oren kept quiet because he was embarrassed."

"Did you notice a change in his behavior at the time?" Cal asked.

June stared off into the distance. "Now that you mention it, he didn't come to dinner as often after that, and he spent more time alone." She shook her head and exhaled hard. "What do you suppose will become of the things he put in my safe?"

Interest piqued, Cal sat forward. "I don't recall you mentioning a safe."

June waved a hand. "It's just some old family jewelry that doesn't have any real value."

"Can I see it?"

"Sure, but I don't see how an old ring and necklace could be related your investigation."

Cal came to his feet. "Why don't you let me be the judge of that?"

"Okay." She stood. "The safe's in the office. I'll be right back."

When she'd left the room, Tara got up and crossed to Cal. "You think the necklace has to do with why he chose necklace bombs?"

"If it has any family significance, yes, but otherwise it may be a coincidence," he replied, though a coincidence in an investigation rarely turned out to be one.

Tara crossed her arms. "I wish Oren hadn't involved June in this mess. She wouldn't hurt anyone and doesn't deserve this treatment."

He met her gaze and held it. "You don't deserve it either."

She opened her mouth to say something, but June returned, taking Tara's attention. Her aunt held a cloth bag with a drawstring top made from flowery quilted fabric.

"This bag belonged to Oren's mother." She pulled the drawstring open, revealing a flannel lining with pockets. "It was filled with jewelry when she passed. Oren and I went through it together, but he only kept two pieces."

She reached inside, drew out an opal ring, and handed it to Cal.

He turned it around in his fingers but found no inscription in the gold or anything unusual about it, for that matter.

June dug into the bag again. "The necklace has a lovely cameo. His mother used to wear it to church quite often. In fact, she was wearing it when the car crash took her life."

She lifted the beaded necklace from the bag and ran the black agate beads mixed with sepia-toned metal beads through her fingers. The cameo dangled from the beads, facing away from them.

Tara stepped closer and took the necklace. "I remember the beads."

Cal pointed at the gold backing of the oval pendant. "There's something engraved there."

"Odd." June leaned over the necklace. "I don't remember it being engraved."

Tara lifted the cameo to inspect it, and Cal bent over her shoulder and read, " 'To Tara, my love.' "

Tara's mouth opened and closed, but words seemed to fail her. Cal flipped over the medallion, revealing a black oval background holding an ivory skull and crossbones.

Tara gasped and stared at her aunt. "The cameo. He . . . he . . ." Tara shook her head. "Why would he deface his mother's necklace like this?"

Cal couldn't share Keeler's addition of the skull and crossbones on the front of the bombs, but he would be an idiot if he didn't acknowledge to himself that the change in this necklace held significance for their investigation.

June touched the front of the oval and jerked her finger away as if it might burn her. "And when did he do it? It's been in the safe since he lost the farm, and he's never taken it out."

"At least not that you know about." Cal's imagination took a dark turn. He visualized the creep stalking through this house. Maybe when June had gone out or even when she'd slept upstairs. His fingers pawing through everything. Touching and messing with June's personal possessions.

The queasy look on June's face told him her thoughts moved in the same direction.

"Cal?" Tara's big eyes, wide and filled with terror, fixed on his. "What are you thinking?"

"It's not something I can discuss right now, but be assured, I'll get to the bottom of what this means." He closed his hand around the cameo to remove the visual threat and wished he could so easily remove the actual threat on Tara's life.

CHAPTER 20

Tara approached the burned-out shell of the pump house and stopped at the fringe of the exploded mess. Her knees were weak and her palms coated in perspiration. If she wanted to remember anything, she had to get closer, but she couldn't get her feet moving forward. She slid her fingers under the thickest rubber band on her wrist and snapped. Once. Twice. A third time, but her heart continued to trip along at an alarming rate.

Cal walked up to her, confidence in his steps. He didn't speak or touch her, but having him at her side gave her the courage to move. She scrubbed her palms down her jeans and took the final steps into the ruins.

An acrid smell lingered in the air and charred fragments of wood lay on the ground. If she hadn't called Cal that night, would she have died in an explosion? Or would Oren have simply shot her and hauled off her body? Simply, right. There was nothing simple about a gunshot. She'd experienced that firsthand.

She took a few more steps and tried to remember June's potting bench, but the sight of the cameo wouldn't leave her brain. Cal hadn't explained the meaning behind the skull and crossbones, but with the inscription on the back of the necklace, she believed Oren had wanted her dead even before the pump house incident. Or perhaps, in his sick, twisted mind he thought if he gave her the necklace, her feelings for him would change, and she'd join his crazy world.

She slid a finger under the rubber band again.

Cal gently took her hand and pulled her fingers free. "I know this is hard."

His voice wrapped around her like a warm blanket, but what touched her even more than his reassurance was his willingness to ignore his need for the same professionalism he'd mentioned in the car and hold her hand in front of his teammates standing guard at the perimeter.

She looked up at him and memorized every plane, every angle of his face and the compassion shining from his eyes. The coldness in her heart evaporated, and with him standing nearby, if she remembered the details of the night Oren had tried to kill her, the memories wouldn't do irreparable harm.

She touched Cal's cheek, a light whisper of

her fingers, then lowered her hand. "Thank you again for saving me in the woods that night."

He squeezed her hand. Dark anger, likely over Keeler's crazy behavior, flashed in his eyes but vanished with a blink. "Why not remember the good times you've had on the farm? I've seen how much you love your aunt. You light up when you talk about growing up here. Don't let Keeler take that away from you."

Cal was right. She had a choice. She could listen to her emotions and let them color her attitude, or remember that feelings weren't facts and didn't convey truth. They were just feelings, and she could control them if she put her mind to it.

She extricated her hand and stepped deeper into the blackened wood. Ash filtered up and swirled around her feet like a living, breathing thing. Raucous sounds of scrub jays crying out in the trees mimicked her internal cry for help. She ignored it. Ignored the birds. Ignored her fear of Oren and closed her eyes.

She thought to pray, but she didn't deserve the help. And yet she wanted it badly. She'd missed casting her cares on God. Had she been wrong in running and counting on herself alone? Maybe if she had stayed and asked for His help, all of this would be over already and three women would be alive.

Was she responsible for the additional women, her friends, losing their lives, or should she believe Cal and Shane when they said Keeler was the only responsible party here? Her fear fluttered away and guilt settled in, but she wouldn't let it stop her. She'd use her remorse to drive her need to remember.

"You can do it, Tara," Cal called out again.

She could. Yes, she could. She tried to pull up an image of Oren. Not the fun memories of growing up, but the expression that haunted her nightmares. As Shane had said, the boy of her youth was gone and she had to recall the man capable of shooting her and killing defenseless women.

Suddenly, the terrifying look he'd fired at her after she'd hit him with the board came back in vivid color. She'd slammed the heavy wooden plank against his chest. As he'd fallen, he'd caught her gaze, anger and hatred spewing from his eyes, but she'd ignored him, run hard and fast, turning to look back only one time. He'd gotten to his feet and chased her, a gun in his hand.

The sound of the gunshot on the audio returned. Her breath locked in her chest, and her throat seemed to swell and close. She gasped for air, wanting to run now, too—flee—as she'd done that evening, but that's what Oren would want. Cal was right. She couldn't let Oren win.

You're there, right, God? You're with me?

For the first time in ages, she felt His presence and the peace that accompanied it. She pulled back her shoulders and let the sights and sounds of the night come racing back. In her mind's eye, she touched the bricks of explosives, ran her fingers over the slick plastic wrap. She shifted her gaze farther down the table and spotted drawings.

Yes! Drawings made by Oren of the bombs. Before he'd arrived, she'd studied them. She mentally flipped the pages to find various views he'd sketched of the exterior of his necklace-shaped bombs, much like the one Cal had shown her. But these sketches had a skull and cross-bones added to the front of the bombs.

No, oh, no.

The cameo necklace *was* connected to the bombs, and with her name engraved on the back, she was even more connected, too.

"The necklace in June's house . . . his bombs," she called out to Cal. "He uses the skull and crossbones as a symbol on the front."

"I know," Cal replied, far too calmly for just having learned of it.

She opened her eyes and shot a look at him. "You knew that already?"

Nodding, he strode across the space, his boots kicking up the ash.

It should hurt that he hadn't shared this with her, but she understood his reasons for keeping parts of the investigation a secret. "Do you think he's visualizing his mother's necklace when he sets off these bombs?"

"It fits his profile."

"But why a skull and crossbones? I don't get the relationship to his cause."

"We think he's taking a literal translation of the symbol." Cal met her gaze and held it. "The skull rests on bones that resemble an X, which in our culture can symbolize being wrong. The skull indicates death. Add them together, and it can be interpreted as man is wrong about the truth and therefore he dies. We think Keeler takes this view, as it fits with ISIS's theology that anyone who doesn't hold their beliefs should die."

"With the symbol on the necklace and my name on the back, this is further confirmation that he thinks I should die." Feeling like she might pass out or be sick, she pressed her hand over her mouth. The need to run came flooding back, to be anywhere but at this scene of destruction that resembled the scenes where so many women had lost their lives.

"Look at me," Cal commanded. "Breathe, honey. Just breathe."

His calming voice helped, but more than that, him calling her honey sliced through her panic. Until the memory of Oren calling her honey replaced the thought.

"He called me honey, too. That night when he asked me out, and then . . . then months later, this is how he responds?" She gestured at the ruins, and a collage of images from the night flashed through her mind.

Red-hot anger replaced her anxiety. She'd been too afraid or consumed with staying alive the last few months to let her anger loose.

"He deserves the same fate that he's meting out." The words came flying out before she could filter them. "To know the same fear."

"But he never will," Cal said. "He'll spend his life behind bars instead."

She turned to look at Cal. "Forget that I said that. No one deserves such horrific treatment. Not even Oren."

"Which is why we have to find him now before he strikes again."

"Yes, and I'll try my best to remember everything I can." She closed her eyes again to mentally return to the table. She continued flipping through pages in the binder. On the back cover, she found laminated yellow notepaper holding a list written in Oren's neat, square printing. He'd scratched the numbers one through ten and behind them listed women's names in bold print.

She remembered running her finger down the list. She strained to remember each and every name, but could recall only the first one.

She opened her eyes, so very glad to be back in the present. Glad to see Cal by her side.

"He had a list of women's names," she said. "Ten of them. I think the first three were women he'd killed. At least they were names I remember hearing on TV. I remember thinking the next seven were the women he'd target next, but I didn't have time to really look at them before he came back." Tara twisted her hands together. "If only I'd thought to grab the binder and take it with me when I ran."

"You were terrified for your life."

"Still, I wish I'd thought of it."

"With Keeler's change in focus to you, these women might not be in danger right now anyway. Or Keeler might think you gave us the names, and he could have moved on."

"Do you think so?"

He nodded. "Would you like more time here?"

"Maybe a few more minutes. Just in case."

She closed her eyes and put her mind to the task, but when it became clear that she wasn't going to remember anything to help, she opened them and suggested they leave.

As they drove away, Tara expected Cal and the team to rush back to FBI headquarters to continue working on the investigation, but instead, he lowered his car window and motioned for Kaci to join him near the car.

"Tara remembered that Keeler had a list of ten names," Cal said. "Likely his first three victims and seven new names."

"I don't suppose knowing there's a list will give you anything to go on?" Tara asked.

"It does confirm that he's planning more bombs, specifically three of them." Kaci leaned down to the window. "Not news any of us wants to hear, but it's true."

"And you can't do anything?" Tara asked.

"Barring finding a connection between Keeler and the Muslim community, we have nowhere to go."

"Let's bring the team together at the safe house and hash it out again," Cal suggested. "Maybe we'll see something we've missed."

Kaci nodded. "I'll let the others know."

She and Cal stopped at the main house to say good-bye to June, and by the time they reached the safe house, everyone except Max had gathered in the living room.

Shane and Rick sat in leather chairs, and Brynn and Kaci on the plump sofa. They were deep in discussion but immediately quieted when Tara and Cal entered the room. Cal gestured for her to have a seat on the sofa, and he leaned against the wall as he brought them up to date on their day.

"I hope you can process the necklace for me." He handed Brynn the evidence envelope containing the necklace. "And could you follow up with jewelers in the area? We might get lucky and find the one who updated the necklace."

"Sure." A no-nonsense expression lodged on Brynn's face as she turned her attention to Tara. "We've been talking. Now that you were able to recall more of the night at the pump house, we'd like you to try it again, here, with us."

"You what?" Cal asked.

Shane sat forward and ignored Cal's question to focus on Tara. "We believe if we guide you through the visit in a nonthreatening place, that you might remember even more."

"You don't have to do it if you don't want to." Cal's words came out in a clipped tone.

Tara really didn't want to think about the pump house again, but she desperately wanted Oren caught before he killed another woman. Besides, they had a good point. Perhaps she'd let her fear from the night keep her from remembering things at the pump house.

"If you all think it will help, I'm glad to do it," Tara offered. "Where do I start?"

Shane smiled at her, his expression kind. "From the minute you arrived at the pump house."

She rested her head on the back of the sofa and stared up at the ceiling. She forced herself to relax. In her mind, she called up the walk down to the pump house. She felt the coolness of the night and forced her mind ahead to the door. She pressed her hand on the cold handle, and a flash of memory played in her eyes as she flung open the door.

Her breathing intensified, but she tried to slow it.

"What are you seeing?" Shane asked. "Feeling?"

"At first, I was mad that the ancient pump was acting up. But when I saw June's old potting table in the middle of the room, thoughts of starting seeds with her for the vegetable garden made me smile."

She felt her lips turning up now. "Then I saw a pile of white PVC pipe on the table and was confused. My first thought was that someone was planning to fix the pump." She shook her head. "Until I noticed the large quantity of pipe, and that it had been assembled in an odd configuration. I was just plain baffled, and I stepped over to the table. The wind caught the door and banged it shut, blocking out the exterior light, so I pulled on the string hanging above the table."

"So you're in the small building, the light burning bright," Shane said, his tone captivating, as if he were in the shed with her. "What did you do next?"

She saw herself in an out-of-body kind of experience moving across the room, the PVC inches from her hands. She reached out. Stopped. "Before I could get to the pipe, I saw a stack of white bricks wrapped in cellophane. I had no idea what they were, but there was a warning label on the box." She ran her gaze over the warning and gasped. "I read it and jumped back to think. I then remembered seeing such explosives in documents I translated for the State Department, and I panicked. Explosives. What were they doing in the pump house?" She got lost in the memories. Breathing became difficult, and she shot a look around the room.

"And then?" Shane asked, his voice comforting and quieting some of her anxiety.

She forced herself to keep going. "I looked at

the rest of the room. The shelves along the wall held discarded gardening and farm items, but on the end of the bench, I saw a three-ring binder. It's black and thick. Three inches. It's open, and I walk up to it. That's where I saw that list of names. I know, right there in the blink of an eye, that the women listed first are the ones who died at the hands of the Lone Wolf Bomber."

"How?" Shane asked. "How did you know these were the women who died?"

"I'd seen their names, their faces, on the news." Tears pricked at her eyes, and she swiped them away. "I asked myself what the Lone Wolf's things were doing there. I stared at the list to find an answer and noticed the square little letters printed on the yellow paper. Realization hit me. Oren. This is Oren's handwriting. He's the Lone Wolf. Oren is the bomber." She shuddered.

"What else is in the binder?" Shane asked, his voice encouraging yet urgent.

The scene became real to her. The night. The cool breeze blowing through the open window, ruffling the edges of paper under the pipe. She moved the piping. "Maps! There are maps with big red Xs on them. All in the metro D.C. area. I can't stop staring at them. What do they mean? Are they the locations of the exploded bombs or of the future bombs?" She sat up and peered at Cal. "Do you think the Xs point to where Oren plans to kill the other women?"

He nodded, his eyes alight with the potential lead. "If I get a map of the area, can you remember the location of the Xs well enough to mark them for us?"

"I don't know. I didn't have much time." She thought back to the map. "Maybe seeing an actual map will jog my memory more."

"We could print one from the Internet," Shane offered.

"I have a portable printer with my computer in the car." Brynn jumped to her feet. "I'll grab it."

"Make it quick," Cal said.

She nodded and hurried out the door.

Tara's temples started pounding. She rubbed the tender skin above her ears and stifled a groan.

Cal eyed her. "I think this is enough of struggling to remember for now."

Tara nodded, glad to have a break. She sat back and waited for Brynn to return with the computer and printer. When she did, she set them up on the dining table.

"One more thing," Rick spoke for the first time. "We now have a good idea of the pump house items thanks to you, and you've given us a better understanding of the things in the house Keeler was renting. Do you know of any other places where he might hide supplies or sketches, that sort of thing?"

She thought back to their time together and one

idea came to mind, but she dismissed it right away.

Rick eyed her, his intense stare digging deep. "You thought of something."

Her idea was so far-fetched that she didn't want to share, but she doubted Rick would give up until she did. "It's a real long shot."

"Tell us anyway," he demanded.

Cal glared at Rick, his protector mode obvious in his expression and his sudden rigid posture.

Tara held up a hand to tell him she was okay. "When Oren and I were kids, we played in his family's barn. He had a hiding place in the wall in the haymow. We kept things there that we didn't want our parents to know about."

"Do you think he could have continued to use the hiding spot?" Rick asked.

She shrugged and was vaguely aware of Brynn's printer whirring in the background.

Shane sat forward. "Keeler likes to keep things. Hide them. That we know from the items you identified today. The more we see of him, the more I'm convinced he's trapped in his past. I wouldn't be surprised if he used this secret hiding place up until the day you discovered the pump house and gave us his identity."

"I'll have Max contact the new owners to get permission to visit the barn as soon as possible." Cal planted his feet and cast an apologetic look at Tara. "Are you up for that?"

"How soon?" Tara worked hard to hide her

hesitancy to visit another spot she associated with Oren, especially another visit today.

"I'll push for first thing in the morning."

She nodded her agreement, but she'd be lying if she said she didn't dread the visit and what they might discover.

What if they found something that exacerbated this horrible, horrible nightmare? How would she handle more bad news?

She'd deal with it, that's what. Like she'd learned to handle whatever was thrown at her since the night at the pump house. But it wouldn't hurt to have God on her side.

She recalled the earlier sense of peace and let it settle in as the group continued to chat. Had God been there all along for her, and she'd let her fear keep her from sensing His guiding presence?

Brynn charged into the room with several pieces of paper and a roll of tape. "I enlarged the map so you can see the roads. Just let me tape the pages together first."

Brynn knelt at the coffee table and set to work. The tip of her tongue peeked out of the corner of her mouth, and she looked far more relaxed than normal. When she'd finished connecting six sheets of paper, she turned them over and dug a red marker from her pocket.

"I thought it might help if you used red to do this." A shy smile on her face, she handed the marker to Tara.

Tara finally got that Brynn wasn't standoffish; she was shy. Maybe socially awkward. Tara smiled her thanks and received a swift nod of acknowledgment in return.

Tara bent over the map and closed her eyes. She willed her mind back to the pump house and the maps. "There were ten Xs. I remember thinking they went with the ten names, but I knew I'd never remember all of the addresses. So I figured the first three went with the women he'd already killed and focused on the last—that's it! I came up with a mnemonic for two of them like I did when I was learning foreign languages and couldn't remember certain words."

"What exactly do you mean?" Rick asked.

"You know, like the old 'thirty days hath September' rhyme many people know for remembering the number of days in each calendar month."

"So what did you come up with?"

"Lone Wolf." She shifted the map and tapped on L Street. "L Street NE for the L and NE in Lone. The word 'lone' has four letters and the cross street is Fourth." She looked up, expecting to see that the team was impressed with her mnemonic. She received skeptical looks instead.

"Not that I doubt your abilities," Rick said, his hesitant tone in direct contrast to his statement, "but you were terrified for your life, and you managed to create something like that?"

"First, I saw this before I heard Oren come home. Second, after using this memory system to learn three new languages, the process is second nature to me."

"Okay, say you're remembering this right," Rick said. "We only have cross streets."

"Oren's map had buildings on it like you see when you zoom into Google Maps. If I have a map like that, I might be able to find the exact house."

Brynn jumped to her feet. "I'll print one out."

"You said you remember two locations."

She nodded. "The second one is W Street and Flagler. You know . . . the W and F from 'wolf.' "

"These aren't addresses from earlier bombs and could be the break we need in the investigation," Rick said.

"Great work, Tara," Cal said.

"Agreed," Shane added. "You really came through for us."

She felt herself beaming under the compliments, but she couldn't pat herself on the back. "I haven't found the actual houses yet, and there are still more names and addresses on his list."

Brynn returned with the detailed map. "I zoomed in on and printed both intersections."

Tara stared at the square boxes of connected homes. She was familiar with the area of row houses that D.C. was so famous for. She located the exact location of the first home and drew an X on it, but the other one failed her. "That's all I can do. Sorry."

"No worries," Rick said. "We can review property records for the area and even go door-to-door if we have to."

Tara sat back. A good thing she did, as the others scrambled to peer at the X.

"I'll call out the address," Cal said. "Who wants to look it up?"

"I will," Shane volunteered.

"And I'll take notes on what we discover." Kaci took out a notepad.

Tara watched and listened as they worked.

Cal leaned back on his haunches. "We can provide protection for the women at this address, and I'll arrange agents to stake out the house."

"You don't want to have the team do it?" Tara asked.

Cal shook his head. "With Keeler going off his plan and targeting people connected to you, we don't even know if he's going to go through with these bombs, so I'd rather spend our resources that way."

"Plus, even if he does," Shane said, "he may not do so until the first of next month."

"And," Cal added, "by protecting these women, we'll have foiled Keeler's plans anyway."

Kaci snapped a picture of the maps. "I'll get my team doing a deep background check on any women associated with this address. Maybe we'll luck up and see a connection between them and the other victims."

"I can also use the information to flesh out Keeler's profile," Shane offered.

Cal nodded. "Thanks, everyone, for your hard work."

"So maybe our idea to help Tara remember was a good one, then." Shane grinned.

"Okay, fine." Cal punched Shane in the arm. "I admit it. You guys occasionally have a good idea."

They groaned in unison, and after they said good-bye to Tara, Cal walked them to the door. Exhausted, Tara remained seated.

He locked the dead bolt behind them and came to sit with her on the sofa.

"So what's next?" she asked.

He grabbed his laptop from the table and set it on his knees. "I'm going to look up the contact information for the new owners of Keeler's family farm and schedule that visit."

"Right, the visit to the barn."

"I wish you didn't have to go, but I promise I'll be with you." He squeezed her hand.

She gazed into his eyes. "I appreciate you being here for me more than you can know." She chewed on her lip for a moment to phrase her next words properly and not hurt him. "But I'm starting to depend on you, Cal, and that's not a good thing for either one of us."

CHAPTER 21

Morning came too soon for Tara, a thought that hadn't entered her mind in months, what with the nightmares keeping her up at night. Last night hadn't been any different. Oren had continued to plague her sleep, and she'd walked the floor most of the night, but she preferred that to stepping up to the barn she'd played in with Oren.

Everything looked the same, but it felt wrong. Very wrong. Ominous.

You're imagining things. Looking for problems where they don't exist.

Cal slid open the door, and Tara chalked up her unsettled feeling to the change in the exterior paint—formerly red, now a crisp white with black trim.

She peered into the haymow that was level with the ground, and the milking parlor sat below grade in a hill, like the barn at June's farm. Sunlight flooded into the large space and dust particles danced in the rays. Three-by-five bales of hay were stacked to the ceiling against the back wall, but the rest of the space held only a thin layer of hay littered across the roughhewn wood.

Tara stepped into the space, and the familiar odor of manure filtered up through the floor. Tara took the caustic scent in stride, but Cal grimaced and covered his nose.

"Does it always smell like this?" he asked.

"Actually, this isn't so bad. It's far worse in the winter months when the cows are inside." She went to the back wall and inhaled the familiar scent of hay from her childhood. "The best time to visit is spring and fall right after the hay has been cut and baled. There's this wonderful sweet smell that fills the haymow and the cows are only in the barn twice a day for milking, so it airs out."

Cal's forehead furrowed. "I've been in some foul-smelling places, but honestly, this is one of the most irritating smells I've encountered."

"You get used to it." She remembered growing up, how even though they'd removed their outerwear in the mudroom before entering the house, the odor had clung to them.

Cal turned in a circle, his gaze focused as usual. "Not many bales in here."

"It's the end of the season. I took a good look at the alfalfa fields on our way in. Looks like they're right on schedule for making hay at the end of this month."

"Making hay?" He tilted his head. "People really talk that way. It's not just part of the old saying 'make hay while the sun shines.' "

She chuckled. "Farmers actually still use the term. And FYI, the reason for the saying is that after hay is cut, it has to lay in the field to dry in the sun, preventing the bales from molding inside." Memories of riding on the trailer behind the baler and stacking bales came to mind and she smiled. "Back in the day I could toss these forty-pound bales around like crazy."

He shook his head. "I believe you, but I can't see you as a farm girl."

"I've really taken a long step away from my roots. From Oren," she added, since he was the purpose for their visit. "Now I need to go back to my childhood again."

Stepping deeper into the space, memories assaulted her, and she stopped moving. The sunshine warmed her back, and she took in a deep breath of country air. Fun times raced through her mind like a slide show. Oren as a child. Chasing her through the yard and racing into the haymow. Climbing the bales to the top, dragging them into a fort, and defending it from Tara's cousins.

"What are you thinking about?" Cal asked from right behind her.

She jumped, her eyes flashing open and her heart kicking into high gear.

"Sorry if I startled you," he said.

"The smell brings back so many memories, it feels like I'm literally walking through them."

"And did you see anything just now that you think might be helpful?"

She shook her head. "I was thinking about my

cousins and the forts we built in the hay. Oren and me on one side of the haymow, my cousins the other. We'd defend our forts from the invading enemy."

"Sounds fun," he said.

She nodded, and another memory flashed in her mind. "Until someone got hurt. One time Oren climbed as high up on the bales as he could with his pretend sword in hand. He jabbed the air and lost his balance. He hit the floor hard and broke his arm in two places that day." She shook her head. "He was on restricted activity, strictly enforced by his mother. She checked on him every few minutes, so most of the time we colored and drew pictures of what we would do once she let him play hard again."

She could easily remember Oren with paper and crayons in his hand, sitting at their oak dining room table. "He was so mad at his mom that he drew some pretty unflattering pictures of her and hid them in his stash."

"Where exactly is this secret spot?" Cal asked.

"Over in the corner." She stepped in that direction, wishing she'd come back for a fun visit for old times' sake. To visit an old friend. A boy she'd once cared about. Who she'd never, ever, believe capable of extreme violence against women.

Instead, they'd come here today to prove Oren had defiled yet one more of her childhood memories, and hopefully he'd left a clue that would lead them to arrest him and lock him up for life.

Cal had to admit he believed they might actually find something Keeler had stuffed into the wall as Tara led him to the far corner of the haymow. Maybe wishful thinking, but his SEAL sense said they were right on track.

"We'll have to move this stack of hay." Tara slipped her hands under the tight twine on the top bale.

"I can do that for you," he offered.

"Sure you can, but can you do it this efficiently?" She hefted the bale, her biceps tightening, her body twisting as she set the bale behind her, then reversed and grabbed another one.

Cal was uncomfortable not helping her, but he loved watching her fluid motions. She was a study in contrasts. Two separate people, graceful yet powerful, but one when it concerned his emotions.

When she moved on to the taller stack where she had to strain to grab the top bales, he stepped in and reached over her to lift the bale. His body pressed against hers, the fresher scent of the hay and her shampoo replaced the hideous barn odor. He was so aware of her as a woman that it took every effort to grab the bale and not turn her into his arms and kiss her.

He lifted the hay, even more surprised at how unwieldy it felt and how easily she had swung them out of the way. He had no idea tossing a hay bale required skill, but he was learning so much in his time with her. Most notably, that he liked being with her, no matter what they were doing. Even if they were tossing bale after bale aside to clear the corner in short order.

Tara planted her hands on her hips, her breathing labored. "I can't believe I used to do this all day long. I sure slept good, though."

"Sounds like my days at BUD/S."

"BUD/S?"

"Basic Underwater Demolition/SEAL. Six months of pure craziness. It was filled with physical and mental challenges meant to push prospective SEALs to the end of their limit and beyond. Things like bursts of three thousand sit-ups and a twenty-station obstacle course that I'm sure the very devil designed himself."

She stared at him like he'd grown two heads. "Three thousand sit-ups? You're kidding, right?"

He would never forget the days of physical torture. "Trust me, it's real."

"And now?" Her focus shifted to his abs. "Can you do that many sit-ups?"

He shook his head. "I try to work out every day, but I've resigned myself to the fact that I won't ever be in such good shape again."

"Nothing wrong with your shape right now." She clapped her hand over her mouth. "I said that out loud, didn't I?"

He couldn't resist smiling over her error, and his whole body relaxed. They were in the haymow to track down a serial killer and they were flirting. He had to admit he liked it, and at the moment, he would rather keep up the conversation than look for Keeler's secret stash.

She suddenly sobered and tipped her head at the wall. "The hiding place. We should check it out."

He nodded, and she climbed over a single row of bales to the corner where she lifted out the last bale and set it on wide floor planks behind her.

He scrambled after her and dropped onto a bale to wait while she pressed her hands against a section of the slatted wood wall that let loose in her hands.

"Oh my gosh." She handed the piece to him. "There's something in here."

"Did you leave anything here when you were kids?"

She looked up for a moment. "No. I remember emptying it out. We fought about who got to keep the candle we used for secret meetings."

"Who won?" Cal asked, surprising himself that he wanted to know more about her childhood than what the hiding spot contained.

An impish grin lit her face. "We arm wrestled for it, and I won."

"Remind me never to wrestle against you."

She rolled her eyes and turned back to the wall.

"Hold on," he said as he dug latex gloves from his pocket and snapped them on. "This item could be evidence. I can't have you touching it."

"Right." She shifted around until she sat next to him with her leg pressed up against his. She didn't seem to notice, but he was painfully aware of her touch and inched away to lift out an oversized padded envelope from the wall.

He opened the clasp and pulled out a stack of pictures.

The top photo was of Dafiyah Jabbar.

"Oren's first victim."

"She was pretty." Tara's voice was barely more than a whisper.

Cal wished they could go back to a moment ago when they were flirting. When she still possessed one more piece of her innocence before Keeler stole it from her.

He flipped to the next picture and the next. All were photos of Dafiyah going about her everyday life, and they proved that Keeler had stalked her before he killed her. Cal turned them upside down on the bale, then removed a sheaf of papers with e-mail headers printed on the top of the pages. Cal scanned the first one, and the word *ISIS* in bold, capital letters immediately caught his attention.

He read the entire e-mail, then sat back, his mind racing to process the information. He didn't recognize the name or e-mail address of the sender or the address Keeler used, but that wasn't surprising, as the Knights had found no direct communication linking him to ISIS prior to locating this message.

"The killing. It isn't about me." Tara looked up at him, her expression flooded with relief. "He says he's targeting Muslim women who turned their back on their faith. That's his reason. It has to be."

"He would definitely see someone who rejected his faith as an infidel who needed to be punished," Cal mused aloud. "FBI profilers once suggested Keeler's use of the necklace bomb was his way of beheading infidels—an action ISIS took from passages in the Quran. We rejected it when we didn't find any evidence to support that theory."

"But it makes sense now."

"Yes and no. If that was his only motive in these bombs, he wouldn't have begun targeting you, too."

"I know, but I . . ."

"But you want this to be true so you don't feel guilty."

"Yes."

"You have nothing to feel guilty for."

"But I do . . . you see. When I took off from the hospital, I didn't ask for God's guidance. I decided that I could only count on myself to stay alive, so I bolted." She shook her head. "But lately

I've been thinking I was wrong. If I'd listened to God maybe I would have stayed, and He could have resolved the issue before more women died."

"You're playing 'what if' again. That's no different than feeling guilty over not letting Keeler down gently. There's no way to know what would have happened in either case."

"But it doesn't change the fact that I didn't trust God and ran."

"So what? That only proves you made a mistake. The God I remember wouldn't hold that against you if you asked for forgiveness."

"You're right, I suppose, but it's a whole lot easier to say I'm forgiven than to actually accept it."

Cal felt like someone hit him upside the head with one of the large fence posts he'd seen on the drive over. The same thing was true of his guilt. He was choosing to hang on to it when he no more deserved the blame than she did. He'd done his job. Followed proper protocol. Worked until he dropped. Done everything within his power to succeed.

Everything? Really?

Surely, he could do more to save lives if only he could focus. Maybe forget about his feelings for Tara and figure out how to render Keeler's bombs safe. Because until he did, women were at risk. Big risk. If Keeler set another bomb, and Cal was lucky enough to get to the woman before it exploded, Cal couldn't stop the explosion. Just as he hadn't been able to save Willy even when he had him in his arms and was running from the kidnappers' compound.

Cal had no time to lose. No time to think about anything but the job.

He turned his attention to the pages in front of him, racing through them to look for key points. "These messages show Keeler growing more and more agitated." Cal tapped the last page. "He's positively spiteful in this last e-mail in January when you two bumped into each other again."

Cal took out his phone and snapped photos of the pages. "I don't want to wait until we get back to the office to begin working on this lead. I'll e-mail these pictures to Kaci so she can get her analysts tracking down the e-mail address right away."

Cal typed a message to Kaci. He attached the photos and set the pages on top of the pictures. When he finished, he looked at Tara, who stared at the envelope.

"Let me check the hole for anything we might have missed." With the light from his phone, he peered into the dark space. He spotted several leather-bound books set deep in the cavity. He drew them out one at a time, counting five books in all.

Cal ran his fingers over the first book's aged binding before flipping it open to reveal journal pages filled with tiny scribbles that he recognized as Keeler's handwriting. Cal used the dates listed in the front of the other books to stack them in order.

He opened the first one and read, " 'Ode to Tara.' "

"What does that mean?" Tara asked.

"These are Keeler's journals," Cal replied.

Tara frowned, her response mimicking Cal's thoughts. These journals were sure to hold secrets and horrors and neither of them would want to read the thoughts of a psychopath.

CHAPTER 22

Ode to Tara. The title of Keeler's journal rolled around in Tara's mind, and she tried to hide any outward signs of her emotional turmoil. Soon Cal would read Oren's personal thoughts about her. Would Oren rant and rail against her rejection? Maybe express in words the crazy infatuation that caused him to steal her prized possessions.

She sighed, drawing Cal's attention. He appeared to want to give her a hug. Feeling so emotionally raw and vulnerable, she'd be glad for a hug, but that was precisely the reason she scooted out of reach and sought her rubber bands. She expected him to try to stop her, but he didn't, and she snapped hard.

Despite his assurance that she had no reason to feel guilty, it continued to bother her, and she knew that until she fully dealt with her issues of ignoring God in her life, her nightmares would continue. She was no more free to hug Cal and lean on him now than she'd been since he'd arrived at the tower to bring her back here.

He tapped the journals sitting on the hay next to him. "Any idea why Keeler would leave these things here and risk them being found by the new owners?"

"None." Tara bent closer to the pictures, and raised holes near the edge caught her attention. "These have pin-sized holes. Like they were posted somewhere."

"The house at your aunt's place, maybe? He could have thought someone might see them there, so he took them down but didn't want to get rid of them."

"Or he could have posted them at his family's house but removed them when he lost the farm. But then it doesn't make sense that he left them here."

"If I've learned anything in chasing down criminals, it's that the things they do often don't make sense even when they explain their reasoning. That's doubly true of someone as disturbed at Keeler." He paused for a moment, seeming to collect his thoughts. "You have to remember he's obsessed with ISIS and killing. He's living in a make-believe world, and his actions don't have to make sense."

"I suppose so." She tried to give his thought some consideration, but her mind was a jumbled mess. One thing, however, stood out bright and clear. "Killing seven women makes no sense in any world."

"You have a point." He came to his feet and held out his hand. "C'mon. Let's stop at the hired hand's house at your aunt's place to see if there are matching holes in the walls for these pictures."

"And if we find them? How will that help?"

"We won't know the answer to that until we look." He tugged her to her feet and bent to put the items back in the envelope and pick up the journals. "Ready?"

She nodded, and he led the way to his car, where he put the envelope and journals in a large evidence bag and settled it in the backseat.

He pressed his finger against his chest, where the mic from his communication device rested. "We're heading over to June's farm. Rick, take the lead. Shane, the rear."

It took only a few minutes to exit Oren's former property and turn down June's drive. Cal sent Agent Ingles inside to get the key for the hired hand's house, and then continued down the drive to the tiny single-story house.

Cal eyed her. "We didn't have a chance to check out this location today, so we'll go straight inside."

She nodded and got out. He escorted her to the front door, his gaze watchful and his head swiveling as he scoped out the area. He broke a seal on the door and unlocked it.

She stepped inside the familiar space, but a coldness seeped into her body rather than the warmth she'd known when she'd visited June's longtime hired hand who'd managed the farm for so many years after Earl died. The door led straight into a spacious kitchen with ancient cupboards and an old turquoise refrigerator from the fifties. A bedroom was located on the right and a narrow doorway straight ahead led to the living room.

Cal gestured at the bedroom. "Keeler had this room set up as an office. Let's start there."

She entered the space painted a blindingly neon blue color.

Cal stepped to an open wall and ran his still-gloved fingers over it. "Lots of holes here."

She joined him and shined her phone's flash-light over the area. "The size is consistent with the holes in the pictures." She continued down the wall. "Looks like he had bigger pictures here, too."

"It could have been papers or other items."

She looked up at him. "Items like what?"

"Souvenirs from the women."

"That's just sick."

"Keeler *is* sick, Tara."

"I know . . . I . . . even after everything I've seen and heard, I can't seem to think of him that way."

Cal gave her an incredulous look.

"You don't get it. I know." She sighed. "Did you have a close friend growing up?"

"I was kind of a loner."

"Then imagine learning one of your Knight or SEAL teammates was behind this and doing sick, depraved things."

"First, none of them would."

"But see, that's how I used to feel about Oren. You've always known him as a killer. I've known him as a friend and then a lost soul when he pulled away. Even as sick and twisted as he is, it's not as easy as you might think to give that up."

"Makes sense, I suppose."

"But you can't see it."

"You've got a more innocent outlook on life than I do." He gave her a sweet smile. "It's one of the many things I like about you. I honestly wish I didn't have to be the one to force you to accept reality."

"You like many things about me, huh?" The question came out before she thought it through.

"You're an incredible woman, Tara. Strong. Courageous. Tough yet soft and vulnerable. I like it all." He peered into her eyes, and the intensity of his passion nearly had her stepping over to him and flinging her arms around his neck.

"We should finish up here," she said instead, and moved on to another wall where one of Oren's rudimentary paintings of a cow hung slightly askew.

She remembered when he'd created the garishly colored picture in a junior high art class. He thought it was so realistic, but it wasn't in perspective and the barn next to the cow was about the same size.

Still, he loved to draw, and she'd encouraged him. *Wait, draw.* Her mind flashed back to the pump house. To the table. Under the binder. Large papers folded. Drawings of devices. The necklace bomb.

"There were more sketches in the pump house," she blurted out. "Diagrams of the bombs and parts."

"What brought that back?"

She pointed at the picture with Oren's signature on the bottom. "Oren loved to draw as a kid. The picture triggered a memory."

Cal's eyes gleamed. "And are you any good at drawing? Can you re-create what you saw?"

"Not really, but I can give you a rough sketch that should do the trick. I know it had words on it. Those I don't remember, but maybe what I do remember will help."

"I'm sure it will."

They walked the rest of the house, not discovering any additional leads, and soon stepped back into the warm sunshine. Cal fixed a new seal on the door and escorted her back up the drive, where he allowed her to run inside and return the key while he waited on the porch.

Tara handed the key to June.

"Did you learn anything?" she asked.

Cal had warned her not to share any information without his permission, and she hadn't thought to ask him about today. "Nothing I can tell you about."

"Then I won't ask again." June frowned. "I hate that all of this is happening, but at least I've gotten to see you two days in a row."

She circled her arms around Tara and drew her close. Her aunt smelled of peanut butter and chocolate, as did the house. When June released her, she picked up a large tin that often held June's famous cookies.

"Monster cookies for Cal," she said.

"Cal?" Tara cried out. "But you know I love them, too, and I haven't had any in months."

"I do, but I can spoil you anytime, and unless you bring Cal back here when all of this is over, this might be my last time to spoil him."

Tara appraised her aunt. "I know you're fishing for something, but I'm not touching that comment."

Tara kissed June's cheek, took the tin, and backed toward the door.

"Honey, I saw the way you two look at each other, and my old heart would be real happy to know you might be interested in him."

"I can't hear you," Tara joked.

"He's a fine man. Handsome, too."

"Bye, Aunt June. I love you." She quickly stepped out the door.

Cal spun, and she handed him the tin. "June's famous monster cookies. Apparently you made quite an impression on her. She doesn't make them for everyone."

She never baked them for Nolan. The thought came unbidden, but she ignored it and slid into the car.

Cal opened the tin and offered her a cookie. She gladly picked one up. The size of a saucer, the cookie was made of oatmeal, peanut butter, chocolate chips, and peanuts. She chomped a gooey bite, but Cal closed the tin without taking one.

She swallowed her bite. "You don't like cookies?"

"No, I like them fine, but my clothes, probably my hair—shoot, all of me smells like the barn, and I can't eat."

"Oh." She was surprised that he was so sensitive to smells, though after seeing his reaction in the barn she shouldn't be, she supposed. "I'm used to the odor, but I should have thought about that and warned you. It lingers."

"We'll have to change clothes before we go back to the office or the team is bound to make jokes for days." He grinned.

She loved his playful look, so in opposition to the large-and-in-charge guy sitting next to her.

She didn't think, but took his hand. "I'm glad you were with me when I found the journals. No one else would have handled it so sensitively."

"Sensitive!" He gaped at her. "Me? Now don't go telling the team that, okay?"

"Mum's the word." She smiled back at him.

Their eyes connected, and she forgot all about the cookie in her hand and got lost in the deep brown color.

He shifted to face her more fully. "What are we going to do about this?"

"About what?" she asked, though she knew full well he meant what was happening between them.

"This . . . us." He let go of her hand and gestured between them. "You may not want to hear this, but I can honestly say I've never felt this way before."

"Me either." She couldn't believe she admitted it.

His gaze darkened, deepened, and he reached up to cup the side of her face, his fingers lingering for a moment before he slid them into her hair, drawing her closer to him. He was going to kiss her, and with her gaze locked on the eagerness in his eyes, she could think of no reason why he shouldn't. Not even his team standing in the driveway. If he didn't care about them witnessing the kiss, neither did she.

He leaned closer, his lips inches from hers, his breath fanning softly over her skin.

His cell phone rang in the tone all his team

members used to communicate with each other. A shutter dropped over his eyes, and he sat back to grab his phone. "I have to take this."

"Of course." She could honestly say she was disappointed in the interruption, very disappointed, and yet relieved, too.

"What's up, Max?" Cal stared ahead.

She could hear Max's fast-talking voice echo from Cal's phone, but she couldn't make out the words. She nibbled on the cookie and watched a rush of emotions race across the wide planes of Cal's face as he listened. He ground his teeth, and his fingers curled into a fist on his knee.

She lost interest in her cookie and waited for him to share additional bad news.

"We'll be right there." He ended the call and tossed his phone onto the dash so hard he'd likely broken the screen. He slammed his fist into the dash, leaving a dent and breaking open the skin on the knuckles he'd injured in the explosion.

"What is it?" Afraid to hear the answer, she held her breath.

"Another bomb." He cranked the engine and revved the motor.

"But it's not the first of the month."

"I've been thinking Keeler would take out his frustration over not getting to you by reducing the time between bombs. He's hurting, and he needs his fix to relieve his pain. Not uncommon for a serial killer."

"But you said last night that we had until the first of the month."

"Yeah, for the women on his list."

"So this wasn't someone on the list?" Nausea threatened her stomach. She'd been so naïve to think they had weeks to find him before he killed again. "Where did the bomb explode?"

"In Oregon. Your fire tower. The new fire lookout is dead."

Tara's heart plummeted and all the warm feelings from June, from the cookie, from Cal's almost-kiss evaporated, a hollow ache replacing them. The poor, poor young woman who'd filled in was dead. Dead! At Oren's hands.

Tara circled her stomach with her arms as if she could protect herself from further anguish, but the pain rolled through like a bowling ball racing down a lane, bent on destruction.

Cal shoved open his door, jumped from the car, and strode over to Shane. Tara watched, not only because she was interested, but because it kept her mind occupied. Cal spoke, his shoulders rigid, and Shane's mouth fell open. Cal said a few more words, then pivoted and marched back to the car while Shane jogged up the drive to Rick.

Cal settled beside her and clasped the wheel so tightly his knuckles turned white. "I should have thought to ask for a man to replace you at the tower."

"You couldn't know Oren would do this."

"No! Don't make excuses for me. I failed. It's my job to know things like that." He revved the engine and pointed the car up the drive, gravel spitting under their tires.

When he stopped at the road, she laid a hand on his arm. "Now would be a good time to remember what you keep telling me. You didn't set this bomb. Oren did, and you can't take responsibility for it."

"Yeah." He cranked the wheel, her hand falling off before he gunned the car onto the road. "It's a good idea in theory, but after all I've seen . . . all I've done . . . it doesn't work for me."

"Maybe talking to me about it would help."

He shook his head. "Been there, done that."

"But not with me."

He shot her a quick look and then stared ahead at the road. She waited for him to speak. One minute. Two. Three minutes passed in silence.

He'd opened up with her a few times, but he had always held something back, giving her insight into his inner being only in dribs and drabs. But now? Now he'd closed down tight and had no intention of volunteering any information and letting her into his life.

Good. Just what she needed to happen.

If she was honest about her feelings, she'd been subconsciously thinking about a possible relationship with him once Oren was behind bars. Thankfully, Cal's stubbornness, that part of him that he refused to share because he needed to be in control all the time, *that* part of him put an end to any hope of a relationship before she foolishly fell for him.

Dressed from her shower, Tara pulled back her hair into a ponytail and checked her appearance in the mirror one last time. Fortunately, Cal had arranged for the team to come to the safe house again instead of her and Cal having to go back into the city. If another life hadn't been lost, if Cal hadn't refused to open up to her, Tara would be grinning over his need to shower off the barn odor.

She stepped into the hallway, and at hearing Cal's raised voice, she stopped to listen before walking into what sounded like a heated conversation.

"You don't know that, Max," Cal stated. "The bomb could be a trap. Keeler has to know we'll hop a plane to Oregon and take Tara with us or leave her here unprotected. Either way, he could have a plan in place to harm her, and we can't ensure her safety." He paused for a moment. "And before you suggest it, I won't take her to Oregon. There's no way she needs to see the carnage at the fire tower."

"We'll compromise and split up the team," Max said.

"What?" Rick's voice boomed down the hallway. "We've never done that on a callout."

"There's a first time for everything," Max

answered. "I'll go to Oregon with Cal and Brynn. The rest of you will remain here to continue working the leads."

"I'd rather not go," Cal said.

"Not negotiable," Max replied. "We need our explosives expert on site."

Cal didn't respond, and Tara wished he'd fought harder to stay with her, but she fully understood that his skills were needed at the bomb scene.

"Kaci," Max continued. "I want you to sit on your team until they find actionable information about the woman whose home Tara mapped yesterday. And you don't look up from your computer until you've got something on the e-mail addresses Cal found."

"Roger that," Kaci said.

"Shane, since Brynn has confirmed Tannerite fueled the truck explosion, you need to step up your game to find Keeler's source so when we hit Oregon soil we can run it to ground. And Rick, get back on the stakeout of Sarra Yasin, and for Pete's sake, get me something we can use."

"Can't do that unless she shows up at her house," Rick said. "I checked with our guy on her detail, and she's still AWOL."

Tara assumed Sarra Yasin was the woman connected with ISIS who was caught on film near the Dallas bomb site. If what Rick said was true, she hadn't come home since the team had staked her place out.

"Then spend the time as you wait going back through the information we've gathered on Yasin. We have to figure out why Keeler would work with a Muslim woman at the same time as killing others."

"His e-mail we read a few hours ago says he's targeting women who turned their back on their faith," Cal said. "Have you looked into Yasin's faith?"

"Sure," Rick said. "But maybe there's something there. I'll dig deeper."

"Good," Max said. "Then each of you have your assignment."

"What about Tara?" Cal asked. "I won't leave her here with just anyone."

"I wouldn't expect you to. Kaci and Shane, with your work predominately on the Internet and phone, you can work from here, right?"

"I wish it was that easy," Kaci said. "But I need our equipment if you want me to investigate these e-mails and not let anyone know I'm searching."

"Okay, what about you, Shane?"

"Sure, I can hang out here, but it would be good to have another agent as backup in case I need to track something down."

"I'll say it again, it can't be just anyone," Cal cautioned.

"What about Phillip Ward?" Brynn asked. "We vetted him for that op last year. He's a former Army Ranger and should fit the bill nicely."

"He meet your expectations, Cal?" Max asked.

"Yeah, if I can't be here, he'll do," Cal said, though Tara could hear his reluctance.

"I'll get on the phone right now and have him reassigned." Max clapped his hands. "So get to it, people. I've already requisitioned the plane and pilot, and I want wheels up in two hours flat."

Tara heard the team stirring and decided she should join them. She had mixed feelings about the meeting and Max's decisions. She didn't want Cal to leave, but not because she didn't feel safe with Shane and this Agent Ward. She did, but she didn't want to be separated from Cal.

How pathetic was that? He'd reminded her in the car why they weren't right for each other, and she still didn't want to see him go.

Staring at his phone, Max stepped into the hallway and almost barreled into her. "Tara, good. Cal tells me you remembered a few schematics from the pump house, too."

She nodded. "Now that I'm cleaned up, I'll get started sketching them."

"Keep up the good work. You may be just the person we needed to break this case wide open." He gave a quick nod of acknowledgment and stepped outside.

In the living room, the others were gathering their things. All except Cal, who stood staring out over the backyard.

"Hey, Tara," Kaci greeted her. "How you holding up after this latest news?"

"Fine," she replied, but kept her focus on Cal.

He turned to look at her. "I need to have a word with you in private." He slid open the patio door.

She joined him on the deck, for once not enjoying the lovely yard or the sweet scent of flowers, as she couldn't look away from his tense jaw and narrowed eyes.

"I'll be leaving for Oregon in the next few minutes."

"I know. I was in the hallway when you were discussing it. I probably should have made my presence known, but I thought you all would want to finish the discussion before I interrupted."

Her admission brought a megafrown to his face. "You likely heard the Dallas woman's name mentioned."

"I did, and I'm sorry. I know you didn't want me to know that."

"Just be sure you don't mention it to anyone else."

"It's not like I'll be talking to anyone but you and your teammates."

"True, but I have to caution you anyway."

"I'm sorry, Cal. I guess I shouldn't have eavesdropped."

"What's done is done." His frown deepened, but he didn't honestly seem upset about her overhearing the woman's name.

Tara knew the guilt that was plaguing him

hadn't lessened. In fact, it spoke to one of his strengths, caring about others so much that he was willing to sacrifice himself for them. Which was why he would go to Oregon.

"I'll have my cell on, so you can call if you need me for anything. Due to the ease of tapping a landline, there isn't one in this house, so be sure to keep your cell charged at all times."

She nodded. "So you'll be leaving right away?"

"Yes. I wish I didn't have to go, but with Keeler shortening the time between bombs, it's even more important for me to work the Oregon scene."

Before he takes another life, Tara thought, but she didn't voice thoughts that would only exacerbate Cal's angst.

CHAPTER 23

Washington, D.C.
3:30 p.m.

"Wheels up in three." The pilot's voice came over the jet's intercom as the plane sat on the runway awaiting takeoff.

Cal heard his teammates clicking on their seat belts behind him. He'd chosen to sit alone in the front of the plane, a photocopy of Keeler's most recent journal on his lap. Cal would use the flying time to read Keeler's tirades. Tara had suggested she keep the journals to read, but even

289

if they weren't evidence and had to remain in the FBI's custody, there was no way he'd let her read even a photocopy before he'd prescreened them. Not only because he wanted to predict how she would react to the information, but also his gut said the journal contained items that the team would need to remain confidential.

The plane lurched forward and taxied, gaining speed. As the wheels rolled over the runway, he rested his head back on the seat. He told himself it was because vibrations would make it hard to read, but in reality, he wasn't up to getting into the head of a crazy man, the killer who was targeting the amazing woman who'd somehow made her way into Cal's heart. If her response to the almost-kiss in the car was any indication, she'd opened her heart to him, too.

How had he let that happen?

She'd been hurt enough lately, and when this was all over, he would hurt her again, because he still had to come to grips with the senseless loss of lives, and it was unfair to ask her to wait around while he did.

Unease weighed down on him, and he concentrated on relaxing the tension in his muscles. He'd used the same procedure hundreds of times before SEAL missions, and he always followed it with a quick catnap. Fifteen minutes and he was good to go for hours.

Breathe in and out. In and out.

He suddenly felt someone standing over him. His hand automatically went to his weapon before he opened his eyes and remembered he was safely ensconced in their jet.

"Whoa there." Brynn's hands went up to warn him off.

He lowered his gun. "Sorry."

"Bad dreams."

He shrugged, but she had to know he hadn't reacted like a normal person might respond. *Normal, right.* Who was normal these days? He'd responded like most people in the military and law enforcement. And for the Knights who'd all seen combat and had their own demons to contend with? His behavior was the norm for the team.

"Mind if I sit?" she asked.

If she planned to try to get him to open up, he'd send her packing, but for now, he gestured at the seat across the aisle and shoved the pile of journal pages between his leg and the cushion. "What's up?"

"I thought you'd like to know that DNA came back on the Remington."

"By your less-than-enthusiastic expression, I'd say we didn't get Keeler's DNA."

"Sorry, no. But we're still in preliminary evidence evaluation, and we could link him to the gun in other ways." She smiled. "At least we have the journals from today. Those should contain touch DNA."

Right. The journals that likely held horrible thoughts about Tara.

"You look a million miles away," Brynn said.

He lifted the stack of papers. "I need to get started reading the journal entries."

"But you don't want to."

"Does anyone ever want to get inside the head of a psychopath?"

"I suppose not." She got up. "The reading might be horrible, but it could give us the lead we desperately need."

He nodded, and she stepped away. He turned to the first page, dated six months before the first bombing. As predicted, the pages were filled with Keeler's perceived mistreatment by society. By the bank who repossessed his family's farm. His employer and Tara, neither of them appreciating his amazing skills and brilliance. He followed each tirade with ways that his affiliation with ISIS would let him seek revenge. The pages contained pretty much everything Cal had expected, but he hadn't expected Keeler to be so cruel when it came to Tara.

Cal dreaded asking her to read the pages of filth uttered about her, but he would have to ask. Sure, Cal could ask her questions about things he'd read in the journal, and he would do that, but just as she'd known things about the items they'd taken into evidence that Cal would never have come up with on his own, she could see notes in the journal that meant something only to her.

He swallowed hard, his hand curled and ready to strike, but he continued on instead, highlighting passages that needed follow-up. On page twenty, Keeler raved about a woman he'd met at temple, a Nabijah Meer.

Temple? Cal sat up. They'd been unable to locate a temple associated with Keeler. Cal read faster. He hit page thirty-seven, and his mouth dropped open.

He grabbed his phone and dialed Kaci.

"You can hardly be in the air yet, so this must be important," she said when she answered.

"It is," he said. "I've been reading Keeler's journal, and you'll never guess what I found."

Mount Hood National Forest, Oregon
5:15 p.m.

Cal stood at the base of the destroyed fire tower and stared at the gruesome scene. The sun hung high in the sky, the temps were in the mid-seventies with a cool breeze playing over the area, and the birds chirped in the distance, all in direct contrast to the sight before him.

The tower's front supports had been severed, leaving the platform dangling from the back with all the windows and one wall blown completely out. The balcony where he'd watched Tara, the room he'd locked her in, all destroyed. A woman dead. For what? Because Keeler was obsessed with Tara and couldn't have her?

Cal shook his head and stepped closer. The ME had already removed the remains and though Cal hadn't wanted to see the woman, it could have helped in his evaluation of the bomb.

How long had this woman sat with a bomb around her neck, paralyzed with fear while waiting for it to explode? Had Keeler needed it to occur at a certain time, or was the time of the explosion random? Did Keeler even place the bomb, or was he still in D.C. and one of his accomplices did his dirty work for him?

All Cal knew at this point was the area was so far removed from civilization that no one had heard the explosion. When the fire lookout failed to call in, her supervisor sent someone to check on her and found the tower in ruins.

Cal continued to stare, and for some reason, the team's mission statement ran through his head.

Readiness. Response. Resolution.

Yeah, right.

Sure, they'd responded and would hopefully resolve the situation in due time, but ready? Nah, they hadn't been ready. Tara had no affiliation with this woman, so none of them had seen this coming.

Nor had the poor woman. When Cal had made that phone call for a replacement, he'd effectively sent her to her death. So what if he understood that he wasn't responsible for the other women who died? This death *was* his fault. All his fault. He should have predicted Keeler's actions and requested a man to take Tara's spot. And worse yet, even as he looked at the scene of another woman's death, Cal felt relief that he'd gotten here in time to prevent Tara from being Keeler's next victim.

He tightened his fist. There was nothing within reach to punch, and his anger climbed to a frenzy. If he spotted Keeler right now, Cal would take the man apart with his bare hands.

His phone rang, and he snapped it from his belt in frustration. He spotted Kaci's name and hoped she was calling about Nabijah Meer, the woman he'd discovered in Keeler's journal.

"Tell me you have something for me."

"I haven't actually located Meer, but I did determine the name Nabijah comes from the Indian and Muslim world and means ambitious, leader, and brave. Meer's a common Indian surname that means prince or ruler."

"So you're thinking she belongs to an aristocratic family?"

"Maybe. I'm going to follow that direction to see where it leads."

"None of the victims were Indian."

"No, they weren't, and neither is Sarra Yasin."

"So it might not mean anything." Cal took a

breath and let it out. "Get back to me the minute you have more on Meer, okay?"

"You got it."

They disconnected, and he looked at the tower with Kaci's thoughts fresh in his mind.

Had Meer helped Keeler with the other bombs and taken out this tower while Keeler headed back to D.C. to kill yet another woman? Or had Sarra Yasin or both women been assisting him all along in planting the bombs?

Cal needed answers. Needed them now. He spun to retrieve his equipment and spotted Max and Brynn in a deep discussion. He started for them, but Max broke away and met Cal in the middle.

"What's up?" Cal asked, though he suspected Max planned to lecture him on how to let go of his guilt and do his job.

"You're blaming yourself for this woman's death," Max said, as if Cal had written his script for him.

"Maybe."

Max opened his mouth, but Cal held up a hand, stopping him. "Before you go spouting some mumbo jumbo about this being Keeler's fault and only his fault, there's no need to say it. I get it in theory."

"Actually," Max said. "I was going to say that Brynn and I understand what you're going through. We should have thought this might happen, too, and we want this killer found as badly as you do. So let's stop staring at the ruins and get moving."

Cal had to admit Max's comment took him by surprise, as did the ease in which he seemed to let it go. "And just like that, you move on?"

"Sure, why wouldn't I? I hate that a woman lost her life. That all these women have died because we underestimated Keeler, but we're human. We only have the abilities God gave us, and we make mistakes. Granted, our mistakes can be more costly than most, but come on, man. In this kind of job where people often burn out. If we didn't move on, we'd soon be paralyzed. Then how many people might die?"

"Interesting way to look at it."

"I suggest you give it some thought. Might help you deal with that anger I keep cautioning you on."

Good advice and something Cal needed to consider, but most important now was finding a strong lead. He nodded at Brynn. "Brynn looks like she's getting antsy."

"Then let's get going so she has something to do."

They marched across the field to join her.

"Despite our warning to the contrary, odds are good that the locals have trampled the evidence," Cal said. "But let's forget that for now and run this like any other investigation. I'll start by evaluating and setting the appropriate perimeter."

Brynn nodded. "Since Kaci's not here, I'll

handle the photography in addition to my usual forensic duties."

"And I'll log evidence and anything else either one of you need me to do," Max said.

Cal never thought he'd see the day when Max did grunt work. "As much as I hate being here, having you as my gopher might make it palatable."

"Don't get used to it," Max replied good-naturedly.

Cal's mood lifted a notch, and he went to the rental car to grab his gear, then marched up to the officer in charge, who happened to be Deputy Andrews. A good thing in Cal's eyes, as it gave him hope that the personnel access log that Cal had explained the importance of at the last bombing would be complete.

"Log, please." Cal held out his hand.

Andrews handed it over, and Cal ran a finger down the list. The sheriff had logged in. Not surprising. The only other people listed were the ME and two additional deputies who first responded to the scene.

Cal looked up. "I don't see any bomb disposal personnel listed here."

"There hasn't been any called to the scene."

Cal gaped at him. "So no one has walked the area to look for secondary devices?"

Andrews narrowed his eyes. "Well, yeah, the first guys to arrive checked things out."

"But they're not trained."

"Before you tell us how we're a bunch of locals and we don't know what we're doing, you didn't call them out for the other bomb either."

"That's because I have EOD credentials, and I checked the scene myself."

"Right." A sheepish look slid over the deputy's face.

"I need you to move back a minimum of a hundred feet and make sure no one approaches until after I finish my inspection."

Andrews didn't waste any time but took off at a quick march. Cal moved in the opposite direction and took his time checking the ground before placing his foot down. As he approached the tower, a caustic smell filtered into the air, but at least the building hadn't burned, and he wasn't smelling torched wood.

He made a wide circle and, each time around, he moved closer to the tower until he was standing near the back wall where the two supports remained intact. Something suspicious sat near the ground at the far post. He slowly closed in on it until he made out a rudimentary bomb similar to the one in the cabin crawl space, but this one didn't have a timer. Which meant it would be remotely detonated.

It could have been set in case the necklace bomb failed. Or was it? Maybe it was intended to take out first responders or the Knights. If so, the person with the trigger had to be close by watching for the opportune time to detonate. Like now. When he stood less than a foot away from the device.

He spun and ran full-out toward Deputy Andrews. Before he traveled more than fifty feet, the device exploded, sending concussive waves through the ground and catapulting Cal through the air.

He landed on his belly, and his hands automatically went up over his head. He lay stunned for a moment, his ears ringing as debris rained down over him. This wasn't the first explosion he'd survived, and it wasn't even the closest call, but he couldn't help but think how horrible it would have been if the device had been detonated with an unsuspecting person close by.

He lifted his head and saw Max racing in his direction.

Cal swayed to his feet. "Can't hear you, Max. Just listen. The bomb was remotely detonated and the person who set it off has to be close by. Watching."

Max spun and said something, but Cal couldn't make it out. All he knew was they were all sitting ducks, and they needed to take cover.

Washington, D.C.

Tara pushed back from the dining room table and dropped her pencil. She wasn't a good artist, and the sketches she'd created were rudimentary at best, but she hoped they would help. Planning to show them to Shane, who was working at a desk in the den, she got up and grabbed the pad. She found him hanging up his phone, his usual easy-going expression dark and concerned.

Cal. Had something happened to Cal?

She forced a calm she didn't feel into her voice. "Is there a problem?"

"We have a few new developments."

She'd seen nothing but straightforward answers from him, and his Cal-like evasive response raised her concern higher. "Can you share them with me?"

He gestured at a club chair by the desk. "Why don't you take a seat?"

"That bad, huh?" she joked, but when the easygoing guy didn't even crack a smile, she braced herself to hear very bad news.

She dropped into the chair. "Did Oren hurt someone else?"

"We're uncertain who placed the device, but a secondary bomb was left at the fire tower in Oregon and was just detonated."

Cal. He's hurt. Her heart refused to beat. "Cal . . . the team . . . are they . . . ?"

"They're fine. Mostly anyway. Cal's a bit banged up. He was checking the area under the tower for secondary devices when he spotted the bomb and took off running. He was hit with falling debris, and his ears are ringing, but otherwise he's okay."

She noticed she had a death grip on the chair. She released it and twisted her hands together in her lap, and her heart seemed to restart. Memories of the truck exploding took over her mind. The ground rumbling under her body. The fireball. Metal and wood shooting into the air. The ditch had protected her, but there wasn't a ditch near the fire tower. A vision of Cal, lying on the ground and debris raining down on him, left her unable to speak.

"If Oren is here in D.C.," she managed to get out past the dryness in her throat.

"He could have placed the device before he left and someone else set it off," Shane said.

"Not a timer?"

"No. It was remotely detonated."

"Then that person was watching. Waiting."

He nodded solemnly.

"For Cal? Do you think they were waiting for Cal?" Her fingers automatically went for the rubber bands.

Shane eyed her fingers and shrugged. "I only have the barest of details at this point. Max said they were in pursuit of a suspect, but he wanted to give us a heads-up in case the news reported the bombing."

She nodded, but the shock of nearly losing Cal before she really got to know him didn't seem to abate. An ache as real as the bullet that had pierced her stomach took her breath. If this was the first bit of news . . ."Wait, you said there were two developments."

Shane held up his hands. "Relax. This has nothing to do with anyone getting hurt."

She nodded but couldn't seem to shake the thought of Cal incapacitated. He'd been so strong, her rock, and if he could get hurt, what might happen to her, to others?

"You care about him, don't you?" Shane asked. "Cal, that is."

She didn't know if she should admit it to anyone on the team, but Shane was such an easy person to talk to. She nodded, and it felt good to finally declare her feelings, even if it was by way of a nod of her head.

"He's a great guy," Shane said. "But you should know, he's troubled about something and maybe—"

"It's not a good time to try to start something with him? Yeah, I know."

"So he confided in you?"

Had he? Was his often-pensive look caused by his guilt over not catching Oren or did it go deeper? "I'm not sure, as he doesn't willingly share what's bugging him—anything personal, really—but I can see it."

"I'm afraid it's more than bugging him."

"Yeah, I got that, too." She suddenly felt

uncomfortable talking about her feelings with a virtual stranger. "The other thing you mentioned?"

"Right." A knowing look crossed his face.

So what if she was clamming up like Cal? Her talk with Shane in no way resembled Cal's behavior with her. She and Cal had something. She knew it, he knew it, and they both also knew his unwillingness to open up would prevent them from moving forward. Maybe that was his plan.

"So there's this program call ShotSpotter," Shane continued, and Tara turned her focus to listening to him. "Basically it's a network of microphones installed in high crime areas so when guns are fired, the microphones record the audio. That in turn details the number of weapons and shots fired and provides real-time maps of the shooting location to first responders so when they arrive at the scene they're prepared. Not only does it keep them safer, but it helps in aiding victims, searching for evidence, and even interviewing witnesses."

"Interesting," she said. "But how is this related to our investigation?"

"Earlier this evening ShotSpotter in a D.C. location picked up gunfire at a construction site. After the police investigated, they determined explosives had been stolen."

"Explosives like the ones Oren uses."

He nodded. "Max is contacting the local authorities to see if we can process the scene. If we're lucky, we might find Keeler's prints or DNA."

Tara's stomach cramped down hard. "But it doesn't really matter if you get his prints, right? I mean, sure, you can prove he committed the burglary, but the real problem is that he's in possession of more explosives. He'll use them to build a bomb and another woman is going to die."

Mount Hood National Forest, Oregon

The world continued to spin, sidelining Cal while the rest of the team and Deputy Andrews combed the woods for the person who detonated the bomb. With subpar hearing, Cal hadn't even been able to discuss things with Max before he called the sheriff to request backup, and he and Brynn donned vests and took off together. If it were any situation other than one involving a bomber, Cal would enjoy seeing Max in action, as he rarely came out in the field and even more rarely participated in a physical pursuit.

Cal pushed off the bumper of the SUV and tested his balance. The area spun less than it had a few moments ago, but his head continued to ring with a high-pitched, piercing sound. He put a hand on the vehicle to end the residual spinning when he spotted movement in the bushes.

It could be a deer or elk, but he'd take no chances. He backed behind the SUV and hunkered down in a position where he could still keep his eye on the area. Leaves rustled and soon bushes parted a fraction. He couldn't make out what or who was peering out at him, but he thought it was a deer assessing the risk of coming into the clearing.

The opening widened, and a pair of eyes, not animal but human, appeared in the space. He shifted to grab his sidearm but knew he couldn't make a shot at this distance if needed, so he crept around the side of the vehicle and to the back door left open by Max. Cal quietly lifted the lid on a weapon case and found an assault rifle. He inserted an ammo magazine and moved back to the bumper.

A hand came out of the bushes, then another, this one holding a handgun. Not a man's large hands, but a woman's smaller, slender pair. He didn't let the surprise hinder his focus, but lifted his weapon and sighted in the area where the woman would emerge.

She didn't disappoint, but soon slipped out low to the ground. Of Middle Eastern descent, she wore American clothing and hadn't covered her face. He focused the scope, taking in her appearance. Could she be Meer or Yasin? Even though she wasn't dressed in traditional garb as Yasin had worn when she'd accompanied Keeler to Dallas, Cal would go with Yasin as the most likely candidate. She'd likely dressed this way as she was hidden from view and needed to move quickly through heavily wooded areas. Or maybe she didn't expect anyone to survive the bomb.

A sense of urgency almost had him moving, but he held his position and watched her scurry across the road, heading toward the front end of his vehicle.

Could she be planning to hop in and take off?

Assuming so, he scooted to the other side of the car and waited. She soon moved around the front, and he eased toward the bumper. A door latch clicked, and he figured she'd closed the back door. He heard the front door opening.

His team wouldn't ever leave a car vulnerable, so the ignition didn't hold keys. Which meant she would have to hot-wire the SUV. A skill she'd most likely learned from ISIS.

Cal gave her a few moments and then peeked into the rear window. She was bent over the wheel and wouldn't notice his approach. He crept along the side of the vehicle and swung his rifle into the driver's space, planting the barrel against her head.

"Hello, Sarra Yasin," he said, and hoped he was right. "So nice of you to drop in."

CHAPTER 24

Fairfax, Virginia
Saturday, August 6
9:15 p.m.

Tara strode across the safe house deck and back again, her footsteps following the same path they'd taken for the last few hours. She stopped to glance at the moon hanging in the distance. Crickets chirped from the lush garden beds surrounding the yard and the sweet smell of lavender from lovely purple blooms perfumed the air. All in all a peaceful and tranquil location. Except it wasn't. Not since Cal called that afternoon telling her he was on his way back, and when she'd asked for details of his trip, he'd been cryptic and terse.

She'd come to know him well enough to recognize the strife in his voice and the underlying unease and anxiety. If big, brawny Cal Riggins with his SEAL savvy and confidence was anxious . . . she should be worried, too. Which she was. Even more so because he was late and she feared something terrible had delayed him.

Maybe it was related to Oren's journals. He'd taken copies on the plane and could have found something horrific that he'd needed to track down. Or had another bomb been detonated since she'd learned of the last one? Did the team discover something in Oregon? Would he even tell her what was bothering him?

"Stop, just stop," she muttered, and searched the garden for peace.

Father, please keep him safe, she prayed as she'd done since his departure yesterday. She and God weren't right, but she couldn't imagine Him not answering her prayers for other people.

She stood, gazing into the night sky, waiting for a measure of comfort, but uneasiness continued to plague her. Over Cal's safety or her discord with God, she wasn't sure. If only she could learn to trust again, but for some reason, she couldn't make the transition to having confidence in God's direction. Maybe it was her guilt over the latest lost lives. Maybe it was stubbornness or fear. No matter which, she couldn't step over that line and trust again.

Could you if Cal's life depended on you trusting God?

Could she?

She heard the front door open and close before Cal's deep voice rumbled through the space announcing his arrival and saving her from having to answer her own question.

She sighed out her relief and caught sight of him as he strode through the house toward the large patio door. Raw cuts slashed across his face, his arms. He'd suffered, but God spared his life.

For a moment, weariness mixed with frustration darkened his eyes, but then his gaze connected with hers and the uneasy emotions washed away. A relieved smile spread across his face, and the knot in her stomach loosened as a warm, languid feeling filled the aching pit.

He stepped outside. She followed him, then unsure how or what to do or say, she paused.

"Hi," he said, sounding as self-conscious as a man on a first date.

"Hi," she responded.

He eased closer, his arms lifting as if he wanted to hug her, then he dropped his arms and searched her gaze. His eyes darkened again, this time with a longing so clear it stilled her breath. He rested a hand on her arm, and her whole body went up in flames. She'd missed him. How she'd missed him. He hadn't been gone for twenty-four hours, and she'd missed him.

In a few short days, he'd come to mean so much to her. The desire to know him better, to have him know her better, left her stunned, and she could only stand frozen in time and stare up at him.

How would she ever handle saying good-bye to this amazing man after they'd found Oren and Cal stepped out of her life?

His eyes narrowed. "Is everything okay?"

"You . . . the bomb," was all she could say.

"I'm fine."

He didn't look fine, and she wanted to know

more, but even if his whole body ached from the explosion, he was the kind of guy who wouldn't talk about his injuries. Wouldn't talk about much of anything.

He gestured at her sketch pad on the table. "Your drawings of the bombs?"

She picked up the pad and handed it to him.

He flipped through the book, his attention razor-sharp before he looked up. "Thank you."

"I hope it will help," she said, feeling like a stranger trying to make small talk when what she wanted was so much more.

"It should." He placed the pad back on the table. "I'll take a better look later and compare this to the device I reconstructed."

She nodded her understanding. "Shane told me you caught the woman. Sarra."

"Yes, but unfortunately she's not talking." Cal rubbed the back of his neck. "She'll be escorted to D.C., and Max will question her again."

"Did the rest of the team return with you?"

"Yes." The warmth that had lightened his eyes disappeared. A darkness that made her head hurt replaced the light. "Why don't we sit down?"

"That sounds like bad news." She watched him carefully.

He didn't respond, but pulled out a chair at the table for her. She sat, and he took a seat next to her, scooting close. Her awareness of him grew, but he didn't seem to be affected by their proximity. Was she the only one whose true feelings had come to light during his absence, or was she assigning feelings to his expression that didn't exist?

He rested his hands on the table. "Shane told you about the break-in where explosives were stolen."

She nodded.

"Our Evidence Response Team lifted prints and confirmed they belonged to Keeler."

Okay, good, talk about the investigation. She'd ignore his nearness, the scent of his minty after-shave, the emotions churning in her stomach, and concentrate on Oren. *Ha!* She wanted to think about Oren more than her feelings for Cal, which should tell her something.

She willed her mind to concentrate on the topic Cal raised. "Don't you find it odd and sloppy for Oren to leave prints behind?"

"I do."

"So do you think he wants us to know he's stolen the explosives?"

"Could be."

"Because he wants us to know he's going to set off more necklace bombs."

"Likely. Or it could be his way of thumbing his nose at us. Telling us that he's so far superior to us that we can't stop him." Cal sat forward. "This is a common thing for serial killers."

"You mean that they want to get caught?"

"No, that's a myth that's often said of such killers. But in fact, as they continue to get away with murder, they begin to feel invincible and get sloppy."

"You think Oren might be getting sloppy."

Cal nodded. "The blood in the tree was his, which suggests he was scrambling and could mean he's not thinking ahead as much."

"Could that be true of ditching the gun, too?"

"Could be, or he actually left the gun so we would find it and tell us that he was the one who tried to kill you, not Hickson," Cal said, his voice strained. "Although we didn't find Keeler's DNA or prints on the gun, tests confirm slugs removed from the tower and the one found near your truck all came from that gun."

"Oren really did set off the bomb, then, and Hickson was a pawn in Oren's plans," she said, not at all surprised by the news.

Cal nodded. "Also Kaci located video that shows Sarra Yasin renting a Toyota Corolla as Hickson claimed. Max stopped by the county jail to show Hickson her picture, and he identified her as the woman who hired him."

"So Hickson told the truth. Oren used Hickson, and now he'll end up in jail." She shook her head. "Another life destroyed by Oren."

Cal frowned. "Once this is over, I'll do my best to see that Hickson gets a fair shake."

"That's very kind of you."

"It's nothing." Cal stared at his hands for a moment before looking back at her. "You should also know, we've learned the name of another woman who we believe is working with Keeler."

"A second woman. Do you think he's choosing women to help him for some reason?"

"Honestly, we don't know and may not know until we catch him and he tells us, but we're wondering if it's because Muslim women aren't as closely scrutinized as men. This would allow Keeler to move about undetected."

"How did you discover this woman?"

"Keeler talks about her in his journal. Her name is Nabijah Meer. Does that mean anything to you?"

Tara shook her head. "Have you been able to locate her?"

"No, and all we know at this point is that the origin of her name is Indian and Muslim."

"India . . . is ISIS big there?"

"There are millions of Muslims in India but only a handful belong to ISIS. Hopefully Kaci will learn more about Meer and her role soon."

Tara nodded and tried to wrap her head around the fact that Oren, the boy next door, had connected with a woman from India who believed ISIS's crazy teachings. "Did you find anything else useful in Oren's journals?"

Cal shook his head.

"Would it help if I read them?"

He sat watching her for a long time, then nodded. "You might see something that I didn't think was relevant. But you should know, when it comes to you, Keeler's not very kind."

"Finding him and stopping him is what matters. I'll read them." She slipped fingers under her rubber bands.

He took her hand and held it between his, his gaze softening.

He needn't say more.

He would accept her offer to read the journal, and now she somehow had to find the courage to read the scathing words.

Tucked into the big bed in her room, Tara dropped the photocopies of Oren's journal onto the comforter and sighed. She didn't want Cal to see how reading Oren's personal thoughts would bother her, so she'd fled to the bedroom.

She'd gotten through three of the journals and couldn't bear to read any more. She pushed the papers aside and got up to pace the room, her footfalls silent on the thick carpet. Thankfully, Cal had settled down in the kitchen to talk to Agent Ward instead of going to his room next door or he would've heard her moving about and investigated.

Her phone vibrated on the nightstand, catching her by surprise. She shot a look at the caller ID. Aunt June? Cal had warned her not to call this number except in an emergency. A knot formed in Tara's chest, and she snatched up the phone.

"June," Tara answered, trying to keep the trepidation from her tone.

"Sweetheart, I have something I need you to do for me." June's voice shook with emotion.

Tara's apprehensions skyrocketed. "Is everything okay?"

"Fine," she replied, but Tara heard a thread of unease in her aunt's voice.

Tara ignored it for now but kept her ears tuned for additional distress. "You know I'll do anything for you, so what do you need?"

"I expect after I ask, you'll change your mind about that offer."

Tara waited for her to laugh after the statement, but she didn't.

"You're scaring me, Aunt June."

A male voice sounding sharp and irritated filtered through the background of the call, but Tara couldn't make out the speaker's identity or his words.

"In a moment a bomb call is going to come into the Lone Wolf hotline," June said. "I need you to make sure that Agent Riggins reports to the callout."

"What?" Tara's voice rang to the ceiling of her room before she controlled it. "Why?"

"There's a woman wearing a bomb around her neck. If Cal hurries over to her, he can disarm the bomb and save her life."

Tara's mouth fell open. June didn't know about the necklace bombs. Only the team and Tara knew. So who could have told June? Cal needed to know that word has gotten out, and he needed to know about the bomb call.

As Tara hurried toward the door, she asked, "Who told you about the call?"

"Oren."

Tara's feet stilled at the doorway. "You spoke to Oren. When?"

"He's here at my house."

No. Oh. No.

Fear for her aunt trickled down Tara's back, and she couldn't think straight. Cal would know what to do.

She turned the doorknob. "Another tech can handle the woman so Cal and I can come over there."

"No! Don't send anyone over here."

"You're making no sense. I'm going to get Cal right now, and we'll be there soon." She opened the door.

"Stop! Oren put a bomb around my neck, too." The words came shooting out like a high-speed projectile.

Oren had put a bomb on June. June! Her aunt, the woman she loved.

"If you tell Cal and he shows up here, Oren will detonate it," June added.

"But Cal needs to know."

"Once you tell him, we both know he'll rush right over here, and Oren will make good on his threat. Promise me you won't say a word."

June spoke the truth. If Tara told Cal about Oren, Cal would force Oren's hand. But what else could Tara do?

She softly closed the door and sank onto a chair to think. To find a plan of action, but what? She wasn't prepared to handle this alone. Not at all.

Think, Tara, think!

"Hello, Tara." Oren's voice slithered through the phone like an asp with its tongue ready to strike.

Oren. She was talking to Oren. The bomber. The killer. She opened her mouth to speak, but nothing came out. Probably a good thing because she'd likely spew her anger at him.

"You must realize by now that I won't hesitate to detonate June's necklace if you don't follow my directives." He laughed, a high, pitchy, almost maniacal sound. "And the other woman . . . I will trigger her bomb, too. And if that's not enough of an enticement to do as I say, she lives near an apartment building, so if her bomb goes boom, there will be other casualties. Who knows how many people will die if you don't obey."

Acid rushed up Tara's throat, and she swallowed hard. "But you love June. You can't kill her."

"When you have a calling higher than your-self, sometimes others must pay even if you care about them."

"No," Tara snapped, and frantically tried to come up with a solution.

"Go ahead and be stubborn and stupid like you've always been, Tara. Your aunt and the others will suffer."

"How do I know you've put the bomb on her? For all I know you're holding a gun to her head and making her lie to me."

"I thought you might ask about that, so I'm sending you proof."

Her phone signaled the receipt of a text, and she tapped on the video he'd sent. June's face filled the screen, an ugly white pipe wrapped around her neck. A skull and crossbones had been drawn on the front of the device with black marker, further ratcheting up Tara's anxiety.

Eyes wide, June blinked rapidly, yet, underneath it all, the quiet strength her aunt always possessed shone through. Tara opened her mouth to say something, but the video abruptly ended. Tara had expected her aunt would tell her not to comply with Oren's demands, but then maybe with so many lives on the line—including Cal's if he went to help the other woman, Tara suspected— June would hold her tongue.

"Did your person try to kill Cal with a bomb in Oregon yesterday?" Tara asked.

"Someone tried to bomb your FBI agent?" Oren sounded honestly surprised. "I don't know what you're talking about."

Perhaps this Sarra woman had decided to detonate an additional bomb without Oren's direction. Or maybe he was lying. Toying with her. Trying to confuse her.

"What I really want, Tara," Oren continued, "is to see you."

"Me?"

Why did he want to see her? If she complied and went to meet him, giving him what he wanted, he wouldn't have a reason not to kill June. The only hope she had, apart from trusting Oren's word, was to tell Cal and the Knights what was happening. But if she told Cal, he'd never let her go to Oren, and Oren would kill June. Of that, Tara was certain. The rest was speculation.

"So, if you want June to live, you need to send Riggins to the callout. If not . . ."

She had no choice. At least not right now. She'd have to abide by Oren's wishes. "I'll encourage Cal to respond to the callout, but I can't force him to go if he doesn't want to."

"Ha! Nice try, Tara. You have more influence on him than you're letting on. And if for some reason I'm wrong, you better find a way to make him obey or June is dead." He blew a noisy breath over the phone. "Once Riggins leaves, find a distraction for the other agent on your detail. Take his car and his phone to prevent him from following you or calling for help. I've hidden a car for you." He rattled off the address. "Now write that down, as you'll only have thirty minutes to get there, and I wouldn't want you to get lost."

Tara jotted down the address, the words barely legible from her trembling hands. "Got it."

"The car is unlocked. I've left a phone for you and will call it in precisely thirty minutes. If you don't arrive on time to answer . . . well, you know what will happen." He laughed. "Ticktock, Tara. The clock starts now."

The phone went dead, and Tara stared at the screen. He'd put her in an impossible situation.

She had to choose between the two people in this world who meant the most to her.

CHAPTER 25

Phone to his ear, Cal paced the living room at the safe house and listened to Max provide details of another necklace bomb threat not far down the road from the safe house.

Cal's immediate thoughts went to the list of women Tara hadn't been able to remember, but their addresses were all located in D.C., not in Virginia where Keeler had activated the latest bomb. "Are you sure this bomb is legit?"

"The woman called it in herself, and the first officers on scene confirmed it was Keeler's signature device."

Something was off in this scenario, raising

Cal's concerns. "Don't you think it's odd that Keeler left a phone near this woman so she could call for help?"

"Maybe something spooked him, and he didn't have time to take it."

"Maybe," Cal said, letting the thought ruminate. "Or maybe he wanted us to be sure we'd find her before he detonated the bomb."

"Or maybe he's changing his whole MO."

Adrenaline raced through Cal's veins as thoughts charged through his head.

Relax. Breathe. Calm down.

He didn't want to make a stupid mistake and further compound the problem. "So where do we stand with the woman now?"

"As of my last update from the scene, the local bomb squad has been dispatched," Max said. "A Bureau team is on the way, too. As are agents who will scout the area for Keeler, but with the location so far from metro D.C., the locals will arrive first. In the event that you're able to remove the device, I also have a containment vessel on the way."

"Good," Cal mumbled, his mind already on the best approach to safely free this woman. "But you should know, even though I've reconstructed one of Keeler's devices, I can't in any way guarantee that I can render this bomb safe."

"You have more knowledge than anyone else, and skill-wise, there's no one better than you for the job." He paused for a long moment. "I'm sure I don't have to say this, but I want you out there ASAP."

Cal's brain revved on high octane. "I'll need a suit."

"I'll arrange with the locals to let you use their equipment."

Max spoke the truth, but Cal couldn't go racing off. He had to think of Tara. With Keeler setting a bomb not far from the safe house, Cal didn't want to leave her behind. He was confident that Keeler didn't know the safe house location, but still, a bomb this close by couldn't be a coincidence.

Max cleared his throat. "We're wasting valuable time, here."

"Fine, I'm on my way," Cal said, already jogging down the hall to Tara's room. "I want you to have one of the officers who saw the device call me. I'll walk him through procedures and have him put the bomb squad commander on the phone, too."

"The local squad will know how to handle this until you get there."

"Maybe, but I'm not taking any chances. Nerves cause people to make mistakes, and this woman can't afford any mistakes."

Cal hung up, and his brain whirred as he searched for what to tell Tara. Rendering a bomb safe was always a risky proposition. Keeler's intricate bombs were even more so, and Cal had no idea if he'd be coming back, so he had to make every moment with her count.

He knocked on her bedroom door.

She pulled it open, and her eyes locked on his. "What's wrong?"

"There's another necklace bomb, and it hasn't gone off. If I leave now, I have a chance to save the woman."

"You have to go, then." She acquiesced so easily that it momentarily stunned him into silence.

Did she not get that he would be in danger? Did she not care about him as he'd thought?

"Okay." He tried to keep his confusion from his voice. "Agent Ward will stay here with you."

"I'll be fine." She suddenly threw her arms around his neck and pulled him close. "Be careful, Cal. Please. Please be careful."

Her frantic, whispered plea touched his heart, and he drew her closer. She pushed back and looked up at him. Pain radiated from her face. She *was* afraid for his life.

Shoot, he was afraid for his life, too, and if this was the last time they were together, he would make sure it was memorable.

He lowered his head and didn't wait for her encouragement, but settled his lips on hers. The touch and taste of her sent a shock zipping through his body. He'd known kissing her would be beyond anything he'd ever experienced, but he hadn't begun to grasp the extent of how she could tangle his emotions into a knot.

Stunned by his response, he lifted his head. He waited for her to comment on the kiss, but she kept her eyes closed. "Take care, Cal. Things may not be as they seem."

She acted like she had insight into the situation, but that was impossible, and he couldn't stay here to decipher her mysterious mood when a bomb was waiting to claim another woman's life.

Tara opened her window and listened for the sound of Cal's car revving to life. *Cal.* Caring, compassionate Cal.

How could she have let him go? Especially after the kiss cemented in her mind how much he meant to her. She'd manipulated him to get him to go, playing on the very thing that drew her to him. His sacrifice for others.

Had she just sent the man who'd broken through all of her fears and defenses and made her want to love again to a callout where he could be hurt, or worse yet, killed?

She touched her lips and remembered his final look holding so many emotions. She'd met his gaze, but then her role as traitor came rushing back, and she'd had to look away. Still, if she had to do it all again, she'd do the same thing. Of all the people in danger, he was the most qualified to handle it. If only she could have warned him.

A car engine roared to life and tires crunched down the driveway.

Good-bye, Cal. Be safe. His life was now in God's hands.

She closed the window and glanced at the clock. Five minutes had passed. She had to go now.

She ran for the door, stopping at the desk to write, *I'm sorry, Cal. So sorry!* on a piece of paper. She flipped it over. Hopefully after she was gone, Agent Ward would find it and pass the message on to Cal.

She crept down the hallway to find Agent Ward. He sat in the dining area reading a paperback mystery. His keys were lying on the table. His phone sat next to them.

Perfect. She hurried back to her room and left the door open.

"Agent Ward, hurry," she called out. "I think something moved outside my window."

His footsteps pounded down the hallway. Bursting through her door, he snapped off the lights. He charged to her window and checked the security of the lock before peering out into the night. "I don't see anyone."

"Can you please go outside and check?" She used her best pleading voice.

"First, let's get you into the hallway where there aren't any windows."

She rushed ahead of him.

"Stay here," he warned, before taking off toward

the front door, drawing his weapon on the way.

She hadn't even thought about him having a gun. He might see her when she fled, think she was the intruder, and shoot her. It didn't matter, though. She'd have to risk it.

She waited until the door closed before running into the dining room to grab his phone and keys and slide through the night undetected.

With each step forward, she waited for him to discover her. Waited for him to warn her to stop. Maybe shoot her.

Please don't let him see me.

She forced her legs to churn faster and made it to his car. She hid on the far side so he couldn't see her. She unlocked the car door, and the urge to climb into the vehicle was strong, but she couldn't risk him seeing the light from opening the door, so she crouched in the darkness. She desperately wanted to snap the rubber bands for relief, but she had this ridiculous fear that the sound would echo through the night, so she held the craving at bay and waited.

Footsteps crunched on the gravel path leading to the house. She rose halfway and peeked through the car windows. Agent Ward stepped inside the house, and through the window in the door, she saw him turn back, likely to secure the dead bolt.

When he pivoted and walked away, she jerked open the car door and climbed inside, then gunned the engine. He would hear the car, but by the time he made it back outside, she'd be long gone, and he had no way of following her.

Cal set his light strobing on his car and floored the gas pedal to race down the highway. His phone rang, and he punched the button to connect via his in-dash program.

"Riggins," Cal answered, hoping the caller was one of the agents who'd first responded to the scene.

"Deputy Yancey here," the guy said. "You wanted to talk to me."

"You've seen the bomb. Describe it to me."

He gave a succinct description of Keeler's signature bomb.

"We need to keep this woman from panicking," Cal said.

"No worries there," he replied. "The bomber told her that he used a motion switch, and if she moves, the bomb will detonate."

Not a surprise to Cal. "Has the local bomb squad arrived?"

"Negative. Last report has them three minutes out."

Cal had to assume Keeler built this bomb as he had the others, and he would remotely detonate it. The squad likely carried something to stop radio frequencies or electromagnetic interference. If they did, they could drape it over the woman to prevent any incoming cell signals from reaching the bomb, thus stopping Keeler from detonating it. Worst case, they could use a metal emergency blanket, though it wasn't foolproof. They would be risking an EOD tech's life to go into the house and place the covering, but in Cal's opinion, the risk was worth it to save the woman and other lives in the surrounding area.

Cal had to make sure the local team acted quickly, but he wouldn't explain this to Yancey and risk the information being changed in a secondhand communication. "I want to talk to the squad commander the moment he arrives. Don't waste even a second but get him on the phone with me. You got that? Not a second."

"Affirmative."

"Okay, set two perimeters. Inside, a minimum of one hundred feet. Outside, another four hundred feet."

"We've already started clearing the area, but there's an apartment complex nearby and it's taking time to evacuate the residents. We have additional officers en route and that should help."

"Keep at it," Cal said, now worried that this bomb could take out even more people.

"We're working on it, but you know it takes time, man."

"We don't have time!" Cal pressed harder on the gas, as saving this woman, and now the neighborhood, rested solely on his shoulders.

• • •

Tara pulled up behind a white sedan parked in the exact location Oren had said it would be. Did he truly want to see her, or was this a way to subdue her? Was he hiding in the woods and when she got in the car he'd attack? Maybe put a bomb around her neck, too?

She opened the car door and heard the phone ringing from the other car. She had no choice. Only two minutes remained on Oren's time clock and she had to move. Now!

She bolted from Agent Ward's car and raced across the road. Her hands trembled and she fumbled with the door handle.

"No, no, no. June is counting on you." She jerked the door open and saw the lighted cell on the passenger seat.

She dove to answer it. She soon discovered it wasn't a normal call; he'd called on Skype. Dreading seeing his face on the video app, she tapped the answer button and averted her eyes.

"Hello, Tara." His smarmy voice sent chills of repulsion over her body. "I thought for a moment you hadn't obeyed."

"Cal's on his way as you requested, so now you can let June go."

"You didn't think it would be that easy, did you?"

She had hoped that would be the case, but deep in her heart she'd known that Oren would require something more. "What else do you want from me?"

"Look at me, Tara."

She swallowed hard and swung her gaze to the phone. Expecting to see his face, she saw her aunt instead.

"June," Tara cried out.

"Enough of that." Oren swung the camera to his face.

Tara nearly gasped at the change in his appearance since she'd last seen him at the pump house, but she managed to bite her lip before she dis-played her shock. He wore a full but scraggly beard, a white woven cap, and a traditional white Indian shirt. His eyes were glazed and piercing at the same time, and she saw nothing of the boy she'd grown up with. Nothing of her friend. It was time to finally admit that person was long gone and evil faced her instead.

"We have no time to lose," he said. "First, I want you to take the agent's phone and yours, too. Smash them on the road. Be sure to aim this phone's camera at it so I can see you destroy them."

There was no point in arguing, so she got out of the car and dropped her phone on the ground, then stomped on it with the heel of her shoe. It took a few tries, but it finally cracked and died. She did the same thing with Agent Ward's phone, severing any hope that Cal could trace her location.

"I want to see a close-up of the cells," Oren demanded.

She bent low and demonstrated the ineffectiveness of the phones.

"Go back to the car and drive to June's house. The car has GPS, and I've mounted cameras inside and outside the vehicle in case you planned to have someone follow you."

"I'm all alone," she said.

"Good, because I'll know if you aren't, and I'll kill June."

Tara wished Oren hadn't planned all of this so carefully or she might have been able to come up with a way to outsmart him.

"Oh, and Tara, you have another thirty minutes. I'll make another video call then, and you best be with June."

He disconnected, and she wasted no time but hopped into the car and raced down the highway to her aunt's driveway. The house was dark, and there was no sign of the car belonging to June's protection detail. Tara wished Cal was there with her, but then, what could he do? He'd told her he couldn't disarm the bomb yet. Besides, her intuition said Oren still wanted something from her or he could have killed her the moment she arrived at the car he'd left for her.

And what about Cal's life?

They were just getting to know each other and starting to like and respect each other. And besides that, he was a fine man and didn't deserve to lose his life because of a choice she'd made.

"But I have to save June," she mumbled, and parked the car by the front steps.

She got out, barely noticing the cool breeze drifting through the fields bringing the fresh scent of recently mowed grass. She stepped toward the house, her shoes feeling like they were encased in lead. She forced her feet up the stairs and found the door unlocked.

Fearing some sort of trip wire or booby trap, she cracked the door open only a fraction and held her breath. When nothing happened, she pushed the door open another foot and yelled, "June."

"In the living room." Her voice came from that direction, but Tara wouldn't take a chance.

"Did Oren really put a bomb around your neck?"

"Yes."

"Do you know if he booby-trapped the front door?"

"No. It's fine."

Tara shoved the door all the way open and flipped on the entry light, casting a glow into the living room. June sat on a wooden dining chair in the middle of the room, her hands folded on her lap, her eyes blinking at the sudden light.

Tara entered the room and stared at the plastic pipe around June's neck. "Are you sure this is real? That it'll explode?"

"I can't be positive, but when he clicked it into

place I heard a whirring sound from inside, so I know it's not empty piping."

Tara circled her aunt to evaluate the device. Right—like she had a clue about what she was looking for. That didn't mean she didn't desperately want to find a way to save June. Tara couldn't lose her aunt, the woman who for all practical purposes was her mother. She loved her so much.

Tara dug deep to find even an ounce of bravery before she passed her fear on to June.

"Wouldn't you be more comfortable on the sofa?" Tara asked.

"There's a motion switch in the bomb. Moving could set it off, and I can't risk that."

Tara was suddenly grateful her aunt had always kept in tiptop physical shape so she had the stamina to remain still for as long as it might take to disarm the bomb.

"Oren left another cell on the dining room table," June added. "He said he'd call you on that one."

Tara stepped across the entryway and turned on the old crystal chandelier. The light fractured across faded floral wallpaper, and memories of the many meals she'd eaten in this very room momentarily replaced her anxiety. She glanced at the chair where Oren had often sat, but instead of seeing the boy, she imagined the man in the video. His narrowed eyes, darkness buried in the depths, and her terror came rushing back.

Would she escape from him and eat a meal here again?

Maybe. If she didn't panic. She carried the phone and a chair into the living room and placed the chair next to June. Tara sat and gently twined her fingers with her aunt's. "I love you, Aunt June."

"You can leave the house if you want," June said. "Take the phone with you and get far enough away. Oren will never know."

Tara shook her head, as Oren had said he would make a video call again, and even if he didn't, she wouldn't leave June alone to face this horrible uncertainty.

CHAPTER 26

Burke, Virginia

Cal swung around the corner where patrol cars and uniformed officers blocked the road at the outer perimeter of the bomb scene. He leaned out the car window and flashed his credentials at an officer standing in the road. The guy nodded and stepped out of the way, allowing Cal to move down the road to the inner perimeter. As much as the delay of having to show his ID frustrated Cal, he was glad that Yancey had listened and set up two perimeters.

Four fire trucks were parked just outside the barrier, and worried firefighters stood at the ready.

Nearer the scene sat a heavy response truck with the county logo painted on the side. A tech had already moved a robot down the vehicle ramp. The device containment truck used to transport bombs to a disposal area hadn't arrived. Perhaps Keeler chose this location outside of D.C. because he knew the county squad didn't have the funds for such a truck.

Cal slammed the gearshift into park and was out of the vehicle with his ID in hand before the car quit rocking from his sudden stop. He charged up to the bomb tech. A disposal suit lay discarded on a storage case, and Cal hoped the suit had been worn to put a protective cover over the woman.

"Where's Sergeant Udall?" Cal asked.

The officer gestured at a strongly built man in uniform leaning over the hood of a patrol car, a map spread out in front of him.

"Is the robot ready to go?" Cal asked the tech.

"Ready when you are."

Cal nodded and marched up to Udall. As the squad leader, he'd phoned Cal and was expecting him, so Cal didn't introduce himself but simply held out his ID. "Is the shield in place over the woman?"

Udall gave a quick nod.

"Good. I'd like your man to control the bot, but I'll be the one suiting up to work on the device if it comes to that."

Another nod.

"Show me the lay of the land."

Udall bent over the hood and tapped a home five houses in from the intersection where they stood. "Subject's house. We don't have a blueprint yet, but it's a two-story, and she's on the first floor in the dining room. It faces east and the front door faces south. Back door, north, but the backyard falls off into a gully, and you'd have to climb two flights of stairs to get to the door."

Cal looked down the road. "So the bot goes in through the front."

He nodded. "Unless you want the dogs to take a look-see first."

"You have dogs?"

"Best bomb sniffers in the country. We can strap a camera on 'em and send 'em in."

"Let's use the robot for now." Cal didn't want to risk a dog's life when a robot could perform the task they needed to complete.

"We're ready, Sarge," the tech called out from the back of his truck.

Cal spun, and tuning out the commotion outside of the perimeter, he joined the tech inside the truck. The young man who looked barely out of college sat behind his control module.

"Let's get the bot moving," Cal directed.

The tech nodded and started the robot whirring forward. Bots didn't move fast, so the drive from the perimeter to the front of the house seemed to take forever.

Cal's phone chimed, and he glanced at it to see a text from Kaci saying she located Nabijah Meer's address in D.C. Kaci had dispatched a team to Meer's house to bring her in for questioning. Kaci had also attached Meer's photo. Cal studied the woman's face and wondered why she would team up with Keeler.

"Nearing the house," the bomb tech said.

Cal's attention needed to be on the bomb, and he could think about Meer after he'd neutralized the bomb. He stowed his phone and turned his attention to the tech. "What's your name?"

"Frankie."

"And the robot. Does he have a name, too?" Cal asked, knowing many teams named their bots.

"She, actually." Frankie looked up and grinned. "Anne Droid."

"From *Dr. Who*," Cal said, recognizing the name. Frankie nodded.

"How long have you been doing this, Frankie?"

"This job, three years. The marines another eight."

So he wasn't as young as he looked. And if he was a bomb disposal tech on a county squad, he'd be certified and have graduated from the FBI Hazardous Devices School in Huntsville, Alabama, as Cal had done when he'd come out of the navy. That meant he and Frankie spoke the same language when it came to rendering a bomb safe. The knot in Cal's gut loosened a fraction.

Anne Droid approached the house, and Cal quit talking to focus on the monitor. It didn't take a great deal of skill to move a robot down a street, even if Frankie faced a flat screen in a three-dimensional world. But to enter a house and approach the woman took far greater concentration.

Frankie took the bot right up the stairs, and with great dexterity, used Anne Droid's pinching arm to turn the knob and open the door. Inside the house, she veered to the right.

"Turn on the speakers so I can communicate with the victim," Cal directed, and Frankie complied.

"Ms. Tabet," Cal said into the microphone. "I'm Special Agent Cal Riggins with the FBI. We've just sent a robot into the room. If you speak up we can communicate through the bot."

"Hello." Her tone was tentative and, even in a single word, her fear evident.

"We're here to safely get you out of this device, but I'm going to need your help."

"What . . . what do you need?"

"Our robot is going to get up close and friendly with you now. The tech will direct it to lift the tent flap and zoom in the camera so I can get a good look at the device, and then we'll take a few x-ray pictures of it."

"Okay."

"In all of this, I need you to remain still."

"Okay."

"We're signing off for a few minutes so we can concentrate on the robot. Do you have any questions before we do?"

"N-n-no."

"Okay, back in a few," Cal said lightly, though the tightness in his gut had moved to his chest, too.

Frankie muted the mic.

Cal took a step closer. "From what I've been able to ascertain on the previous bombs—"

"Previous." Frankie's head shot up and he stared at Cal, who could almost see the thoughts racing through the guy's head like sports scores on the bottom of a TV screen. "This is the work of the Lone Wolf, isn't it?"

Cal nodded.

Frankie clutched a hand to his chest, then let it fall with a thud to his knee. "Man, oh, man."

"Relax." Cal rested his hand on Frankie's shoulder. "This is the same job you were doing a second ago. Nothing has changed."

"R-right. Same job."

"Do you need me to take over?" Cal wasn't familiar with this robot and, even nervous, the kid would likely do a better job.

"I got it."

"Then as I was saying, the explosives will be

packed in the rear of the bomb. I'd like a clear picture of that section along with x-rays for the entire device."

He nodded and started Anne Droid moving to the tent where her pinchers lifted the fabric. Cal forced himself to breathe as the first pictures came over the monitor. The woman sat in a dining chair, her back rigid and shoulders level. She had a square face with a broad nose and her dark brown eyes were wide with terror. Her gaze darted around, but she remained seated and motionless. The white pipe circled her neck, and the front coupling held a crude drawing of a skull and crossbones as Cal had expected.

"We saw the design when we placed the tent," Frankie said. "Is that the Lone Wolf's signature?"

"Yeah, and I need you to keep that bit of info to yourself."

"No problem," he replied.

Cal doubted, despite good intentions by Frankie, that he would be able keep this quiet. Best case, he'd share it with his wife. Worst case, he'd pass it on to his sergeant, who would run it up the chain of command and word would spread, but Cal couldn't worry about damage control right now.

At the moment, the most important thing was to get his mind into the game, as it was clear that he would be donning the eighty-pound suit waiting for him outside the truck. Even if a cell signal couldn't pierce the tent to set off an explosion, Keeler packed his bombs with many hidden switches, and Cal had to be careful if he didn't want to go boom right along with the device.

Spotsylvania County, Virginia

Tara's palms were slick with sweat, so she scrubbed them over her jeans. She'd sat with June for thirty minutes now but time dragged. Each second, each moment an hour. Tara's mouth had gone dry long ago. She wanted to get a glass of water, but June couldn't risk tipping her head back, and she didn't have any straws in the house, so Tara wouldn't seek creature comforts for herself while June suffered.

"How did we find ourselves in such a situation?" June asked.

Tara shook her head. "I should have seen how unstable Oren is."

"Now, don't go blaming yourself. I spent more time with the guy than you did." June swallowed hard. "Besides, Cal once told me that guys like Oren were good at hiding their psychopathic tendencies, and it wasn't uncommon for people around them not to see it."

"It's one thing to hear that. Another to believe it."

"So," June said. "What's the first thing you're going to do when your Agent Riggins comes riding in with his White Knights and saves the day?"

Tara smiled at the vision of Cal and their team on horses galloping across the field to save them, likely June's intent.

"Maybe you should start by asking him out on a date," June suggested.

Tara swiveled to stare at her aunt, who was grinning.

She smiled. "Come on, sweetheart. I'm old but not blind. There's chemistry between the two of you."

"If you got to know him better, you might not be encouraging me."

"Whyever not?"

"He has many of the same controlling tendencies as Nolan."

"Hogwash." June's chin jutted out, and Tara could see she worked hard not to move her body to express her vehemence. "He might take charge and know what he wants, but he's nothing like Nolan."

"You hardly know Cal. How can you be so sure of that?"

"Easy. I can read people, and I pegged Nolan for the louse he is the first time I met him."

Tara gaped at June for a moment. "You never told me that."

"When a woman thinks she's in love, she doesn't always listen, so I kept my mouth shut."

"But I could have married him."

June smiled. "I would have stepped in long before that happened."

Tara shook her head and wished she could clear her mind from the immediate danger to think about Cal, but all she could envision was him walking up to the woman with a bomb like the one around June's neck and the device exploding, taking Cal out with it.

She shuddered. "I sent him over there. To the woman with the bomb. What if it's gone off? If he's—"

"Now don't even think such a thing," June warned. "He'll be okay. We have to believe God will watch over him."

"You're right," Tara said, but despite her earlier prayer, she didn't feel confident.

The phone chimed in her hand, and she jumped a foot from her chair.

"You ready for this?" she asked June.

"Yes," June replied, but fear darkened her eyes for the first time.

Tara accepted the Skype call. "Hello," Tara answered.

"Let me see June," Oren demanded.

Tara turned the camera to June.

"Good work, Tara," Oren said. "I know you came alone, and my people tell me your Secret Agent Man has arrived on site and is busy trying to save Hadil."

Hadil. That was her name. The woman. The one with the bomb that Cal was trying to save. Tara forced the image of another woman wearing one of these hideous bombs from her brain and with it went the sight of Cal in danger.

She turned the phone back to her face so she could see Oren's expressions and judge his sincerity. "You'll let June go now."

"Um," he replied, and tapped his chin. "Not quite yet."

Tara glanced at June to see her response, but she sat stoically, her emotions tucked away where only she could know them.

"When?" Tara held her breath in wait for an answer she doubted she would like.

"Soon." Irritation deepened his voice. "First, you must follow my directions. Get back in the car and head up Highway 17 going north. Take this phone with you and stay on the road until you hear from me again."

"But where am I going?" Tara hated how desperate she sounded.

"It's a surprise, but it's worth it. Trust me. I've wanted to see you ever since the night of the unfortunate incident between us. And now . . ." He paused, the time ticking by in excruciatingly painful seconds. "Now we'll have the chance that we've always dreamed of. Oh, and Tara? I know all about you and Secret Agent Man. Unfortunately, he'll have to die or you'll never be free."

CHAPTER 27

Cal picked up the EOD suit's cumbersome helmet that resembled a deep-sea diving helmet. He lifted it over his head and slipped it into a padded high-profile collar. He'd already turned off his phone to keep a wayward call from accidentally triggering the device, donned the suit pants and jacket, and now slipped on the gloves.

He gave Frankie a thumbs-up, then he stepped forward in the bulky suit that forced him to walk like a lumbering elephant down the road. Moving this slowly gave him plenty of time to think about the device x-rays taken by the robot. Keeler had used several switches including a collapsing circuit that would trigger the bomb if any wires were cut. To render it safe, Cal needed to know the safe arm, which he didn't see on the x-ray. So right now Cal planned to only look inside the PVC before taking additional steps.

At the house, he climbed the stairs and entered the dining room.

"I'm here, Hadil," he called out. "Can I call you Hadil?"

"Yes." Her tiny voice came from the other side of the tent flap that Frankie had lowered when he'd backed Anne Droid out of the house.

"I'm coming in to join you now." He bent low and lifted the flap.

Hadil blinked hard before her eyes widened and she gasped.

"Don't be afraid," he said. "Remember, I told you this suit is a precaution, so don't let it freak you out."

"But I . . ."

"I know this is hard." He made sure to use a comforting tone. "But think about the fact that I'll have you out of here soon."

"Honestly?"

He nodded, though he still didn't know if he could follow through on his word.

"I'm going to come closer and put down my tools." He stepped ahead and set his bag on the floor next to her. "Next I'm going to bring in a chair and lower the flap over both of us." He backed out to retrieve the chair and positioned it so he could face her. With thick gloves, he opened the bag, removed a light, and clamped it on the back of her chair before aiming it at the device.

"Now." He sat. "It's time to get to work."

She swallowed. "And you're sure you know what you're doing?"

He nodded, but the padded collar held his helmet in place, so he had to move his entire upper body. "Besides being trained and certified, I've had years of experience with explosive devices. You ever heard of Navy SEALs?"

"Yes, yes, of course. They're amazing."

"I was a SEAL for many years and have been in far tighter spots than this one."

"Oh . . . okay . . . good, then."

He dug a cordless drill from his tool bag. "All I'm going to do right now is drill into the side of the pipe with a very small bit." He displayed the bit so she could take comfort from the tiny size. "I need you to sit very still."

"I haven't moved since he programmed a number into my phone, and I pressed the dial button an hour after he left like he told me to."

"Good job." He bent closer. Her face was shiny with perspiration, her mouth and chin trembling. He felt her emotions to his core, but he couldn't let it get in his way and display any concern or he might unsettle her, exposing them both to an explosion.

He put the drill against the PVC and pressed the switch. Shards of white plastic fell from the pipe like a heavy snowfall, but he ignored it and concentrated on feeling the way as the bit moved through the PVC. He had to make a complete hole in the plastic, but he couldn't apply too much pressure and drill too deep into the space behind it.

When the movement changed, he released the switch on the drill before he did irreparable damage. The seam on the right side of the device suddenly released and the front popped open.

No! his mind shouted, and he cringed, preparing himself for the blast impact.

Nothing.

Silence. No explosion. No concussive wave.

He studied the device now hanging open.

"Can you take it off now?" Hadil begged.

Could he? Either he'd gotten very lucky and the device failed or this was a dummy device. But why would Keeler plant a dummy?

Had he meant this as a distraction? If so, he could have exploded the bomb to get the same effect. Cal would think this was a ploy to take him away from Tara, but again, why not blow up the bomb? That was guaranteed to bring him to the scene, too.

Why a hoax?

Unless it wasn't a hoax. Perhaps there was a second bomb like in Oregon. One meant to take them all out once they'd let their guard down. Perhaps someone else who was helping Keeler had gone rogue and wanted to do more than kill one woman at a time, or maybe Keeler was escalating and wanted to take more lives, too.

"Is it over?" she asked more insistently now.

"Hold tight." He flipped up the tent and stepped out. He raised his face shield and searched the room for anything suspicious but didn't find any trip wire or other devices.

He lifted the tent flap again. "Did the man who

put the bomb on you do anything but strap on the device while he was here?"

"No. He barged in with his gun and forced me to sit. He had a woman with him. She held the gun to my head while he put this thing on me. He programmed my phone and put it in my hand, then warned me not to move. Then they both walked out the door."

Cal found this incident very odd, but he had the opportunity to separate Hadil from the bomb, and he wouldn't miss the chance. He eased the collar from her neck and carefully set it on the empty chair. He took her arm and escorted her out of the house.

Hadil started crying and she sagged against his hand. "Thank you. Thank you."

Cal nodded but didn't say anything. They weren't out of the woods yet.

Which is why the officers stood stoically by, their gazes rapt and searching the area. Until Cal proved the bomb was a dummy and gave the orders to stand down, they had to believe an unexploded bomb sat in the house, leaving them in a dangerous situation, and they were trained to act accordingly.

With each step, Hadil faltered more and more. If Cal wanted to get her to the medics without carrying her, he needed to redirect her thoughts.

He dug a picture of Keeler from the suit pocket

and displayed it. "Is this the man who put the bomb on you?"

She nodded.

"Do you know him or have you ever seen him before today?"

She shook her head hard as if it felt good to move. "Should I know him?"

"Probably not," he said as they reached the perimeter. "But take some time to think about him. He might have been in the periphery of your life. Maybe following you."

She shot him a terrified look.

"Don't worry, we'll make sure you're safe, and he's not going to get anywhere near you again." He gave her a comforting smile and kept her moving forward. At the ambulance, he handed her off to a medic and smiled. "I'll check back later to see if you remembered anything."

He turned and lumbered over to the sergeant.

Cal studied the area, his training warning him to pay attention to even the tiniest detail. "Something's not right here."

"Like what?"

"My gut says there's another device. To be safe I want everyone to fall back to the outer perimeter."

"You're sure of this?"

"Sure enough that I want everyone to move. Get the command vehicle to a safe position and the people in harm's way out of here. I'll shed this suit so I can move more freely and go in search of another device. You get Frankie suited up to deal with any bomb we locate."

Cal stripped out of the suit. Sure, he'd be safer wearing it, but eighty-plus pounds of Kevlar would slow him down on his search, and he wouldn't risk others' lives to save his.

Udall barked orders at his men. They instantly mobilized and started evacuating. Cal needed a better look at the area than he could get driving his SUV, so he left it parked and headed toward the outer perimeter. He kept his head on a swivel looking for anything out of the ordinary, but he reached the barricades without locating anything suspicious.

His mind racing, he let his gaze run over the crowd.

"C'mon, c'mon, c'mon," he whispered. "Figure it out, man."

Just then, his gaze caught on a slight male with a ball cap pulled low over his eyes. He stood in the middle of the crowd. Nothing about him drew Cal's attention other than the way he kept looking up and furtively glancing away, like Sarra Yasin in Oregon. They had Sarra in custody, but could this puny guy standing before Cal be a woman? Perhaps Nabijah Meer, the woman Oren mentioned in the journals?

The next time the guy's head popped up, Cal took a better look.

Yeah, he could be a she, and her bone structure matched the picture of Meer.

Cal turned away before he scared her. He crossed the road and resisted the urge to look back at the woman as he stepped into the parking lot of an apartment complex. If she had a remote for a bomb, it wouldn't do to startle her. He had to play it cool and act like he was looking for something totally unrelated to her, then double back behind her and take her into custody.

Once out of sight, he radioed Udall and shared his plan. "I need you to get eyes on the woman and keep me updated on her movements."

"I'll radio my men."

"No," Cal said. "I can't take any chances that one of your patrol guys will spook her. Make your way over there yourself, but keep it on the down low." Cal described the woman and her exact location.

"Roger that," Udall said.

Cal hurried through the complex and onto the street a block behind the location where he'd last spotted her.

"Got her in sight." Udall's voice came over the radio. "She's holding steady."

"Good. I'm about to cross over to the crowd."

Cal employed every stalking skill he'd learned as a SEAL to slip in and out of onlookers until he stood directly behind the woman. She lifted a feminine hand to the back of a slender neck, confirming she was female.

It didn't mean that she was Meer, and he'd cause the Bureau a world of hurt if he was wrong, but he couldn't take a chance that she had a remote in her pocket. Inches behind her, he shot out his hands, sliding them under her arms and jerking up high to keep her hands away from her pockets.

She screamed, and fought him with surprising strength, but she was no match for him.

"Special Agent Cal Riggins, FBI," Cal shouted, making sure his voice carried through the crowd to Udall, who leapt the barricade and joined Cal.

"Check her pockets," Cal instructed.

Udall frisked her and came up with a gun and cell phone.

"Let's get that phone into a Faraday bag." Made of specially coated metallic shielding, Faraday bags were a much smaller version of the tent used in the house and prevented connectivity to cellular networks, Wi-Fi, and Bluetooth. If the cell was programmed to trigger a device, once in the bag, it would be worthless.

Udall passed the phone to a deputy. She hurried toward the truck as Udall cuffed the woman.

Cal removed her cap. Her face matched the photo to a T, and he couldn't contain his victory smile. "Nabijah Meer. So nice of you to join us."

She gaped at him for a moment, her shock further confirmation of her identity. She started spewing obscenities at Cal, but he ignored her and escorted her through the crowd to the nearest cruiser.

"She could do with a more thorough search," Udall told a female deputy who stood nearby.

She patted Meer down. "No ID."

"Not a problem," Cal said. "I know all about Nabijah. She's the coward too afraid to show herself, letting bombs do the dirty work for her."

She spat at him.

He jumped back, and she missed the mark. He grinned over being able to rile her and having another suspect in custody, meaning they could pit them against each other and maybe convince one of them to turn on Keeler.

His mind traveled to the phone. "I know the first bomb was a decoy, and I suspect you were told to use the phone to set off a secondary device. We need to find it ASAP."

A sly smile slid across her face. "I have no intention of helping you locate it."

"Don't worry," Cal said. "I don't need your help."

"Time for the K-9s?" Udall asked with a smile of his own.

"Time for the K-9s," Cal confirmed and had the pleasure of seeing Nabijah frown.

Tara glanced at June. Her aunt, the woman who'd been so instrumental in Tara's upbringing. Memories came rushing back of their annual

Thanksgiving celebration for all of the neighbors with a huge spread of food and games for children that June spent weeks arranging. Tara had dug for coins in mounds of sand and plunged her hands into big aluminum troughs of icy-cold sodas. Some years, she cupped hot chocolate in her hands. She'd loved the scavenger hunts, tag, and spoon races, all watched over by her precious smiling aunt. Even when Uncle Earl passed, June had thought of others, putting them first and quietly grieving his death.

And here Tara stood, planning to abandon her special, wonderful aunt, and they might not be together in November. There might not be a celebration.

Tara dropped onto the chair. "I can't leave you."

June smiled at Tara and despite the circumstances, her eyes were filled with love and encouragement. "I'm fine here. God is with me."

"But I . . ." Tears Tara had barely kept at bay brimmed over. "What if Oren doesn't follow through on his promise to let you go? What if he detonates the bomb?"

"Then we'll see each other in heaven." June didn't flinch or seem the least bit worried. "I've had a full life. I know where I'll go if I die, and I'm not afraid. Don't be afraid for me."

Tara thought about Cal and Oren's claim that he planned to kill him. She was almost paralyzed by fear of his death. "I wish I had even a fraction of your faith."

"Oh, you do, sweetheart. You do." June took Tara's hand and met her gaze with the same encouraging look she'd shared with Tara for years. "Remember. There is no problem that trusting God won't fix. Nothing is bigger than He is."

The stakes were so enormous, Tara doubted she could manage it.

"Just trust in your faith, honey." June squeezed Tara's hand. "I'd love to give you a big hug, but that's impossible. So give me a kiss on the cheek and get going."

Tara's tears fell in earnest now, and she angrily swiped them away. "I love you, Aunt June."

"I love you, too, sweetheart."

Tara bent over and kissed her aunt's smooth cheek, then stood and gazed down on her. "I can do this. I won't let you down, and I'll be back here with a way to remove this bomb and move you to safety."

"That's my girl." June smiled again.

Tara turned and walked toward the door, taking the hardest steps of her life and fearing that Oren would make sure they became even more difficult before the night was over.

From the bomb control truck, Cal watched Sparky and his handler Deputy Randall work the area. Randall had the German shepherd on a thirty-foot leash, giving him free rein to sniff the area. Today wasn't the first time nor would it be Cal's last time seeing bomb-detecting dogs in action. In Afghanistan, dogs and their handlers walked out in front of soldiers, risking their lives to clear the path for others.

Cal would never forget heading outside the wire and feeling like every step he took could be his last, but with a dog going before them, he could rest easier. Unfortunately, dogs were so effective in bomb detection that terrorists were targeting them overseas before they even set their sights on soldiers.

Cal could also see the day when certified explosive detection dogs working for local police came under fire, too, as they were being used more than ever. Nothing was more effective at detecting hidden bombs than the nose of a working dog. Especially Vapor Wake dogs who could trail the scent of a bomb as a terrorist on the move carried the device through a crowd. Cal hated that this was the world we lived in, but at least man's best friend could help in the fight to keep people safe.

Near a set of silver community mailboxes, Sparky stood on his hind legs, sniffed one of the larger boxes meant for packages, and then sat to look back at his handler.

"We've got something," Randall said over the radio.

A bomb, just as Cal had expected to find. There might even be more of them, but Sparky and Randall would help them figure that out. Right now, Cal needed to get the squad to render this one safe.

"Get me a good look at the device," he said to Frankie, who sat at the screen ready to move Anne Droid into range.

Once Sparky and Randall had cleared the area, the robot whirred down the street. At the mailbox, Frankie snapped an x-ray revealing a rudimentary bomb controlled with a remote timing device.

"Not much of a bomb," Frankie said. "Would've destroyed the mailboxes and injured anyone standing nearby, but nothing catastrophic."

"Pretty much a noisemaker is all," Cal agreed. "Makes me wonder if there's another device, too."

Cal grabbed the Faraday bag holding Meer's phone and slid his hands inside to check phone numbers programmed into the contacts app. He found three phone numbers, but they had no names attached. He checked the call and text history and didn't see any outgoing calls or texts. Didn't mean Meer hadn't made calls on this phone. She could have deleted the history, but he thought it reason enough to believe that there could be three devices hidden in the area.

Cal grabbed a marker, jotted the numbers on

the whiteboard, and turned on his phone to call Kaci for help. As he dialed, he noted five missed calls all from the same number, but he needed to text the numbers to Kaci before finding out who'd been trying to reach him.

I need owner information for three phone numbers, he tapped into his phone, then added the phone numbers.

I'll get them to you ASAP came her reply.

Cal stowed his phone and turned to Frankie. "Has the containment truck arrived?"

"Boy, has it." Frankie grinned. "You feds get all of the cool toys."

Cal had to agree. "I know we'd normally detonate a puny device like this right here on scene, but the parts used in constructing this one could help in our investigation. So I want you to move it to the containment truck instead. I'll step out to arrange that with the team, and we'll get Sparky on the hunt again."

Cal hopped down from the truck and caught sight of Max and Rick arriving at the barricade. They marched forward with a purpose Cal recognized in himself . . . and all of his teammates, for that matter.

Cal informed the containment truck driver of the plan before heading back to the command truck. "We're good to go, Frankie."

"On it." Frankie maneuvered the bot forward, and with no errors or even hesitation, he soon had Anne Droid rolling and the package placed in the containment truck.

Cal clapped Frankie on the back. "You must be hard to beat in video games."

He grinned up at Cal. "No one will play with me anymore, so I don't know."

Cal dug out his business card and handed it to the guy. "Call me next time you need a run for your money. I'd be glad to take you on."

"Hey, thanks, man." A big, goofy grin crossed his face.

Cal turned his attention to his radio to put Randall and Sparky back in action.

"A minute of your time," Max called out from the open door.

"I'll be right back," Cal told Frankie, before jumping down from the truck and joining Rick and Max.

Cal assumed Max wanted an update, so Cal obliged without being asked. "We're mopping things up here and—"

Max held up his hand. "It's time we turn this over to the locals."

"What? Why? After we get these bombs contained and transported, I'll give them a good look, and they could give us something to go on."

"That's not happening."

Cal had shown great patience in waiting to tear apart the necklace bomb, in hopes of finding a way to locate Keeler, but he'd held back to clear the area. Now Max wanted him to stand down? No way.

"It's our best lead right now," Cal argued.

A low growl of frustration sounded from Max's throat. He was normally a serious man, but right now his intensity was off the charts. "Your attention is needed elsewhere."

Cal glanced at Rick and saw something unsettling in his eyes, and if Rick looked unsettled, they had a problem. A big problem.

Cal sucked in a breath. "What's going on?"

"It's Tara," Max said. "She's gone."

"Gone? What do you mean 'gone'?"

"Agent Ward has been trying to call you, and when you didn't answer, he called me."

Cal remembered the five missed calls he'd spotted a few minutes ago, and his heart sank. "I turned off my phone to safely approach the bomb. What happened?"

"Tara claimed she heard a noise outside her bedroom window. Ward went out back to check it out. She grabbed his car keys and phone from the counter and took off. With no landline at the safe house, he hiked next door to use their phone."

Cal's thoughts jumbled into a tangled mess, each thought trying to find purchase, but nothing made sense. "Why would she take off?"

"That's what we're trying to figure out at the same time as trying to locate her," Rick said.

Locate her.

The reality of the situation hit Cal. Tara was out there. Missing. On her own. Maybe in Keeler's hands. Cal's knees threatened to give out, and he thought he might drop to the ground.

No. He couldn't afford to be weak. Tara needed him. She needed him *now,* and he had to find her.

Max eyed Cal for a long moment and pinched his lips together.

"You've got something else to add, so out with it," Cal demanded.

"Tara left a message on the desk for you."

"What did it say?"

" 'I'm sorry.' "

"Sorry. Sorry for what?" Cal's mind went back to his last conversation with her.

She'd been acting odd, but he'd chalked it up to the fact that he was leaving her in someone else's care again. But now it looked like her eagerness to be rid of him may have been planned.

"Does Ward have GPS on his car or his phone?" Cal asked, but didn't manage to keep the panic from his voice.

"Doesn't matter." Max widened his stance. "We found his car a few miles from the safe house, and his phone and hers have been destroyed."

Cal hissed out a breath. "So you don't have a clue where she is."

"Sorry, man," Rick said. "But something made her run, and since you know her better than we do, we thought you might figure it out."

Could he? Maybe if he could clear his brain and focus, but all he could think of right now was that the woman he'd come to care for was in the hands of a raving madman.

"Cal?" Max asked. "What would motivate Tara to leave the safe house?"

Cal curled his fingers into his palm and called up the precision focus BUD/S had taught him.

"June," he said. "She'd leave if June was in danger."

"I'll call the agents on her detail." Max dug out his phone and dialed.

Time ticked by in slow, excruciating seconds.

"First agent's not answering. I'll try the other one." Max dialed again, then shook his head. "No answer."

"Then something's going down at June's house," Rick said. "And odds are, it involves Tara."

Max sucked in a quick breath, and Cal would have done the same thing if he could draw even an ounce of air into his lungs, but he swore an armored tank had parked on his chest.

"Keep your focus, Cal," Rick said. "Otherwise your head won't be in the game, and we know what happens when we're not in the game."

Yeah. People die. People like the women Keeler's been killing.

Something Cal would move heaven and earth to keep from happening to Tara.

CHAPTER 28

Fear and anger erupted in tandem, and Cal slammed a fist into the barricade. He welcomed the splitting of his knuckles, the pain that followed.

"Calm down," Max said. "Tara needs you level-headed not a raving lunatic."

Cal tried to banish the raging red tinting his vision and keeping him from doing his job.

Job? Right.

He'd always been the one who knew what to do in every situation. How to remain calm under pressure. Think on his feet. Well, he wasn't thinking now. At least not anything good or helpful.

"C'mon, Cal," Rick said. "Tara needs you."

Yes, Tara. Forget Keeler for now and think only of Tara.

He took deep breaths, blew them out, and lost count of the number of times he inhaled before finding the control he so desperately needed. Finding the agent who could think logically and reason out his options.

Figuring only one option existed right now, he dug out his car keys. "I'm going to June's house."

Rick grabbed his arm. "You're in no state to drive. We could dispatch locals to check it out first."

Cal shrugged free. "I might be a bit on edge,

but we're not sending a local team to June's house and risk them botching this. June deserves our best effort, as does Tara."

"And our best means not letting you go in on your own." Max held Cal's gaze, warning Cal not to argue. "We have no idea what's happening at June's place. I shouldn't let you go at all."

Cal planted his feet on the concrete. "It's not like you're going to stop me."

"I'll go with him," Rick volunteered.

"Guess that's the best I can hope for."

"Grab your gear while I retrieve my car," Cal said to Rick.

Cal didn't waste time waiting for Rick's response or Max's blessing, but ran across the inner perimeter and got his car going. He parked near the outside perimeter, engine idling as he waited for Rick. His mind went to Tara. She would do anything she could to protect June, and Keeler had to know that was Tara's Achilles' heel. As much as Cal would rather not believe Keeler enticed Tara from the house, Cal had to wonder what Keeler had done or said to get Tara to run from safety.

Rick jerked open the passenger door.

Cal jumped and chastised himself for being so jittery.

Rick eyed him as he dropped onto the passenger seat and settled his bag on his lap, but he didn't say anything.

Cal wrapped his hand around the gearshift, the trembling in his fingers a foreign feeling for him.

Rick's focus went to the shifter. "I've never seen you rattled like this."

"Me either." Admitting it aloud unsettled Cal even more.

"You've got a thing for her," Rick said, an understatement for sure. "And you need to find a way to put it aside by the time we get to June's place or let me take lead."

"Not happening, man. I'm calling the shots." Cal eyed Rick until he held up his hands in defeat.

Struggling for calm, Cal inched the SUV through the workers, honking when they didn't yield the right of way. He'd faced down invading terrorists. Had knives and guns pointed at him. Bombs explode near him. But nerves like this? Tara missing? That was beyond him.

He needed help. Much more than Rick could provide. They were both just men. Skilled men, but men failed. Tara was too important for even a hint of failure.

Father, help us, please, he implored. He had to let go of his anger at God. Let go of his stubbornness and trust Him to save Tara. It was the only hope.

Please, he pleaded again before turning his attention to the perimeter ahead and honking at the officer moving the barricade at a snail's speed.

Cal wanted to race through the opening, but

reporters and looky-loos stared at him and failed to yield the right of way until he flipped on his lights and siren, and laid on his horn.

Ten minutes later, he finally reached the main access road leading to the highway and another hour passed before GPS announced their destination a mile ahead on the right. Cal eased the car onto the shoulder and flipped off his headlights. Rick rummaged through his bag, came out holding night-vision goggles, and strapped them on.

Cal killed the engine and peered ahead. The house sat in the dark, shadows cloaking both stories. A light shone through the living room window.

"Look for June's protection detail," Cal directed. "They should be blocking the drive before the house."

Rick sat forward and stared out of the window. "No sign of them."

Cal curled his fingers but held his anger in check, as he couldn't risk damaging his hand when he might need it. "Let's get suited up and hike in."

Rick didn't have to be told twice, and he exited the car with Cal. A cooling breeze rushed over Cal as he opened the back window to retrieve combat vests and fill pockets with extra ammo and tools.

The action felt so similar to suiting up for his days at war. A fitting sentiment in Cal's mind.

The entire country was at war with terror, and men like Keeler had to be stopped.

Cal tucked a backup gun behind his vest and settled his NVGs on his head. After a quick check of the thirty-round magazine for his assault rifle, he was ready to roll.

He nodded at Rick, then made a sweep of the area, the green tint from the goggles familiar and comforting as he scanned. Not seeing any threat, he signaled his intent to move and stepped off.

Despite darkness and heavy clouds obscuring the moon, Cal could see a clear path to the house. He tightened his hold on his rifle and moved silently down the drive. A single cow mooed in the distance, breaking the quiet. Despite the lack of noise, Cal didn't have to look back to know that Rick was right on his heels. He was as silent and deadly as all of the Knights, and if Cal *had* heard Rick's footsteps, something would be very wrong.

Cal eased off the drive and approached the house, pausing at the living room window. He signaled for Rick to hold. The light from inside cascaded into the night and illuminated the shrubbery below, forcing Cal to lift his goggles as he crept closer to the window.

He shot a quick look inside, then retreated, his heart plummeting. A brief glance told him that June sat in a chair, Keeler's telltale white PVC circling her neck. Cal returned to the window again and held his breath as he ran his gaze over the room, looking for Tara in a similar situation. He determined June sat alone and confirmed that, other than the bomb, no additional danger presented itself.

He dropped to a squat and froze in place as he tried to figure out where Tara could be. Rick duckwalked closer and cast a questioning look at Cal. He signaled to look inside. Rick took a long look and came to squat next to Cal.

"A bomb would definitely bring Tara out here."

"No sign of her, though," Cal whispered. "But she could be in another room."

"We need to gain access to the house and not through a door," Rick whispered back.

He was right. Keeler could have booby-trapped the doors and windows. Still, they could cut a hole in a window and insert a camera to determine if it was safe to open.

Cal signaled for Rick to follow him to the back of the house where, if Keeler was watching from the road, his finger perched over a remote, he couldn't see them enter the house. Cal dug into the bag attached to his vest and located a glass-cutting tool. Rick stood at the corner keeping watch. Cal made the hole and inserted a snake camera through the opening. He swiveled the camera to capture every inch of the window frame.

"We're clear," he whispered, and unfastened the lock. "We're good to go."

Rick backed his way over to Cal. "We need to steer clear of the living room. If there's a leveling device on the bomb, we don't want to spook June."

Cal nodded his agreement and silently climbed inside. He and Rick both knew the first-floor layout from prior visits, so Cal stepped straight ahead and gestured for Rick to move right. Together they crept through the first floor until they'd cleared all rooms save the living room and headed up the stairs.

Four bedrooms and a bathroom later, they hadn't found Tara, and Cal's worry for her safety almost had him running down the stairs and bursting in on June to question her.

Rick faced Cal. "Now what? We can't go barreling down the stairs and scare June."

Cal forced Tara from his mind and ran their options until a sound idea took hold. "I saw an answering machine on the kitchen counter. A ringing phone shouldn't freak her out too badly. I'll leave a message telling her that we're in the house and coming down the stairs."

Rick nodded his approval. Cal made the call. A ringer pealed from a bedroom down the hall and from the kitchen. On the sixth ring, June's cheerful message played. Cal left a message after the beep.

"Agent Riggins," June called out. "Are you really here?"

"That I am," he replied from the top of the stairs. "Are you alone?"

"Yes."

"I'm with a fellow agent, and we're coming down now."

Cal took lead. He wanted to march straight into the living room, but they needed to take care, as a remote possibility existed that they'd missed something on their sweep and June was compromised by Keeler, saying anything he instructed her to say.

Nearing the bottom of the stairs, Cal swung around the corner to run his gaze over the room and confirm their earlier assessment. Once cleared, he lowered his weapon and smiled at June.

She stared up at him, her usual smile absent. "Now don't the two of you look fierce."

Cal stepped to the side and introduced Rick, who remained in the archway where he could see the porch and driveway.

June gave Rick an earnest smile. "Nice to meet you, Agent Cannon."

"You too, ma'am," Rick replied, his southern accent especially thick, as if he hoped his lazy drawl would help June relax.

Cal crossed over to June. "Not that I don't appreciate exchanging pleasantries, but we need to arrange the proper assistance to deal with your bomb."

"This little thing." She smiled, and Cal was amazed at how calm she was being.

"I'll call Max to get the bomb squad dispatched," Rick said.

"Make sure they have a Faraday cloak for June, too, and let's get someone on looking for the agents on June's detail."

Rick gave a clipped nod and dug out his phone.

"I assume you want to know where Tara is, and if I know where Oren went." She patted the chair next to her. "Come sit down, and I'll explain. You're making me nervous standing there like an intense warrior."

Cal took the chair next to her, but Rick remained at the entryway, a stance that would allow him to protect them should Keeler breach the front door.

June planted her hands on her knees. "All I know is that Oren strapped this thing on me and had me call Tara. He instructed her to make sure you responded to that bomb threat."

So Cal had been right. Keeler *was* the reason for Tara's apology. It was just like her to take the time to say she was sorry.

"Now before you get upset with Tara," June continued. "She didn't want to do it. She really cares for you, Cal, but Oren threatened to detonate not only this bomb, but the one on the woman you went to help. And he's done something with the agents out front. Tara figured you could handle yourself better than anyone else could."

"She was right," Rick said.

"But where is she?" Cal asked, trying to keep his anxiety at bay.

"I wish I knew." June wrung her hands together, raising Cal's concern. "Oren left a phone on the dining room table, and he told her to come here to wait for his call. When he phoned, he instructed her to get in the car and take Highway 17 heading north."

"Did he provide a destination?" Cal's voice came out like a strangled cry.

June started to shake her head, then sat perfectly still. "I keep forgetting this thing could go off if I move."

Anger over the mistreatment of this wonderful woman churned in Cal's gut, but he swallowed it down so he didn't agitate her even more.

"Oren didn't give a specific destination."

"Do you know what kind of car she was driving?" Cal asked.

"No. Sorry. I didn't think to ask." She twisted her hands together in her lap.

"It's okay, June," Cal soothed. "We'll find her."

"Squad's on the way," Rick broke in. "They'll figure something out to cloak June with."

"Cloak?" June asked.

Cal turned his attention back to her. "They'll cover you with a specially coated metallic shield that will prevent a radio signal from getting through and arming the device." Cal continued to keep his focus on June while sneaking quick looks at the bomb, trying to see anything different from the dummy bomb. He spotted a hole on the right side and got up to circle her.

"I feel like an animal in the zoo." She laughed.

Cal found no reason to laugh. He dug out his phone. "I'm going to snap a few pictures of the device."

"Should I smile?" June chuckled again.

Cal admired her attitude. He doubted he would be so relaxed in her situation. "You're taking this awfully well."

"You're here to remove this, so why should I be worried?"

Why? Because I don't know how to render this bomb safe, and until I figure it out, I can't remove it.

June continued to peer up at him. "Will you start working on it now or wait for the bomb squad to arrive?"

The six-million-dollar question. He could grab tools from his car and try to remove the device like he'd done with Hadil, but if that device hadn't been a dummy, both he and Hadil would be dead right now. Once he had a chance to study that bomb, he might be able to figure out what went wrong with the device and finally discover how to render this one safe.

"If you're worried about Tara, she's strong and resourceful," June said. "After all, she managed to evade you for months."

Despite the turmoil, Cal smiled.

June's expression turned hopeful, and Cal came to a decision.

He was willing to risk his own life, but June's? The woman who meant so much to Tara? No, that he wouldn't do. He opened his mouth to tell her that her bomb was like a disease and there wasn't yet a cure, but he couldn't get the words out.

"You're going to look for Tara instead. I understand, and the local squad will be fine."

"No, it's not that."

Hope faded from her face. "You can't disarm it, then."

"Not yet, but I'll figure it out."

Her chin lifted. "I know you will, and I can wait."

His anger flared over the situation. Over Tara missing, over all of the evil in the world that ended precious lives. He raised a hand to strike something. The wall, the chair, anything within spitting distance to release the pressure cooker in his gut.

"Looks like you have the weight of the world on your shoulders," June said, catching his attention and distracting him.

"Not the whole world," he joked, and shoved his hands into his pockets to contain the urge to lash out.

"Maybe not, but you're worried about Tara and me, and if I've read you right, I suspect you're carrying more than that around."

Cal wasn't about to share his struggles with her. "Something like that."

She studied him, her perceptive eyes digging deep. "You guys might be these big strapping men with skills that simple country folks like me can't even begin to imagine, but you're just that. A man."

"I know."

"Do you, or do you think that you need to be perfect? That you don't have flaws or know that there are times that you can't figure something out?"

"I know. Trust me. People have died on my watch."

"But how many people have you helped? Saved? Embrace that and let the other things fall away."

Her words gave him hope, but then she hadn't a clue about the cost of his failures. "You don't understand."

He waited for a judgmental look, but it never came.

"Did you do your best when these people died?" she asked.

He nodded.

"That's all that can be expected of you. Just like now. You'll do your best. I know that. Rick knows that. Shoot, even Tara knows that." She firmly met his gaze and offered a smile so reminiscent of Tara's that his heart ached.

"But," she added, "if whatever's eating at you today continues to linger, you could make one of those mistakes you're talking about. I know how much you care for Tara, and I'm certain you don't want that to happen."

Tara drove down the highway. She'd placed Oren's phone on the passenger seat and kept glancing at it to see if somehow she'd missed a text or a call with additional directions. The cell sat there silently taunting her. Worrying her.

Worry. An old friend that had been eating her alive for far too long. She looked at her rubber bands. At the marks from her frequent use. She was tired of letting the anxiety steal her peace. It was time to break up with such a noxious friend. But how, when people she loved might die?

Words came to mind from her precious aunt who'd lived through so much and remained peaceful even with a bomb around her neck. *Just trust in your faith,* she'd said.

Sounded easy, but it was hard. So hard. Perhaps she hadn't actually trusted God since her parents died. Then Oren. A gunshot wound. The bombs. And now . . . now with June and Cal in jeopardy, the trusting became even harder. Especially since she'd encouraged Cal to head into danger without warning him. Now Oren planned to kill him.

What have I done?

Tears brimmed in her eyes and ran down her cheeks. Her vision blurred, and she pulled to the side of the road to swipe at the tears and pray.

Maybe she deserved Oren's wrath because she'd lost her patience with him and hadn't handled rejecting him in the best way, but June and Cal didn't. They were both good people—fine, compassionate, and caring.

She loved June. And Cal? . . . The terrifying ache in her heart said she loved him, too. This brave man she'd sent into danger.

She bowed her head and prayed, begging God for His intervention for both of them.

The phone rang, and she jumped.

She reached for the cell, and the air seemed to disappear in the car, so she lowered her window and let the cool night air wash over her face.

"Yes," she answered.

"I suppose you're wondering where I need you to go," Oren said.

The sound of his voice sent her stomach roiling, but she swallowed hard. "I am."

"I'll text directions to you, and I want you to keep this call connected with me for the rest of the drive so I can monitor your actions."

"That's not necessary," she said. "You have the cameras. Besides, I care about June and won't do anything foolish." *Unlike you.* "I'm not going to go anywhere else or alert anyone and risk jeopardizing her life."

"All the same, keep us connected."

She didn't offer an additional argument but waited for the directions to arrive. Time ticked slowly by. Panic raised its ugly head, but she breathed it out. In with good air. Out with the stress. Again and again.

She could do this. If she focused on one step at a time and if . . . if she didn't look ahead to the danger she most certainly faced.

CHAPTER 29

Cal paced up and down the driveway outside June's house. The bomb squad had arrived and cloaked her for safety. As long as she didn't move and no one tried to disarm the bomb, June would be safe. But Tara was far from safe.

He kicked a rock, sending it skittering down the drive. Kicked another one and stormed ahead, his hands curled and vibrating with anger.

"Hey, man." Rick came up behind him.

Cal turned and glared at him.

"Get a grip," Rick said. "You know Keeler better than anyone. If we're going to find Tara, you have to calm down and think."

Right. Calm down.

Rage took over, and he jabbed a fist into his car, striking the driver's door and relishing the pain.

He pulled back his hand to toss another punch.

Rick grabbed his arm, and Cal spun, lifting his fist to his teammate.

Rick planted his feet wide, ready to take the brunt of Cal's anger. Staring. Breathing hard. His hands hanging limp, but standing rock solid. His buddy's willingness to take a beating was enough to break through Cal's fury. He dropped his hands.

"I'm sorry, man," Cal said on an exhale that carried more of his anger.

"Hey, I get it, but you have to pretend Tara's another hostage. Someone we need to rescue. What's the first step?"

Pretend. He couldn't possibly, but he could gain control. At least enough to move forward. One step at a time.

"We need to find her, of course." His mind raced with thoughts of how to accomplish the task, until he settled on one. "We'll pick up the dummy bomb, and when we get back to the office, I'll study it and the x-rays the techs are taking. The rest of you pore over the evidence again, all of us looking for anything out of the ordinary."

"Let's go." Rick held out his hand, palm up. "I'll drive so you can think."

Cal handed over his keys, not because of the offered time to think, but because he was too shaken up to drive. Not something he'd ever experienced even in the thick of mortar shells pummeling the ground in Iraq.

Love will do that to you. The thought came out of nowhere. He'd never been in love before, and he couldn't fathom why such a notion popped into his brain. He'd never even seen real love modeled on a day-to-day basis. Not with his parents. They barely tolerated each other, much less displayed any affection or sign of love. His only experience with unconditional love was with his SEAL team and God.

His SEAL teammates would give their lives for each other, no questions asked. Sure, they served their country, but the willingness to die was born of love for each other. To give up their lives so others could live. God had done the same thing. Gave His son for everyone. And that meant Cal, too. Even if he'd given up on God, He hadn't given up on Cal.

Who was he to carry around guilt over lives lost? He'd done his best as June had said, and he had to leave the rest to God. Cal's guilt was misplaced. Maybe an excuse to not open himself up. An excuse to not let people hurt him the way his parents had.

Well, he was done with that. Starting now, and it was time to admit that even as he'd tried to fight it, he was in love with Tara. Totally in love. He didn't yet know what to do with that, but he wasn't going to lose her and miss the opportunity to find out.

He phoned Max and brought him up to speed.

"I need Frankie to check the dummy bomb to see if Keeler packed it with real explosives or some sort of clay. If it's not hot, I'm stopping by the site to pick up the device along with the x-rays."

"I'm not at the site anymore. I'm questioning Meer and Yasin," Max replied, and didn't sound the least bit put out by Cal's demands. "But I'll give the locals a call."

"Frankie has my cell number. Have him text me with an update."

"Roger that. Oh, and you should also know that the K-9s found an additional bomb large enough to take out the apartment complex."

Cal let out a low whistle. "Thank God for K-9 officers."

"Affirmative. Frankie handled the situation like a pro. We should consider recruiting the guy for the Bureau. I'll get him to text you."

Cal hung up and filled Rick in.

"What are the odds that the dummy isn't packed with C-4?" Rick asked.

"I'm guessing pretty good. If Keeler didn't actually plan for the bomb to detonate, he wouldn't use up pricey explosives."

Cal focused out the window and ran through steps he'd take once he reached the office to keep from wasting valuable time. His phone soon dinged, and he glanced at it. "It's from Frankie. Keeler used modeling clay on the necklace bomb."

Cal texted Frankie to box up the device, and they met at the perimeter, where Frankie signed out the device and x-rays to Cal. When he arrived at the office, he collected his files and papers from the back of his car along with the items from Frankie and marched straight to the situation room while Rick went to round up the rest of the team.

Cal took the device out of the box and set it on the bench, then grabbed the x-rays and mounted them on the wall along with Tara's drawings. He studied them but didn't see anything new.

He moved to the device and ran gloved fingers over the housing seam that had remained intact under the drill's vibrations. It was smooth and neat, meaning Keeler must have used silicone gel, sanded it, and buffed it with an electrostatic cloth. Precision work. Not surprising since he worked as a security system assembler.

Cal examined the open seam. Keeler hadn't secured it at all. No wonder the drill vibrations caused the seam to let go. Keeler was meticulous. He wouldn't forget to glue the seam. So he left it loose on purpose. Likely to cause Cal to let down his guard, then cause mass casualties with the larger bomb. If so, Keeler had escalated to an extreme level.

The door lock clicked, and the team members minus Brynn filed into the room. Kaci took a seat behind her laptop at the table. Max, Rick, and Shane joined him at the workbench. Shane set down stapled copies of Keeler's journals.

"How'd the interrogations go?" Cal asked Max.

"I didn't get much," Max said. "Except that they know each other and met when they started working together."

"Where?"

Max shrugged. "I have Kaci trying to find employment records right now, but it's looking like they were involved in a cash operation, making it harder to find."

"Okay, so cash could mean something illegal." Cal looked away to think, his gaze passing over the bags of evidence from Dallas. "Counterfeiting is illegal."

"Where'd that come from?" Rick asked.

Cal pulled out the switch he'd studied. "This action circuit is counterfeit. I already have analysts looking for Keeler's source, but so far we haven't come up with anything actionable."

"I'll call my contacts at Customs to see if they've got anyone on their radar for counterfeiting electronic parts," Max said. "That could be a long list, though."

"China is the main importer of these parts, but India is known for it, too," Cal said. "With Nabijah having an Indian background, we could cull the list down to those leads."

Max gave a firm nod and strode to the far corner of the room to make his call.

Rick tapped the x-ray on the wall. "What I don't get is why go to all of this work for the dummy bomb? He might as well have given us a blueprint of the device."

Cal had questioned the same thing. "I'm guessing he thinks I'm dumb enough to believe this is the entire device, but he left out a switch or two."

"But why?"

"He thinks I'll try to disarm June's bomb, and he'll end my life, too."

"That's right on target with his profile," Shane said.

"Explain," Rick said.

Shane rested a hand on the stack of photocopies. "I've been studying his journals where he documents his infatuation with Tara. He may not know it yet—shoot, he may never know it—but he wants her more than anything. So far, she's been elusive, and he needs to alleviate the pain somehow, which is a logical explanation for why he's detonating the bombs and killing women."

Rick frowned. "I still don't see why he'd tip his hand like this."

"Simple." Shane smiled. "He failed to get to Tara because Cal is protecting her. So he hates Cal, too. But, as our bomb expert, Cal's a worthy adversary in Keeler's mind. So he wants to show Cal how smart and skilled he is. To point out that he's better than Cal, and he can take Tara out at any time despite Cal's protection." Shane faced Cal. "And maybe, as you said, let you try to disarm a device with limited knowledge and take you out along the way as well."

Cal pondered Shane's statement, and many things that Keeler had done now made more sense. "Then if Keeler has Tara, we'd better pray she can remind him of how he once cared for her. If not, he'll release all of his pent-up anger on her."

Dulles Airport area

Tara headed down a narrow walkway between large metal buildings until she found suite C, as directed by Oren. The closer she came, the faster her heart beat, pounding as if wanting to escape her chest. She rounded the corner. The hairs on the back of her neck stood up, and she paused to listen.

The wind whispered down the path, but she heard only traffic whizzing past on the nearby freeway. She started walking again, moving ever closer to suite C. Deep in her soul, she knew she would soon feel the cool PVC of one of Oren's bombs circling her neck.

Would she trust God then? Remain calm like June, or would fear cause her to panic?

If her perspiring palms and rapidly beating pulse were indicators, the latter was more likely. She prayed again as she continued on.

A door down the narrow alleyway opened and light flooded into the darkness.

"Hello, Tara." Oren's voice stabbed through the air like a bolt of fear grating on Tara's nerves.

Her footsteps faltered for a moment, but then thoughts of the bomb circling June's neck, of Cal perhaps in equal danger, urged Tara forward until she saw Oren. He wore the same shirt as in the Skype call, but now she could see that it hung to his knees over pants narrowing at the ankle.

He ran his hands over his clothing with a flourish. "I look a bit different than when we last met. An improvement on my Western ways, don't you think?"

Her negative response would only serve to anger him, so she didn't say anything.

He frowned and waved his handgun. "Come inside. Now!"

She brushed past him, making sure she focused ahead to avoid looking into the evil lurking in his eyes. She surveyed the cavernous space filled with large cardboard cartons and wooden crates in neat stacks. The musky scent of incense lingered in the air, and the lights were low. She looked for an incense burner but soon realized the smell came from within the crates. She saw no indication of bomb-making materials, but she suspected Oren was more careful with his supplies since the pump house incident.

She turned to look at him. His gaze flicked over

her like a serpent's tongue, leaving her feeling dirty and unsettled. His dirt-brown eyes were rimmed in red, his chin jutted out, and a challenge was building in his body language.

Needing to stall and at the same time figure out how to get away from him once he'd deactivated June's bomb, she forced a calm into her voice that she didn't feel. "What is this place?"

He arched a brow, his narrow face appearing longer. "A warehouse."

Duh! She bent down to read an address label. "What does Unique India Arts do?"

"It's an online business specializing in quality Indian imports."

She remembered Cal saying that Nabijah Meer might have been Indian. "This is your connection to Nabijah."

"Wait." He shot across the room so fast he blurred in her eyes. "Say that again."

"Nabijah Meer. Your accomplice. This is where you met her."

"You are not fit to say Nabijah's name." He hauled back a hand and swung it toward Tara's face, but she stepped back before he could connect.

His rage sent panic rushing through her veins, but she took a breath and let it out. "She's special to you."

"Special?" He seemed confused. "Oh, I get it. You think she's my girlfriend, and you're jealous."

"Right," Tara said to keep him talking.

He scratched his head, shifting the cap and messing up pageboy bangs that he must have hoped would cover his receding hairline. "Nabijah and I are only friends with the same goal."

Now they were getting somewhere. "Which is?"

"To kill women who have turned their backs on the Islamic faith and let American infidels have their way with them. The way you did when you turned your back on me." His words flew out like a curse, letting her see the depth of his anger, not only at her, but at these women, too.

"So that's what your bombs are all about?" she asked, pretending calm when fear inched along her nerves. "Women who renounced their faith to have a relationship with American men?"

"Not a relationship. Letting these so-called Christians defile their purity." He shuddered. "Nonmarital sex is punishable by execution, so they have to die, don't you see?"

"I can see where in your very deluded mind that this makes sense, but how do you justify killing my friends? They weren't Muslim. They'd done nothing wrong."

He waved his gun in the air, and his eyes lost focus. "No, but they still fornicated."

"Please. Bombing them was all about getting back at me."

He gasped and advanced on her, his eyes narrowing into cold shards of ice.

She'd pushed him too far. She backed away, putting a large crate between them.

He raised his gun, pointed it at her forehead. "We'll see who gets back at who."

His focus fixed on her, he eased around the box like a large cat hunting its prey.

Panic cut deep into her being, sending her head spinning, but she took a breath. Then another. She refused to give in to the terror that he obviously wanted. He placed the gun against her forehead and smiled. His minty fresh breath wafted over her. Odd. She'd thought the odor would be as foul as his attitude.

"Turn around," he commanded.

She complied, and the gun came up against the back of her head.

"Now walk straight ahead until you reach the office."

She moved slowly, hoping, begging God to send Cal to her aid before Oren trapped her in a confined space. But all too soon, they reached the office holding a desk and three chairs. She stopped in the doorway to run her gaze over the walls displaying rainbow-colored tapestries, wooden flutes, drums, and exotic apparel like she'd seen in Bollywood movies.

He shoved her forward. "Sit."

She settled into a wheeled chair, and the gun never left her head.

With his free hand, he opened a cardboard box

on the table and withdrew a zip tie. "I only have one hand, so you'll have to help me fasten your wrist to the chair."

"And if I don't?" She tried to put bravado into her tone.

"I detonate June's bomb." He chuckled.

His laughter held a hint of the boy she'd once played with. "What happened, Oren? To us, I mean. We were such good friends. I once thought nothing could ever come between us."

"Until you discovered the one thing most boys wanted from you."

She swiveled to look up at him, and the gun briefly left her head until he jabbed it back into place. "You think I was sleeping around in high school?"

"Tommy Simmons said you were."

"Tommy Simmons? I would never have gone out with him. Besides, no one believed a word Tommy said."

"But he shared the intimate details with me. Told me about the birthmark on your lower back."

"That wasn't a secret. Anyone who'd seen me in a swimming suit could have described that."

"He was very convincing, all right."

"And so you shunned me."

"What else was I to do?"

"Gee." She filled her tone with sarcasm. "I don't know. Ask me about it."

"I couldn't talk to you about that. It's forbidden in my religion."

"Please don't tell me that a lie Tommy Simmons told our freshman year is the reason all these poor women had to die."

"They had to die because of their promiscuity. You, on the other hand—"

"I what? Have to die because Tommy lied to you?"

He glared at her, his anger burning through the air. "Help me with the zip tie, or I *will* detonate June's bomb."

She believed he meant it, so she took the hard plastic strip from his hand and laid it over her wrist. Together they slipped the tab into the hole, and he jerked it tight. He placed the gun on a shelf out of her reach and fastened her other wrist.

He stepped around her, smoothed his beard, and pressed his hand down the front of his tunic as if she'd ruffled him. He opened another box, and from it, he withdrew a terrifying white PVC contraption she'd come to know as a necklace bomb.

CHAPTER 30

Washington, D.C.

Cal paced through the room as his teammates worked their assignments. He'd been leaning over the device for an hour now, and the muscles in his neck had stiffened, so he'd taken a break. He paused by the pictures he'd snapped of June's device and mounted on the wall next to the dummy x-rays.

He was missing something, but what?

He noticed again the small hole on the right side of her bomb. After seeing Keeler's perfectionism in aligning the seam of the dummy device, Cal doubted the hole was made in error. Which meant it had a purpose.

He flipped through Tara's drawings and noted a bright red circle drawn around a small hole located in the same place as the one he observed on June. Okay, so Tara must have seen it in Keeler's drawing this way, and the hole wasn't an error. Cal needed to see the x-rays of June's device to determine a reason for the hole. Problem was, he didn't have them.

He'd left June's farm before the tech had finished taking x-rays, and when Cal called to follow up on his lack of an e-mail copy, the tech had said they were having internal server issues, and he couldn't forward them on until the issues were resolved. If that didn't happen in the next fifteen minutes, Cal would pick them up himself.

His cell rang, and hoping it was the tech now, Cal eagerly grabbed his phone. Brynn's name popped up instead.

"Tell me you have something for me," he said.

"It's a long shot, but maybe."

"Go ahead." He wished she was in D.C. rather

than at the lab so they could talk face-to-face, but a call would have to do.

"I was waiting for a DNA sample to process and started looking at Keeler's journals. I—"

"I've read those things cover to cover and back again too many times to count," he interrupted, and continued pacing. "So has Shane. You couldn't have found anything we missed."

"It's not Keeler's words that are intriguing me. It's the paper."

Cal came to a stop. "Say what?"

"I noticed that the pages of the two most recent books were more textured than the paper found in mass-produced journals. So I analyzed a sample of the fibers. I discovered it's treeless paper made from grasses and bamboo. This type of paper is frequently produced in India."

India. Cal's heart started pounding. "We think one of the switches Keeler used could have come from India," he said. "If the paper is from there as well and we find a place where the import of both items intersect, we might find Keeler."

"Okay, good."

"You're brilliant! If you were here, I'd kiss you."

"Then it's a good thing I'm not there." She laughed, but he could tell she was proud of her discovery, and well she should be.

"I'll get Kaci on searching for a connection right away." He almost ended the conversation, but stopped. "Thanks, Brynn. I mean it. Thanks a lot."

"Yeah, well, name that lovely child after me that you and Tara are going to have someday." Laughing, she hung up.

"Kaci," Cal shouted as he rushed across the room. "I have a lead, and you're just the person who can save the day."

The cold PVC pipe rested against Tara's neck. Ironic, she thought, when it contained items that if Oren so chose would combust and create a swirl of fiery warmth.

He bent over her wrists and snipped the zip ties. "There. Now that you know I can end your life at any moment, you won't do anything foolish, and I don't want you to be uncomfortable."

Really? Did that thought actually make sense in his twisted brain?

"So you plan to kill me," she said, no longer avoiding the elephant in the room.

"I have no choice."

"Because of your belief that I'm promiscuous."

"No, no, you cleared that up for me."

"Then why go through with it?"

He sat in a chair facing her. "Because of the hold you have on me. You distract me from my cause. I can't let that happen."

Unbelievable. "I have to die because you can't control your thoughts."

He jutted out his chin, the scraggly whiskers

catching the overhead light, making him appear even more evil. "Everyone who doesn't embrace our beliefs will die eventually. So why not now?"

He was crazier than she thought. "You really think ISIS is going to kill off every person who doesn't embrace their ideology?"

"Eventually."

"You're delusional." She needed to get up. To move. "Can I stand or did you put the same motion control in this one?"

"You can stand."

"Why change up my device?"

"I'm not going far before . . ." His voice fell off, and he shrugged. He didn't have to say any more.

She got it. "Then what about June?"

"I don't plan to harm her. Never did. She's always been kind to me."

Tara sagged in relief. "But I'm different, right? I haven't been kind in your eyes?"

He ran his hand over the beard, and she thought he was trying to look scholarly or wise. "Exactly."

"As much as you say your bombing tirade is about your religion, I think it's about rejection. These bombs started at the time I told you I wouldn't go out with you."

"Fat lot you know." He jumped to his feet and shot a look around the room.

"So it's a coincidence that your first bomb went off right after we ran into each other again?"

"Yes." The word hissed out.

She'd hit a sore spot. "You say yes, but your body language tells me something else."

He glared at her. "I saw you at the farm. You kissed Secret Agent Man."

"And your point?" she asked, though technically she hadn't kissed Cal in the car.

"You're in love with him."

His comment turned her thoughts to Cal, the honorable, honest man who was willing to do everything it took to stop criminals like Oren. Who gave of himself in sacrifice for her since the day she'd first spoken to him. Sure he was pushy, but he was also kind and caring and compassionate. She was thrilled that she'd found a man like him, and yes, it was time to admit aloud that she was in love with him.

"I do love him," she said, and it felt so good not to question or doubt her feelings. "He's an amazing, principled man who works for the good of others. Most women would fall for him."

Oren's frown deepened, but at the same time, resolve claimed his expression. He spun away from her and stepped across the room to turn on a small television sitting on a long credenza. He flipped the channels until settling on a local news special report on the bomb that Cal had gone to disarm.

A blond reporter with perfect teeth stood outside a police perimeter. A county bomb truck sat in the background and lights from police cars strobed behind her as she indicated she was reporting live from the scene.

Tara searched the screen, hoping to catch a glimpse of Cal, but didn't see him.

"The FBI in a joint operation with County deputies disarmed a number of bombs here tonight," the reporter said. "Several hours ago, police arrested a woman believed to be behind the bombing attempt."

The video cut away to a Middle Eastern woman dressed in a man's Western attire. Cal had her by the arm, urging her into the back of a police car.

Yes! Cal was fine.

Oren cursed and slammed a fist into the screen. "Your boyfriend has gone too far. He cannot arrest Nabijah. Allah has big plans for her."

Nabijah. So Cal *had* found her. "Looks like those plans are going to have to be achieved with her in prison."

Oren spun on Tara. "He'll free her. Just you wait and see. She'll be back by my side or taking her prisoner will be the last thing your boyfriend does."

Washington, D.C.

Cal paced behind Kaci, his heart racing as fast as his mind.

Max stepped over to join them. "My Customs contact e-mailed a list of import companies. We can compare it with Kaci's research."

"No need." Kaci shot to her feet and handed Cal a slip of paper.

" 'Unique India Arts,' " he read, and recognized the address as being near Dulles Airport. "Is this the company?"

Kaci nodded. "I'm ninety-nine percent certain. The address I gave you is an industrial park where they lease warehouse space."

"Make that one hundred percent," Max said, looking at his phone. "The company is on the Customs list."

Cal's excitement had his hands trembling. "We need a warrant and blueprints to raid the place."

"I'll handle that," Max offered as he jogged to the door.

"I'll print satellite photos." Kaci sat behind her computer.

"Shane and I can gather our gear for a building breach," Rick said.

"Oh, yeah," Shane replied, already on his way to the door.

Cal's phone chimed. Hoping the text was from the bomb tech, Cal glanced at the screen. "It's from an unknown number."

"It could be from Tara," Kaci replied without looking up from her computer.

Cal navigated to his messages and found a picture message. Cal tapped on the image and it popped up, revealing Tara sitting at a desk, one of Keeler's bombs circling her neck.

Blood rushed from Cal's head, and his knees buckled. He grabbed on to Kaci's chair and took deep breaths to keep from losing all control. Nothing had ever sent him spinning like this. Nothing.

Protect her. Please protect her, he begged.

Kaci peered up at him. "What's wrong?"

Unable to voice the horror racing through his body, he held out the picture.

Kaci gasped. "I'm sorry, Cal."

He didn't want her sympathy. He wanted a way to find Tara. "Can you track this text?"

"Give me the phone, and I'll try."

Cal handed it over and fought down his paralyzing fear.

Kaci's fingers flew over her keyboard, and then she glanced up. "The number is one of the ones listed on Meer's phone. I've already tracked those numbers. It's unregistered, and we won't locate additional information."

Cal's gut tightened. "This at least confirms Keeler has Tara."

Kaci handed the phone back to him. "You think the picture was sent to taunt you?"

"Keeler's sick and sadistic like that, so I guess that could be his reason."

"On the bright side," Kaci said, "Tara appears unharmed in the photo."

"True." Cal's phone dinged. "Another text from the same number. This one has a message."

Cal read it aloud. " 'Free Nabijah and I will let Tara live.' "

"Looks like he wants to make a trade," Kaci said. "That's a good sign."

"Good sign. How can this be good? Our country never gives in to terrorists' demands, much less frees an ISIS operative."

"It's good because if Keeler wants Meer bad enough, he's not going to harm Tara."

Cal's anguish eased a fraction.

"Send me the photo so I can take a good look at it," Kaci said.

Cal forwarded the picture to Kaci, who wirelessly transferred it to her computer. She put it on the big screen and used a magnifying tool to search the background. She let the tool hover over traditional Indian clothing hanging on the walls.

"Unique India Arts?" he asked.

"Let's check their website for matching clothes." Kaci brought up the site. She flipped through clothing in their online store, finding several outfits matching the ones on the wall.

"Good. Good. Keeler's likely taken her to their warehouse."

"And Max will soon have our warrant to raid the place."

"We'll need a plan," Cal said, his mind already on ways to breach the building while ensuring Tara remained unharmed. "We can dress an agent in a hijab and have her sit in the car so

Keeler can see her from the front door and think she's Meer. I'll go to the door and tell him I've cuffed her in the car and won't allow her inside until I have some assurance that Tara is unharmed. While I keep him occupied, the team can enter through the back and disarm him."

"Sounds like it could work."

Cal could visualize the scenario in his mind. See himself at the front door, the team in the back, sneaking inside. Easing up to Keeler, and then . . . oh, yeah, then they would test the veracity of Keeler's bravado.

Dulles Airport area

Oren continued to flip through television channels and pace the room. Tara had asked him several times to disarm June's bomb, but he'd refused, as he planned to use it as additional leverage in convincing Cal to release Nabijah.

"Why hasn't your Secret Agent Man responded to my text?" Oren stopped moving to glare at her. "Or doesn't he care about you?"

There was nothing she could say, but she had been wondering the same thing.

A sick grin twisted his mouth. "Wouldn't it be ironic if he doesn't care? You'd finally find out what it's like not to lead your charmed life and have a man reject you."

"I've been rejected."

"I doubt it."

She'd never actually had a man choose someone over her, but Nolan rejected her in the most important way, by turning against her. She would never tell Oren about Nolan, though, so she opted to remain silent.

He faced the television again. The same reporter appeared on-screen with an update, but she rehashed her prior report.

"Still no news on Nabijah," he muttered.

"What's there to say beyond the fact that she's been arrested?"

Oren looked up, a puzzled expression on his face. Perhaps he knew something about the bombing, and he expected the reporter to figure out the information and share it with the public, making him seem like a hero in his sick mind. As Shane had said, Oren sought attention, which could mean he wanted to hear his name on the news.

She met his gaze. "You're not waiting for them to mention you, are you? Because I'm sure Cal and his team would never share Nabijah's connection to the Lone Wolf Bomber."

His eyes narrowed. "I don't like that name. Stop using it."

"Or what?" She had less fear of angering him now that he wanted to free Nabijah and wouldn't kill her or June until that happened.

He glared at her but didn't speak, perhaps because he didn't know what to say when his plan wasn't going as well as he'd hoped.

Tara had a sudden thought. What if he wasn't the mastermind behind the bombs—not the savvy man who'd been pulling one over on an incredible team of FBI agents? Perhaps Nabijah was the brains behind the plan and had succeeded in keeping Oren out of jail thus far.

With Nabijah in FBI custody, maybe Oren worried that he couldn't keep things together. His demand insisting Nabijah be released was further evidence that he wasn't thinking things through. Anyone who watched the news understood that authorities in the U.S. didn't negotiate with terrorists, and Nabijah would be no exception.

Which meant Oren wouldn't give Cal their location for the exchange, he wouldn't be coming to her rescue, and the only way to save June was to immobilize Oren so he couldn't detonate her bomb.

CHAPTER 31

Washington, D.C.
Sunday, August 6
1:45 a.m.

Cal promised to trade Meer at the location where Keeler held Tara, and Keeler went for it. Not that Cal and the team needed the address for the exchange, but Keeler had no idea the Knights were onto him, so Cal had to ask where to bring

Meer. Keeler promptly texted his location, confirming he was holding Tara at the Unique India Arts warehouse. By that time, Max had gotten their warrant and the team had gathered the items needed for a successful raid. All that was missing was time to fully plan and run the drill to perfect it.

Cal was faced with another rescue, this one the most important of his life, and he didn't have time to prepare properly. The consequences of failure? Lost lives.

Father, please, he pleaded as the group gathered around the table to view satellite photos. *We can do this together, God. Please be with me—us—so we can bring Tara safely home where she belongs.*

The tightness in Cal's chest loosened. A little, anyway. At least enough so he could get a deep breath. He joined the group.

Max jabbed a finger at the edge of the complex. "We'll set up our command post here. Then converge on suite C from the south."

Cal rolled out blueprints of the building. The warehouse was roughly two thousand square feet with a ten-by-ten room in the rear. He pointed at the room. "The picture from Keeler is of an office, and he's likely holding her back here."

"Perfect," Rick said. "It has an exterior wall, so we can detect their exact location."

When the Knights arrived on site, they would begin recon by sliding a radar detector tha looked like a big stud finder along the exterior wall. With a 95 percent probability in detecting the slightest of human movement, as slight as breathing, they could pinpoint Tara and Keeler's exact location.

"If they're both still on site," Shane added. "I wouldn't put it past Keeler to be long gone and the exchange is a trap."

"I've got that covered," Cal said. "I told Keeler that before I meet them, I'll insist on seeing a live video of Tara with him in the shot to prove he's with her in the same location, or I'll bail on the exchange."

"Nice work," Max said. "It will also give a second confirmation that she's in the office."

"This isn't a typical rescue, and we can't rush in," Cal cautioned. "When I draw Keeler away from the office, you all can move in from the loading dock and subdue him before he has a chance to know what hit him and activate the bomb."

"Just double-checking, but Keeler hasn't shown signs of being a suicide bomber, right?" Shane asked. "So if he's in the blast radius, he's not likely to detonate the bomb."

"Right," Cal confirmed. "That will give us extra comfort regarding Tara, but that doesn't mean he won't try to detonate June's bomb. Of course, she's protected right now, but bombs are unpredictable."

"If I were Keeler, I'd bring Tara to the door with me so you could see her and hope it would distract you," Kaci said.

"It would fit Keeler's profile to hide behind a woman," Shane said.

Rick leaned forward. "But if there's a motion switch on the bomb, Keeler won't want her to move."

Cal nodded. "I'll try to determine if she has freedom of movement in the video feed. If she does, and it's possible he could bring her to the door, we'll have to count on the radar detector to tell us she's on the move."

"And we can assume he'll insist on disarming you," Rick added.

"That's a given, but it can't be helped."

"I could take him out when he answers the door," Rick offered.

"The potential trauma for Tara in witnessing what a sniper shot can do to a body would be too great," Cal said. "I'd like that to be our last resort."

"Okay," Max said. "Rick, you'll take a stand and be ready for Cal to signal if needed. If he gives the go-ahead, don't wait for my approval. Take the shot."

"Roger that," Rick said.

"We're dealing with unknowns here, and we

haven't drilled it," Max said. "But it's a strong plan. Anyone disagree?"

No one spoke up.

"Then I'll coordinate communications from the command post." He pointed at the warehouse's south wall. "Kaci, you and Shane do the prelim surveillance and enter through the rear. Cal will signal when you're clear for takedown."

They both nodded their understanding.

"Any questions or additional thoughts?" Max asked.

When no one raised any questions, he began gathering up the items and looked up at Cal. "Give me time to get our stand-in agent updated on the plans, and then you can get on the horn with Keeler and confirm the rendezvous."

Dulles Airport area

Tara shifted in her chair and dug deep for a smile. When Cal had demanded a live video feed to demonstrate she was alive and in the warehouse, her hope for rescue soared. Oren was no match for the Knights, who she suspected would right now be in their situation room planning to come to her rescue. With their incredible skills, she had no doubt they would succeed.

"Stupid, demanding agent," Oren mumbled.

Tara opened her mouth to suggest he say that to Cal's face when he arrived, but she didn't want to anger Oren. He clicked on his mouse to connect his computer to Cal's video feed. Tara kept her focus glued to the screen until Cal's face appeared.

She drank in the sight him, and when she caught a good look at the worry on his face, tears burned in her eyes. She wished he wasn't so concerned about her, but she was happy to see him in any state, and she forced back her tears so she didn't increase his distress.

Oren poked her in the back. "Move, Tara. Show Secret Agent Man that you're alive and well."

She could raise a hand or a finger, but she wanted Cal to see that Oren hadn't put the motion sensor in this bomb so when the Knights arrived, they'd know she could move about freely.

She bent forward and to the side, mimicking a stretch. She heard Cal gasp as if he'd expected the bomb to explode.

She smiled at the camera, making sure the realization of her newfound feelings for him carried through. "I'm fine, Cal, and I'm so glad to see you."

"What's the date and time?" he asked.

She rattled it off, then added, "I miss you."

Surprise lit his eyes, his concern momentarily vanishing, but as he opened his mouth to respond, Oren pushed her out of the way.

"Such a touching display of affection that we don't have time for." Oren held his phone to the camera, and Tara saw a clock counting down on the screen. "The timer is set. Sixty minutes. No more. Have Nabijah here by that time, or June will go boom. If another sixty minutes passes" —he paused and a sick grin slid across his mouth—"then Tara will go boom, too."

Thirty minutes had raced by since Keeler's clock had begun. An imaginary timer ticked down in Cal's head as the team finished dressing out in tactical gear at the command post. Thankfully, they'd expected Keeler to set a time limit, and they'd had a chopper standing by to wing them to Dulles. From there it had been only a five-minute drive to the industrial park.

Cal helped Kaci with her combat vest, and the desire to dress out and burst inside the warehouse with guns blazing hit him hard. Of course, he wouldn't risk Tara's life to ease the pain in his gut, but the satisfaction of taking Keeler down? That was something he hoped to experience once she was safe.

Max clapped his hands to gain the team's attention. "Okay, people, let's move out."

They stepped forward, heading in different directions, but their movements were in sync in a way that years of working and training together had brought. They reminded Cal of synchronized swimmers who moved in perfect harmony. They'd start with the exterior surveillance, noting any security cameras, trigger wires, or other oddities, and when they reached the back of the building, they'd confirm Tara and Keeler's location.

Cal waited to hear the first update on the undercover comms unit that had a hidden mic and a minuscule earbud. He'd never been on this end of an op, standing and waiting while it went down without him, and unease ate at him, even though they could easily do the recon without him. If anything went south, he trusted his teammates to lay down their lives if necessary.

The clean, crisp air blew over his face as he looked up at the stars peeking through gaps in the clouds. Tara's comment at the safe house in Oregon about him being a romantic made him smile despite the active op.

"Tango One and Two in office," Shane announced.

"Roger that," Max responded.

"Security cameras at both entrances," Kaci reported. "Once Tango One heads to the door, I'll disable the rear, but we should leave the front camera in case Tango One is watching and expects to see the package arrive."

"Affirmative," Max replied. "Let us know when Tango One is on the move."

"Sniper in position?" Max asked.

"Roger that." Rick's voice came over loud and clear.

"You're a go," Max said to Cal, and then into his mic he added, "Phase two under way."

Cal jogged to the car where Agent Vera Brevard waited. She clipped on her seat belt, and he noticed her shaking hands. Not an odd reaction. She might be an agent, but still, an op with a bomb would make most law enforcement officers nervous.

"Relax," he said. "You won't have to do anything but sit in the car."

She nodded but didn't speak while Cal started up the car and put the vehicle into gear. He drove the short distance to the warehouse and parked far enough from the door to allow Keeler to see Vera but not make out her true identity.

"Remember to keep your arm down as if I've handcuffed it to the door," Cal said. "Listen to the chatter on the comms. If Max tells you to bail, the keys are in the ignition, and you hightail it out of here."

"But you . . . the others."

He smiled at her. "This isn't our first rodeo, and we can take care of ourselves."

He climbed out, and keeping his head on a swivel, he strode to the door and pounded hard. He peered straight into the security camera so Keeler could get a good look at his face.

"Both Tangos on the move." Kaci's voice came over Cal's earbud. "Disarming rear camera now."

Cal ignored the agitation in his gut that said he could die, that they all could die in the next few minutes. He'd felt the same flutter many times before, and today would be no different.

He'd give his life in a heartbeat to save others, and it wouldn't take even the length of a heartbeat for him to offer his life for Tara.

CHAPTER 32

Oren dragged Tara toward the main entrance. She had to work hard to keep up with him. She wasn't sure whether she should be glad that he was taking her with him. She was glad that she would see Cal in a few moments, even though his arrival meant he'd put himself in harm's way.

Near the door, Oren clamped a rough hand on her shoulder and shoved her in front of him, then took out his phone, which she knew controlled June's bomb.

"Open the door," he said from where he hid like a coward behind her. "But remember one tap of my finger, and June goes up in smoke."

Tara stepped forward and unlocked the dead bolt. "Don't do anything foolish," she warned Cal right up front. "Or Oren will detonate June's bomb."

Cal made eye contact and held her gaze for a long moment, before a dazzling smile lit his face. "It's good to see you."

"You too." Despite their peril, she returned his smile.

"Enough with the small talk," Oren barked. "Where's Nabijah?"

"Handcuffed in my car," Cal replied calmly, and she saw his gaze shift to the bomb.

"Go get her," Oren demanded.

Cal faced Oren. "Not until I have some

assurance that you'll give me the location of the safety arming switch on Tara and June's devices so I can remove them."

"If I do that, what's to keep you from taking Tara and running right now?"

A flash of relief lit Cal's eyes as if he'd learned something important about the bomb from Oren, but the light extinguished as fast as it appeared, and Oren didn't seem to notice. Cal still didn't respond but tapped a finger on his strong chin. Oren probably thought Cal was thinking, but to Tara it looked like he was listening.

Was the team communicating with him through an earpiece? She assumed they were and that Cal was trying to stall while they enacted a plan to take Oren down.

His eyes cleared. "The first step in reaching a mutually beneficial decision is for you to put down your phone and relinquish control of June's bomb."

Oren snorted. "So you can overpower me?"

"You could draw your weapon and hold me at gunpoint. Unless you don't think you can keep me at arm's length even with a gun."

Oren's chin shot up, and he eyed Cal. Just as Cal hoped, Tara suspected.

Oren jerked his gun from his belt and jammed it against Tara's back, eliciting a growl from Cal before his stoic expression returned. Oren placed his phone on a nearby box.

Cal frowned. "I won't be happy until you put that somewhere well out of your reach."

Oren eyed Cal for a moment before picking up the phone.

"March," he yelled at Tara.

She moved with him across an aisle where he set down the phone. He shoved one hand in his pocket, and with the gun in his other hand, he pushed Tara back toward Cal. "That make you happy?"

"Nearly," Cal said. "Unless of course you have a remote or other device in your pocket that will set off Tara's necklace."

Tara spun to look at Oren, and he was grinning. "Our agreement was for June's bomb only. Now I'd like to see Nabijah."

Cal stepped to the side. "Go ahead and take a look at my car where you can see her."

"I meant in here."

"One step at a time, Keeler. One step at a time."

Tara was impressed with Cal's negotiating skills and his utter calm. She'd known he could do anything he set his mind to, and yet he constantly amazed her.

Oren jerked the gun from Tara's back and gestured at Cal to move inside. "Stop next to the door where I can keep an eye on you."

Cal stepped in.

"Okay," Oren said. "Now give me your gun."

Cal didn't hesitate but lifted his weapon from

his holster and handed it to Oren. Tara doubted Cal would give up a gun so quickly unless he had a backup plan. Maybe he had another weapon. Or he possessed the skills to take Oren down even with a weapon pointed in his direction.

"Face against the wall," Oren said, surprising Tara at his ingenuity.

Cal complied slowly, his gaze going around the room, and a sudden dawning light appeared in his eyes before he gave a sharp nod.

Had the team entered the room, and he'd signaled them?

When Oren peeked outside, Tara took a quick look around. Of course she saw nothing. If the Knights were in position, no one would see them, especially not a novice like her.

Cal turned his head to stare at Tara. She smiled at him but soon realized he'd focused on the bomb. He motioned with his eyes for her to turn toward her right, and she did so slowly to keep Oren from noticing her movement.

A smile broke on Cal's face, and he tried to silently transmit something to her, but she couldn't understand what he was trying to say.

He eased toward a wooden crate and placed the hand that Oren couldn't see on the box. Cal acted like he was lounging against the crate, but his fingers worked to remove a nail from the wood. Perhaps he wanted the nail to stab Oren. At least that was the only reason she could come up with. Seemed like if he got close enough to do that, Oren would shoot Cal first. She believed he wore a vest under his shirt, but she didn't know if the vest would protect him at such close range.

She couldn't—wouldn't—let Oren shoot him. If Oren opened fire, she'd try her best to step between them.

Oren spun toward Cal.

"Satisfied?" Cal asked.

Oren scowled. "I won't be satisfied until Nabijah is standing next to me."

"Why don't we find a place to sit down and talk about the next phase of our negotiation?" Cal asked, but it wasn't a request. "You must have an office, right?"

"I do, but I'm not leaving this door where I can keep an eye on Nabijah."

"What if I have a sniper out there?"

"Do you?" Oren growled out.

Cal shrugged.

"You wouldn't warn me if you did."

"Wouldn't I?"

Oren shot a quick look outside and moved the hand in his pocket. "Your sniper takes me out, I press the remote."

"Actually," Cal replied. "When my sniper takes you out, he'll make sure to sever your brain stem, and you won't have a chance to even flinch, much less trigger a remote."

Oren lifted his chin, but his eyes were uneasy. "Why hasn't he done it already?"

"Good question," Cal said. "Are you willing to take a chance of finding out by standing there out in the open?"

Oren snarled at Cal, but he stepped back and slammed the door.

"The office," Cal said pointedly.

"Tara can lead the way," Oren said.

Cal pushed away from the box and crossed to her before she even turned.

"Easy," Oren said.

She and Cal started forward and Oren hung back, likely because he was afraid of being close enough for Cal to take over the situation.

Cal moved next to her and whispered, "Did Keeler pull something out of the hole on the right side of the device when he put it on you?"

She thought back to that terrifying moment and remembered him fumbling with something on that side of the bomb.

She glanced back to make sure Oren wasn't suspicious, and when she was confident he was far enough away not to hear her, she whispered a yes.

Cal nodded. "Do you trust me?"

Trust him? What kind of question was that? Especially now.

"Do you?" he asked again.

She didn't even need to think about it, but nodded.

"Good. When I tell you to, spin around and face me."

"Shut up," Oren shouted.

"Okay, okay," Cal answered. "Take it easy."

They marched farther forward.

"Get ready," Cal whispered.

Her heart rate kicked up higher, and her mouth went dry.

How could Cal possibly be planning to take control of this situation when Oren had his hand on the remote?

That's why she had to trust him, like she had to trust God. To believe the unseen and know that it would all work out for her good.

"Spin," he whispered urgently.

She pivoted. His hand holding the nail came up. He slammed the nail into the hole in the bomb that he'd asked about. Something whirred inside the pipe.

"No!" Fear washed over her, and her legs gave out. She latched on to Cal's arm. He stood strong and unwavering.

Shane catapulted from behind a stack of boxes and slammed his fist into Oren's arm. The gun went flying.

"I'll detonate," Oren warned.

Cal smiled as the middle section of her bomb suddenly released and opened. "Go ahead, Keeler. Press the remote all you want."

Shock overcame Oren's anger, but Tara didn't

have a chance to appreciate it before Kaci flew from the sidelines to tackle Oren.

The moment Oren hit the ground hard, Cal removed the necklace from around Tara's neck and placed it on a crate on the other side of the room. He turned back, and his lips lifted in a bright smile unlike any she'd seen from him. She stood transfixed in the impact that his smile had on her heart.

He took slow steps toward her, his gaze fixed on hers. The look of raw vulnerability in his eyes sent her blood racing. He swept her into his arms and kissed her neck. Then her mouth, his lips urgent and hungry. He held her close, firmly, as if he might never let go.

She was safe in Cal's arms. Safe!

Oren was in custody and she was free to return Cal's kisses with her own urgency, which she did with abandon.

He lifted his head for a moment to look into her eyes and whisper, "I've been waiting to kiss you like this since we first met." He grinned mischievously and kissed her hard again.

Tara gave herself to the kiss, fully and completely, and as soon as they stopped to catch their breath, she would declare her love and tell him that she thought they belonged together.

Applause and catcalls from the background finally broke through her senses, and she remembered that she and Cal weren't alone. Heat flooded her face, and she pushed from his arms. This was definitely not the place or time to confess her love, but at least the kiss told her all she needed to know—he thought they belonged together, too, and she could wait until they were alone to talk about it.

Cal stood motionless a moment, then jammed his hand into his pocket and pulled out his phone. He dialed and held it up to his ear. "We have Keeler in custody. The safety arming switch can be released by inserting something like a nail into the hole on the front of the device. I'll hold while you do it."

"June," Tara said, feeling foolish that she hadn't even thought of her aunt.

Cal marched over to Oren where he lay handcuffed on the floor, Shane's knee in the jerk's back.

"Thanks, Keeler," Cal said, staring down on him. "Nice of you to give me the dummy bomb to study. If you hadn't, I never would've noticed the hole in the one you put on June and Tara."

Oren grumbled something under his breath.

Tara nipped on her lower lip. "Was that from the callout I urged you to go on?"

Cal nodded. "The bomb was a fake, and Keeler here chose not to add all of the components. But he gave me enough so I could figure out how to release you from your bomb."

"Way to go, man." Kaci clapped Cal on the back and offered Tara a beaming smile. "It's over. You're free, and we couldn't be happier."

"I second that," Shane said.

Tara's eyes welled up at the display of affection from Cal's team members, but more than anything, her heart soared at Cal's affection, and she couldn't wait to get him alone.

"Yeah," Cal said into his phone and listened. "Hold on."

He crossed to Tara. "It's June. She's free from the bomb and wants to talk to you."

Tara grabbed the phone. "Aunt June."

"Is it really all over, sweetheart?" A loud exhale followed her question. "Did Cal arrest Oren, and you're safe, too?"

"Yes, it's all over." She smiled up at Cal.

His face glowed. She'd never seen such joy from him, and this moment, the glorious moment free from fear and worry, was filled with a new beginning for them.

Cal needed to talk to Tara alone, but she'd been waylaid in the office by Max to take her statement. Cal watched through the window as she recounted the events, her shoulders back, her amazing strength displayed. He loved her and wanted to be with her, that was clear, but could he take the next step?

Max shook Tara's hand, then came to the door. He clapped Cal on the back. "Good work on bringing Keeler in."

"It was a team effort," Cal replied, his mind more on Tara than Keeler.

"You can take her home now," Max said.

Cal wasted no time, but entered the office. When Tara looked up at him, he suddenly felt as if he were back in junior high about to ask a girl on a date. Her expression reflected the same apprehension.

"Max says you can leave now," he said, sticking to business where he felt secure. "I'll drive you home."

"Would you mind if we went to see June first?" She stood. "I have to get my eyes on her to believe she's okay."

"I'd like to see her, too." Cal stepped back so Tara could exit. She stopped to look at the commotion in the warehouse, and he took her hand to move her forward, as it would do her no good to watch the forensic team and agents who'd descended on the place.

Outside, the air somehow felt fresher and cooler. As they walked toward his car, he couldn't seem to get enough of touching Tara to prove all danger had passed. He tried to come up with the right words to express his thoughts, but he wasn't used to talking about his feelings. And now, when it was so vitally important, he didn't want to mess it up.

He tightened his hold on her hand. "I . . . we . . ."

Tara stopped by his car and peered at him. "What is it?"

"I've skirted your questions about my personal life," he said. "It's not because I didn't want you to know about me. I just don't like to talk about my past."

She lifted his hand and kissed the palm. "None of that matters anymore. Not after what we've been through. We can be thankful to be alive and happy to be together."

"No, I want to tell you."

"If it's because I pushed you before, that was only because I thought you were a lot like Nolan."

"Your ex? You think I'm like him?" he asked, now fearing he was her rebound guy.

"Like Nolan, no." She shook her head so hard her hair swished over her shoulders. "At first, I thought you were. You see, he was a great guy until we got engaged. But once he put a ring on my finger I became like property to him, and he started making decisions for me. Telling me who I could see. What I could do. When I could do it."

Cal doubted she could have said anything that would have surprised him as much as her comparing him to this man. "And you thought I was like that?"

"You are—were." She held up a hand. "No, wait, I'm making a mess of this. You were very controlling when you came to Oregon."

He thought about their first interactions and

didn't much like what he saw. "You're right. I could have handled it better. Not that it's an excuse, but that was work and lives were at stake. I'd never do the same thing in my personal life. At least not on purpose."

"I know that now, but I had to get to know you to see that." She squeezed his hand. "At the same time, I saw you were bothered by something, and you wouldn't open up about it. Nolan became secretive, too, and when you didn't talk to me, I thought you were purposely hiding something."

He opened his mouth to explain, but she quickly pressed her finger to his lips, sending a jolt of electricity through his body, and he had to force himself to focus on the topic.

"Again, I realize that it was my problem, not yours. You're not being secretive. You have something on your mind that you'll talk about when you're ready."

"I'm ready now. I'm not sure I have it all figured out, though." He explained Willy's failed rescue, trying to stay factual and not let emotions sidetrack him. "If only I could change what happened."

"I'm so sorry." She took his other hand and twined her fingers with his.

"Since Willy died, I've been trying to make up for it. I thought God was letting the bad guys win, so if I did something about it, Willy wouldn't have died in vain, and I'd feel less guilty. But each time a woman died at Keeler's hands, the

426

guilt ate away at me more. So I tried to control every little thing around me."

"And now?"

"That's the tricky part, I guess." He took a deep breath. "I realize I have no control over life and death. I had to come to the end of what I could do before accepting God's way is right and to know guilt is a useless emotion. I wish I could say I'm back on solid footing and trusting Him to keep the people I love safe, but I'm not. That's going to take some time."

"No worries there," she said. "I'm actually in the same spot. We could work on trusting God together."

She smiled at him, a soft, sweet smile that told him everything would be okay. That she'd give him the time he needed to sort out his life and still be there when he could commit. "You have to know right up front that I could fail."

"As could I." She moved closer to him and touched the side of his face. "But we have real motivation not to fail now, don't we?"

"Oh, yeah." He breathed out a sigh. "I love you, Tara, and I want this thing between us to work."

"I love you, too." She let his hand go and slipped her fingers under her rubber bands to slide them off. "These were necessary so I didn't lose my mind when I was all alone." Her eyes fixed on his, she pressed the rubber bands into his hand. "I don't need them anymore. Not with you by my side."

He curled his fingers around the rubber bands, surprised at how he couldn't tighten his fist in anger right now if he wanted to. All of his anger at God for the lost lives, at the world, at injustice, had burned out. He no longer needed to prove anything. To make up for anything. He just had to be the man God called him to be, and right now, he was sure that meant a man who moved forward with Tara.

He smiled at her, and she flung her arms around his neck. Before he could lower his head to kiss her, her lips connected with his. He dropped the rubber bands and lifted her into his arms to kiss her hard. He reveled in the warmth and hope filling his heart, but soon pulled back to look at her. To memorize everything about her.

Her eyes were filled with yearning and love, sending his heart racing more.

"So," he said while trying to gain his breath. "Now that everything's out in the open, what do you think about dating?"

"I think it has its merits." A cute little smile claimed the lips he'd kissed. "With the right person, of course."

He caught her flirtatious tone. "I don't suppose you know that right person, do you?"

"Hmm." She mocked a serious expression. "Let me think about it, and maybe I'll come up with someone."

He laughed and crushed her to his chest.

"You, my sweet," he whispered into her ear, "will not be seeing anyone except this man who is totally in love with you."

EPILOGUE

Spotsylvania County, Virginia
Saturday, November 26
12:25 p.m.

Cal clutched the potato sack, one leg inside the rough burlap and pressed tight against Tara's leg. She fit perfectly next to him, and he circled his arm securely around her waist, drawing her closer. She clasped her arm around his back, the gentle pressure and warmth from her touch nearly bursting his heart with happiness.

"Now don't forget," she said, shielding her eyes from the bright sunshine. "I'm the expert here, so match my stride, and we'll leave your teammates in the dust."

"Yes, ma'am." He smiled at her and winked. "I forgot how bossy you were."

She laughed, her face filled with joy.

He didn't care about the many neighbors or his team lined up at the starting line for the potato sack race but bent down to kiss her soundly. He thought she might pull away, but she curled a hand around his neck and tugged him closer. The slight chill in the fall air evaporated, and he felt cocooned in warmth.

"Ah, Cal," Kaci called out. "You might want to pay attention, or we're going to skunk the two of you."

Cal lifted his head, his brain clearing, and he looked around. His teammates were paired in sacks of their own. Rick and Brynn. Kaci and Shane. All lined up at the starting line in the grassy area that had once held the pump house while Max watched them. Cal and the team had worked several backbreaking days to clear the debris and resod the area, but the work was well worth it when the ache that appeared on Tara's face every time she'd looked at the ruins had been erased.

Shane peered at Kaci. "No need to warn him. Even without his distraction we can take them."

Tara lifted her chin. "You may rescue people and free hostages, but potato sack races? That's my wheelhouse, and you are going down today."

Laughter burst from Cal's chest. He was so proud of Tara. Of how she'd overcome her night terrors and moved on with her life. She'd lived with June the last few months while she looked for a job, and Cal had spent many days on the farm with them.

Having grown up in a city, he hadn't been able to imagine farm life, but Tara had done her best to teach him, which even included a stint in the barn to milk the cows. Cal loved Tara, but he never wanted to experience that again.

"On your mark!" June, acting as the starting official, shouted through a megaphone.

"I love you, Tara," Cal said. "And I'll do my best in the race, but no matter the outcome, I hope you'll still love me, too."

"Of course I will, but where's that SEAL resolve you're so famous for?" Her face filled with grit and determination. "Come on, man. Remember, the only easy day was yesterday."

Cal grinned at her. "Um, honey. This is just a race."

She gaped at him. "It's my reputation at stake."

"Get set!" June shouted.

Tara faced the field ahead. "Here we go. Now focus. We've got this."

Cal tightened his hold but also took a moment to pat his pockets, content to find the envelope and small box right where he'd put them.

"Go!"

Cal shot his free leg forward and paid attention to Tara's rhythm as she hurled her body ahead with abandon. He wanted to glance down and see her fierce look of competition, but he had to focus to keep from falling on his face. He felt his teammates all around him, but he kept facing forward as they fell into a rhythm.

Free leg. Bagged leg. Free leg. Bagged leg. Over

and over. Like an approach in one of his rescues if he'd ever had a woman attached to his side. The thought made him chuckle, but then he sobered. In a moment, he hoped to be attached to this woman for life.

They powered ahead, the finish line only three feet away.

"Ready," Tara called out. "Now!"

She hurled her body forward, taking Cal with her. They crashed through the bright red finish ribbon and tumbled to the ground. Cal took the fall on his free arm and rolled to protect Tara from hitting hard.

"We did it," she cried out.

"Yes, we did, honey." He hugged her to his chest. "Our first test as a couple, and we passed."

He'd said *first,* but they'd been mightily tested the last few months as they worked to get over their issues and come out the other side stronger and still together.

"I demand a rematch," Rick called out as he and Brynn stumbled over the finish line.

"Yeah," Brynn said. "You had a ringer."

"I agree," Shane added. "We'll go with the best two out of three."

"Um." Tara sat up, sounding like she was considering it. "No!"

Cal laughed and sat up next to her. Consternation was written on his teammates' faces. None of them liked to lose, Cal included, but today wasn't about them. It was about Tara.

Cal got to his feet. "No can do on the rematch. June has our Thanksgiving meal waiting for us, right, June?"

She nodded and lifted her megaphone. "Can I have everyone's attention?"

Her voice carried over the neighbors and friends gathered for her annual Thanksgiving celebration, and their conversations stilled as they turned to look at her.

"This year I'm very thankful for the brave men and women who saved my sweet Tara's life." She waved a hand over the Knights, surprising all of them. "There is no fiercer or braver team than the Knights, and I want to publicly thank them for their service to our country."

Applause broke out, and Cal felt himself blush. He and the others didn't like or need public acclaim. All they needed was the satisfaction of knowing they'd helped others.

"You're blushing." Tara gaped at him.

"I . . . we don't need this."

"But you deserve it. You're the White Knights, and you ride in on your white horses to save people like me."

He rubbed the back of his neck and looked away.

"Did I say something wrong?"

He shook his head. "We're not special in the sense of being put on a pedestal. We're men and women like the average Joe. Sure, we're highly trained, but we just do our jobs, which happens to be helping people in crisis."

"Take it from someone whose life has been saved several times by you. You're not an average Joe. You really are special."

He shook his head. "No more than anyone else. We're gifted by God with special skills, but everyone is. They just don't demonstrate them in such a dramatic fashion."

"Now," June said, ending the applause. "I want to thank them privately as well. We had scheduled a Thanksgiving Day meal earlier, but they were called out to an incident. So today, I'm going to disappear for a bit and sit down to my table with these amazing people. Please, carry on while we're gone, and we'll be back soon."

She set down her megaphone and looked at them. "Well, what are you waiting for? Let's move, people."

"Yes, ma'am." Tara saluted and winked at Cal. "You're about to find out that June is tougher than your drill sergeants or even Max."

"I heard that." June's laughter trailed behind her.

"As did I," Max grumbled good-naturedly.

Tara fired him an impish grin before heading for the house, and Max actually laughed.

"Oh, and I should mention." Tara turned back to the group. "There's always the egg toss after lunch if you need to prove something."

"You're on," Rick replied. "No steadier hands than mine."

They moved through groups of smiling people and passed the pole barn holding tables filled with potluck dishes brought by June's neighbors and church friends. A big water trough sat at the entrance and held icy-cold drinks. In an empty cornfield, June had added a bouncy house, huge piles of sand where children could dig for prizes, and of course, the race area. The sense of community almost overwhelmed Cal, but in a good way.

"June sure knows how to throw a party," Tara said.

"The closest I've ever come to this was my church picnics growing up." Cal took Tara's hand. "But then I was alone. Now I have you."

"Your parents didn't attend?"

"It was another Sunday to them, and they dropped me off at the door as usual." He shook his head. "It's strange to say this, but I didn't mind. Church was my solitude. Time away from my parents arguing about money. Just peace and love."

Tara frowned, and Cal didn't know what he'd said. "What's wrong?"

"Nothing now, but I should never have gotten so far away from all of this. I let the stresses of life separate me from it."

"So strange, isn't it?" He met her gaze. "We

435

ignore the obvious thing right in front of our faces and try to fix our own problems."

"Like fighting the attraction to the person meant for you when it's the best thing for you." She threaded her fingers in his. "But we're done with that."

He nodded and walked in contentment up the stairs to the porch.

Tara let go of his hand and held the screen door. "I'll take coats, and there's a bathroom down the hall where you can wash your hands before taking a seat in the dining room."

She gathered the jackets, and Cal helped hang them in the foyer closet as he inhaled the wonderful scent of roasted turkey. He was looking forward to a traditional Thanksgiving meal without the bickering that had always been present at his family's table.

He and Tara washed up in the old-fashioned farm sink in the country kitchen with gingham wallpaper and frilly curtains.

As he dried his hands, he turned to June, who'd settled a flowery apron over her clothes. "What can I do to help?"

"Carry, carry, carry," she replied. "I have a ton of dishes that need to go to the table." She turned to Tara. "You need to finish setting the silverware."

"I told you she's a drill sergeant." Tara laughed and grabbed napkins with an autumn leaf pattern before opening a mahogany chest to remove gleaming silverware.

June went straight to the refrigerator.

"Start with these, Cal," she said, and placed a spaghetti salad and another fluffy green salad with marshmallows on the island. "Then you can come back for the hot items."

He picked up the bowls. "I appreciate all of your hard work."

"I'm happy to do it anytime." June rested a hand on his arm and smiled. "Now get going before my turkey gets cold."

All told, he carried out salads, mashed and sweet potatoes, stuffing, two gravy boats, large fluffy rolls, and three bowls of vegetables that June had raised in her garden and preserved. On the final trip back to the kitchen, he retrieved the golden-brown turkey and placed the platter at the head of the table.

"You'll sit here, Cal. I want you to carve." June took off the apron and tossed it into the kitchen.

"I've never carved a turkey," he protested as chairs were scraped against the wooden floor and his friends took their seats.

"I would think in all your SEAL training some-one taught you how to use a knife," June replied.

"They did, but this is—"

"Just a turkey." She marched to the other end of the table to sit. "C'mon everyone. Take a seat wherever you'd like."

Cal pulled out a chair for Tara and met her gaze. "Now I know where you get your bossiness."

"Hey." She gave him a playful punch. "I keep telling you, I'm not bossy."

Cal opened his mouth to respond, but Kaci stepped up to them. "Before you say anything, Cal, 'yes, dear' is the right answer. It's always the right answer and the sooner you get that, the sooner your life will be filled with bliss."

Kaci and Tara shared a conspiratorial look as they sat, and Cal smiled over the way Tara fit in so well with his team. He took his seat at the head of the table and felt like a fraud with the big carving knife and fork in his hands. But if June wanted him to carve, and Tara hadn't disagreed, he'd do his best not to mutilate the turkey.

Once everyone was seated, June clapped her hands to gain everyone's attention. She bowed her head and the others followed suit.

"Thank you, Father, for this time together to share this meal. You brought these special people into our lives to save my precious Tara, and for that, I am so thankful. Bless all of them, keep them safe in their work and, Father, let them know how important they are in keeping our country safe. Amen."

A chorus of amens came from the group, but no one moved.

"What's everyone waiting for?" June asked. "Cal,

start carving, and the rest of you, grab a bowl."

While food was passed around, Cal stood to carve, and he didn't actually mutilate the turkey, more like critically wounded it.

"Perfect job for your first time." Tara took the plate of turkey and handed it down the table.

"Yeah, man," Kaci said. "If we ever have a callout where turkeys attack, you can lead the charge against them."

The group erupted in laughter, and Cal joined in.

"Hey, it's not so far-fetched," Shane said when they'd settled down. "Where I grew up in Florida, we had wild turkeys that roamed our neighbor-hood, and they didn't like the mailman so they attacked him almost every day."

"Seriously?" June asked.

Shane nodded.

June shook her head. "With all the hunters around here, those turkeys wouldn't last long."

When silverware clanked to empty plates, Cal patted his pocket again. For a moment he worried that he might botch this very special day, but then he let it go. He'd prayed about this decision, and he was confident that proposing to Tara was the right thing to do.

He reached into his pocket and palmed the ring box. Standing, he turned Tara's chair to face him and got down on one knee. Her mouth fell open, and he heard June gasp, then clap at the end of the table. He waited a moment for his teammates to offer smart-aleck comments, but no one spoke.

"Tara." He opened the ring box, revealing the diamond Brynn and Kaci had helped him pick out. "You've changed my world. Dramatically. I couldn't be more thankful for having you in my life, and I couldn't be any happier. Well, except if you agree to marry me. I love you. Will you be my wife?"

He expected her to take her time, to think about it, but she threw her arms around his neck. "Yes!"

He drew back and settled his lips on hers, putting every ounce of his love in the kiss. His teammates erupted in applause and congratulations, and he remembered the day when he'd stood on the porch watching June and Tara and wished for a family in his life. He didn't have to wish any longer. This group *was* his family, and with them, June, and Tara, he'd come home at last.

Tara leaned back, her heart overflowing with love as she held out her hand for Cal to slide on the princess-cut solitaire. She twisted and turned her hand to admire the ring. Overhead light caught the diamond's brilliance, sparkling in Tara's vision.

"It's beautiful, Cal," she whispered, tears in her eyes.

"It's nice to see happy tears in your eyes." His voice was so choked with emotion that her tears started to flow in earnest.

She was happy for herself, yes, but even happier at seeing Cal's joy. She started to swipe away her tears, but he gently erased them with his thumb.

She circled her arms around his neck again and stood on tiptoe to hug him. She wanted to forget that everyone else was with them, but movement at the end of the table caught her attention.

June stood and came to join them. "Congratulations, sweetheart."

Tara extricated herself from Cal's fierce hold and hugged her aunt, the sweet scent of honey and vanilla wrapping around Tara and reminding her of how thankful she was for her precious aunt.

"I'm so happy for you." June released Tara and turned to Cal. "You're a fine man, Cal, and I'm proud to have you as part of our family."

June gave him a quick hug, but Max requested everyone's attention and cut it short.

"A toast," Max announced, holding up his iced tea glass. "To Cal and Tara and many years of happiness."

They grabbed their glasses and clinked with the others while the group called out additional congratulations. Tara basked in the joy filling the room, knowing full well that days like this could always be interrupted by pagers going off and the team rushing into danger on another callout. A moment's apprehension lit in her heart, but she forced it away as she'd learned to do the past few months and smiled up at Cal.

He set down his glass and met her gaze. "One more thing before we go out and trounce everyone in the egg toss."

Amidst groans, he reached into his pocket and drew out an envelope. He pressed it in her free hand. "I wanted to give this to you ever since you told me about the scarf your mother bought for you. It wasn't appropriate to do so at the time, but now I can think of nothing more fitting."

So many questions in her mind, she set her glass on the table and opened the envelope. Inside, she found two first-class tickets to Paris for next spring.

"Oh, Cal. How amazing. It's perfect."

His smile widened, and he pulled her into his arms.

"Springtime in Paris with you," she whispered for his ears only. "I'd be happy going anywhere with you, even the barn, but once again, you've made my dreams come true."

"Let's stick to Paris," he said, and chuckled. "And never talk of visiting the barn again."

"I suppose now that you two got engaged it means you'll be too busy making googly eyes all day and will change your mind about participating in the egg toss," Rick said, a note of humor in his tone.

"Nothing is out of the picture for us," Tara replied as she squeezed Cal's hand and smiled at him. "Nothing ever again."

ACKNOWLEDGMENTS

Thanks to:

My daughter, Emma, and husband, Mark, for help with plot issues and technical details in this book and many others.

My agent, Chip MacGregor. Without you, this book wouldn't have been possible.

My editor, Christina Boys. I'm so blessed by your insight and suggestions for crafting a stronger novel and for your publishing wisdom.

The wonderful romantic suspense author Elizabeth Goddard, for always being my sounding board and a friend I can lean on when needed. I am blessed to know you, Beth!

The very generous Ron Norris, who gives of his time and knowledge in police and military procedures, weaponry details, and information technology. As a retired police officer with the La Verne Police Department and a Certified Information Systems Security Professional, the experience and knowledge you share with me is priceless. You go above and beyond, and I can't thank you enough! Any errors in or liberties taken with the technical details Ron so patiently explained to me are all my doing.

The Portland FBI agents and staff for sharing your knowledge, expertise, and heart for your job at the Citizen's Academy. Our day at the firing range still brings a smile to my face. Who knew shooting a semiautomatic rifle could be such fun. I hope my respect for your dedication to the job comes through in my FBI agents in this series.

And most importantly, thanks to God for giving me the opportunity to share stories filled with the hope He gives to all of us.

READING GROUP GUIDE

1. Tara is shocked when she learns that the Lone Wolf Bomber is her former friend, and she struggles to accept that he could be a killer. Have you ever had a friend who surprised you, perhaps betrayed you, and you struggled to come to grips with it? If so, how did you handle it? How long did it take for you to accept—or maybe you are still working on it?

2. When Tara sees that the agent who is supposed to protect her has disappeared, she panics and decides to rely only on herself. She doesn't consult God. Doesn't talk to Cal, but runs. What do you think she should have done in that situation? What would you have done and why?

3. Cal promises to be by Tara's side to protect her, but he no sooner offers the promise than he leaves her in the care of others. Do you think he had a good reason for leaving her behind each time he does so? Have you ever promised to do something and had to go back on that promise? How did that make you feel? Make the other person feel? If you

could go back and change your decision, would you? If so, what would you have done?

4. Tara had to come face-to-face with the Lone Wolf, a very traumatic experience for her, but she chose to trust God to get her through the situation. Have you ever faced a difficult situation where you wanted to panic but relied on God? What was the outcome and what might the outcome have been if you hadn't trusted Him?

5. For a long time, Cal blames himself for the loss of the young boy and the women Keeler killed. Do you think Cal was justified in blaming himself? How do you think you would have felt in such a situation? How might his life have been different if he'd let go of the guilt earlier?

6. At first, Tara thought Cal was controlling and rigid like her former fiancé, but as she got to know Cal she learned there were many sides to his personality. Have you ever pigeonholed people when you first met them and had to change your opinion? Do you think most people do this, and if so, what can we do to stop it from happening?

7. Both Cal and Tara let their past take over, and as a result it changes their future. Have

you ever let something from your past change the course of your life? Are you glad you did so, or do you regret it? In either case, why?

8. Trusting God—so easy to say, but if you're like Cal and Tara, it can be very hard to do. Is there an area in your life where you aren't trusting God? Do you want that to change? If so, what can you do about it?

9. Cal doesn't open up to his team, as he's afraid they'll find out that he's letting the loss of Willy and the women get to him. As a result, he's alone when he could use a friend. Do you share yourself with others or are you more reserved like Cal? Do you like how you handle this part of your life or would you like to change? If so, why?

10. When Oren put a bomb around Aunt June's neck, she embraced her faith and sat peacefully and without worry. Do you think you could have done the same thing? If not, how do you think you would have reacted?

Center Point Large Print
600 Brooks Road / PO Box 1
Thorndike, ME 04986-0001 USA

(207) 568-3717

US & Canada:
1 800 929-9108
www.centerpointlargeprint.com